ONE
SEPTEMBER
MORNING

ONE
SEPTEMBER
MORNING

ROSALIND
NOONAN

KENSINGTON BOOKS
http://www.kensingtonbooks.com

KENSINGTON BOOKS are published by

Kensington Publishing Corp.
850 Third Avenue
New York, NY 10022

ISBN-13: 978-0-7582-0929-0
ISBN-10: 0-7582-0929-0

First Printing: January 2009
10 9 8 7 6 5 4 3 2

Printed in the United States of America

Acknowledgments

My sister, Nurse Maureen, put the brakes on single parenting, her job at the hospital, and real estate ventures to advise me on medical issues and share what it's like to work in a psych ward. Cory Noonan is my new sister, unofficial publicist, and generous source for all things marine and aquatic. To Sofia, wellspring of joy and purity—thanks for the inspiration, love bug! My good friends Nancy Bush and Lisa Jackson generously share the glory, the publicity ops, and the lunch special at Gubancs. Many thanks to my friend and free therapist Wendy Handwerger, who helps me laugh at life. A shout to my very functional siblings, Denise, Larry, Mo, Jack. Mom must have done something right. And to my mom, supportive, smart, and great company—you're the best!

I am eternally indebted to my editor, John Scognamiglio, who lets me seize stories that grab me and run like crazy with them.

A big thank-you to my kids, who both have great writing instincts and will occasionally talk through a scene with me. My husband, Mike, former cop and born psychologist, is always generous with information he soaks up like a sponge. Thanks, Sig.

Prologue

Iraq, 2006

The king is dead.
Americans will no longer turn on their televisions to watch
him run the ball through a pack of hulking football players,
breaking free to lope into the end zone. Viewers of the nightly
news will not see him in a combat helmet and desert khakis,
flashing a smile and telling a reporter about a community program he facilitated to get school supplies for Iraqi children.

He won't come bounding into the barracks to roust the guys
for a race or to hand out the candy or nuts or clean cotton
sheets he just received in a package from home.

No more soldiers gathering to bask in the presence of the
king.

No more jokes from the big guy.

No more photographers aiming their cameras to capture the
king in a battle stance, the almighty warrior.

The king is dead, slain with this weapon cradled in the hand
of the man who knows him so well. Chee-ee-oom! He pumped
the hero full of lead. That was all it took to bring the big man
down.

Now the sweet, biting scent of oil stings his sinuses as the
new king rams the cleaning rod down the barrel of his M-16,
removing all traces of the crime.

Not that it matters, as no one has a clue that he fired off the rounds that spawned a flurry of gunfire in the dark Fallujah warehouse.

Nobody realizes he deliberately aimed and killed Army Specialist John Stanton, big-ass football player, All-American hotshot with a charmed life and a trophy wife.

Nobody knows that a new king will soon take Stanton's place.

He checks the spring, and then lubes it—lightly. Oil it up too heavily and you're in trouble—one of the tips he's learned and heeded in military training. He learned from the best of them. His old man used to tell him, you never break the law unless you can get away with it. Well, he's getting away with it now, and it feels damned good. He felt a surge of adrenaline when the bullets exploded from his rifle, a swell of satisfaction as the impact pushed the body back in the darkness. The first shot was nice and clean upper arm, in through the armored vest. Thank God for the NOD, the night operation device that illuminated hot spots, making it easy for him to find to his target.

Just like a freakin' Xbox game.

And the sheer beauty, the perfection of the killing, is that no one will ever suspect him. Why would they? People thought they were friends, buds. No one could see the hatred he felt for John. The great John Stanton, football hero, patriot, and philosopher. Such a load of crap. John with his megabucks job, celebrity profile, beautiful wife. John with the picture-perfect family, the old man retired army, Mom a freakin' saint, a brother who was his best friend, and a kid sister who idolized him. When you have it all, people adore you and want to give you more. But why should John have all those things when he has zippo?

Yeah, yeah, life is unfair. But nobody says you can't make a few changes to even the score.

He fits the two parts of the rifle back together and replaces a pin. John's death is just the first step in restitution. With the king out of the way, he can move in and scoop up some of the goods left behind. What guy wouldn't want a piece of that wife . . . a place in the perfect family? And who knows, if he can get close enough he might have a shot at some monetary gain, too.

Rest in peace, Johnny boy.

And don't worry about the good life you left behind. He smiles as he removes the soiled patch from the end of his cleaning rod. *I'm ready and willing to jump in your boots.*

PART I

September 2006

Chapter 1

Fort Lewis, Washington
Abby

It's wrong to wish your life away.

Abby Fitzgerald knows that. Still, resting one hip against the porch rail that's been painted over so many times it's taken on a new, snakelike shape of its own, she wishes away a beautiful September morning. The green stretch of lawn, the yellow and orange mums bursting like a dozen suns in the community flower bed, the expanse of cerulean sky and Mount Rainier huddled on the horizon like a gentle giant—let them be gone.

Vanished.

Abby would trade them all for the grim, gray rain of December, the month her husband returns from Iraq. Gripping her hot teacup with both hands, she closes her eyes and wills away the day, the months . . . September, October, November, December.

Which does not work. When she opens her eyes, September reigns, dammit.

A few feet away, birds swoop onto feeders John tacked in place. Chickadees and house finches quickly snatch up black sunflower seeds, then bounce down to the bushes. At the saucer dangling from the porch overhang, the buzz of a hummingbird is slightly alarming, and Abby catches sight of the tiny bird just long enough to see the patches of iridescent violet on its head. Busy creatures. So damned chipper. She should follow their example—wake up and get to work. She needs a clear head to pull her notes together for tonight's presentation.

But the dream absorbs her.

Last night, John seemed so real that it felt more like a visitation—a spark of contact with the warmth of his body—than a dream. Her mind replays the sequence, the sensation of John moving beside her, twisting the sheets away from her the way he always does, then flopping onto his side with a relieved sigh. Abby was so caught up in the ebb and flow of her own rhythmic breath beneath the quilt that it required great effort to open her eyes through the mask of sleep. But she did. She turned to him and observed him settling in beside her, his head a halo of dark hair, his broad back a wall of comfort for her as his solid body sank into the mattress.

The citrus scent of his aftershave clung to the bedding, and she heard him, too. Heard him calling her name, his voice a tidal wave washing through their small bedroom, breaking through her consciousness, then crashing into the street outside to resound over the neighborhood, the military base, the wide patches of green lawn and suburban sprawl that stretch north to Seattle and east to Mount Rainier.

"Abby," he called, the tenor of his voice both heartbroken and exalted, and so heavy it rumbled the bed, shook the room, causing their wedding photo and the tiny porcelain bowls on the dresser to shimmy and clink. Abby recalls bracing herself for the earthquake, having experienced them a few times since moving to the Pacific Northwest. But it was only the ripple of her husband's voice stirring the air.

Even as her eyes searched the dim landscape of her room, the wide expanse of pale sheets beside her, she knew John wouldn't— *couldn't*—be here. Of course not. He was on the other side of the world, where their night is our day and our day is their night. While she slept, the sun was already blazing over the desert plain of Iraq. Thousands of miles away.

And yet his presence felt so real.

"Just a dream," Abby says aloud, for only the chickadees and nuthatches to hear. "Just a dream," she reassures herself, knowing that it still can't explain the vividness of the moment. The smell of sweet clove from his aftershave.

Or the warmth of her husband's body beside her.

She's not sure when she dozed off, but this morning she awakened to an empty bed and a beautiful morning. The golden September sun warmed the earth with one last sigh of summer, the air crisp and brash and bright. A gorgeous day, but Abby Fitzgerald has learned not to trust a beautiful morning. She's seen tragedy dance in the arms of happiness, dance without missing a beat.

The morning her father was stricken with cardiac arrest, Abby was rolling on the grass of the junior high, playing Ultimate Frisbee with her gym class. The day John told her of his discontent with professional sports and his desire to enlist in the army began in Paris with a walk through a farmer's market with all the color and texture of an Impressionist painting. And the most deceptive morning imaginable etched itself deep within her memory: the September day that dawned with a clear, blue sky over Manhattan five years ago, the morning she looked out from her dorm room and spotted smoke billowing from the North Tower of the World Trade Center across the harbor.

Digging her fingernails into the thick paint of the porch rail, Abby turns toward the kitchen. *You can't keep going back to that.* If she's losing her mind, she's not about to go down without a strong cup of coffee.

While coffee brews, she flips open her laptop and checks her e-mail. Nothing from John, but then sometimes he is assigned to shifts that keep him away from the computer for extended periods. She dashes off an e-mail, telling him about the vivid dream. I knew I missed you, she writes, but now I'm dreaming you into our bed. Sure sign that I'm losing my mind without you. December can't come soon enough.

Although this is John's second deployment to Iraq, this time the detachment feels more acute, the parting more intimate, and Abby still wonders how she fell into this role of military wife. It was not something she foresaw for herself when she was making plans, thinking she'd make very conscious choices, as if life were a route that could be charted on Mapquest. She'd never imagined saying good-bye to her new husband and trying to patch together a life on an army base with other women married to the military. Although Abby has always been independent and competent, this separation from the man she loves seems endless, as if she's put her life on hold, sealed into an airtight container until the day of John's return.

You've got your job to do, John e-mailed her when she mentioned her feelings. *Remember the deal? Finish that master's and study for the licensing exam.*

The plan made perfect sense when John departed on the drab green bus. While he was gone, she would focus on her psych degree, finishing up her course work before embarking on clinicals. But she hadn't expected to be distracted with worry, flipping on CNN, *Nightline,* the *Today* show in search of news that might involve John. Tuning in to NPR while driving. Naively, she'd thought it would end soon. Saddam Hussein's Baghdad fell in 2003; wasn't that the goal of the U.S. Army? They'd found no weapons of mass destruction. Recently, she'd heard a politician compare the use of force in Iraq to trying to fix a wristwatch with a sledgehammer. But the word was, our armed forces were in it for the long haul.

Outside, she lowers her laptop and books onto the table. Their yard backs up to a common area that John rallied residents to refurbish soon after they moved here. Japanese maples and boxwood shrubs were planted, a brick barbecue was built, and a play structure installed for children of all the military families housed here. "Don't you think you should ask permission to do all this stuff?" one resident asked, squinting at John suspiciously. Abby sips her coffee, recalling John's answer: "It's easier to ask forgiveness than permission." Looking at the play structure, Abby can still see John drilling while Suz's husband, Scott, kneeled on the ground with the level, ready to pour cement over the anchors.

Funny, but she can feel John's presence here, too.

Now the scent of apple blossoms and September roses sweetens the air as Abby waves to Peri Corbett, who is mowing her lawn on the other side of the commons. Peri lifts one hand, then cautiously steers around a flower bed, and for the bazillionth time Abby wonders how the woman manages so well with three kids, and her husband deployed overseas. "You just do it," Peri always says when she and Abby run into each other at the commissary and chat over fresh tomatoes or blocks of cheddar.

Abby sinks into a chair and drags the textbook into her lap. As if she has time to mope around and fantasize about making some telepathic connection with her husband. She's got a Power-Point to write on solution-focused family therapy. This evening she is scheduled to present this approach to the rest of the class. She works steadily, spurred, as always, by the impending deadline. Having typed five bulleted points, she frowns, not sure where to go next.

"You know I love you, so you won't mind my saying that you look like hell." A familiar voice calls from the kitchen window of the attached duplex.

Her neighbor Suz.

"I couldn't sleep last night," Abby replies to the dark window screen.

A moment later Suz appears at her back door, stepping onto the patio, hands on her hips. "I never sleep anymore, but that's no reason to be nodding off at this time of the morning."

It's as close as Suz has ever come to complaining. In the four months since her husband, Scott, was killed outside the city of Baghdad by an IED, a roadside bomb, Suz has pushed herself, sometimes stoically, to "shut up and move on," as she puts it. The army allows widows and their families to remain in base housing for six months after the death of the service member; Suz will need a new place by December.

"Where's Sofia?" Abby asks. Suz usually keeps her three-year-old daughter within reach.

"Day care. I dropped her off for a full day today. Got some leads on apartments near here, and I figured I'd check 'em out without the mommy baggage. One of them's supposed to have a hot tub," Suz adds, an enticing lilt in her voice. "Want to come with and check 'em out?"

"I wish. But I'm beat. I didn't sleep well last night."

Suz tilts her head, the concerned mother. "You feeling okay, sweet pea?"

"Just hallucinating in my sleep. I dreamed John was in my bed last night."

"A juicy dream, I hope." Suz grins wickedly.

"It was sort of reassuring . . . except that it felt so real. I swear, when I woke up, there was a warm spot in the bed beside me. I could smell his aftershave on the pillowcase."

Suz rubs her arms. "I'm getting goose bumps. Come with me and you can fill in all the details."

"Can't. I'm pulling some notes together for a presentation due tonight."

"Well, you were in a funk when I caught you. You got to visualize success, honey."

Abby reaches back and twists her hair into a loose knot. "Does that work for you?"

"Hell, I'm always too busy visualizing whirled peas. That and wrapping up dolls for a three-year-old. As of this morning, we've got another baby in the box."

"Really?" Abby bites back a grin. In the past few months, three-year-old Sofia has insisted on having her baby dolls tucked into shoe boxes and wrapped up as if they were gifts, which she carries around in a large shopping bag. Abby suspects that the behavior has something to do with the loss of her father, but as she's pointed out to Suz, it's a harmless practice. "Maybe Fia is onto something," Abby says. "I'm going to try that the next time I'm feeling blue. Wrap up something I own and give it to myself as a gift. Maybe carry it around for a few weeks so that everyone will know I've got something special."

"Well, good luck with that," Suz says. "'Cause my daughter has cleaned every last shoe box out of your closet."

Abby smiles at her friend, who looks almost professional with her ginger-colored hair swept back with a skinny headband. She's wearing a lime green tank with a matching polka-dotted sweater, a denim skirt and black polka-dotted flip-flops. "You're all dressed up today." When Suz works the counter at Java Joe's, she sticks to shorts or jeans and a T-shirt. "What's the occasion?"

"Just trying to look respectable for my potential landlords."

Suz yanks off the headband and shakes out her hair. "Re spectable, but not loaded. Rents aren't cheap around here."

"True." Abby is relieved that her friend wants to stay in the area. At first, she thought Suz might take Sofia home to Nebraska. Suz and Scott both enlisted years ago to "get the hell out of Dodge," as Suz likes to say.

"I thought you were going to look for a place closer to Seattle?" Abby says.

"Yeah, I was, but those places are *really* expensive. I don't know what to do. I'd sort of like to stick nearby and keep Sofia in the same day care. Continuity and all. But part of me wants to make a clean break and start over somewhere else."

Abby nods, slipping her feet out of her sandals and hugging her knees. "Joe should give you a raise. You certainly deserve one."

"Yeah, well, I'm not sure that Joe can afford me much longer. With Scott gone, I need a real job. A career. That's the only way Sofia and I will get anywhere."

"I like the way you're thinking," Abby says. "The way you're always pushing ahead. You're amazing, Suz."

"Talk is cheap . . . a helluva lot cheaper than housing in the Seattle area. Besides, I've got a deadline breathing down my neck. The army wants me outta here in December, and with the holidays coming, it just complicates things for a move." She slides the headband back into place. "You sure you can't come along? I'll buy you a latte."

"Next time." Abby leafs through the pages, searching for the chapter's end. "And if I've got any say, I vote for the place with the hot tub."

"Yeah, I'm going to need it for all those wild parties I throw . . . for three-year-olds." She slides the patio door open. "Listen, I've got the sprinkler going out front, so's we don't get our own version of a dust bowl. Do me a favor and turn it off in, like, half an hour."

"Got it." Abby waves good-bye even as her eyes skim down a page of the textbook.

Talking with Suz has energized her, and she works more efficiently now, organizing the material, writing an outline for her presentation and inputting the presentation into the Power-Point format. When she's done, she clicks on the Save icon, then notices the time in the corner of the screen.

"Damn! The lawn's going to be a swamp." Leaving her sandals on the patio, she clamps a textbook under one arm and races through the house and out the front door to find the sprinkler silently rotating. The lawn isn't too soaked, though a puddle of excess water is now running over the sidewalk and down toward the street.

She steps off the narrow brick porch, gasping as her feet sink into the wet mulch behind a shrub John planted. Her fingers close over the handle of the spigot and twist toward the right. Right tight, lefty loosey. Out on the lawn, the fountain of water dies down as the sprinkler stops whirling. Straightening up, Abby wipes her hand on her shorts as a dark car rolls slowly up the quiet street. It's not Suz's boxy Volvo wagon, and not one of the neighbors'. She takes in the shiny black sedan, which slows and then parks right in front of her house.

Her focus sharpens on the two officers inside the vehicle—a man and a woman who exchange a word, then reach for their hats.

Their *dress* hats, she notes, as they step out in full dress uniforms, pants creased, shirts smooth and starched.

Abby is stung by adrenaline, alarm coursing through her. It's the casualty notification team, the messengers all the army wives talk about, the sight every military wife dreads seeing outside her door.

Don't panic, she tells herself. *Maybe they're John's friends. Maybe someone you know on leave here, come to bring one of John's creative personal greetings.*

But she does not recognize their faces, and there's no joke in the demeanor of this woman who stares down at her well-shined shoes, no animation in the face of this man who stands, jaw clenched, regret embedded in his eyes.

And suddenly, she knows.

She knows they bring her the absolute worst news.

"Are you Mrs. John Stanton?" the man asks.

She nods, feeling like an actress playing out a melodramatic scene. Despite the panic beating like a hummingbird's wings deep in her breast, she wants to laugh it all off. This can't be true. They must have the wrong information.

He gives his rank and introduces the female soldier, but it's drowned out in the deafening roar swirling in her head and her acute awareness of bizarre details. The sergeant must have cut himself shaving this morning, and there's a pinpoint of tissue stuck to the edge of his jaw. A flock of small birds rises from some nearby laurels. They circle, then return to their spot. The woman wears a ribbon that's green and red, reminding Abby of Christmas. Home by Christmas, that's what John keeps writing in his e-mails.

"Mrs. Stanton, it's my duty to inform you that—"

"No." The textbook slides from her grip to the wet lawn. She leans down and grabs it quickly, noticing the strangest details. The splatter of mud on her calves. A blade of grass stuck to the side of her foot. Two pairs of shiny dress shoes, facing her dirty bare feet.

It's all wrong.

"Mrs. Stanton . . ."

She hugs the book to her chest, turns and lunges toward the door, hoping to find escape and safety in the house.

But he blocks her way. "It's my job, ma'am," he says, and, meeting his eyes, she sees that he's not as old as she originally thought. "Mrs. Stanton, your husband was killed in the line of duty yesterday in Iraq."

She presses her eyes closed, thinking how wrong it all is. She's not Mrs. Stanton—that's John's mother. And John cannot be dead. Not the John she knows, the man with the charmed life. He's always the lucky one.

It's all wrong, but these soldiers are just trying to do their job, fulfill their duty to their country, just as John is doing . . . *was* doing?

"We're sorry for your loss, ma'am," the woman, lieutenant something, says quietly.

Abby lets the woman press the written notice into her hand, unable to stop the small cry that escapes her throat.

Chapter 2

Iraq
Emjay

Corporal Emjay Brown is still in a daze when he steps into the orange light of the bungalow shared by eight soldiers. Despite the darkness outside, sunglasses shield his eyes against the curious gawkers who know that he was there, right beside John when he went down.

Another few inches and it would have been him.

Bam!

The slam of the door behind him sends him jumping out of his skin. His heart thuds in his chest, sweat trickling down his back.

And suddenly he is back in the warehouse, in the rapid hammer of gunfire, the muzzle-flash in the darkness, the alarm of John's cries, and the blood . . . so much blood.

"Corporal Brown," a leaden voice orders, and Emjay whirls, hands gripping his rifle.

"Lieutenant Chenowith, sir."

"At ease," the lieutenant says, as if he thought Emjay was moving to salute, which he wasn't. The lieutenant removes his helmet to reveal a round mop of hair on the top, like a friar. Most guys in combat units shave their heads, best way to escape the vermin and bugs. Chenowith nurtures his grassy knoll, but it's been a point of speculation among the platoon, some guys figuring he had rows planted in, others figuring he's got some weird birthmark underneath, an inappropriate shape like a swastika or a dick.

"I've asked the others to assemble in quarters," Chenowith says. "I'll be addressing the platoon regarding my investigation."

"Yes, sir," Emjay says, and he waits for the lieutenant to pass, then follows him into the common room used for their quarters, the tiny bungalow where every inch is taken up with bunks, cots, desks, and small plastic tables and chairs, the kind they sell outside the hardware store back home in summer months for five bucks a piece.

This Forward Operating Base—FOB for short—is officially called Camp Desert Mission, though the men have dubbed it Camp Despair, because once you land in this bombed-out-highway town that is Fallujah, you've reached the end of the world. The base, rows of prefab bungalows that formerly served as a government retreat, sits on a desperate stretch of treeless terrain now encircled by sandbags and strung barbed wire. Although the officers were allotted more space, the rest of the platoon was packed into one bungalow—eight men sharing a space smaller than a chicken coop back home.

The Marines who were in here before nailed shelves into the plywood walls, and in the months since Bravo Company arrived, the walls have come to reflect the personalities of the men in the platoon, with pictures of half-clad girls taped to some walls, Christmas lights shaped like chile peppers to remind Lassiter of Texas, a Pacific Northwest calendar over John's bunk, and a large mirror so Hilliard can check out his pumped muscles.

Emjay doesn't like living in such close quarters, not at all, but he's learned that opinions are worth shit in the army.

Doc looks up from the bag of licorice. "At ease!" he calls, as Lt. Chenowith enters the common room.

A card game is on at the table where Lassiter complains he's got another losing hand. Doc returns to separating strands of cherry licorice, apparently part of a care package Antoine "Hillbilly" Hilliard just received from his wife.

Over in the corner, Spinelli, the greeny, remains prone on his cot, plugged in to his iPod. He must be pissed that his injury didn't get him out of here, Emjay thinks. Spinelli can't wait to get the hell back, back home to his mama—that's what Doc says. But no one knows the kid's whole story yet. Spinelli just joined the platoon a month ago, after they lost Spec. Willard Roland to a land mine. All they know is that he's eighteen and lived with his mother, but Emjay knows that, eventually, Spinelli will spill. Everyone does.

The men playing poker pretend that they're not tiptoeing around John's brother, Spec. Noah Stanton, who sits on a bench organizing his gear.

Stone-faced and silent, as if sleepwalking, Noah splits his M-16 in two for cleaning. Cracked open like a Chesapeake hard-shell crab, the weapon seems useless, harmless, definitely not powerful enough to take down a big man like John.

Emjay goes to him, the elephant in the room. Trying to ignore the others who are pretending not to stare but watching anyhow, he squats down real close and whispers, "Sorry about John."

Noah just nods, his dark eyes trained on his disassembled rifle.

Emjay wants to go on, wants to tell Noah that he was right beside John when he got hit, that the shots came out of nowhere because the power was out in the windowless warehouse and Emjay's night-vision goggles weren't working. Does Noah know that Emjay did everything he could to stop the bleeding? The blood . . . Christ, it was everywhere, smeared between his fingers, blossoming over John's shirt so fast that Emjay knew it was real bad. Emjay wants to lean his head close to Noah's and talk, really talk, but he doesn't want Lassiter and Doc and the others listening, and besides that, Chenowith seems to be in the middle of some half-assed speech.

"Bravo Company lost a good man today," Lieutenant Chenowith says. "Every casualty is a great loss, but I know you'll all agree John Stanton was a special individual, a man of courage and moral strength, a leader and a fine soldier. He will be missed."

Silence. Emjay lets his eyes run up to where the cheap plywood walls meet the ceiling. The air is charged with pain and alarm. Even Spinelli reacts, hunching over the side of his bunk wistfully.

"I miss him already, sir." Gunnar McGee folds his cards, his baby face as earnest as Charlie Brown's. Beside him, Lassiter gestures to Noah and smacks Gunnar in the arm, as if he's said the wrong thing. But Gunnar stands firm. "It's true. John's the heartbeat of this platoon. *Was,* I mean."

The men glance nervously at John's brother, but Noah continues cleaning his rifle, ramming the rod down the barrel methodically, as if there is some therapeutic value in the ritual.

"Sorry, man," Gunnar says.

Noah nods but doesn't meet his eyes.

"Specialist Stanton," the lieutenant begins, then clarifies, "Specialist *Noah* Stanton . . . you'll be dispatched stateside just as soon as you've been debriefed. Corporal Brown, I'll want a full report from you, as well."

"Yes, sir," Emjay responds, a thorny branch spiraling through his chest at the prospect of recounting the incident to his commanding officers. Part of him wants to let it all come spilling out, even as he is sickened at the prospect of reliving the event.

"And any other personnel who witnessed anything in the warehouse incident that might be helpful to our investigation should report to me. That is all." Chenowith steps toward Noah. "Sorry for your loss," he says, and though his voice is brusque, Emjay thinks it's probably the kindest act of Chenowith's sorry life.

"Sir," Noah answers, trancelike.

The day's events rush through Emjay's mind like a rip cord, and he cranes his neck, writhing uncomfortably. It was a nightmare day for him, but it had to be a horror show for Noah, who's the medic for their platoon. Christ, he was already outside the warehouse, stitching up a gash on Spinelli's leg, when he sees his own brother hauled out of the warehouse, bloody and fading fast. That must have smacked him hard, the moment of realization that the man dying on that stretcher was his own brother. At least Noah wasn't in the warehouse when John went down, but the sting of seeing his brother carried out, the sudden knowledge that he was unconscious, bleeding out, almost dead, the fact that Noah couldn't save him even after the guys had carried John out of the warehouse and into the stark sunlight . . .

It's all fucked up.

Somebody should have gotten to Noah Stanton first, pulled him aside, got him out of the way so he wouldn't have to live with that image of his dying brother stuck in his head.

And Noah's immediate reaction—the curses, growling at the other guys to stay back. The tears in his eyes. So fucking humiliating, in front of the other men. And now Chenowith telling Noah he can't head home for the funeral until he gets grilled by the higher-ups.

"Unbelievable," Doc says, bringing Hilliard's cardboard box of licorice over to Noah, who shakes his head. "You should be in Kuwait already, buddy. On a flight to Frankfurt, out of here. And the COs are going to hold you back for debriefing? That sucks." Doc, their platoon leader, doesn't usually talk against the brass that way.

Shows you how out of control it all is, Emjay thinks. Noah's own brother was killed and they still won't let him go. As Lassiter always says, *The only way out of Iraq is in a body bag.*

"Here's a news flash for you." Lassiter lowers his cards beneath his homely face, those big ears and a nose like a carrot. Emjay has chalked it up to Lassiter's insistence that everything is bigger in Texas. "The army sucks."

"Amen to that," Doc says, extending the licorice toward Spinelli, who peels one out and lies down again with the strand balanced on his chest. Odd bird, that Spinelli.

"Where're the goddamned peanuts?" Hilliard digs into the care package from home, causing bags of bubble gum and chips to squeeze out and topple to the dusty floor. Hilliard likes his treats, and since Camp Despair is nearly fifty miles away from the small PX in Baghdad, he's got to rely on packages from home. "She sends me Jelly Bellies, but no peanuts?"

"Are those the jelly beans from the Harry Potter movies?" Gunnar McGee asks. He's the only guy called by his first name, as the guys in the platoon enjoy the irony of a soldier whose name is Gunnar. "They taste like vomit and snot and poop and shit?"

Lassiter smacks Gunnar's shoulder with the back of one hand. "Idiot! Shit and poop are the same damned thing."

"Is that the kind?" Gunnar's eyes twinkle at the prospect of a taste of home, even if it is a foul taste.

"I don't know." Antoine Hilliard tosses a handful of foil packets to Gunnar. "Take 'em. Like I need to be popping jelly beans in the desert. I married the goddamned Easter Bunny."

Normally the men would laugh over a wisecrack like that, but the airless room is void of humor. Emjay sits on his cot and watches unobtrusively through his dark sunglasses as Noah sets his rifle aside and turns his attention to a pair of combat boots, which he begins to unlace. There's a dark stain on the side that extends over the toe of the boot. Blood, most likely. John's blood? It's possible, though with Noah's medical assignment, it could be any number of things.

Still . . . as Noah rubs polish into the black leather, Emjay fights off a sickening chill at the thought of one brother cleaning off the blood of another. It seems to make this war too small and personal, and way too close. Beside the boots Noah has laid out his belongings—ammo, desert fatigues, a few canned rations and books, skivvies, and equipment like his rifle, a gas mask, and an NOD, a night operation device, goggles that clip over your helmet.

"You getting everything in line for the trip back home?" Emjay asks Noah, who nods over one boot.

Emjay shoots a look to the cot behind him, where John used to sleep. The floor beneath the metal frame is bare. John's gear is gone.

"Hey, what happened to John's stuff?" Emjay shouts to the room at large.

"Whaddaya think? Chenowith," Lassiter says, venom on his tongue.

Lieutenant Chenowith, a West Point graduate, views the army differently than these enlisted soldiers, many of whom came to this career by default. Lassiter worked in a shoe store, Gunnar

McGee mowed lawns, Hilliard drove a beer truck till he fucked that up by getting a DUI. Most of the guys in the platoon are here because they have no direction and they need to get out of debt, while Chenowith's direction has always been to rise up the ranks in the U.S. Army, just like his old man, who was some hotshot in another war.

"The lieutenant confiscated all of John's gear," Doc explains. "Pending investigation. He wouldn't even let Noah here go through and take out some personal items for John's wife."

"Goddamned army," Hilliard grumbles over a mouthful of licorice. "They fuckin' own you, even when you're dead."

Unresponsive, Noah briskly swipes a stiff brush over the toe of one boot.

Weary to the bone, Emjay shakes his head and stares at the NOD lined up with Noah's stuff. What the hell happened to his today? Last time he used the night operation device it was working just fine, but today when he lowered the equipment over his eyes, he saw nothing—just blackness. He'd been complaining about it to John when the first shot rang out in the dark warehouse.

Now he kicks himself for not having working equipment. If the device had worked, he would have seen the shooter. Maybe he would have seen the gunman taking aim, closing in on John. Maybe, he might have saved John's life.

His heartbeat picks up, thumping in his ears as he pictures the scene. After the two shots, Emjay had grabbed John's NOD and soaked up everything around them. That was when he saw the soldier—one of them—walking away.

A goddamned soldier.

But John must have seen the guy. That's why he was yelling that he was a friendly, that he was John Stanton, U.S. Army. John knew who shot him, and it wasn't some Iraqi insurgent.

Had the raid of the warehouse been a staged mission? A way for Lieutenant Chenowith to get rid of John so that the media would stop dogging his platoon?

Crazy theories from a crazy man, but Emjay can't think who else would have wanted to kill John. He removes his helmet and presses two fingers into each temple. *Wish I had an NOD in that warehouse, a way to see the shooter.*

Who was it? One of you?

Did one of you fuck with my NOD? Screw it up so I wouldn't see your face when you took out my friend?

His eyes obscured by shades, Emjay studies the faces of the men in quarters. Hard to believe it could be one of your own. Noah and John are brothers, and Doc played football with John back in college, so those three are pretty tight. Antoine Hilliard isn't the aggressive type. He's been goldbricking the army since they got here, claiming a back injury so he could stay behind the wire to do paperwork—until a mortar round came through and took out an Alpha Company soldier while he was asleep in quarters. But Hilliard, he and John got on okay. Gunnar McGee is too much of a pansy, which leaves Lassiter, who was obviously jealous of John's popularity. It could have been Lassiter, but Emjay would have trouble buying that, given Lassiter's lack of follow-through. The guy is a big talker, but Emjay suspects he's all talk.

So who else was in that dark warehouse? Who hated John that much?

Emjay removes his helmet and sits down on the edge of his cot. There will be no sleep for tonight. No rest. No escape.

"Just a tip, Brown," Doc says, one blue eye squinting in half a wink. "You can lose the shades at night. Especially in this pit."

Emjay stows his helmet and flak jacket but makes no move to remove his sunglasses. "Didn't you know?" he says as he leans back on his bunk, hands crossed over his chest like a corpse. "I'm legally blind."

Doc and the guys chuckle for a moment, but their attention quickly shifts to the poker game. Hilliard is munching through a can of macadamia nuts as Noah Stanton methodically laces his combat boots.

Through the dark shield of his shades, Emjay watches them all. It's a damn shame the sunglasses can't cover everything, can't hide the shaking of his hands or the sour pucker of lips on the verge of sobbing. If only he could be alone, walk into the cocoon of nightfall, the dark wrapping around him like a forgiving blanket. You never get to be alone in the army. In that way, it's like a prison.

He misses the privacy of home, the freedom to fly out the door and walk the farm, any time of the day or night, without getting his ass shot at. Sometimes he walked to the back acres of the farm, past the chicken coops, the thicket and the pond, night opening to him like a dark blossom. Walking to get away from his old man, to escape the arguments, the drunken fits, the smell of the stale beer and chicken shit and malice. Truth was, nobody enjoyed culling dead chicks or sucking in the ammonia smell, so acidic in the chicken houses it burned right through your sinuses into your brain. Emjay signed up to get away from that chicken farm on the Maryland shore, and damned if he didn't trade one hell for another. Only, this new nightmare was bigger and more twisted than anything he could have imagined.

Without turning his head, Emjay can see Noah Stanton pulling on his boots. He doesn't bother to lace them, but strides out of the bungalow without his helmet or flak jacket or rifle, defying regulations.

"What the hell's he doing?" Lassiter asks, scowling toward the slamming door.

"Living dangerously," Gunnar agrees, "but, really, what are the chances? Taking down two brothers in one day? Odds are against it, I'd say."

"Sometimes grief will make a person act recklessly." Doc picks up his helmet and removes the gold medal he keeps tucked into the camouflage mesh for good luck. It's a replica of a Purple Heart he got in Afghanistan, and Doc's so proud of it he wears it like a fishing hook in his hat, even when they go out on missions. Doc's sort of a dick that way. "And I have to say, I get it. I still can't believe he's gone. Goddamned sniper. Goddamn them all."

Emjay's mouth goes dry as silence pervades the room. Usually he resents Doc's declarations of pop psychology—the nuggets of mental health tips Doc tosses off each day in his role as what the army calls field counselor, which they all know means head shrinker. But this time Doc seems sincere, and rightly so. Before he was Dr. Charles Jump, Doc played football with John back in college. This had to cut deep, even for a cat like Doc. They were old friends, but then John was a friend to everyone. He was that kind of guy.

Doc goes to a calendar on the wall, grimaces at the breathtaking photo of a huge potato-head rock in the surf, and marks off a square with a felt pen. "One more down," he says, and for a moment Emjay thinks he's referring to a man down instead of a day to mark off on the calendar.

"You gonna take on the calendar now?" Lassiter asks.

"Guess I'll have to," Doc says, capping the pen.

John was the one who had hung the calendar with photos of the Pacific Northwest on the wall, the one who'd kept their spirits up, counting down the days until their deployment ended, crunching the numbers in countless different ways. Three months is ninety-one days. Less than a dollar in pennies. Less than eight dozen eggs for the son of a chicken farmer like Emjay.

Spinelli rolls up one pant leg and lifts a fat bandage to press at a raw cut underneath.

"You get that sewn up?" Doc asks.

"Noah gave me two stitches," he says flatly. When Spinelli fell outside the building and sliced into his knee, he'd been sure it was a serious injury. "Look at all that blood," Spinelli had said, awed by his gruesome knee. "You'll probably have to medevac me to Germany."

"I don't think so," Noah answered solemnly as he pressed gauze to the wound. "See? It's deep enough for stitches, but no tendon damage. I can sew you up right here, if you want."

Chenowith tipped his head to the side, obviously put out by Spinelli's latest injury. "All right, okay. We'll pull you two from the operation."

Which left Doc partnering with Hilliard, who couldn't tell his ass from his elbow under the best of circumstances.

Now Emjay bites into the licorice strand and wonders what

it all adds up to. It must be the eighth time he's gone through the details of this day, but he can't seem to piece it together.

"I'd love to take down the bastard that got John," Gunnar says, extending one arm and pretending to stare through the scope of a rifle. "I wish they'd let me go out of the wire and track him down. I would."

"Who the hell *did* fire at him?" Hilliard asks, his jaw working on a handful of nuts. "Did anybody ever find the sniper?"

"Hell, no." Lassiter reaches toward Hilliard and grabs some macadamia nuts for himself. "Alpha Company searched the perimeters after it happened, never located the insurgent. But let me ask you, Hilliard, did you see us nabbing the sniper? Where the hell were you, anyway?"

"I guarded the door, like Doc told me to do," Hilliard says defensively. "You know I don't want to be doing that crap."

"Yeah, we know, Hillbilly," Lassiter says. The platoon is well aware of Hilliard's reticence to do the patrols.

Hilliard stops chewing. "You gotta wonder, what the hell were we doing in that warehouse in the first place?"

"The mission objective was to detain suspected insurgents and search for rocket-propelled grenades," Doc says succinctly. Sometimes he acts as if he's keeping everyone in line, though Emjay thinks it's mostly an act. Without rank, nobody gives a shit.

"Anybody find RPGs?" Gunnar asks.

Lassiter shakes his head. "Chenowith said there were reports of insurgents taking back some buildings in the warehouse district." He wipes his palms against each other, brushing off salt. "I'd love to know how we got that intelligence. From the goddamned sniper, probably. And some officer believed it, some boss with his head up his ass."

For once, Emjay suspects Lassiter's got something right.

Chapter 3

Fort Lewis
Jim Stanton

He is going to be late for work.

Checking for cars, Jim Stanton jogs across the street and onto a path that cuts through a densely treed park bordering the army base.

You cannot report for duty late in the army without repercussions, and this fact has been so ingrained in Jim in the fifty or so years since he entered West Point that he still feels guilty calling in a bit late now that he has retired and moved over to the civilian side of the armed services.

"No worries," Teresa told him when he called in to the office at I-Corps, the elite Army Division here in Fort Lewis where he now taught at the Joint Readiness Training Center. "A retirement job," Sharice called it, knowing that he'd go stir-crazy if he totally detached from the military after thirty-some years with Uncle Sam.

"Wait . . ." Teresa paused, and he heard her shuffling through some papers. "Your classes don't even meet until this afternoon? Easy does it, Jim. You don't need to come in this morning if it's not convenient."

He resisted the urge to accuse her of colluding with his doctor and assured her he would be there, his voice tight from lack of sleep. The damned dream was back, and though he spent the night fighting it, the pattern persisted: He would fall asleep, fall victim to the dream, wake up in a panic, then spend the next few hours trying to relax and clear his head. By the time he finally fell asleep, the sun would be rising, a spiteful orange ball bouncing in through the tall round window of the master bedroom.

The goddamned dream.

It had returned, a monster scuttling out of hibernation and roaring in the night.

He lengthens his stride, trying not to favor his left leg as he cuts off to the right on the path that turns into the woods. As he jogs, he is vigilant, his eyes darting quickly from side to side, watching for movement in the trees. The slightest movement of a branch, the smallest jangle of leaves can mean danger.

The enemy.

An ambush.

Well . . . he does not expect to find those things here but these are things that he teaches his soldiers, survival skills he learned by doing.

Odd that the same memories that lend credibility to his days now haunt his nights. Sometimes he wonders why the dream has returned after having been gone for so many years. And how did he chase it away after his return from 'Nam? He can't even remember, though he's damned sure he didn't employ the help of a head shrinker. Don't need those guys to interfere and start telling him what to do.

A man's got to make his own decisions.

Some of it's obvious, of course: that the dream returned when American soldiers were once again dispatched to combat duty. Not to mention the kick in the butt that came when his own two sons dropped their career paths and enlisted in a Special Forces unit three years ago. If the act of packing up your sons and sending them off to basic training doesn't send you rewinding back through your military career, nothing will.

As he jogs, he notices movement in a lone tree standing in a clearing. His eyes dart over to catch a squirrel leaping off a leafy branch and somersaulting to a limb below. Rodent trapeze. Just a squirrel.

Another lone tree appears in his mind, the last tree standing after B-52s came through the night before and dropped bombs in an attempt to clear the area of Viet Cong. His platoon had been sweeping through in search of the enemy when they came across the single tree. They paused there, curious that the tree had survived the holocaust of fire, and that it was occupied by a monkey who kept scrambling up and down.

"Very entertaining," said Riley. "Hey, Amitrano, you got peanuts to go with the show?"

No one laughed. They didn't do much laughing on forward patrol.

"Weird," Shroeder said, scanning the barren landscape scraped out by last night's bombs. Eighteen and freckle faced, Shroeder was a kid from Wisconsin who should have been home scooping ice cream and polishing his car for his date at the drive-in with Betty Sue. "How'd that monkey survive?" When no one answered, he added, "You think any of those bombs hit Charlie?"

"Bombing the jungle at night's like shooting into a pickle barrel," Jim said. "The chances of hitting your target are one in a million."

"Yeah, but sometimes you get lucky, right?" Shroeder asked.

Don't count on it, Jim thought, taking a last look at the eerie tree swaying in the early morning mist. The poor monkey was probably scared out of its gourd, traumatized by the firestorm of the night before, only to awaken at dawn to find itself islanded in this tree. Isolated. Alone.

Like the last one on earth.

Don't go there, Jim warns himself as he pushes past the pain in his left leg, pushes on, as always. "I see no reason why you can't do some running, if the pain is tolerable," the orthopedic surgeon had told him when his physical therapy was ending back in 1970. "Light running—no marathons for you." Jim had taken a bullet in the upper leg and one in the chest during an ambush outside Lai Ke in 1967. Serious injuries, but he counts himself lucky to be alive. His company lost more than half their ranks in that disaster.

By the time he rounds the corner and sprints toward home,

sweat drips down his back, drenching the collar of his T-shirt. His bad leg throbs, but the pain is tolerable, no more than a persistent reminder of where he's been. As he closes the distance, his mind races ahead to a quick shower, coffee at 7-Eleven, then a beeline to the office.

But the person waiting at his front door sounds an alarm in his brain. Jim breaks stride and slows his pace to see that it's someone in uniform, who is turning away from the doorbell to shoot him a glance.

"You looking for me?" Jim calls out, checking his watch. "I may be AWOL, but not by that much." He smiles at the kid, but as he grows closer he's able to see that the young man does not return his smile.

In fact, the corporal seems nervous. "Are you James Stanton?" he asks, and realization dawns within Jim, blinding and stark.

Just then a shot cracks the air.

Jim Stanton braces himself, eyes closed and fists clenched, knowing it's the beginning of the onslaught, unaware that the explosion he heard was only in his mind.

Chapter 4

"I hate MapQuest." Suz Wollenberg leans closer to the steering wheel, as if that will help her read street signs that are not there. "Can I have a street sign? Just one goddamned sign?" She tosses the printout of her directions onto the floor and grips the steering wheel with her fists. "Dear Lord, please give me a sign!" she moans dramatically.

How's a person supposed to get around without signs? Maybe the city of Greendale can't afford them. Or they were stolen by a bunch of kids. She's seen movies where they make it a fraternity prank to steal them, then use them to decorate the frat house, bringing new meaning to signs like DEAD END and DANGEROUS CURVES and SLIPPERY WHEN WET. You betcha.

Oh . . . her sick mind. Like she's ever going to have a chance to have sex again in this millennium. Scott took care of that by dying. Sometimes she gets so pissed off at him for getting killed and leaving Sofia and her alone. But that's when she's not aching for him and wondering if there is some sort of afterlife and gaping at this whole big world where she's supposed to find a place for herself and her baby to live beyond the safety net of an army base.

Which, so far, has not been as easy as it might seem.

Bottom line, she's never going to find this apartment complex if she can't locate NW Walnut, and even though the rent on this one is a little beyond her comfort zone, she doesn't want to piss off the apartment manager by making an appointment, then not showing up. She can't afford to burn any bridges. Now that she's a widow with a three-year-old, she's got to behave more responsibly and not fly off track like a bat out of hell, which in her book is all easier said than done.

Even if the town of Greendale is more than a tad disappointing. Yes, it's close to the base, but it's not so much a town as a cluster of one-story storefronts offering tire service, pawn shops, fast food establishments, and OTB. She might be a desperate housewife, but this place is no Wisteria Lane.

She rolls past another street, this one with a twisted sign surrounded by laurel leaves. But before she can eyeball the name of the street, her eyes flit over to a group of kids, eight or maybe a dozen if the ones sitting on the concrete sign that says WELCOME TO GREENDALE are a part of the group. The kids are milling around the spit of lawn between the convenience store and gas station, holding signs that say "WE NEVER DECLARED WAR!" and "GET OUT OF IRAQ!" and "VOLDEMORT FOR REPUBLICAN PRESIDENTIAL CANDIDATE!"

Hmmm. At last, some signs she can read.

And right in the center of the goths with their fluorescent orange hair, pierced noses, and thick, charred black eyes is a thin blond waif waving a sign against the spanking blue sky.

Suz narrows her eyes in recognition. That's Madison Stanton, Abby's sister-in-law. Abby's in-laws are all-army—good people. Suz knows because Madison's mom, Sharice, really extended herself when Scott was killed, cooking for her, helping her tidy the house and send out thank-yous, sending Madison **over** to sit for Sofia. Yeah, the Stantons are good people, but **they**'re going to freak when they find out about this.

She pulls into the convenience store parking lot and heads inside to ask directions, smiling slightly at the chorus of "Give Peace a Chance" from the small green mall behind her. Kids! If only it were that simple.

Inside the store she winces over the long line but heads over to the wall of fridges to grab a drink, so she's not asking directions without patronizing the place. Water is better for the bod, but she snags a Diet Coke with every intention of getting jacked up on caffeine. She's addicted for sure, but at least it's legal.

She joins the line behind a large teenage boy who appears coy behind his scruffy hair, and begins the internal debate of where Scott would want Sofia and her to live. He'd always joked that they could return to Oklahoma, but that was a joke, wasn't it? Especially the part about living in his parents' basement? Suz sighs. She knows her parents would take her and Sofia in in a heartbeat, and wouldn't it be so reassuring to tumble into their arms and leave the big choices to them, as well as the electric bill? That would be a huge relief. Her parents and Scott's could help with Sofia while she worked—but at what kind of job? Stocking shelves in the Wal-Mart or waiting tables at the diner? And all the while Suz knew she would just be itching for escape, some star to hitch on to, some other way to get the hell out of Oklahoma.

As the teenage boy points to something behind the counter, Suz presses the cool can of soda to one cheek. No, no, no . . . she can't go backward. Got to move forward.

But does that mean an apartment at the edge of the military base? In a town like Greendale, where their yard might back up on a pawn shop? Where most of the neighbors will come and go with their two- to three-year tours of duty?

The store clerk, a broad man with a military buzz cut and bulldog jowls, has some issue with the teenage boy. The man reaches under the counter and slides out a wooden baseball bat. "No ID, no cigarettes, kid," he says, sliding one palm menacingly over the smooth wood of the bat. "Now don't be giving me any trouble, or I'll whoop you from here to the Canadian border."

The sight of the bat, solid and deadly, sends a tingle of alarm running down Suz's spine. It would be crazy to start a fight with it, and yet she's not convinced that this man wouldn't take a swing.

"No trouble," the kid says, rubbing the back of his neck. With his broad shoulders and doughy face, the teddy bear of a boy clearly outsizes the man, but his fear is palpable. "I told you, they're for my old man."

"Yeah? Then let your old man come in and buy his own cancer sticks," the clerk says before mumbling something Suz can't discern under his breath.

"Then I'll just take this." The teenage boy gestures to the two long sticks of taffy and bottle of water on the counter.

"Yeah, okay," the man with the square jaw and shaved head grunts. "That's two ninety-nine, and I'm happy to keep the change." He snatches a five-dollar bill out of the kid's hand and points him toward the door. "Now get the hell out of my store, you and your liberal-ass friends, and don't come back. This is a marine you're insulting with your asinine protest."

"Sorry, man, but you're kidding, right?" The teenager squints, frown lines obvious in his forehead. "What about my money?"

"It's mine now," the store owner growls. "And I'm not your *man*. That would be *sir* to you."

Suz steps back, her head down, one hand closing over the cell phone in her pocket. She will not allow this kid to take a beating, even if she has to call 911 or fling a bag of frozen peas at the man.

"Okay . . ." The kid backs away warily, as if the store clerk might snap at any minute.

Which he does.

"Now get the hell out of here!" the clerk growls, raising the baseball bat high and revealing pumped, tattooed biceps.

The boy tries to gather his purchases and flee. As he scrambles toward the door, a stick of taffy drops to the floor but he leaves it behind. Better to lose part of his purchase than a quadrant of his brain, Suz thinks.

As soon as the kid is gone, the man chuckles and slides the bat out of sight. "Wimpy kids. Can't even get a fight out of 'em anymore."

"He was frightened," Suz says, nodding toward the bat. "I hope you really wouldn't use that thing."

"Only when necessary," he says, a gold tooth glinting from the back of his mouth as he smiles and rubs his hands together.

"Though I've done some damage in my day. Now, what can I get you?"

"Just the soda," she says. "And a promise that you'll stop torturing America's youth."

He scowls at her. "Just the soda, then." He rings it up. "Don't you know caffeinated beverages are bad for you? Put pits in your bones."

"So I've heard." With the sorry state of her life, a few holes in her bones are the least of her worries. She hands him two dollars and wonders if this man, who reminds her of one of her sergeants in basic training, will steal her change, too. Forget about asking directions to NW Walnut. When her time in base housing is up, she's going to take Sofia and move on . . . north toward Seattle.

Get the hell out of the military.

She doesn't need Colonel Major Buzz Cut–types barking orders at her anymore.

When she returns to her car, two of the teens from the protest group approach her.

"Could you spare some change for the liberation of the oppressed?" the boy asks. Scarecrow thin, with stringy hair dyed fiery orange, he delivers the line with the futile tone of someone who expects to be rejected.

"We're working for peace," the girl beside him says, with more enthusiasm. "If you could spare a quarter or even a dime . . . we're using the money to pay for poster board and supplies and stuff."

Suz looks to the scattered group beyond the two kids, where Madison Stanton and another girl are listening to Teddy Bear Boy's horror story about the clerk with the baseball bat. Madison makes eye contact, then looks away, as if caught in the act of committing a crime.

"Nope, no money." Suz turns to her car and locks the door. "But I will give you a hand." She walks past the kids to the stack of signs leaning against the brick posts that bear the WELCOME TO GREENDALE sign. She can feel the kids watching her as she picks through their poster boards and lifts a square of cardboard decorated with flowers drawn by marker. "Where have all the WMDs gone," she reads aloud. "My question exactly."

Madison's face is pink with embarrassment as Suz crosses to the kids circling the lawn with signs.

"Oh . . ." Suz stops in her tracks and reaches into the pocket of her skirt. "I almost forgot." She pulls out a stick of taffy and hands it to the Teddy Bear Boy. "You dropped this. And your change is there, too." Two dollar bills are wrapped around the bottom of the stick.

"Whoa! I can't believe you got the money out of that old geezer."

She didn't, but Suz can't stand to let it go.

"I told you he'd give it back, Ziggy," Madison says, turning to Suz. "We knew he was exaggerating."

"I wouldn't be so sure." Suz lifts her protest sign, spots Mount Rainier in the distance, and faces north toward Seattle. Come December, she'll be out of here.

She started her day looking for a sign, and dammit, she found one.

Chapter 5

Fort Lewis
Sharice

You can always learn something new. Sharice Stanton likes the style of the new chaplain, a young man who is trying to lecture on the ways to ease into reunion after your spouse has been assigned overseas for so many months. After a lifetime in the military, first as an army brat and now as an army wife, Sharice has weathered her fair share of reunions. As a girl, she waited for her father to return from exotic-sounding places like Vietnam, Germany, Guam, Korea, and Thailand. How the days would stretch out into plodding weeks, and when at last he returned, the reunion was over so fast. A kiss and a toy doll or necklace, and then he was just a boring normal father again, going to work, sitting at the head of the dinner table, taking care of small projects in the house or yard.

Still, a childhood in the army made her the perfect wife for Jim, who was a career man, a graduate of West Point. When he proposed to her on one knee one spring day at Fort Drum, he warned her that, as a lifetime soldier, he couldn't promise her a settled home in one place. And she said that was good, because she got bored being in one place for too long.

She smiles, thinking of how they'd laughed at that . . . laughed so hard that one of the MPs had come out of the guard booth to make sure they were okay. Yes, she and Jim had lots of laughs over the years . . . and many trying yet fulfilling reunions when he returned from overseas assignments.

Of course, her husband has been a fixture at the training academy here for so long, she doubts he'll be deployed again, but both her two sons, Noah and John, are currently in Iraq, and she wants to be on her game to help them ease back into life stateside when they return.

The new chaplain asked them to take the chairs out of rows and put them in one big circle, and Sharice liked the approach, which allowed her a chance to see the adorable baby boy who had been wailing in his mother's lap in the row behind her. Sometimes it seems like minutes ago that she was holding a baby of her own, little John with a full head of dense black hair, and Noah, whose bald head had made him resemble an old man until wispy brown hair started sprouting at eight months. And then, years later, her surprise baby whom Jim called "Oops!", sweet Madison with downy hair so pale she could have been mistaken for an Easter chick. Now Maddie's in high school and her baby boys are in their twenties, soldiers, grown men, one with a wife.

"They grow up so fast," she whispers to the young mother, who is now burping the baby over one shoulder.

"Not fast enough when they're crying," the mother answers wryly, and they exchange a smile.

From this spot in the room Sharice is one of the first to notice when the door opens and two uniformed officers enter. One of the men is Lt. Col. Mitch Preston, a chaplain Sharice has known for years, the minister who baptized her youngest, Madison.

The other officer, a captain, appears exceedingly nervous, beads of sweat on his brow and a pinched look around the mouth. Together, the two men have the look of a CAO—casualty assistance officer—the team that notifies family members when a soldier has been killed or wounded. Since the war in Iraq began, Sharice has been part of many a CAO team. Usually, wives from the Family Readiness Group wait in the car while the officers make the notification. Then the women approach the home to offer support. After that, any number of scenarios might follow, usually involving tears, hugs, phone calls, stories, and covered casserole dishes.

With so many soldiers from Fort Lewis deployed in Iraq, Sharice has been a part of this process more times than she'd ever imagined. The war has taken a huge toll on the men who serve, and their families, and sometimes Sharice wonders if the rest of the country is half aware of the sacrifices that have been made by military families.

With an apologetic gesture, Mitch makes an apology to the young chaplain as he moves around the circle of chairs. When Sharice meets Mitch's eyes, his look is sobering, and she gathers her notes and purse, knowing it's time to make a notification.

"Sharice," he says softly, "would you step outside with us?"

"Of course." She excuses herself as she quietly rises from her chair and follows Mitch to the door.

"Are the other women from the FRG outside?" she asks once they're outside the door. Although she's tucked her notepad away, she's not happy to be wearing chartreuse dress shorts for such a somber task. She smooths down the hem of her black tank top. "I'd like to go home and change."

"No." The reluctant tone of Mitch's voice snaps her head up. The gray pallor of his face makes panic bubble up inside her. "We're here to talk to you, Sharice."

Me?

She thinks of Jim, who is at the NCO Academy this very minute. Could it be . . . ? No, more likely it's the boys, Noah and John, assigned to a Forward Operating Base in the al-Anbar Province, that vast no-man's-land in western Iraq.

Oh, dear Lord, her boys . . .

Whoever it is, let him be injured, she prays. Wounded. Able to heal.

Despite the heated panic in her chest, Sharice maintains her composure as she follows the men out of the building, into the cool, surreal sunshine of the small Northwest garden. Mitch invites her to sit with him on a bench beside yellow black-eyed

Susans and a wild lavender bush, and her heart is thudding so furiously she can barely hear the details when he tells her that there's been a casualty in her sons' unit in Fallujah.

She holds up a hand to stop the white-washing words. "One of my boys?"

"John."

Her eldest. "Is he dead?" she asks.

"Yes."

The earth's rotation comes to a crashing halt, its momentum a stone on her chest.

Her oldest, her firstborn. The impact squeezes a squeal from her throat that resembles the cry of a wounded animal.

Mitch squeezes her hand as the other soldier glances away, awkwardly.

Don't do this to yourself, Sharice thinks. *Do not lose control; it is not your way.*

"And John's wife has been notified?" she asks.

Mitch Preston assures her that she has, as well as Jim. "Jim was the one who told us where to find you," he says.

All right, then that part is done.

"I need to go home," she says, rising.

"Of course." Mitch slides his arm around her waist, as if he's escorting an elderly woman when, really, she can walk just fine.

Sharice wants to drive home, but Mitch insists it's the least they can do.

During the ride, inside the shell of her skull, her mind checks off the to-do list. She'll have to call the salon and have Mindy cancel her appointments. Though there's no need for Jim to come home right now if they need him at the academy. She'll get those boneless pork chops started in the Crock-Pot, and she can make a large portion of rice in the steamer Joyce loaned her. Sharice will call the rest of the family. Madison will be crushed, and Noah . . . the army will send him home for the funeral.

She needs to touch base with Abby soon to warn her that scads of people will be stopping over to pay their respects.

Sharice will stop by the bakery for fresh rolls and bread, and maybe Eva will bring a cold cut platter . . .

"You know," Mitch says as he turns toward base housing, "considering John's popularity and his reputation as a football star, a burial at Arlington Cemetery might be appropriate."

"Yes." She nods, visualizing the hills of white gravestones and a dark limousine with U.S. flags flapping in the wind. "I'd like to honor John that way."

Her heart solidifies, a cold, hard stone in her chest as she proceeds with the details she's spent her entire adult life learning, married to the military.

Chapter 6

Washington
Madison

As Ziggy waves a match over the ends of two cigarettes—one for him, one for Sienna—Madison lets out a sigh over the injustice of it all.

Why do her parents think she's a criminal?

They always suspect her, the straightest, most cautious kid in the pack. They're sure she's dabbling in drugs and booze and sex, when the truth of the matter is she's just a sixteen-year-old innocent.

Ziggy's lower lip pokes out, releasing a stream of smoke that lifts the stringy hair over his forehead. "I can't believe he wouldn't sell me a pack of smokes." He sulks.

It is a little surprising, since Ziggy looks about ten years older than he is, with dark circles under his eyes and a barrel chest that you'd figure more for a prize boxer than the leader of the high school marching band.

"Do you think your friend'll score some for us?" Ziggy asks.

"Don't even ask her," Madison says, shooting a look over at Suz, who's talking with some old man gassing up at the station. "She doesn't want to contribute to your sick addiction. And you know the word will get back to my parents that I'm smoking. Which I'm not." She waves a hand through the air, trying to fend off the smoke. "You're disgusting."

Sienna and Ziggy exchange a look and giggle.

"Pollyanna." Sienna accuses with thinly veiled disdain. "It's a good thing we like you."

"Since when did this become about scoring cigarettes?" Madison holds up the sign in her hands, which reads: NO MORE BUSHIT—GET OUT OF IRAQ! "I thought we came here to launch a war protest, get the message out."

"Whatever," Sienna says in that sing-song tone she thinks is so clever but in truth is quite irritating.

Sometimes Madison has to ask herself why it is she hangs out with this crew. She is the only squeaky-clean freak here, despite her parents' suspicions.

She has never been arrested.

She doesn't do drugs, and the few times she tried alcohol it was in small doses in safe venues, at the houses of friends, none of whom would be so boneheaded as to get behind the wheel of a car after downing a beer or a few drinks of vodka and orange juice.

Madison is an A student, honor roll, National Honor Society, just one apple short of being teacher's pet.

She's a vegetarian, a runner, and she showers on a regular basis.

So what's so incredibly wrong with me?

For her parents, it's all wrapped up in her political activism, which could be summed up with the sign she's holding up to block the blinding sun.

Get out of Iraq.

She really believes this. She wants her brothers home— J-Dawg and Noah-Balboa. She wants all those young guys and women home. All those poor kids, not much older than she is, from places like Alabama or Ohio, who enlisted because they had no other job choices.

Her mother says it's wrong to hate anyone, but she hates the president. He claims that a soldier is obliged to serve his country without questioning decisions from a higher authority, but how can anyone not question? How can anyone not see how useless it is for our people to be dying, unappreciated and without gain, thousands of miles from home?

And how could one man—the president—get away with it? Signing off on a few documents, giving a few orders and—

POOF!—we were at war. And suddenly thousands of kids and fathers and brothers are sent off to a strange place where the air is dryer than Mars and the roadsides explode in your face.

That's what happened to Suz's husband, Scott—a roadside bomb. One of Scott's commanding officers wrote Suz a letter saying that the IED came out of nowhere, that Scott never knew what hit him, that he didn't suffer. Which has to be a load of crap—the suffering part. And somehow, for a guy like Scott with a wife and baby at home, maybe he'd want a few minutes' warning, a chance to say good-bye, to send last messages to Suz and Sofia.

Of course, Madison is not supposed to know any of this stuff because it is strictly AW—Adult World—but she's always listening, and when her mother gets engrossed in her military wives' network stuff, she forgets anyone else is around.

But Madison hears everything.

She heard her mother's cry of outrage when the base commander announced there would be no more individual memorial services for soldiers killed in Iraq—because they couldn't friggin' keep up with it, that's why. And she's heard the endless stories, the families whose sons or husbands signed up for a stint in the National Guard, thinking they'd be called in during an earthquake or flood or something, but finding themselves shipped off to Iraq and returning in a body bag. Those stories hit all the papers in Washington and Oregon, though no one on base wants to talk about it because they have to believe they're doing the right thing serving their country. Otherwise, they'd go crazy.

Un-fucking-believable, as Ziggy says when his head is screwed on straight. That would be when he's not floating on a cloud of weed or trying to scrounge some money to cop some. Ziggy is one of those untapped geniuses. He'll probably become an engineer, or a scientist who comes up with a cure for cancer, if he ever kicks the weed and survives high school.

Madison holds her sign up to passing motorists, motioning for them to honk if they support peace. Behind her, half the people she came with are already flaked out on the mall, and the other half seem to be dropping like flies, abandoning their march to sit in the grass, search for four-leaf clovers, and contemplate their navels. Ziggy and Sienna are working the edge of the gas station, bumming money from people who come in to fill up their cars. Cameron, Matthew, and Lily are stretched out, sunning themselves beside the WELCOME TO GREENDALE sign, but no surprise there. She knows they just came along to get in Sienna's good graces and prove they can fly their freak flag whenever.

Suz comes up from behind her, her sign held high. She gets a passing motorist to honk in support, and both girls wave back.

"Thanks for doing this," Madison says, feeling awkward. Every time she's been with Suz, it's been orchestrated by her mother, who's in that group of ladies who intervene when a soldier dies, trying to cure grief with casseroles and coffee cake and conversation.

"No problem," Suz says. "It's a hell of a good cause, and I can think of a lot worse things to do with my morning off."

Madison was happy to help Suz when her husband got killed, and Sofia's a cute kid, no trouble at all. But this is weird. Madison is here to prevent other guys from getting killed the way Scott was. But still, when she turns to look at Suz, a sickening feeling soaks through her. It's too late for Scott, right? He's dead. And Sofia, their little kid with brown eyes as wide as buttons, who loves to sing the alphabet song and lace her fingers through yours, Sofia is never going to have a daddy. And that's so wrong.

Madison's cell phone chimes. When she sees that it's her mother, she definitely does not want to answer, at least not until she considers the alternatives. What if Mom persists and then calls the school to leave a message in the office? What if they tell her Madison is absent for the day?

Suz is watching her hesitate when her cell phone starts ringing, too. When she snaps it open Madison decides to answer her mom. She'll pretend she's between classes or at lunch or something.

"Hello?" her mother's voice sounds surprised, but she recovers quickly. "Honey, I'm on my way to pick you up," she says. "You need to come home."

Madison panics, thinking of her driving down the street, closing in on the school. "No don't come," she says quickly. "I'll . . . I can drive myself. I've got the Jeep."

"Then come right home," her mother says emphatically.

"Mom—" Madison wants to argue, but something in her mother's voice scares her. She's shaken, not her usual self. "What is it?" Madison asks.

And then her mom lets loose. In a sobbing voice, she tells Madison it's John. Something happened in Iraq. "Is he . . . ?" Madison can't say the word. Neither can her mom.

"Just come home," her mother orders, her voice cracking.

And that's when Madison knows the terrible reality.

John's gone.

Goddamn George W! This is all so wrong, and now it's too late. John is dead for no fucking reason.

There's a hand on Madison's shoulder.

"I'll drive you home." It's Suz, her brown eyes soft with sympathy. Does she know?

"My brother . . ." Madison starts to say it but a huge knot in her throat chokes off the words.

"I know." Suz pulls Madison into her arms, where the younger girl sobs against her lime green polka-dotted sweater.

"My J-Dawg cannot be gone," Madison whispers against the petite woman's shoulder. He can't be gone. The world is not going to make any sense without him.

Chapter 7

Iraq
Noah

He cannot speak.
If he opens his mouth the rage will spew forth, a roiling fireball of anger, bitterness, and contempt. Anger at his brother for leaving him here alone. Fury at John for selling him on the patriotic notion of signing up in the first place, his sweeping enthusiasm that brought Noah along for the ride, that led him to believe they could do something to make the world a better place. Hell, if you listened to John you'd think that the two of them could protect their country from nuclear war, intercepting the weapons of mass destruction like two star football players. The ultimate power play.

When Noah left the bungalow, where he was supposed to be getting rest, and set out into the windy desert without his helmet or flak jacket, he knew it was a foolish thing to do. But now, as he considered that the worst-case scenarios were death or court martial by the army, he calculated that there was so little to lose at this point. Life had suddenly become cheap and tenuous and fluid, like a splash of water that dripped through your cupped hands. So what if it was gone in seconds? It was just a fact of life . . . and death.

The temperature is bearable—maybe in the seventies—but a brisk wind blows dust and grit into his face. The Sharqi, a south-easterly wind that kicks up this time of year, can be unrelenting, and he reaches under his desert fatigues and pulls the neck of his undershirt up, stretching it over his mouth.

He passes the guard at the door of the Communications Center, then steps into the dimly lit, air-conditioned room, the only place on the makeshift Fort Liberation where soldiers have access to computers and the Internet. Sgt. Dawicki, or Sgt. Dweeb, as most of the men call the officer who runs the Communications Center, looks up from the eerie blue light of his terminal.

"Specialist Stanton," he says, one eyebrow cocked as he sits back in his chair and rests his folded hands on his slight paunch. "What the hell are you doing in here at this ungodly hour?"

It's one a.m. in Iraq, and most of the soldiers at Fort Liberation are either on duty or asleep in their quarters. "I need to use a computer." Noah pushes out the words, only half lying, and he is relieved to see that the two PCs designated for use by soldiers are both free.

"Sign the log," Sgt. Dweeb reminds him. "And sorry for your loss. Your brother was a fine soldier and a good man."

My brother was a hothead, he wants to say, but instead he just frowns as he signs the log book and takes his place at a terminal.

It takes less than a minute to insert the thumb drive and access it. And there, beaming at him from the monitor, is the list of files stored in the thumb-size drive that he shared with his brother. All of Noah's files are titled with the initials NS, while John's begin with JS.

Got 'em. Noah's nostrils flare as he savors the victory. They had taken away John's physical possessions, but he had access to his brother's written legacy.

The need to view these files swelled inside him as he was scrubbing blood from his combat boots, worrying about the army's wiping all memory and details of his brother clean. His brother's body was barely cold when Colonel Waters's goons were already in the quarters, confiscating John's possessions, taking his photo of Abby, his letters from Ma. Christ, they even took the bottle opener Maddy gave him with the personalized "J-Dawg" nametag she'd made for him. The army's voracious claim over all-things-John heightened Noah's sense of loss and injustice. He wanted to tear John's journal out of the M.P.'s hands, but then reason descended upon him.

You may own his body, his possessions, Noah thought, *but you cannot own his thoughts.* And John's rational arguments for peace would not be articulated in the chicken scratch of his journal; the polished debates would be on the computer.

They could hold John up as a hero, but in reality he was a vocal opponent of the way this war developed, an adversary of violence, an advocate of peace. Noah knows his brother wrote extensively to this effect, and he wants to have a copy of John's writings—no matter how polished or rough they might be—so that no one can remake his brother into a dutiful soldier who followed blindly. He opens one of John's files and finds a journal entry that might also be considered a call for peace.

> I spoke at length to a man in the marketplace today. He doesn't understand why the American soldiers are here, and I had to agree with him. I told him we'd come to free the Iraqi people from the rule of a tyrant, but he told me things were much better before we came. The women and children are afraid to leave their homes, fearful of the big American soldiers. And since the Americans arrived, the people have no electricity, no water, no gasoline. "When will you be going?" he asked me.
>
> Of course, I had no answer. When will we leave these people to rebuild their society the way they want it? Yes, things are chaotic here, but conflicts among the Sunni and the Shiite Muslims and the Kurds predate Saddam Hussein. Our armed forces will never have the power to bludgeon these people into peace.

John should have told Noah what to do with his essays, but then no one had ever guessed things could turn out this way. They'd had such high hopes when they'd signed up. To end terrorism by fighting Osama Bin Laden's terrorists. To maintain peace by defusing Saddam Hussein's Weapons of Mass Destruction in Iraq.

Only they got to this desert to find that there were no WMDs, only mortar rounds exploding in marketplaces and schools, homes and city streets. He and John came to stop death but landed in a world of fireballs and shrapnel and screams.

More death than Noah had ever imagined.

It wasn't supposed to be this way; John wasn't supposed to die. He wasn't supposed to cut out and leave Noah alone here, fighting in a war he had never believed in.

Contempt burns in the back of Noah's throat, contempt for the unseen war planners in the top brass, the strategists sitting in a command center somewhere who send down futile, meaningless orders for guys like him. Mission objective: break down doors of dark homes and apprehend insurgents. But no one tells you what an insurgent looks like, and no one can prepare you for the frightened faces of women and children huddled in windowless rooms, their eyes glowing in the green illumination of your NOD.

Or there's always the order to "secure the perimeter," another useless request.

"Orders from Oz," John always used to joke. "The wizard wants us to reclaim the city block we secured and lost yesterday, but I say we click our boots three times and say 'There's no place like home.'"

Noah swallows past a lump in his throat as he opens another of John's documents. This was not the way John planned to go home.

Rage flares in his chest. He wants to mourn John, wants to think benevolent thoughts, but whenever he thinks of him, Noah's perverse mind goes to the negative things his brother has done. He can't help but remember the times John bullied him as a kid, wrestling him to the ground and pressing marshmallows down his throat at a Cub Scout cookout. The way John ostracized him because he enjoyed growing things in their little plot of a garden, because he used to get a thrill out of nurturing a plant until it brought forth cucumbers or carrots or watermelons. Punching him in the jaw when he beat John in the Fourth of July race when they were kids. Sticking

Noah with the blame when they got caught snooping in forbidden caves when their dad was assigned to Okinawa. Giving him a wedgie, slap-fighting behind their parents' backs, embarrassing Noah in front of countless girls . . .

I hate him for all those things, and for the times that I was invisible, lost in the shadow of John Stanton.

Hatred is a sour taste in Noah's mouth as he scrolls through his brother's files, sure he is going to hell for thinking ill of the dead.

"I know your brother leaves a wife behind," Sgt. Dweeb calls over in the conciliatory tone of a father. "A beautiful woman. Seen her picture online. Did they have any children? Any pets?"

"No."

"Probably a blessing, given the circumstances."

Noah nods, an image of John's wife tugging at him, her dark eyes always full of questions and concern. Someday, he would share John's writings with her but for now . . . now, he would just send the documents to himself as attachments, a way to have a backup in case anything happened to this thumb drive.

Noah's chest feels lighter as he logs on to the Internet and starts sending John's files into the electronic cosmos. At least, he would have this. The army could take his brother's body, his clothes and worldly possessions, but these—John's thoughts— would not be put under lock and key.

That, Noah vows, picturing his brother handing out pencils to Iraqi school children, *is my promise to you.*

Chapter 8

Forty-two Miles Away
Flint

Damn technology.
You can order groceries online, send a message to a friend on the other side of the planet, or buy a song through your computer, but now that he really needs his laptop to work it keeps freezing up on him, when he's thousands of miles from home with no malls or Apple Stores where he can slap down his credit card and purchase a replacement.

Dave Flint runs two fingers along the seam of his open laptop, wiping the powder and grit of sand out of the crevice. He was working outside under a tent when the Sharqi started blowing with a violent burst that sent sand and debris and anything that wasn't anchored whipping through the air. Now the screen is frozen and his final story from Iraq isn't transmitting back to his editor in Seattle as it should be. If that's not enough bad luck, his flight home that's scheduled to leave at noon, just eleven hours away, is probably going to be cancelled due to the sand storm spewing a wall of sand and dust into the air. Nobody can get in or out during one of these storms; Sharqis have been known to last for days this time of year.

Just his luck.

He's been embedded with the 121st Airborne Division since July, and though he didn't really want the assignment in the first place, it provided him with his first chance to file breaking stories—pieces printed above the fold, nearly every other day—

as well as an opportunity to step away from his life in Seattle, a rote routine coordination of job, girlfriend, online gaming, and late-night drinking. Not a horrible life by any means, but one that will definitely require some fine-tuning when he returns home. It's time to make some adjustments, shake things up a bit.

He's already broached the topic of change with Delilah during their few spare phone calls, his attempt to seed their inevitable parting but, typical of Delilah, she only picks up what she wants to hear. And right now all she seems to want to hear is the "C" word. Commitment . . . it's the bane of Flint's relationships. Nothing can make him feel like he's looking down the dark barrel of the rifle of unhappiness quite like the prospect of having to sign on with one person for a lifetime. Not that he's ever cheated on Delilah or any of his girlfriends before that. He's a monogamous guy, just not ready to sign it all away for eternity.

Why do women want the big commitment? They want you to promise something that no person in their right mind can truly guarantee. Forever and always . . . like those songs played at friends' weddings, right around the time when Flint grabs a glass of scotch and heads out to the terrace to join the cigar smokers. He hates the smell of old stogies but even the scent of burning rubbish is preferable to the glaze in a woman's eyes when she's smitten with the notion of idyllic love.

Yes, he's going to have to end it with Delilah. Even if it means ending up a lonely old crone, as Fanteen always threatens.

Flint leans forward and blows dust from the keyboard, then tries turning the laptop on one more time. At last, an Internet connection. His fingers moving deftly over the keyboard, he e-mails the piece to the *Seattle Trib,* and it uploads quickly. Done.

He lets out a grunt of relief, then lets his eyes scan headlines on the server's homepage. John Stanton's name catches his eye, and he clicks on the link to find just a few lines of copy, reporting that John was killed by a sniper's bullet just outside

Fallujah. He was with Camp Desert Mission, a Forward Operation Base some forty miles west of Baghdad.

Shit.

John Stanton can't be gone. He's one of those guys you expect to see going on forever, charging through life with voracity and determination just as he'd charged through linebackers on a football field.

Flint knew Stanton through Abby Fitzgerald, one of his suitemates in college back in New York. Ancient history, but they were good friends back in the day. For a time, Flint and Abby had a little flirtation going, but Abby fell hard when she met John Stanton, her Scarlet Knight. Suddenly Abby was a football fan, coaxing them on a road trip to see a Rutgers game. It was a beautiful fall weekend and they had papers due back at the Wag, but who could stand to hole up in the library all weekend when you could kill yourself late Sunday night? Abby, Fanteen, Hitch, and him—they'd been inseparable until John came along and stole Abby's heart. Once she got an eyeful of him in a football uniform, Abby never looked twice at anyone on campus, Flint included. If anyone was destined for a happily-ever-after, it was John and Abby.

And now this.

It sucked. It was the shorthand of the newsroom: shit happens.

Hopefully, you can find some meaning along the way before everything goes bad.

Flint searches for more information about the incident with John, but so far details are sparse.

When was Abby and John's wedding? He counts back to a year ago June when they walked together under the crossed swords of John's fellow soldiers. It was the last time they'd all been together, Abby and Hitch and Fanteen and him. Fanteen was pregnant with her second, and Hitch kept joking about how he was going to quit his job and become a househusband. Flint had brought Delilah to the wedding, and Abby had joked that she wanted an invitation to *their* wedding. Ha-ha. Again, the commitment thing. Delilah had loved hearing that, though she was still waiting. Waiting for Flint to become the marrying kind? Waiting for freakin' Godot.

John's death here in Iraq is going to be a huge story. The guy was already considered a hero. One of the best college running backs this decade, and then a star player for the Seattle Seahawks who left a promising career in the NFL to enlist in the army with his brother. And now that John had made the ultimate sacrifice, well, the media is going to go wild.

"Can you say 'feeding frenzy'?" he mutters.

Will Abby give him an exclusive interview? Is he slimy enough to ask?

Any reporter worth his salt would have been on the phone already, but Flint is still unsure. Abby was his friend. She *is* his friend, unless you factor in the fact that they haven't had any contact beyond joke e-mails for the past year. Is he a scumbag for thinking about swooping in on her? It reminds him of the joke: When you X-ray the chest of a reporter, is there any dark spot for a heart?

On the other hand, shouldn't he e-mail and offer his help? Abby is his friend, and she could use someone from the inside to help her field the media. He'd like to help, and it looks like he's stuck here for at least another day or two with this wind storm brewing. On second thought, the wind storm is going to keep other reporters from flying in. He opens his mail files to send Abby an e-mail.

In the meantime, he can always join a convoy heading over to Camp Desert Mission and see what's what. Stanton's brother, Noah, is stationed there, too, a medic, the report says. Maybe Noah wants to talk. He scrolls through his address book and clicks on Abby's name. He'll offer to help, and if it delays his return to Seattle, he can tell Delilah it's business.

Which it is.

Sort of.

Chapter 9

Fort Lewis
Abby

"What time did it happen?" Abby asks.

"I don't have that information," Sgt. Jason Palumbo answers, thoughtfully tapping one finger against the rim of his mug of tea.

Having spent the past few hours in her kitchen with him, Abby no longer finds him intimidating. The sergeant is the messenger, her only line of access to John's whereabouts, and oddly she feels compelled to hold on to this man as if he offered a lifeline.

"We do know that he was shot during a warehouse raid, sometime yesterday," he adds.

"Yesterday . . ." Abby says.

"And their day is our night. They're eleven hours ahead," Suz reminds her, dumping the wet coffee grounds so that she can start a fresh pot. "What time did you have that dream?"

"In the middle of the night. Though it wasn't so much a dream." Abby bites her lower lip. "It felt like he was right here with me. His side of the bed was even warm." She hugs herself and closes her eyes, trapped between the memory and the raw pain of here and now. She has said too much, exposed an open wound. "I know it sounds crazy."

Suz leans back and fingers the charm strung around her neck, a golden "S" that was a gift from her husband. "Honey, when you look up crazy in the dictionary my picture's printed there. What did John say to you?"

"He just said my name, over and over." Abby rakes one hand through her dark hair and holds it in a knot at the back of her neck, remembering. "At one point, the room was rocking and rumbling. The pictures and bowls on my bureau were shaking. Did we have an earthquake last night?"

"Not that I know of, but then I've been known to sleep through tornadoes." Suz turns to Sgt. Palumbo. "You read about anything rocking the Richter scale, Sarge?"

"Nothing that I've heard about," he says. The casualty assistance officer does not strike Abby as a man who believes in the supernatural, though Abby doesn't sense that he's judging her. Instead, she perceives concern, sympathy. And she's come to appreciate that tiny spot on his chin where he nicked himself shaving. Against the smooth fabric and shiny buttons of his dress uniform, it's nice to know he's a human being.

"Well, I say it's all more than a coincidence, you seeing him in your dream and now this." Suz punctuates the end of her sentence with the whirring bean grinder, then dumps the fresh-ground coffee into the filter. "Quite a coinkeedink, if you ask me. I wonder what he was trying to tell you."

"I don't know." *Was there a message?* Abby wonders, feeling revived by the earthy smell of ground coffee beans. *Or was John just making one last connection, saying good-bye?* She presses her lips together to ward off tears. And here she was thinking she'd gone beyond tears to numb denial.

"I didn't hear Scott's voice when he was killed," Suz says, leaning against the kitchen counter. "I sure would have liked to. Could've used a few tips on how to get the car started on wet days, where to reinvest his four-oh-one-K."

Pressing a napkin to her eyes, Abby feels comforted by her friend's ramble.

Beyond the kitchen, her house is swollen with people who've brought casseroles, cold cuts, and fruit, flowers and deepest regrets. Glancing out at them from the arched kitchen entry, watching two women move respectfully past her Monet print, Abby has the feeling that her entire life is being turned inside out, giving all the world a view of the snags and broken fibers she has held in her pocket all these years. It's a raw, vulnerable feeling only somewhat softened by the warm support of the military community, which she did not fully embrace in her time here at Fort Lewis. John was the one who dove in willy-nilly, and now Abby, a more private person, is being forced to open up and let strangers in.

You're going to love the Northwest, John told her when they first learned of his assignment at Fort Lewis. *It's a beautiful slice of the planet.*

And Abby was beginning to share his love for all the green grass and trees, the more mellow pace in which people took the time to look you in the eyes. She didn't mind trading the East Coast humidity for the dry air, even if it meant skies were gray for much of the year. They had met back east while John was at Rutgers and Abby attended Wagner College on Staten Island. Geographically challenged from the start, the logistics of their relationship only got worse as John signed on to play football with the Seattle Seahawks while Abby remained in the dorms on Grymes Hill to finish her senior year at Wagner. New York to Seattle, tough commute.

Abby presses her palms to the familiar kitchen table. This place became her home in the past year. *Their home.* Although she stopped making three-egg omelets and buying green salads that wilted in the refrigerator, she still considers herself part of a couple, half of a whole.

And now the other half is gone.

The sergeant holds up two pamphlets and then places them on the kitchen table. "I'll leave these here for you to go through when things quiet down. They've got everything you'll need to know about benefits, burial, and setting up the funeral."

A funeral. She's supposed to bury her husband. It all seems incongruous. "I'm having trouble processing at the moment," Abby says flatly.

"And that's no surprise." Suz places a fresh mug of coffee in front of her, tips some cream from a small pitcher into it, stirs for her.

Abby wonders who had the presence of mind to bring cream. She and John are strictly one percent milk people.

John *was*. Would she ever get used to saying that?

"We can handle all the arrangements for you, Abby," he is saying. "As much as you like."

As her CAO, Sgt. Palumbo has already explained many of these things for Abby, but although she has been sitting politely and trying to listen, she feels as if she's playing a role, pretending to be herself in her own home while friends and strangers pass through the kitchen extending regrets and condolences. Now that the initial shock has worn thin, she's operating on autopilot, going through all the motions of talking and breathing though her mind is a million miles away fighting the information that John is gone. She cannot believe it. It seems ludicrous that such information could simply be passed to Sgt. Palumbo to pass on to her. Maybe the information is wrong. "Can I ask you . . ." She lifts her face to the sergeant. "Has the army ever made a mistake in something like this? I mean, maybe they've got the wrong guy."

He sighs. "I've never heard of it happening. At least, not in our lifetime. When John's remains arrive at Dover Air Force Base, they'll run tests to verify his identity."

"Oh." She would like to hang her hopes on the delusion that a huge mistake was made, and she would if she could just get rid of this sick feeling in her stomach.

"Have you thought about a final resting place?" the sergeant asked.

A grave. Abby shakes her head. "John wanted to be cremated," she said. "We both do." At least they had discussed that much at the funeral of one of John's college teammates who had died in an accident. The kid's parents had made the unfortunate choice to have the casket open, and the body laid out in a bed of satin looked nothing like the vibrant defensive end who had helped the Scarlet Knights to victory. "No open coffin," John said. "That's just creepy. And burn what's left of me. Ashes to ashes."

"Cremation is a viable option," Sgt. Palumbo says, "but you don't need to make any decisions right now. Sleep on it. Discuss the possibilities with family if you like, and I'll be here to assist you when the time comes."

"And you know I'll help, too." Suz reaches across the table and squeezes Abby's wrist. "I've been through it before." The tip of Suz's nose turns bright red and tears shine in her eyes.

Abby places a hand over Suz's and nods. The wounds are still fresh from Scott's death and now Suz is here to suffer again. It's so wrong.

Sgt. Palumbo excuses himself to talk to someone in the living room, and Abby takes a deep breath.

"This is surreal. These people in my house. All the food and conversation. It seems festive, and maybe that's not wrong. John would hate for anyone to wax morose over him."

"At least you've got Sharice. She's quite the diplomat," Suz says, and they both glance out toward the living room. Although Abby cannot see her mother-in-law she can hear her remarking on how she's going to extract the secret recipe for someone's sour cream noodle casserole.

"Sharice is so good with things like this," Abby says. She had long admired her mother-in-law's ability to hostess with charm and grace.

"And she's all-army. She really knows the culture. She and Madison were a tremendous help when we lost Scott."

Over on the rocking chair, John's teenage sister Madison holds Sofia in her lap, reading *The Very Noisy Morning* for the umpteenth time. How good of Madison to entertain Sofia when she herself is hurting. She and John were close.

"Yes, Noah will be home just as soon as they can get him the flights back," Sharice is saying. "Certainly in time for the funeral. It will be good to see him."

Abby's mouth puckers involuntarily. "Thank God Noah

didn't get taken out, too. At least he'll have some answers when he gets here, some specifics of what happened to John."

"I'm sure he will, sweetie," Suz says.

"As if that matters. I mean, if he's really gone, knowing the details isn't going to bring him back. I'm sorry, my mind isn't working properly anymore."

"No need to apologize. You're not supposed to be sweet and rational right now. You're supposed to throw up your arms and holler and blubber. Let it go like an elephant trumpeting over the savannah." Her arms flailing, Suz lets out a wild, bestial howl.

Silence falls over the house. A moment later two women peek into the kitchen. "Everything okay in here?" a woman with short-cropped black hair asks cautiously.

"We're just mad as hell," Suz answers. "But all things considered . . ." She shrugs. "Whatcha gonna do?"

"It's a difficult time," says the woman with black hair.

"I am so sorry for your loss," the other woman says, crossing to Abby. Her startlingly blue eyes shine with compassion, and Abby realizes it's Peri Corbett, from across the way. "Please let me know if there's anything I can do for you."

"I will," Abby promises, warmed by the genuine sincerity of the people who've dropped everything to come to her house this afternoon.

"I got a fresh pot of coffee here," Suz says. "Can I get you a cup, Peri?"

As normal chatter resumes, Suz serves up two mugs, then heads out to the living room with the coffeepot in hand. She passes Sharice under the arch, offering a refill.

"No, thanks." Sharice shakes her head briskly. "Any more coffee and I'll be bouncing from wall to wall." She places her mug in the sink and then turns to Abby, who can sense her mother-in-law gearing up for an important question.

Abby glances up at her, encouragingly.

"I want you to know," Sharice says confidentially, "Jim just got a call from his C.O., who says there's a good possibility that John will be honored posthumously. There's talk that the president might even attend his funeral."

Abby feels her lips shaping an "O" of surprise, but she cannot form a response.

"That would be wonderful," Peri says, "and well-deserved. After all, he is a hero. He made the ultimate sacrifice for his country." The woman with the dark hair sniffs, and suddenly her eyes are glossy with tears, her nose red. Without a word she grabs two tissues and blots at her eyes.

"What happened?" Suz returns with the empty coffeepot. "Did I miss something?"

"John's going to get some medals," says the woman with dark hair. "He's a national hero."

Why? Abby wants to ask. *Because he used to be a football player?* She turns away from everyone, looking down at the table. John used to sit in this chair. When he wasn't deployed, he ate breakfast here. They dined at this table, sometimes by candlelight. She presses one palm flat against the wood, knowing that John would not want to be favored. Suz's husband, Scott, also lost his life in Iraq, but there was no talk of the president attending his funeral. Why do they want to make a fuss over John?

"I don't see that we have any choice now," Sharice says. Leaning against the counter, she lifts her chin and stares off with a lofty expression, as if she can see destiny shining in the distance. "We're going to have to bury him at Arlington Cemetery."

With those words, Abby feels control slip through her fingers like white sand drizzling onto the beach. Having grown up in Sterling, Virginia, she was well aware of the national cemetery at the edge of Washington, D.C., its white-studded hillsides reserved for veterans and the historically famous. Heroes and presidents and Supreme Court justices. It hardly seemed a fitting place for the man she loved, the man who'd written of his doubts recently, of the futility of war, the darkness in taking another man's life.

"It would be wonderful to see John honored that way," Sharice goes on. "A military procession, twenty-one gun salute . . ."

"Arlington Cemetery . . ." Jim Stanton appears in the doorway, his gray-peppered head just clearing the arch—a tall man, like his sons. Since this morning's news, his skin seems pale, his posture somewhat stooped, contrary to his usual proud military bearing. "I've read that they're running out of real estate there, but no doubt they'll make an exception for us. John was loved by all. If he's there, people who don't know him personally will have a chance to visit his graveside."

"It can be tough to get into Arlington Cemetery," says Sgt. Palumbo, stepping up beside John's father. "But I don't think it would be a problem getting John a burial there."

"John wanted to be cremated," Abby says, feeling as if no one is listening.

Ashes to ashes . . . he used to say.

She closes her eyes and suddenly she is viewing a young couple honeymooning in France. The dark-haired young woman walked arm-in-arm with her husband through a flower market, surrounded by towering stalks and colorful blossoms. In the market he bought her a single rose, a powdery shade of coral with a burst of sweetness. The satin petals were smooth against her cheek as she and John strolled through the sunny square of Montmartre, passing an artist at work, a vendor selling homemade jewelry, a kiosk.

"When I pop off, I want to return here," he said. "Promise me you'll bring me back and toss my ashes into the Seine."

She laughed, happy to be by his side, amused at the notion of the two of them growing old together. "What makes you think I'll outlive you?" she teased. "Besides, I don't think you can dump someone's ashen remains into a river like that. It's illegal."

"Who would notice?" he insisted. "And then you'll be free to hook up with a Frenchman, a man who can feed you baguettes and café au lait every morning, make love to you every night."

"Every night? When am I going to get my beauty sleep?" she'd argued. . . .

"Abby? Are you okay, honey?" Suz's voice breaks into her memory, and she opens her eyes and finds herself back in the kitchen, crowded with people fighting to preserve John's memory, arguing for their notion of right.

"I've never been comfortable with cremation," Sharice says. "Leave it to John to push for the extreme."

"It's done more and more often these days," Sgt. Palumbo says. "The truth is, the space for cremated remains is more plentiful in most national cemeteries."

"Arlington Cemetery would be quite an honor," Jim says, nodding.

"Abby?" Suz leans close and rubs Abby's back between her shoulder blades. "Maybe you need some fresh air."

Abby nods and follows Suz out to the back patio, where a sunny autumn afternoon resounds with haunting beauty.

"I can't do this," Abby says.

"What? The military funeral? The in-laws? The mourners who are going to wear down your carpeting and consume all your chips and soda?"

"All of it," Abby admits. "I don't want any of this in my life. I just want my husband back."

Biting her lower lip, Suz just nods, and Abby knows that she gets it.

Chapter 10

Madison can't take one more minute of this coffee talk. She's going to scream if she hears one more speech about what a great hero John was or how he made the ultimate sacrifice (like he had a choice!). And if she sees one more person rubbing their hands greedily over the prospect of the president awarding her brother a posthumous medal, she'll go ballistic.

No way will she let that asshole present anything to John—not even to John's memory. It's the sort of thing that would have pissed her brother off if he were alive, and if they let it happen now, John is going to rise up and haunt them all!

"This is all happening so fast," her mother says, fanning herself with a magazine from Abby's coffee table. "What's your take on it, Jim? Do you think the Congressional Medal of Honor . . . really?"

"I'd say it's a distinct possibility." Her father speaks in a lowered voice, probably so people won't overhear him and know him for the greedy mercenary he is, counting his son's medals before he's even buried. He leans close to Mom to add: "Our son died a hero, Sherry."

"Oh, my God, listen to yourself," Madison says, unable to restrain herself any longer. "Do you hear what you're saying? Don't you remember that John didn't believe in this war? He enlisted to stop terrorism and violence, not to encourage more war."

"Madison . . ." Jim Stanton's voice is a low growl. "That's enough. Don't muck this up with your personal politics."

"My politics? What about what John believed? That war is wrong. Even back in college he wrote his senior thesis on the cost of war."

Her mom is shaking her head. "He did not, and you were only eleven when he graduated. How would you know, Maddy?"

She points toward the door. "I know because I've got it in my room—right in the desk drawer."

"That's enough, Madison," her father says in the authoritative tone born of military life. "Maybe you'd better step outside and calm yourself. You can return when the hysterics have ended."

She has to bite back tears as she pushes herself out of the rocking chair and steps around them. What a nightmare! Her brother's gone and already they're trying to make him into the model soldier embodying all the crap be was fighting against.

Weaving through the throng of neighbors, she feels her face pucker, on the verge of tears. John would hate this! To be mourned by a bunch of army wives gossiping over casseroles and kids.

On her way out, Madison grabs the frosted glass from where she stashed it on the third shelf. She pushes the door to the back patio and takes a slug of the hard lemonade—the second one she's pilfered behind her parents' back. She thought it would dull the pain, but instead it seems to intensify it, as if someone took a photo of her edgy nerves and enlarged it ten times. Still, she takes another sip, liking the taste. She swallows until the cup is empty.

Behind her, the screen door creaks. Caught, Madison wonders what to do with the empty cup—the evidence—until she hears Abby's voice. "Hey, you."

Madison puts the cup on the table and turns to find Abby looking so incredibly calm in the midst of this storm. Her dark hair shines in the sun and her shoulders are set back, her head lifted high like a flower in the sun. "Oh my God, you look so normal."

Abby tries to smile but her lips crinkle in a pucker. "I may look that way, but inside, my heart is breaking," she admits, her voice cracking.

"Abby! I am so sorry."

Abby opens her arms and Madison falls into them, and, for a moment, Madison feels like her true emotion can flow in front of this girl who loved her brother with all her heart. Loved him so much she gave up an exciting life in the capital to move to this army base and be a military wife.

"I can't believe it, Maddy," Abby says, her voice thick with tears. "I can't believe he's gone."

"Barely gone, and already they're screwing him over." Madison steps back and swipes at the tears on her cheeks. "Are you hearing what they're saying in there about him?"

Abby frowns. "The hero stuff?"

"They're talking about medals and . . . and an audience with the fucking president!" Madison spins on her heel, stomps toward the back yard and takes a seat on the edge of the patio. "It's disrespectful to John. They might as well kick dirt on everything he stood for. But when I point that out they act like I'm an idiot."

"Everybody is out of sorts," Abby says from behind her. "Grief does strange things to people."

"They're vultures. Did you hear my mother? It's like she's looking forward to the funeral. Giddy about John getting medals. Can't wait to have Noah back so she can show him off to her friends." Madison closes her fingers over a clump of crabgrass and tears at it. "Better show him off before he gets killed, too." A sob rises in her throat and she hugs her knees, grateful to be able to wipe the hot tears against her bare legs.

"Oh, Maddy."

She feels Abby's hand rubbing her back, is conscious of her sitting beside her.

"This is hard for all of us," Abby says.

"It sucks."

"Harder for you in a lot of ways. You've grown up an army brat, but I came into this much later. And right now it's really hard for me to face those people in there without feeling like they're part of the problem, part of the system that took John's life. You can bet I'm angry at the army, but I'm still cognizant of the fact that I can't take that out on Sergeant Palumbo . . . or on the neighbors who are trying to maintain a normal life in the shadow of this war."

"So what about my parents? Are they driving you nuts yet?"

"I've been trying to avoid them," Abby admits, "but whenever your mother corners me I feel a panic rising. I don't want to cross her, but it might come to that."

"Welcome to my world." Madison flings the handful of grass into the air, but some of the blades stick to her sweaty palm. "How could they not know that John didn't want this war, that he was having doubts about his country?"

"I suppose they didn't want to hear it. They don't know John's views on politics and war. That was something else they didn't want to hear."

Madison nods. "It does suck."

Abby squeezes her shoulder, silently agreeing.

"You know, Mom is all excited about Noah coming home. A mixed blessing, she calls it. As if getting him out of Iraq for two weeks is going to save his life." Madison turns to look at Abby, whose dark hair is tucked behind her ears. From close up she sees that Abby's eyes are shadowed by gray sadness, shadows that might never go away.

Abby loved John so much. Madison doesn't even have a boyfriend, and she can't imagine losing the love of her life.

"Are you nervous about Noah's trip?" Abby asks her. "About him traveling home?"

Madison shakes her head. "I'm nervous about him going back. I want to kidnap him, lock him in a closet so he'll miss his flight, then throw him into my car and drive him up to Canada or down to Mexico."

"I can see why you feel that way," Abby says. "But honor and patriotism mean a lot to your parents."

"Maybe. Or maybe they don't have a clue about it. Maybe they don't know what patriotism means. Just because you love your country doesn't mean you have to go off and kill people."

Abby nods. "I agree with you, Maddy, but it's just not that simple."

"It could be," Madison says. "Peace is simple. It's people who make it seem so complicated."

Chapter 11

Iraq
Lt. Peter Chenowith

The procedure is clear: the possessions of a soldier killed in the line of duty are to be secured and inventoried by his superior officer and transported home along with the remains. So technically, Peter Chenowith has every right to go through John Stanton's belongings. Maybe it just feels wrong because Chenowith knows Stanton would have hated having his lieutenant go through his things.

Chenowith can almost hear Stanton grousing about invasion of privacy as he dumps the black plastic bag onto the table of the airless briefing room and starts making a list in his notebook. A wristwatch. One wallet with one hundred and ten dollars cash, one Amex card, a Washington State driver's license, and assorted photos.

Whoa—apparently Stanton went for the dark, intellectual type. The brunette has to be Stanton's wife, and though Peter figured a football star like Stanton could have done better, the Mrs. is tight. He'd definitely do her, though after a few weeks in Iraq, most guys would do just about anything on two legs. But the little blonde, there's a hottie. She looks a lot younger than Stanton, and chummy in the photos. Probably the sister. He's read that Stanton has a younger sister.

There isn't much here, as Stanton's stash of PowerBars was left in the bungalow for the other men. There is a homemade name tag with macaroni letters, and a bottle opener that had been decorated with glittery stars. A football, a bunch of books, letters from home, a box of pens, a framed photo of the wife. For such a superstar, Stanton didn't own much.

Chenowith regrets the death of any soldier, but honestly, his job will be easier without Stanton in his platoon. This is Chenowith's first combat assignment out of West Point, and it hasn't been easy having the media breathing down his neck, always watching because he had a celebrity soldier in his ranks.

He tosses the books to see what Stanton was reading and notices that some of them are journals—those blank bound books you fill in. Stanton had written in two and a half of them.

Peter pulls out a chair and cracks open one of the journals, starting in the middle.

Many Iraqis don't understand why American soldiers are still here, and I have to agree with them. We've overstayed our welcome. Saddam has been dethroned, and Operation Iraqi Freedom should now be called Operation Colonization.

Chenowith's lip curls as he remembers the way Stanton always used to talk to the locals. What a schmoozer. You'd think the guy signed up for the United Nations instead of the U.S. Army. Stanton argued that it was good to let people vent, but Chenowith knows no good will come of stirring the pot, whipping these people into a political frenzy.

The more Chenowith reads, the more his teeth grind against each other.

Soldiers are programmed to follow orders without question. But I believe that if a soldier is given an order that he knows is not only illegal but immoral as well, it is his responsibility to refuse that order.

It's this sort of philosophical bullshit that cripples the U.S. Army, Chenowith thinks, stewing over the pages. Peter Chenowith grew up wanting to serve his country, just as his father had done, and his grandfather before that. He was the third generation of Chenowiths to attend West Point, and he sees this deployment in Iraq as his opportunity to prove himself as a man, as a soldier, as a leader.

Unlike whiners like Stanton, he can handle the pressure. He follows orders, and he has the mettle to push his soldiers to make sure they follow, too. His company has suffered some casualties here—every unit has been hit—but that sort of loss is a fact of war, and a good soldier eventually learns that you carry on no matter what the adversity.

His eyes alight on another entry . . . his name.

The army wants "yes" men like Lt. Chenowith who do not question the legality of the policies of the administration. These warmongers will have the lifelong guilt of murdering innocent Iraqis on their conscience and the indelible images of seeing their friends blown up in a war whose purpose is illegal.

And if I stay, what am I? No better or worse than these warmongers.

Canada looks better and better every day.

A burn rises and blossoms in Chenowith's head. So the bigshot hero was thinking of leaving. A sissy. How he'd love to give this to the media. But how can he, when the disparaging remarks about him are laced in those pages.

Goddamned Stanton.

No one is going to see these journals. No one.

This is one time when a rule needs to be broken.

He grabs a few pages and tears them out, cracking the first journal in the seams. The pages fit into the shredder without a problem. It will take a little while, but once he rips these journals up, everyone will be better off.

Stanton is not going to have the last word here. Let the resistance die with the man.

Chapter 12

"I want to go to him," Abby says. "Wherever he is . . . in Kuwait? Or Europe? I'll fly to Iraq if they're holding his body there. I just . . . somehow I feel the need to be with him. To meet him."

Her announcement is greeted with silence in the kitchen. Suz is the only one nodding in agreement, but then Abby knows she can count on her friend's support no matter what she decides.

Sharice pauses at the kitchen counter where she has been consolidating leftover coffee cake and cookies brought by friends. She does not answer but lifts her head, as if a large knot of disapproval is stuck in her throat.

"Oh, Abby . . ." Jim Stanton's voice is laced with worry. "You don't want to go to Iraq."

"Iraq is out of the question. He'll be airlifted to Kuwait by helicopter in the morning," says Sgt. Palumbo, checking his watch. "Their morning, which is just hours away. The body will probably leave Iraq before any of us turn in tonight. He'll be on a Hero Flight with other . . . fallen soldiers. You may have seen the photos. Each case is draped in an American flag with a special light on it. The remains are taken to Dover Air Force Base."

"In Delaware?" Abby asks.

"Dover, Delaware."

"Then that's where I'm going," Abby says.

"But the facility there . . ." Sgt. Palumbo strains to explain. "It's a mortuary. They ID bodies, embalm them, and ship them home for funeral services. There would be nothing for you to do there, Abby."

"I know it probably sounds strange, but that's how I feel, and I can't stay here and just wait for administrative work to be done while he's over there all . . . all alone."

"Abby . . ." Sgt. Palumbo shakes his head. "This is not a good idea. Dover is a military facility. They're—"

"Don't worry," she assures him, "I'm not expecting any special treatment there. I just need to be there, for John. I'll book a flight for tomorrow, pack tonight, and . . ." She turns to Sharice. "You'll tell me if I'm missing something—something important that I should be doing? I don't have any experience with . . . this sort of thing." And Sharice, she knew, had helped other women through it, more than a dozen times in the past few years.

"Of course." Sharice's countenance softens. "But, really, you're doing just fine." She looks down at the cake platter. "I suppose there isn't a wrong or right way to do any of this."

It's the first visible streak of compassion that Abby has seen in her mother-in-law all day, and she is reminded that grief strikes people in different ways, at different times. Sharice has just lost her oldest son; who can fathom the emotional journey that lies ahead of her?

By the time the visitors thin out, leaving Abby with an exceedingly clean kitchen and half a fridge of leftovers, Abby is sure she has weathered a month of Mondays. In truth, it's just after seven.

"I'm taking this one next door for a bath." Suz nods at Sofia who is playing a game in the living room with a stack of Abby's coasters, pretending they are plates containing "very delicious foods" that must be kept in a very specific order on the coffee table. "Do you want us to come back and stay with you?"

Abby remembers the night Suz learned Scott had been killed, how Suz had put Sofia to bed, then spent most of the night on the floor with Abby going through photographs of Scott from boyhood, his college days, their wedding, Sofia's baptism. She'd been happy to be there for Suz, but right now all she wanted was to be alone.

"I'll be okay." Abby shoots a glance into the kitchen, not sure where her mother-in-law is lurking. "Actually, I just want to be alone right now."

"Well, give a holler if you need me." Suz swoops down and lifts Sofia to her hip. Sofia objects that she hasn't given out all the delicious foods yet, but Suz promises the coasters will be here next time she comes to play. On her way out, Suz stops to put a hand on Madison's shoulder to say good-bye.

Madison's face is illuminated in the light of the computer, and Abby thinks she looks so mature for her age. On looks alone she could easily be mistaken for a college student, with wise periwinkle blue eyes and honey-blond hair streaked with pale gold that falls in a curtain over her shoulders. But beneath the smooth veneer of beauty, Madison possesses a naiveté that is very much sweet sixteen, a quality that Abby hopes will endure.

"Here's something you might want to look at," Madison tells Abby once Suz has left. Needing to escape the annoying conversations around her, Madison agreed to send out a mass e-mail with pertinent details about John to friends and relatives, and manage the deluge of responses that Abby didn't have time to handle. "You got an e-mail from a guy named Flint. Wasn't he one of the college friends at your wedding?"

Abby nods. "Dave Flint. He was one of my suitemates in college. Suite, as in we shared a set of rooms," she clarifies with a slight smile.

"He's in Iraq," Madison says. "Is he a soldier?"

"A reporter. Actually, he likes to be called a journalist. He works for a newspaper up in Seattle." She leans over Madison's shoulder to read Flint's email.

Abs, sorry to hear about John. There are no words. . . .
I'm on assignment in Iraq, not far from his FOB.

Will head over there and see what I can find out.
Reach out if you need me.
—Flint

"Why is he going over to the base where John was stationed?" Madison asks.

"Because he thinks the information he can gather will help me," Abby answers. "Or because there's a story in it for him. Flint is a good friend, but journalism runs deep in his blood."

Madison looks up from the computer, the blue screen reflected on her pale face and hair. "Would you give him John's story? Not the hero profile they all want to hear, but the real story of John."

"I don't know. I won't sanction inflating John's life or death just because it makes for better entertainment, and I'm not sure that Flint would be able to work within those parameters." She closes Flint's e-mail, scans a few others, then shares a few personal things about the people Madison is writing to, to help fill her in.

"Thank you for doing this. I want to get the word out, but I don't feel capable of sitting at the computer and fielding e-mail right now."

"I don't mind. And you'd better get packed. I got you on a morning flight to D.C." Madison opens some papers that were discreetly folded closed and hands them to Abby. "It leaves kind of early, but it was a choice of early morning or take a red-eye tomorrow night."

"This will be fine," Abby says, eager to be out of here and on her way. She'll stay with her parents in Sterling, Virginia, until John's body arrives at Dover Air Force Base, which is about a half day's drive from D.C. Staring at the flight itinerary, which shows a short stopover in New York, Abby senses the small segments of reality falling into place around her, like autumn leaves covering her path.

She's flying off to meet John's body. He's dead.

This is all horribly real.

The door to the back patio slides open, and Sharice returns

to the house, along with her husband and Sgt. Palumbo. From the way their conversation stops when they see her, she suspects they're discussing John. Or, more specifically, the many mistakes she's making by flying to Dover.

"It just occurred to me that we should place an obituary in the papers," Sharice says, joining Abby and Madison at the computer. "Would you like me to handle that?"

"It would be a huge relief," Abby says honestly. "I won't have time to do anything here, since my flight leaves early in the morning. But do you think we could get the media to play down the hero angle and point up what a wonderful human being John was? Keep it short and to the point? I'd hate for them to puff him up as a war-loving hero." *Especially since he didn't believe in this war.*

Behind Sharice's back, Madison glances up from the computer and rolls her eyes, but Abby forges on. "John would want something simple. As he used to say, 'Give it to me straight.'"

"I'll mention that," Sharice says, "though the obit writers will do what they want. No keeping them in line."

"I know you'll do your best," Abby says, forcing herself to smile. She's been forcing it so much today, her jaw aches.

"I'll say good night now," Sgt. Palumbo says, "but Abby, I'll call you on your cell in the morning. We'll pin down the details for the ceremony over the next few days."

"Arlington Cemetery," Sharice says knowingly. "I'm counting on it."

Abby thanks the sergeant and turns toward her bedroom, suddenly feeling exhausted but knowing she won't be able to sleep. No . . . sleep is not the thing she needs. What she longs for now is the solace of a hot shower, a chance to be alone and cocooned within the rush of water, a place to let the tears flow freely, to sob and howl without someone patting her back and trying diplomatically to make her stop crying.

"Well," she tells Sharice, folding her arms in front of her chest, "thanks for all your help today. I'll call you from the East Coast."

"We're not finished here. I'm going to help you pack for your trip," Sharice tells her.

"You don't have to do that," Abby says. "We're both tired, and I'm just going to throw a few things together."

"And then you'll be across the country without the things you need. Don't be silly. I'm happy to help." Sharice marches into the bedroom. "At times like this, you forget to pack important things, and suddenly you find yourself across the country without a toothbrush, or minus your favorite slippers, or, God forbid, without any clean underwear. I remember traveling home when my father passed. The boys were young yet, and Madison wasn't even born, and when we got word there was no time. We had to throw together a few essentials and jump on an army transport from Okinawa back to the States. . . ."

Abby sits on the edge of the bed, listening as Sharice talks from the closet.

"Needless to say, there was no time to pack properly. I threw things into a suitcase and a duffel bag, trying to remember to pack the right dress clothes for the ceremony, as well as coats for the weather. Of course, when we arrived in Minnesota, nothing was quite right. I'd forgotten to pack dress shoes for the funeral. Had to borrow a pair from my sister. Those shoes gave me the worst kind of blister on my heel. Noah was angry about the blue suit I packed for him. He complained that it made him look like sailor boy. And John . . . apparently, just before we left the house, John dumped out all his clothes and replaced them with his collection of stuffed animals, so that they wouldn't get lonely without him."

She emerges from the closet rolling a suitcase, another bag slung over her shoulder. "So there we are in Minnesota for my father's funeral and John has nothing to wear. I was so angry with him."

"What did you do?" Abby asks, grateful for Sharice's rare anecdote.

"I made John wear Noah's sailor suit. That taught him not to repack." Sharice removes a garment bag from the closet. "You'd better take your dress clothes. Might as well have what you need in case the funeral is back east, which sounds very likely."

And that's that, Abby thinks as her mother-in-law starts going through the garments hanging in her closet, looking for a suit or a dark dress.

Thinking of comfort, Abby opens a drawer on her side of the dresser she shares with John and pulls out short white socks and panties, shorts and T-shirts. One pair of jeans should be enough, and she'll need a sweatshirt. She pauses, then slides open John's bottom drawer, where her hands dig into his old football jersey, scarlet red with the number nineteen on the front in white. Pressing her face into the soft folds, she inhales his scent, a mixture of salt and soap, a scent that creates a pang of longing deep in her soul. The jersey goes into the bag along with everything else, then she changes her mind and pulls it out. She'll carry it with her on the plane, burrow into it when she has nowhere else to turn.

As she closes the drawer, photographs on top of the dresser catch her eye. Two photos from their wedding, and a picture of John in his gray dress uniform, the sky behind him so blue that his dark hair and broad shoulders cut a bold silhouette. That smile . . . it tugs at her heart, even in a photo. She used to tease him that he could appear in a toothpaste commercial, and he'd flash her a wide grin, saying something inane like, "Brightens *and* whitens!"

The black-and-white wedding photos have always reminded Abby of a classic film, one in which the soldiers return from the front in World War II to their joyous wives clad in sophisticated gowns. In one photo, John, in dress uniform, escorts Abby beneath an archway of crossed silver swords. John was so tall he had to duck, and a glint of light off the sword over his head makes it look as if he has a halo. The other photo is a close-up of Abby and John dancing, their eyes fixed on each other, each utterly mesmerized by the other.

She never imagined herself as a soldier's wife; the sword-crossing ceremony at their wedding made her feel like a princess, the bride of a knight. "I don't see myself as an army wife," she used to tell John, who would roll his eyes and remind her that labels are so limiting and often inaccurate. Abby didn't want to be married to the military, but by the time John had come to the decision to enlist, she had already fallen for him, and the attraction, like John himself, was so huge and overwhelming and brilliant that she could not imagining spending her life with anyone but him. And now she is a military widow, a tag that seems just as ill-fitting and all the more unavoidable.

"Slowing down on the job?" Sharice zips the garment bag closed and steps closer to view the photos. "I don't know if Jim has ever told you, but he's never been so proud as the day John and Noah enlisted. When John signed on to play for the Seahawks, we'd thought it was over—our family legacy in the military. And then . . ." She shrugs. "The terrorists attacked, and everything changed."

"To be honest," Abby admits, "it wasn't a change I welcomed. I never imagined myself as a soldier's wife. It was a world, a culture, so foreign to me, and I prided myself on being in control of my own life."

"I sensed that about you," Sharice says, heading back to the closet.

"It's hard to give up your freedom to 'orders.' I didn't want to be married to the military, but suddenly it became part of John, part of the whole package if I wanted to be with him. And I did. I couldn't imagine my life without him." Her lower lip begins to curl as a sob threatens, but Abby bites down on it, tamping down the inevitable pain. Not here, not in front of her mother-in-law, who always seems to be silently questioning Abby's mettle.

"Your feelings about military service aside"—Sharice steps out of the closet to make eye contact—"no one has ever questioned your love for my son. We could tell you adored him, and he was just crazy about you, too." Sharice sighs. "And although you didn't choose military service for him, you also did not stand in his way. That's admirable."

"I don't know how you did it all these years, moving across the country when orders came up, being a single parent while Jim was deployed."

"You just do it. You adapt." Sharice picks out a pair of

black pumps from the floor of the closet and shrugs. "At least you've come to understand the dedication of the military community—unlike the rest of the country. I swear, they believe we sit here on base and hold Bingo tournaments. It's always been an issue for me, the lack of support for the military community. Too many people don't appreciate the sacrifices made by soldiers in the armed forces and their families. People just aren't patriotic anymore."

Does Sharice think she's lacking in patriotism?

Picking up the photo of John in dress uniform, Abby studies the folds of the American flag flapping in the wind behind him and has to steel herself to keep from choking up. Her eyes still fill with tears when she witnesses the lowering of the flag at dusk here at Fort Lewis. Since 2001 she has not been able to witness a ceremony with the Stars and Stripes without choking up, recalling the image of the firefighters who raised the flag at Ground Zero, the resounding choruses of "America, the Beautiful" that filled sports arenas and hearts at a time when the country was so shaken by acts of terrorism against innocent people.

Was it patriotism that made her throat tighten in a lump as she watched the soldiers in John's brigade line up to board their buses, their desert fatigues a speckled sea of muted tones? So many of them, men and women . . . and which ones would return healthy? Which would lose their lives or come home damaged and traumatized?

Or was she unpatriotic to want her husband out of the war? Was it wrong to want to keep him here in the States, out of harm's way? Was it selfish to wish he'd stayed in pro football, playing out his battles on Astroturf a few Sunday afternoons during the season?

"I'm not sure what patriotism means anymore," Abby says, surprised at her own honesty in front of Sharice. "But I have to admit, when John got on that bus to go to Iraq, I didn't want him to be like the other men. I wanted him to be special, protected, as if he had a guardian angel watching over him." She can still recall the eerie feeling as she scanned the long line of men, some turning to wave, others facing away, anonymous heads. "I knew some of those men would die, but I didn't want it to be John. And knowing how strong and tall and courageous he was, I was sure he would survive. So sure."

"I'm sure he died in a state of grace," Sharice says, "knowing that he gave his all for his country."

Abby suspects that Sharice has it all wrong, that John would be frustrated by his own pointless death, but she doesn't have the energy to go there. She and Sharice have a long history of political friction, and after heated discussions of the exigencies and tragedies of war have come to a silent agreement not to venture to those dangerous territories in conversation. They agreed to disagree, but here is one occasion in which Abby wishes she shared her mother-in-law's views. She presses the framed photo to her heart, hoping that Sharice is right, and that John found some peace as he left this world. At the very least, a glimmer of peace.

Chapter 13

Camp Desert Mission, Iraq

The ritual of sending off a fallen soldier can bring tears to any man's eyes, but today is special. As if the hands of God descended to the earth to shield this region of Iraq from the desperate winds that blew through the night, a stillness looms over the desert now. A sudden break from the vicious Sharqi winds.

A miracle, just in time to allow the pomp and circumstance of a hero's farewell, John Stanton's final departure from Camp Desert Mission.

He straps his rifle on—the stealthy cause of death, no doubt—and joins the other soldiers, the sea of desert khaki. Marching at parade rest alongside the stretcher, he feels a frisson of excitement, a tingling awareness that he is observing history. John's send-off is unlike any event that has ever transpired on this Forward Operating Base.

Not that they haven't sent scores of bodies home on Hero Flights. This unit has seen mass casualties. During bad times they've had days with twenty or thirty people dead, and each body got a send-off, a guided procession to the helicopter that bore it off to Kuwait. Yes, the soldiers of Bravo Company have sent plenty of fallen soldiers home to their final resting place.

But none of the previous casualties came close to John Stanton's status as a celebrity, a star, a hero. And true to his legendary status, he is getting a hero's exit, complete with an opening in the heavens that allows pink and gold sunlight to emanate over the pale horizon like a photo on a goddamned greeting card.

A picture-perfect moment, and a huge turnout. Many final ceremonies attract fifty men, maybe a hundred, but today it looks like every soldier from Camp Despair and neighboring outposts turned out to honor John.

The sight of so many somber, silent men is quite the spectacle—further proof of the king's stature. A person could easily feel a twinge of jealousy. Except, of course, for the obvious fact that Stanton is dead, no longer able to suck up the adulation.

All the king's men are in attendance: dutiful brother, loyal friends, fellow soldiers, surly superior officers. Hell, even a handful of reporters got here for the early-morning service, sandstorm and all. That's fame for you. The guys from the media stand among the nearly three hundred men who line the path to the ambulance when the litter bearing John Stanton's body emerges from the temporary morgue, carried by John's favorites.

Everyone knows who the king's favorites were.

But no one realizes that one of them betrayed him.

John's death will go down in history as a combat casualty.

And it's all rather beautiful. The snow-white litter bearing the body. The crimson, white, and navy of the flag draped squarely over his body. The hard-jawed, somber male soldiers standing in a line so long their desert fatigues form a ribbon of muddy brown that ripples against the stone color of the sand flats.

The beauty of the ceremonial send-off on a Hero Flight has eluded him until this day when the body of a fallen hero is borne by his buddies down the path of soldiers.

An American flag with a light shines on the hero, a fallen man, yet his light shines on.

The pallbearers pause at the ambulance as a soldier wearing a purple vestment around his neck says a prayer. "Lord, we pray that this soldier's life was not in vain, that his hard work on earth furthered your cause of peace and justice. Heavenly Father, into your hands we commend the spirit of John Laurence Stanton . . ."

Words, words. They buzz in his head, often too loud and distorted to decipher. He wishes the chaplain would finish so that the hero's grand ceremony could continue, the king's litter progressing down the line so that every mourning soldier could bear witness to his fallen power.

The greatness that once reigned.

The power and light that passed into me the moment I took his life.

"Amen." The soldiers' voices are a thunderclap as the chaplain closes his prayer book. The litter is loaded into an ambulance and the mourners march on in silence, forward to the helicopter pad.

No one flinches when the winds kick up dust and grit.

No one misses a step in the hero's last march.

At the helicopter pad, the ambulance rolls to a stop. Two men from Stanton's platoon open the vehicle's rear doors, and the priest steps forward to lead another prayer. This time the chaplain dashes holy water over the body, then over the crowd.

A clot of thick holy water lands in the new hero's hair, and he imagines it seeping into his scalp, into the follicles, his pores soaking it up in the same way he has soaked up John Stanton's soul.

"Remember, man, that you are dust," the chaplain says, "and unto dust you shall return."

A soldier steps forward, lifts a bugle to his lips, and blows taps as John's boys lift the litter from the ambulance and carry it to the helipad. With gravity and reverence the snow-white litter is lifted into the helicopter, like some ancient emperor who has been granted the gift of flight. The men duck low and scurry away as the chopper blades begin to rotate.

And then the soldiers stand at attention and salute their fallen hero.

The final salute.

The king has fallen. The survivors will battle on.

Sleep well, he thinks as the copter lifts from the ground. *Sleep on into eternity, and I will take care of the living.*

To the victor go the spoils.

Chapter 14

The minute Sharice steps out of Abby and John's house she faces her husband with the question that has been nagging at her all evening: "How am I going to work around Abby?"

"I don't want her to get hurt any more than she is," Jim says, unlocking the car door and opening it for his wife. "She's very vulnerable right now. In too much of a state to handle the media with real control."

"She wants to play down John's accomplishments," Sharice says in disbelief. "She'd have the press minimize all the things John fought for, the things he gave his life for."

"That's not going to fly. If you doth protest too much, the media is going to pump him up all the more."

"Mmm." Sharice stares through the windshield as Jim starts the car. "I don't know how Abby's going to handle all this considering the state she's in. Poor thing. She's an emotional wreck. Thank God I intervened and insisted on packing a few things that she can wear to the funeral."

"I heard her ask you to keep the obit subdued and understated," Jim says. "How are you going to do that?"

"I've got to be guided by my best instincts."

"Which means, a hero's tribute?"

"Which means the truth," Sharice confirms. "And if some people are looking for a strong, courageous role model to inspire them, then let them honor John."

By the time they arrive home, it's all decided: Sharice will reach out to the media and encourage them to use all the bells and whistles in telling John's story, and if Abby doesn't approve? Well, eventually she'll get over it.

Downstairs, from the trail of discarded flip-flops, backpack, hoody, and empty yogurt cup, Sharice can see that Madison has blazed through here on her way up to her room. And she's left the computer on. Well, for once, Sharice has good reason to go online.

Sitting at the unfamiliar computer, Sharice searches online to find contact information for the Seattle newspapers, as well as the local TV stations affiliated with national networks. She starts by drafting an e-mail to one of the TV stations, but halfway through, she realizes this is going to be a time-consuming process for someone who's not computer literate.

"Sometimes you just need to make a good old-fashioned phone call," she tells Jim, who is tucked into in his old blue recliner, watching the ten o'clock news.

While she's on hold, Sharice paces into the small laundry room to start a load of colors, and there, hanging on the "wall of fame," as the kids dubbed it, are three framed montages, one devoted to each of her children. She quickly pours in detergent, then takes the framed pictures of John from the hook on the wall, studying the photos of her oldest son, from infancy to manhood, the most recent shot taken last Christmas right here in this house.

Still holding the phone to her ear with one shoulder, she closes the door to the living room, leans back against the filling washer, and allows herself to gape, open-mouthed, over the photos of her son, her first baby, her oldest child, who is never coming home again.

A sharp howl escapes her throat, but she staves off feeling, wanting to see her son, his life in its entirety, captured in still photographs.

Her eyes dash from the photo of John potty training with a rebellious smirk on his face to a shot of him pressing a ball to his mouth below a miniature basketball hoop. There he is as a baby, swaddled in a downy blue blanket, looking so innocent you'd never believe he was a howler, that she'd spent night after night trekking up and down the stairs in their quarters outside Stuttgart, Germany, because the gentle jostling was the only thing that seemed to ease the discomfort of his colic. My, how the baby weight melted for her that time.

With apple red cheeks, John the toddler hangs from his dad's arm, those red cheeks the tip-off that he was sick with fever. How sick, Sharice had not realized until the doctors admitted him to the army hospital at Robinson Barracks. An abscess in his throat, swollen to the size of a golf ball . . . a wonder he could breathe or swallow. Sharice remembers the sleepless days spent sitting beside his hospital bed, an IV line strapped onto his tiny arm, telling him what a brave boy he was, assuring him that everything would be just fine when she was actually quivering at the thought of losing him.

There's John at age ten, looking dark and serious in his Boy Scout uniform. Barefoot on a summer day, chasing his brother through a shallow stream. At dusk, he'd loved to catch lightning bugs but refused to put them in a jar like his friends because he didn't want to harm a living thing.

John at twelve, when she home-schooled him during a short tour of duty in Japan. Twelve years old and he was reading Kierkegaard, discussing existentialism and the search for the "true self" like a seasoned philosopher. Another shot of him holding baby Maddy at that time, singing her the ABC song, using her Elmo puppet to teach her to count and say words. What twelve-year-old nurtures and teaches an infant, sharing joy with such alacrity?

He was an exceptional child; she realized that years ago.

Not that he was without flaw.

John could be stubborn. Bullheaded. How many times had he defied her and Jim, standing his ground because he felt that his actions were justified. "I'm doing it in the name of right!" he told her, time and again. After he'd chastised her father for smoking cigarettes. Protested that enlisted men weren't welcome in the Officers Club. Convinced some of his friends to join him in tree hugging so that a grove of trees wouldn't be cut down by the base maintenance crew. Such a tough nut, he could be. Uncompromising and determined.

She recalls Jim's disappointment when John graduated from high school and chose to attend Rutgers University. It had been Jim's dream for his oldest son to attend West Point and become a commissioned officer, but although John was accepted there he bucked his father—"I just can't hide in my father's shadow," he'd said—and taken the scholarship offered by Rutgers. Such a disappointment to Jim, despite the fact that John developed a national profile as a running back and was drafted to the NFL right out of college.

That he'd landed in Seattle, not too far from Fort Lewis, had been a stroke of luck. And playing the first year that the new stadium opened. Sharice will never forget standing in the new stadium on opening night, her arm linked through Jim's, as the stadium and the sky above it glowed from festive fireworks. And though Jim's pleasure may have been tempered by disappointment, Sharice was proud that John was achieving his goals—playing professional football, performing beyond all expectations. That night, when he broke away from the pack and ran the ball into the end zone, leaping and bounding like a stag in the woods, she couldn't deny the swell of pride and pleasure.

He achieved so much in his twenty-seven years.

Her throat tightens at the sight of him in his dress uniform—so stern and strong. When he'd called to share the news, told them that he and Noah were signing up together.

That day that John and Noah enlisted . . . perhaps it was the happiest day of their lives, hers and Jim's. It changed something in Jim, made him stand taller, knowing his sons would be serving, following in his footsteps.

She hugs the montage to her breast, unable to imagine the world without him . . . her son, her oldest. How could he be gone?

Sharice's face crumples as a quiet whimper escapes her throat.

Her son, her baby boy, who grew into a beautiful, responsible man . . .

She presses her eyes closed and purses her lips with deep resolve. If he's really gone, she will not let his life end with a whisper. She'll make sure everyone knows of his heroic decision to leave pro football to serve his country because, despite Abby's hesitance to attract publicity, she knows John did it all for a reason. Sharice will dedicate herself to making sure people remember that John Stanton stood up for his country and gave his life to keep America free of terrorism.

"Hello?" someone says on the line, and Sharice realizes she has passed through the black hole of a telephone system to a real person, whose voice becomes alert when she mentions that she's John Stanton's mother.

"I'm so sorry for your loss," the woman on the phone says. "I'm a segment producer, and this is certainly newsworthy." The woman wants to ask Sharice a few questions over the phone, then send out a camera crew for some video footage. "Would tomorrow morning be okay?" asks the producer, Lacey Phelps. "I know this is a difficult time for you, but this is definitely a story with local appeal . . . probably even national."

"Tomorrow morning is fine," Sharice says. She presses the framed montage to her breast, unable to view the photos of her son and keep the tremors from her voice. Preparing to answer Lacey's questions, she braces herself and takes a deep breath.

Stay focused on the mission. Maintain composure. Don't fall apart and play the overwrought soldier's mom. You can do this . . . for John.

Chapter 15

Al Fallujah, Iraq
Emjay

From high up in the warehouse, Emjay stares down at a stain that won't go away.

Some of the guys from Alpha Company were here last night and again this morning scrubbing the hell out of the bloodstain for hours, pouring on bleach and cleansers. Emjay heard them cursing under their breath, unaware that he was watching from above.

But it won't go away. Damned bloodstain. You'd think John was freakin' Superman or something. The whitewashed surface continues to ooze rusty brown, as if the blood is now running from beneath the floor, an underground spring.

Perched some twenty yards above on a loft that was probably once used to store tiles, Emjay Brown stares down at the dark spot on the ground, which seems to darken and grow before his eyes. Like a curse, a scourge, it will never go away.

What's that Shakespeare play where the woman tries to scrub out a bloodstain but can't get it out? "Out, damned spot! out I say!" Emjay can still hear his junior high teacher acting out the scene for the class. Lady Macbeth, he thinks. She became a chronic hand washer. Shakespeare's attempt to point the finger at obsessive-compulsive disorder before Freud was even born. Emjay doesn't have an advanced degree in psychology like Doc, but he's read enough to know about the psychosis of the month. When you live on a chicken farm there's a lot of time for reading, and unlike his old man, he wasn't ashamed to make the trip into town and borrow a bunch of books from the library. That old library became his refuge, a safe place to go when the old man was on a tirade and his friends dried up. By the time he finished high school he'd read through more than half the fiction section, women's books included. Not that he was like that or anything, but Emjay didn't really care who was telling a story, as long as it was interesting.

Yeah, that was Lady Macbeth, scrubbing the skin off her own hands.

Could use a neurotic scrubber like that to work on the stain three stories below.

And all because of . . . what?

The army wants to make it sound like a raid gone bad, an insurgent who turned on them, but Emjay knows better. The man he saw running away was no Iraqi insurgent.

"It was one of our own, sir," he told Lt. Chenowith and Col. Waters at the debriefing.

Waters sat back in his chair and pressed a finger to the bridge of his dark glasses. "What are you saying, Corporal? Do you mean you saw a U.S. soldier shoot John Stanton?"

"No, sir, when the shots were fired I could only see the muzzle flash. But I saw the gunman running away."

Chenowith leaned over the table of the briefing room, a small spartan space in a bungalow that held only the table with an ancient slide projector and a few wrinkled maps and satellite images on the wall. "Did you see who it was?"

"No, sir. Only that it was one of our guys. An American."

Col. Waters rubbed the stubble on his chin, considering this. "And why would an American soldier kill John Stanton?"

"That I don't know, sir." Emjay set his teeth tight, bracing against the colonel's disdain. Either the man didn't believe him, or he was furious that Emjay would open up this can of worms in his company.

"Have you mentioned this to anyone, Corporal Brown?" asked Waters.

"No, sir."

"Good. Information like this is of a sensitive nature. You're to repeat it to no one, understand, Corporal?"

"Yes, sir."

Chenowith squinted at Emjay, then turned to the colonel, who opened a folder and started leafing through it.

"You're dismissed, Corporal," Col. Waters said.

Dismissed . . . just as the truth had been dismissed.

A man killed in cold blood, and damned if the army would do anything about it because, if the truth got out, they might look bad.

The stain blurs and moves before his eyes, and Emjay crawls on his belly to the edge of the platform, staying low in case another phantom bullet flies through the dark warehouse. His fingers dig into the dusty wood of the platform of the warehouse that used to hold dates. Canned dates, it seems. Which led to the usual wry comments from jokers like Lassiter, who made cracks like, "Now there's not a date to be had in Iraq," or "This building couldn't get a date now if it were the last warehouse on earth."

This dark, dismal place. Nobody would have figured John's life would end here. A life so huge isn't supposed to fade out in a dark dead end like this. John was a freakin' football hero back home, a rising star on the Seahawks. Even Emjay had seen him play once or twice on television.

Not that John ever allowed anyone to grant him special perks. "I played football," he used to say. "Big fucking deal. It's inconsequential compared to what American soldiers have been doing to protect our country from terrorists." John hated to be pumped up or given special treatment. He often took the night shift, which nobody else wanted. He was always good that way, volunteering for the shit no one else would do. A team player, a good guy.

Those bullets that took him out nicked the heart of this platoon.

Emjay stares down at the spot and wonders if he did the wrong thing. Maybe he shouldn't have applied pressure to

John's chest. The head wound might have been the thing that killed him, but Emjay hadn't seen it, with blood everywhere, everything so dark. Or he could have gone to get Noah—get real help instead of trying to stop the bleeding himself. And then there were the seconds wasted when he scrambled for John's NOD to get a look at the shooter. What a boner move! He could've saved Stanton.

Instead, he did the unforgivable . . . let his partner die.

The silence of the warehouse says that he's alone, but Emjay stays low and crawls closer to the edge so that one arm can dangle over the site. Letting it drop down to the pull of gravity is somehow freeing. He watches the brown skin on the back of his hand swing to and fro, a dark pendulum in the darkness, ticking off the seconds until eternity. Resting his jaw on the edge, Emjay watches the patch of blood and fantasizes about flying down to it. Splat, right on top of it.

A one-way ticket home sounds sweet right now.

You are not supposed to kill yourself in the U.S. Army. The officers got in hot water for that one, and if the public found out about it there was hell to pay in the public relations office—probably bad for recruitment. Rumor has it that a marine committed suicide, right here in the Al Anbar province back during the first invasion. That's why most companies have a shrink like Doc, tagging along to help them with their problems.

So Emjay is supposed to talk to Dr. Jump if he has any thoughts of suicide. Which would be great, except that Emjay does not talk to anyone but John. He doesn't trust Doc. Doesn't trust Lassiter. Noah Stanton is totally closed off. Gunnar McGee is a moron and Hilliard is in love with himself and Spinelli is just a scared kid who wants to run home to his mama.

John was the only person who made the days bearable, the nights peaceful. Once, when Emjay asked him how he could shut his mind down and sleep at night, John just said: "You gotta sleep, buddy. Regenerate. Tomorrow's trouble can wait till tomorrow." Somehow Emjay had found his words soothing. John could convince you of just about anything. And Emjay had started finding a way to sleep with John around.

But no more. Never again. Can't sleep or eat. Can't even breathe half the time. His heart thuds in his chest, his breath burning. Christ, why can't he breathe? Can't get air and can't move from this spot. A panic attack, something no soldier is allowed.

But it hurts to breathe.

He tries to distract himself, focus on the bloodstain. Lose himself in the dark abyss of the warehouse—four stories of half-empty shelves and pallets that hold a sickeningly sweet odor. He leans over the edge, feeling gravity pull on his thudding heart. From this height, what kind of damage would he do?

Broken bones, maybe. The right break could get him home, in physical therapy. It needed to be bad, because after an incident like this he was going to be marked within the platoon as as a malingerer, a loser faking an injury to avoid duty.

Or there could be spinal damage. A wheelchair for the rest of his life. That'd suck.

Could bust his head open. That would probably kill him.

And maybe that wouldn't be so bad, to end the fear. Take out the unknown.

Kill the pain and go home a hero.

He shifts his weight closer to the edge and lets his head dangle, free.

Free.

Just push away from the side and you're free . . .

Chapter 16

Fort Lewis
Jim Stanton

A whimpering sound wakes Jim Stanton, and he's not sure whether it's the weary sob grinding in his own throat or the cry of one of the guys sleeping nearby. Although they have huddled in the dried reeds in an attempt to take cover, they know that no amount of camouflage can save you from the skilled eye of a sniper or the determined stealth of a night patrol.

"With my bad luck, I'll wake up dead," Riley had joked as they settled in for the night. Although Riley had a joke for every occasion, none of the men laughed or even cracked a smile. What used to be funny now yawned painfully in the dark, a grim reality.

Because how can you wake up, when you're already dead?

Jim rolls over onto his side, adjusting the helmet on his head. His shirt is damp with sweat, and there's moisture in his eyes. Perspiration or tears? Before 'Nam he'd been sure a real man never cried.

He flops onto his back, shuddering as sweat runs down the center of his chest.

Above him, the singular tree looms, listing to one side in the mist.

The tree is the only sign of life in view, the last tree standing, just as he is the last man alive in this desolate jungle.

"Hello?" he calls out.

But there is no answer.

"Is anybody there? Someone . . . Riley? Where the hell are you. Shroeder? Report!"

Silence.

There is only desolate silence, isolation.

"No!" he shouts. It can't be. He can't be back in Vietnam, surrounded by death. After the injuries he sustained in the ambush, the docs said it would be his last tour of duty.

Why was he back here, goddammit? Paralyzed in the jungle, soaked to the bone in sweat and dread. His heart pounds painfully in his chest, a dark pulse thrumming in his ears. It wasn't supposed to happen this way. He was never going back. Never!

He pounds a fist into the ground beneath him.

It bounces back, the earth spongy beneath him as he yanks himself up . . .

And finds himself sitting in his bed.

It was the dream again, the nightmare.

Ever since troops were deployed to Afghanistan in Operation Enduring Freedom, Jim suffered from the recurring dream, the sinking vision of himself back in the game, back in 'Nam, exposed and scared shitless.

Each time he's in a panic over being deployed again.

Each time he jolts awake soaked in his own sweat and tears.

This time the pounding beneath his ribs is disconcerting. He presses a hand there, as if to control the wild rhythm as he glances over at Sharice, who sleeps soundly, her silver-and-gold hair still, her shoulder rising and falling gently under the sheet. A heavy sleeper, thank God, so she didn't have to know about his weakness.

Then again, she took a sleeping pill tonight. She had to. Sharice is a high-wattage lamp, without the turn-off switch.

The reality of it hits him again, sitting there in bed, and he pushes the sheet away and slides to the edge of the mattress, head in hands.

His boy's gone. Killed.

And it's all on my shoulders.

He never wanted to put his kids out there in harm's way. Never. Other soldiers were so proud to have their sons follow them into the military, but not Jim. The eerie sense of responsibility and dread that pinched him since the boys enlisted came to a head yesterday when his commander called him into the office to tell him about John.

Killed in combat. All because his old man was never quite man enough to speak honestly about military service.

Jim tosses back the sheet and slides around, bringing his bare feet to solid ground. No use trying to go back to sleep. Once the dream tears through your night, he's found, there will be no rest, at least not in the dire hours till dawn.

Stealthily, he makes his way through the dark to the door of the master bedroom and closes it quietly behind him. At times like these, he's found the mindless chatter of the boob tube to be the most reassuring company available in the middle of the night. The blanket on the couch and the sound of a human voice sometimes make him feel human again, even if that voice is Rachael Ray telling him how to make spaghetti squash from the gourds in his own garden.

At the top of the stairs, he pauses in front of Madison's room. Since she was a kid, afraid of being too far from her parents at night, she has kept the door open, and now he can't resist looking in, reassured by the slender form slumbering beneath a summer quilt in the blue light from her night-light. Yes, sixteen and she still sleeps with a teddy bear and a night-light. Somehow Jim feels relieved that his daughter, who's old enough to drive a car, sit for the SATs, and see "R" movies, still clings to some of the more reassuring vestiges of her childhood.

God knows, she's going to need them in this world.

He is turning away, stepping over the threshold, when she stirs, sweeping in a deep breath.

"Daddy? Are you okay?" she asks, her throat so tight with sleep that he is reminded of the chipmunk voice she used to have, the voice that used to croon Christmas carols and spiral up to the high notes of the "Star-Spangled Banner" in school assemblies.

"I'm fine," he lies, wondering if she remembers, caught in the haze of sleep. Has the pain of her brother's death seeped so deep into her psyche that her whole being is crushed, her dreams tainted?

God, he hopes not.

His permission to sleep was revoked years ago, ruined, but he wants better for his daughter. "Everything's fine." Another lie, but a necessary one. A fifty-seven-year-old man can hardly tell his daughter that he's exploding from within, dying of a broken heart. "Go back to sleep, honey."

Chapter 17

"**H**ello?" Flint calls through the empty warehouse, feeling like a dick because places like this scare the shit out of him.

As they should.

Although the soldier posted on watch outside told him that the building's perimeters had been secured since the shooting, you could never be too sure. And frankly, a dark warehouse would be hazardous enough during peacetime, but in a war zone like this Flint knows it's exponentially more dangerous.

Stepping forward tentatively, he shifts his protective eyewear onto his helmet and waits while his eyes adjust to the interior darkness. Sunlight arches through two windows high on the wall, but the interior brick seems to swallow the light in the extreme contrast of dark and light. According to the report, which Flint had bamboozled his way into viewing, those windows were shuttered yesterday, making the warehouse dark inside—"dark as night," one soldier claimed. Now the space reeks of overripe fruit, though the shelves are empty, supplies either depleted or looted in the instability that swept over this region with the invasion of U.S. forces.

Something scurries behind a wooden crate a few feet away. Some sort of vermin.

Why is he here?

Scene of the shooting. After the memorial ceremony, Flint

started asking around, trying to get details of how John had been killed, and two guys from John's platoon, Jump and Lassiter, had sent him this way. Although he can't imagine this abandoned warehouse contains anything to assist Abby in the grieving process, his reporter's instincts require that he return to the scene, the place where it happened.

Danger be damned.

Like it's not already dangerous enough just being in Iraq. His eyes land on an unmoving shadow on the floor. Here the pungent scent of bleach cuts the air, and yet the stain remains on the porous floor.

A bloodstain. This, he suspects, is the sight where Spec. John Stanton went down.

He pauses, sensing a weird energy in the air. Not the sort of thing you could write into a piece, but real nonetheless.

"John . . ." *What happened here yesterday? How did it go down?*

Flint lowers his head, makes the sign of the cross. He's not a religious man, but every man's got to possess a certain reverence for death, and he refuses to believe that a man's energy just dries up when life leaves the body.

He is staring down at the maudlin stain of blood when something shifts, disrupting the silence of the warehouse. Flint's shoulders rise as he braces himself and steps back, looking to take cover as something falls from above.

Something heavy and round. It lands a few feet in front of him, bouncing on the hard-packed floor before Flint loses sight of it in his frantic scramble to take cover.

His heart races, his pulse pounding in his ears as he flattens himself against a wall and covers his head. The explosion he is waiting for does not come, and he lets out a whimpering gasp of relief, daring to open his eyes.

Holy Christ. It's a helmet.

Braced against the wall, Flint looks up in the darkness and sees a flurry of movement high up, thirty or forty feet, atop a wooden pallet. His jaw clenches and he pulls back, ready to retreat. It looks like one of our guys, a U.S. soldier, stretched out on his belly.

"Sorry, man." The soldier, an African-American man, now without a helmet, pushes himself up and shifts so that his legs dangle over the side.

"You scared the shit out of me," Flint shouts up at him, though in this hollow space it's not necessary to raise his voice. "What the hell are you doing up there? The guard outside told me this place was secure."

"This is a dangerous place to be, sir," the soldier answers. "If I were you, I'd leave."

Flint's been trying to do that since he arrived in Iraq, greeted by an IED as he traveled the five-mile stretch along the Route Irish from the airport to the goddamned hotel. He tries to get a bead on the soldier dangling from the scaffold. "You on guard duty, soldier?"

"No, sir."

"So what the hell are you doing hanging up there?"

"It's a personal matter, sir. You should leave."

Which makes Flint suddenly want to stay. "You okay, buddy?"

The soldier's hesitation is heavy with desperation. Flint takes a moment to reassess the man clinging to the edge, and now he gets it.

A jumper.

Flint knows the signs. As a rookie reporter in San Francisco, he covered the Golden Gate Bridge, where a suicide occurred just about every two weeks. This guy is a classic jumper, on the verge of pushing off and cutting it all off.

"You hold on up there, 'cuz I got a question for you." Flint points a finger toward the man, as if to hold him in place there. He knows he needs to engage this man, get him to talk. "You're going to wait right there till we have a chance to talk, okay?" All caution fades as he circles the tall platform, looking for a way up. "How the hell did you get up there?"

"You don't need to come up, sir."

"Cut the 'sir' crap," Flint tells him, though he knows that in the military community that's easier said than done. "I'm not in the army. How do I get up?"

"Over by the door. Climb the pegs."

Easier said than done, Flint thinks when he sees the worn, splintered pieces of wood nailed into the structure. He reaches for a handhold and hoists himself up, feeling the weight of his flak jacket and equipment. By the time he reaches the top, Flint is sweating like a pig and trying to remember how he's supposed to approach a person in this state of mind. He was trained to talk to people in crisis, but he's no shrink. Aren't you supposed to keep them talking? Engaged? Frankly, it's the last thing he feels like doing when he should be getting his information, getting the hell out of here, getting home, but he can't just walk out of here and leave this guy hanging, both literally and figuratively.

"That's some climb," Flint says, his breath ragged as he pulls himself onto the platform at the top. The soldier remains sitting at the edge of the precipice, his eyes wide and impossibly white against his dark skin. "I told my editor I'm too old for an assignment like this." Flint starts to stand, but his legs feel too wobbly and he doesn't want to be a high target, so he falls back to his hands and knees and moves forward in a crab crawl.

"Yes, sir," the man answers.

"Dave Flint. I'm a journalist, an embed with the 121st Airborne."

The soldier turns to study him, and Flint notes the hollow expression in his eyes, as if he's staring off at a bitterly sad sight in the distance.

"You came here by choice?" The soldier seems astounded.

"Sort of. It was either this or finish off my career covering city council meetings and the crime beat."

The soldier shakes his head. "Bad choice."

Flint sees the name "Brown" on the man's uniform. "So what the hell are you doing in here, Brown? Did you know a man was shot in here yesterday?"

"Name's Emjay, and I know all that. I was here."

Flint takes all this in with a deep breath. He heard the name earlier when he was asking around about John. Although John was a friend to every man in his platoon, people thought he and Emjay were close. "You knew John Stanton."

Emjay nods.

"Want to tell me what happened yesterday? How it all went down?"

"Nah." Emjay glances down, and Flint follows his gaze to the dark stain below. The view from here gives him the shakes, a mild vertigo. How the hell is he going to get down from here?

"Tell me a story," Emjay says quietly.

"I was hoping you would tell me one," Flint says.

"Nah." Emjay Brown lowers his head, as if it's too heavy to hold up anymore. "I need to hear something that isn't about this place. A good distraction. You're a writer; why don't you spin something for me."

"A story? Hell, you're going to make me work?" Flint leans back on his elbows and tries to take some comfort from the rays of sunlight squeezing through an opening in the decrepit brick wall. He wants to keep things light with Emjay Brown, but it seems they both crossed that line months ago. Maybe they crossed it the minute they both arrived in Iraq.

"You ever been to San Francisco?" Flint asks. When the soldier doesn't respond, Flint takes that as a no. "You've heard of the Golden Gate Bridge? In San Francisco? I used to live there. Anyway, the Golden Gate has a strange claim to fame. It's a destination for jumpers. Easy access, great view. A suicide magnet. Hundreds of people have jumped from there. Something like twelve hundred altogether. But only three people have jumped off that bridge and survived, and you know what all three say?"

Emjay rocks forward over his folded arms, as if there's an ache deep in his belly.

"The minute they jumped, they wished they hadn't. All the unfixable things in their lives that made them jump suddenly seemed fixable once they went over the edge—all except the fact that they had jumped. They wished they could take it back. They wanted to live."

"They weren't deployed in Iraq."

Flint lets out a breath. "No, I'll give you that. But deployments end. When are you scheduled to head home?"

Emjay shrugs, a gesture heavy with hopelessness and ennui. "Come on, man. Everybody knows their exit date."

Emjay brings his knees to his chest and pushes back, away from the edge of the platform.

A move toward safety, no longer on the verge of plummeting off the edge.

Flint allows himself a modicum of relief. "So you like it so much here you want to stay?"

Warily, Emjay shifts his eyes toward Flint. "December. They say we're out in December, but that means shit. This is our second deployment. We were in Baghdad in 2004, then home again. There's a good chance they'll redeploy us back here. Hell, they'd do it in a heartbeat."

Flint nods, familiar with the schedule of deployments, which had only accelerated in the past few years, but right now his main goal is to keep this guy talking. Emjay Brown is in a state of shock. Flint is no shrink, but he'd guess post-traumatic stress disorder. Hell, Emjay should probably be in the hospital for the next forty-eight hours until his psyche found some sort of normalcy. But then, even then, Brown would be returning to the same tortured world, the same battered country stripped to the bone by Americans, loaded with danger.

"You know," Flint says, "I knew John. Went to college with his wife, Abby. I was even at their wedding."

Emjay cups his chin in one hand, squeezing his jaw, as if to clamp down all pain and emotion.

"I hear you and John were a team," Flint says.

"Yes, sir. We were partners, so to speak. I was beside him when he took that first bullet."

"You were with him?" Flint turns away from Emjay Brown, not wanting the soldier to feel his scrutiny.

"I was right beside him when he went down." He eases his grip on his rifle and scratches at the ruff of shorn hair over his forehead. "I was there. I saw it all. I tried to save him. I applied pressure to the wound . . . to where I thought he was bleeding from. I tried, but then he came at us and fired again and I . . ." His voice is thick with emotion. "I had to back off or he was going to shoot me, too."

"You saw the shooter?" Flint says softly, belying the acceleration of his pulse. "But I heard that the building was shuttered, that it was dark—"

"I saw enough. My NOD wasn't working right and I was messing with it when the first round whirred over my head and John went down, told me he'd been hit. I was beside him, on my knees, trying to put pressure on his chest, stop the blood. But John was so angry, screaming and yelling at the shooter. 'You fucking shot me!' he kept yelling, over and over."

"Like he knew the shooter?" Flint adds. He'd read as much in the report, but Emjay's take suggested a new dimension.

Emjay nods. "It was so crazy and dark, I couldn't see right then, but John had his night-vision device, and I think he was looking right at the sniper. And he was goddamned pissed."

"Because it was someone he knew?"

Emjay scratches at the stubble over his forehead, blinking back tears. "Like it's not bad enough these Iraqis try to blow us up? You got to defend yourself from your own guys, too?" He squeezes his eyes shut. "Someone on our team."

"Are you sure of that?" Flint presses. "I mean, in all the commotion—"

"I saw him," Flint interrupts. "At least, I saw that it was a soldier, one of our guys. The second shot hit John in the neck, and as I was scrambling I grabbed his helmet, thinking at least I'd be able to see and help him. His night-vision device worked, and I saw him, the shooter. One of our guys. Someone in Bravo Company, heading right out that door."

The silence in the decrepit building swells between them as Flint tries to process this new information, none of which was in the report he'd read. "Did you tell your platoon leader about this?" he asks quietly. "Does Lieutenant Chenowith know?"

"Chenowith, there's a piece of work. He's threatening to court-martial me because I went on a maneuver with a piece of broken equipment. Like we have a choice out here, when the army gives us shit for vehicles. Flak jackets from World War Two." Emjay lifts one shoulder, sinking into himself. "Chenowith would like to see me hang. He doesn't want to hear that someone in his platoon is a rat."

A journalistic spark bursts inside Flint at the knowledge that this is a story—a huge piece with significant implications. Of course, he doesn't have clearance to embed in this unit, but what the hell. He's always subscribed to asking forgiveness, not permission.

But whoa, boy. Remember your goal here—to help out a friend, to be Abby's eyes and ears here.

Hell, he doesn't know what to do.

Emjay Brown swings his rifle across his chest and cradles it like a baby. "They bury the truth just as easily as they bury the dead. The army is good at that, you know, glazing over the truth. From the day the recruiter tells you you're serving to defend America and preserve freedom, you step into a shitload of lies, a big con."

"You think they'll cover it up?" Flint asks.

"I guarantee, they've already made up some story about who killed John, too. They'll blame it on Iraqis to cover their asses. But I was there and I saw what I saw. It was another soldier. One of our own killed John."

"Another soldier . . ." The enormity of the accusation makes it difficult for Flint to wrap his brain around the evolving truth.

"Someone in our platoon," Emjay says solemnly, fingering the strap of his rifle. "And I wish to God I could tell you who it was."

Chapter 18

New York City
Abby

While waiting at New York City's JFK airport for her final connection to Washington, D.C., Abby hears John's name mentioned on one of those canned soundtracks and freezes in her vinyl seat. Is that John's college football photo illuminated on the television set hanging from the ceiling of the waiting area?

In the video, shot before he left for Iraq, his dark eyes are impossibly round, his brown hair gleaming in the lights set up for a press conference. God, he was so handsome in his scarlet jersey. Number nineteen.

Funny how a person can come alive on a television screen, their face animated and full of mirth, and that image doesn't fade with death.

As a childhood photo of John flashes on the screen, Abby leans forward in the chair. How did the media get that picture? Sharice . . .

Snatching her purse, she digs for her cell phone and rehearses the scolding she'll give her mother-in-law. *I asked you to keep a low profile! A low-key obituary . . . something short and dignified, but instead I'm seeing my husband's baby pictures broadcast on national television!*

She speed-dials her in-laws but a busy signal blares back at her. Damn. Ending the call, she glances back at the television screen, where the on-air personality continues to detail John's life.

". . . however, John Stanton was no ordinary soldier. Friends and family were astounded when the rising young star left a promising career as a running back for the Seattle Seahawks to join the U.S. Army. At the time, John Stanton, who enlisted with younger brother, Noah, said that it was his duty to serve his country."

And there is John, dark eyes locked on the camera, handsome and earnest. "This war on terrorism, I believe, stands to be one of the most significant battles of our generation. I can't justify sitting idly by while our freedom is at stake."

When John spoke he commanded attention, imparting immediacy. *As if he's talking to me.* From the many travelers who now tip their heads up to the television to watch, Abby sees that John's appeal stretched far and wide.

"And now that he's been killed in the line of duty," the journalist continues, "Americans are ready to embrace Stanton as one of the great heroes of our time. Senator Phil Woodsmith of Washington calls him a model American. 'Here's a young man who sacrificed everything for his country. He left a career in the NFL—every boy's dream—to serve in Iraq because he believed in this war.'"

No! Abby wants to shout. John didn't want the war . . . not really.

A Republican senator speaking from the steps of the Capitol remarks on the country's "huge loss of an American patriot, a true freedom fighter," and a spokesperson for the president says: "The United States Armed Forces will honor John Stanton by proving that his efforts in Iraq were not in vain."

They're all linking his name with the war, Abby realizes. She's tempted to climb atop the row of airport seats and pull the plug on the television, but that would be like plucking one weed from an acre of crabgrass.

The word is out: John Stanton is named a martyr of the Iraq War.

Politicians crown him a hero.

And it's all so wrong.

Not wanting all the travelers in the terminal to see her cry,

Abby clutches her bag to her chest and cuts around a bank of chairs to stand at the floor-to-ceiling window, facing out at the tarmac. Part of her does not want to share John with the world at all. She wants the peace and privacy in which to nurture his memory and say her own good-bye. On the other hand, since she cannot have that peace, she feels it's her duty to protect John's image, guard his memory from politicians and spin doctors who twist things around to suit their cause.

"Ladies and gentlemen, this is our preboarding announcement for flight three-oh-two to Washington's Dulles International Airport . . ." The airline representative announced Abby's flight. Since John's remains wouldn't arrive in Dover for another day or so, she was going back to the home of her childhood, and while she welcomed the comfort of her dad's arms and her mother's cinnamon-walnut buns in the morning, it wasn't truly her home anymore.

Home was at Fort Lewis with John.

And soon that home would be gone, too.

She presses a hand to her mouth to suppress a sob, and when she closes her eyes, Abby feels a slight pressure at the base of her throat, right in the nook John used to massage with his thumb.

It's almost as if he is here, haunting her, unwilling to move on to the next world. She takes a deep, calming breath, and suddenly he is with her, the scent of his aftershave filling her nostrils, sweet and lemony. . . .

John.

She can almost hear strains of his laughter, his rumbling voice, gregarious and flippant. *Don't let those stuffed shirts get you down. They're just wordsmiths, and I'm a man of action. They can try to sum me up with a trite label, but you know the truth, Abs. I'm just a man. Not an ideal, but a person.*

"I know," Abby whispers. "I know." She presses a hand to her throat but there is nothing there—the moment has vanished, and she is simply a woman in an airport waiting to board a flight.

As she joins the line, a young couple sprawled on the carpet in one corner catches her eye. They are sharing a slice of pizza, bite for bite, and passing a bottle of Vitamin Water, talking quietly. They remind Abby of the way she and John were in their first years—college students with no responsibilities beyond getting to class on time and making decent grades. Of course, Abby worked her collection of on-campus jobs to offset tuition, and John pumped iron and hit the turf, leading the Rutgers team to victory. At the time, Abby felt she was stretched thin, but looking back now she realizes those were golden days. College offered all the freedom of adult life without the responsibility.

Looking past the young couple, down the corridor of the terminal, Abby realizes that she and John had met for the first time right here at JFK. That was six years ago, and the airport was packed with holiday travelers, with flights delayed and cancelled due to the icy snow that had been falling continually since noon. John was waiting for a flight back to Seattle, and Abby was trying to get home to Virginia for Christmas.

Certain things about that Christmas are still pinpoints of memory in Abby's mind: the scarlet red of John's football jersey, the voice of Karen Carpenter singing "Merry Christmas, Darling," the curl of jealousy she felt over her roommate's relationship with her boyfriend. "He's the love of my life," Fanteen said with the crisp British accent that lent grave authority to such pronouncements. Fanteen was so into Hitch that she had moved all her possessions into his dorm room and would take up full-time residence there after the holidays. Which really burned Abby, who had never really connected with a guy—never!—despite the fact that she was a sophomore in college.

Everywhere Abby went that season, she heard the Carpenters song playing. "The lights on my tree, I wish you could see . . ." Karen sang, and it burned Abby. She didn't have a damned tree, at least not till she got home, and there was no one to share it with. Right around finals week it became hopelessly stuck in her head, an anthem that kept her awake nights, guided her footsteps as she trudged up the hill to the Student Union. "I've just one wish on this Christmas Eve . . ." she would sing in the shower when her suitemates were out. Her wish was for a boyfriend, someone she could really connect with.

In the back of her mind, she thought it might be Flint. They'd become good friends in freshman year, and they hung out together sometimes, listening to music and watching *Friends* and lingering over coffee in the dining hall on sundae night. It was okay for a while that Flint had never made a move, never kissed her. She told herself that they were building a friendship first.

Then she heard about the sorority girl. Flint was taking some girl named Talia to the Alpha Delta Harvest Ball. How could he, after all that he and Abby had shared? Fanteen told her to confront him, give him a chance to explain, but Abby hated confrontations. Instead, she made a choice to keep her friendship with Flint just that—a friendship. Which probably saved their relationship in the long run, considering Abby's pattern of getting bored with a guy once she had him hooked.

Enter one extra-large, extra-loud scarlet football jersey, its white number "19" stretched across one very buff chest. Abby tried not to notice him as he sat down across from her in one of the few empty seats in the crowded terminal but, come on! First, how could you miss that loud red shirt? Plus he was cute, the tall, dark, and handsome type with killer eyes. But not her type. No jacket, but a jersey in twenty-degree temperatures— definitely a jock, and maybe a poser. Maybe he didn't play ball at all, but wanted to nurture the jock thing.

She opened up the Arts & Leisure section of Sunday's *Times* and tried to block him out.

"Hey, do you mind if I borrow a section?"

Abby froze. He couldn't be talking to her.

"Hey, *New York Times* Girl! Can I take a look? I'll give it back."

She lowered the paper to find his wide brown eyes disarming her. "I guess." She handed over the sports section, but he shook his head, stood up, and chose The Week in Review. Surprising.

"You sure about that?" she said. "It's not *TV Guide*."

"That's cool. I don't have a TV."

"Really? So how do you watch the Super Bowl? And the Hula Bowl, and all those other . . . bowls?"

"Other people's televisions." He unfolded the newspaper and started reading.

The ensuing quiet closed around them, and Abby felt oddly disappointed. Okay, the guy could read. So why did she feel compelled to keep talking when the last thing she wanted was to strike up a tedious conversation when she had plenty to read? Shifting in her seat, she picked up the sports section, deciding that if he could go against type, so would she.

And there, on the front page, under the fold, was a splash of red—a color photo of number "19" in his scarlet jersey, all smiles and broad chest, and brown eyes so warm they could melt a Popsicle. She glanced up at him, then back at the photo in the newspaper, as if her eyes were playing a trick on her. The headline read: THE KNIGHT WHO WOULD BE KING, and the article mentioned that "19"—whose name was John Stanton—had been a Heisman contender this year. She tried to read on without letting him know she was reading. The writer thought "19" had a good shot at winning the award next year, as a senior, if he kept up the "incredible momentum" he'd stirred up on the Rutgers University Scarlet Knights.

When she glanced up from reading, he was watching her. "No wonder you didn't want to read this," she said, tossing it over at him. "I bet you have it framed on your bedroom wall."

"Not true. But my mom probably does."

His smile was apologetic, but she noticed that he caught the newspaper section without wrinkling it. "Nice catch, nineteen."

"My friends call me John," he said. "And you seem to have some anger management issues regarding football."

"I don't care one way or another," she insisted, glancing up as an airline representative called for her flight to board. "That's me." She rose, tucking the rest of the newspaper into her backpack.

"So why don't you come see a game, see if I can make you care?"

"I don't think so."

"Come on, *Times* Girl. What have you got to lose?"

Not much, Abby admitted to herself. The possibility of making a "love connection" at the airport seemed highly unlikely, but then he *was* cute, and it *was* Christmas, and wouldn't it be great to go back to school in January with a boyfriend?

She wrote down her cell number, asking, "Where are you headed, anyway?"

"Washington."

"D.C.?" she asked, sensing true synchronicity.

"Seattle."

"I gotta go." She handed him her information and hurried over to the gate, allowing herself one last sliver of a look at him, yummy as the last slice of pumpkin pie the morning after.

"Have a nice flight," he called, tucking the slip of paper into a pocket, where it would probably shrivel and fade in the wash. She was sure that she would never hear from him again.

Fortunately, her instincts were wrong.

Two hours later, the pilot announced that the flight was "not going to make it out tonight, folks," and Abby bit her lip as she headed through the jetway, trying not to hope that "19" would still be there, that he'd still smile at her as if she held the treasures of the ancient world.

Her spirits sank when she didn't spot him, and she chastised herself for being so foolish. What a stupid thing to get all excited about; he was just a guy.

She was heading out of the terminal, toward Plan B, when she heard a shout: "Hey! *Times* Girl!" And John Stanton waved from a hot dog stand, where he was paying for his food.

Tossing off caution, Abby grinned and told him she was happy to see him. She shared his cheese dog and told him about her cancelled flight. He topped her bad news by telling her that his flight was cancelled, as Denver, his stopover point, was facing blizzard conditions. Abby's flight was tentatively scheduled for the next day, but John, and hundreds of travelers, were stuck without a guarantee of a flight until the weather in the Midwest cleared.

"So why don't you come with me to D.C.?" she said, knowing that what she was doing was beyond crazy, but it was time she started being more of a risk taker, and how risky was it inviting a guy to stay in the guest room at your parents' house? Besides, holiday spirit filled the air, and this seemed a small thing to do for a person stranded for Christmas. "I'm taking the train out of Penn Station. It might be standing room only, but what the hell?"

He tilted his head, dark hair falling over one eye. "Serious?"

"Sure, why not. But you would have to pretend that we're friends. At least for more than, like, an hour. My parents might freak if they find out I've started adopting strangers."

"So we'll get to know each other fast. Like a crash course." He reached a napkin to her cheek and wiped off a swath of cheese, such an endearing gesture. Just five minutes and already he didn't seem like a stranger anymore. "I can be a decent student when I focus."

"Oh, sure. Everyone knows they throw the A's at you football stars."

"But this is one course I'm going to do well in, totally on my own," he said, putting a hand on her shoulder. "Abby one-oh-one."

Chapter 19

Iraq
Col. Billy Waters

"This thing is so full of holes, I could drain spaghetti in it." Colonel Billy Waters stacks the pages of the casualty incident report neatly, closes them into the folder, and slides it across the table to Lt. Chenowith. "The question is: Who shot Specialist Stanton? And I have to tell you, Lieutenant, I don't know any more about the answer now than I did before I read your report."

Chenowith's face pales as he flips open the folder and stares at the report, as if some new conclusive fact might catch his eye. "Sir, procedure was followed in the course of the investigation."

"I'm sure it was. But it was a pointless investigation if you can't draw any conclusions, and that's exactly what the media is going to say when they get wind of this." He sat back in the molded plastic chair and cracked open a bottle of spring water. "You mention an insurgent sniper, but did anybody see this shooter?"

"No, sir," Chenowith says, his eyes still on the report, "but we had reports of an insurgent in the warehouse."

"The building's perimeter was secured, and yet none of our guys saw him leave the warehouse? And you have one witness who claims he saw one of our soldiers flee from the shooting. And M-16 shell casings were found at the scene. Sounds like one of our weapons. Did you check the weapons belonging to the troops in the platoon to see which ones had been fired?"

"No, sir."

"Well, that doesn't always work, with guys taking target practice and firing off rounds at anything that moves, but in the future, Lieutenant, it's worth a try." The colonel took a swig of water. "And then we've got the issue of Corporal Brown's night-vision goggles not working. Isn't there an equipment officer in the platoon in charge of this sort of thing?"

"Yes, sir. Captain Jump, and he's been reprimanded."

"But Specialist Stanton's NOD was working. He saw the shooter, and what were his remarks?"

Lt. Chenowith seems to sink lower in the chair as he reads, "According to his partner, Corporal Brown, he said 'Don't shoot. Friendly. Friendly. I'm John Stanton, U.S. Army. Your army.'"

"He recognized the sniper as one of us."

"It appears that way, sir."

"Why didn't you make that clear in your report, Lieutenant?"

"Do you want me to rewrite the report, sir?"

"What I want is for all this to go away," Waters says, waving a hand over the file on the table, "but we rarely get exactly what we want."

The lieutenant screwed up the investigation, and Colonel Waters wants to make sure he learns from his mistakes. Furthermore, the colonel doesn't like the fact that this incident transpired on his watch, that and the fact that he's been left to piece it together long after the incident.

As it stands, it's an administrative nightmare. John Stanton wasn't a bad guy, but Waters never asked to have a celebrity in his ranks. It puts the entire company under a microscope so that nothing can slide when screw-ups like this transpire. After twenty-three years in the army, his record is scot-free of blunders and scandals . . . and now this. Waters has a feeling he's looking down the barrel of a loaded political rifle.

As the company commander, it's his responsibility to investigate this incident. However, his resources are stretched thin, and his mission objective has nothing to do with cloak-and-dagger crime solving. He has orders to follow, perimeters to

guard. It seems that every day he is dispatching troops to rese-
cure an area that was once considered a safe haven. And a few
weeks after occupation, that same area must be resecured again.

If the U.S. military's occupation of Fallujah were to be
mapped out with pushpins and flags, those markers would
move daily. And casualties of war like John Stanton are an unfortunate reality, tangential to the mission.

There's a knock on the door of the briefing room. The lieutenant goes toward the door to answer, but Waters waves him
off, tilts his chair back, and reaches for the knob.

Captain Charles Jump salutes, and Waters nods. "At ease.
Have a seat, Captain. We were just discussing your platoon. I
spoke with Noah Stanton before he left. The men seem to be
taking it hard."

"Yes, sir. I've been trying to keep them talking. Noah Stanton
exhibited some symptoms of shock, which isn't surprising, considering they were brothers. But I wanted to bring another one
of our guys to your attention, Colonel. Corporal Emjay Brown
was partnering with Stanton when he was shot."

"I'm aware of that." The colonel takes a swallow of water.

"I'm concerned about Corporal Brown, wondering if some
action should be taken." Jump places his helmet on the table,
his shiny scalp giving him a wise visage, the face of a philosopher. "I observed that he was shaky even before the incident
with Stanton happened, and this has put him over the edge. I
have doubts about his stability, and I honestly have to question
his readiness to engage in combat. He's displaying symptoms
of post-traumatic stress disorder."

Lt. Chenowith has been squirming during Jump's assessment.

"Lieutenant?" Waters calls on him. "Do you agree with
Sergeant—or should I say, Dr. Jump's assessment?"

"Are you sure Brown's not just looking for a ticket home?"
Chenowith asks. "I mean, PTSD? What soldier out here isn't
suffering from a touch of that?"

Jump frowns. "It's not the sort of thing you can get a touch
of. Many of the men are depressed, yes, and with good reason.
They hate it here. But this is different. He's got every symptom

on the list. Avoidance symptoms. I've seen Corporal Brown sweat and become breathless when the episode is brought up. He's experiencing difficulties sleeping, and hopelessness. He's easily startled."

"Those behaviors could apply to any soldier who's seen his buddy killed," Chenowith argues.

"Don't shoot the messenger," Jump tells him. "I thought the colonel should be aware of my observations."

The colonel downs the last of his water and caps the bottle. "Chenowith is right. We're living on a Forward Operating Base, in a combat zone. There's going to be an emotional toll; it's inevitable."

Jump presses his lips together and nods. "Yes, sir. But one of my jobs here is to recognize these symptoms before a soldier becomes a threat to himself and a danger to others."

"And is Emjay Brown at that point? A danger to his platoon?"

Jump sighs. "He's close, sir. My honest opinion? If it were up to me, I'd send that boy home."

"I'll take it under advisement, Captain." Colonel Waters taps the empty bottle against the table as he stares off blankly.

"Sir?" Chenowith straightens. "In my dealings with Corporal Brown, I've found him to be attentive and focused. He doesn't seem like a threat. He'll be able to finish his deployment. I think we should let the army realize some benefits from all the time and money it's invested in him."

"A good point. Both viable positions," the colonel says. "I'm losing ranks. Roland and Stanton dead. Noah Stanton on leave for two weeks." He shakes his head. "I'd like to give Brown some time to recuperate mentally, but it would be foolish to let him go right now. Let me mull this one over."

"Thank you, sir." Jump stands and salutes, but Waters is the first one out the door. He's heard enough. Jump is a whiner, and Chenowith is a man to be taken in limited doses; sometimes Waters thinks his lieutenant truly believes all the operations and maneuvers in this desert arena are just a training scenario for West Point—a competition, a game, a chance to prove himself against all obstacles. The kid definitely has balls, just not enough to compensate for his lack of healthy fear.

As he crosses the compound, a journalist talks with one of the soldiers from Bravo Company, obviously gathering material for hero pieces on John Stanton.

Waters wishes that story could have a happier ending.

Maybe he should leave good enough alone, let the world think Stanton died defending his country from terrorism. In the end, who would know the difference? A handful of people, and most of them did not have knowledge of all the circumstances of Stanton's death. Most people wouldn't have the information to piece things together.

Chenowith would have to rewrite his report, shift the focus. After twenty-three years in this man's army, Waters had learned that history was simply the spin you put on what happened yesterday.

Chapter 20

Fort Lewis
Madison

Another interview!
Madison Stanton presses her cheek to the cool molding of the kitchen doorway, shrinking from the superwhite lights that flood their living room, making it look as if some alien vessel just landed and focused their ray guns on her parents, who sit side-by-side on the sofa like a married couple from a '50s sitcom.

What are these people doing in their house . . . and why is her mother talking to them as if they're her best friends from college? Doesn't she know they're here to carve out a story for themselves? Doesn't she have a clue that every word she says here will be pumped up and amplified and twisted to draw viewers or make snappy headlines?

And the really creepy part is that weird light in her mom's eyes, a spark of pride that wasn't there before. You'd think she'd just been voted prom queen or something.

At least the two of them gave up on having *her* sit in on the interviews. That was painful. Especially when a reporter tosses you an inane question, like, "Madison, I suppose you're feeling sad today"—Duh!—or "Where were you when you heard the sad news?" When the female reporter asked that question, Madison had to sink her nails into the cushion of the sofa and restrain herself from jumping on the couch like Tom Cruise and putting her cause on the air to rally support.

Man, she would have loved to answer that one honestly.

Actually, Diane, I was marching in protest with my friends. An antiwar protest! The talk show host would have loved that one, and her father would have gone into shock. And her mom, what would she do if Madison blurted out the truth? Probably squeeze her hand gently and lead her back to the bedroom to rest, then return to glaze it all over and ask them to edit her out. Mom was good at that sort of thing—ice the dry cake, wash down the bitter pills with something sweet. Not a terrible habit, except that her mother was so accustomed to smoothing things over that she'd lost contact with the truth festering underneath that sweet glaze.

You see, Diane, I've always known this war was a travesty. Ever since the day our president sent the troops into Iraq for the fictitious weapons of mass destruction, one of the great mysteries of our time. I'd love the president to send one of his daughters. Put them in the line of fire and we'll see how long the troops linger there!

Madison wishes she had the nerve to say something like that, but when she'd had her chance she'd withered respectfully under the lights and avoided looking into the camera. She couldn't do it. One look over at her parents served to wilt any thoughts of defiance.

How long is this media circus going to last? she wonders as a cameraman tilts a photo of John in the background to minimize the glare of the lights. Dad sits tall in full-dress uniform, his medals like LEGO blocks of color on his chest, and Mom perches stoically beside him, wearing the yellow blazer that brings out the blond highlights in her hair. The yellow blazer is her way of waving a big yellow ribbon, as in, "Tie a Yellow Ribbon 'Round the Old Oak Tree" and Let-the-Hostages-Go. Shiny pins on the lapel of the blazer snap in the light of the cameras—an American flag pin and one shaped like a black ribbon that says SUPPORT OUR TROOPS in tiny letters. Tacky, tacky, but her mom loses all sense of style when it comes to showing her patriotism.

Madison turns back to the kitchen, neat and shiny enough to pass inspection, as always, and circles the table, not quite sure what to do with herself. She didn't eat breakfast, she couldn't even swallow toast, not feeling this way.

So empty. An emptiness of the soul.

She considers sneaking out the back door. She could walk to school, get a late pass from the office. If she left now she would catch the tail end of chemistry, where the students are probably sitting with safety goggles, observing the color change of some liquid in a beaker. The math part of chem is a struggle for her, but the social part of it rocks. Besides, she gets a large charge out of seeing the gorgeous football players and perfect popular girls trapped behind geeky plastic goggles.

But no, she was not allowed to go to school today.

"It's not appropriate," her mother said earlier that morning as she swept a dust cloth over the living room shelves in preparation for the media visitors. "When there's a death in the family, you take a break from life out of respect."

"But I want to go to school," Madison said. "It'll be a good distraction for me. Plus I have a history quiz." Not to mention the trip to Olympia she'd planned with her friends after school. They would visit the state legislature to protest any allocation of funds for the war in Iraq. Sienna wasn't sure if it was the right venue for that sort of issue, but they all figured it was a good place to start. Would Sienna and Ziggy and everyone go on without her? God, had they even heard about John? It wasn't as if they had a direct line to the military wives' clubs on base.

Sharice Stanton grimaced as she lifted a photograph of John set in a heavy brass frame and rubbed the corner diligently. God forbid there was a smudge on John's photo, Madison thought grimly.

"So can I go?" Madison pushed, realizing her mother was lost in thought. "I'm going."

"Over my dead body," Sharice said in a sharper tone than usual, prompting Madison to wheel toward her.

Madison's dad appeared in the kitchen doorway. "Is there a problem?"

"I'm sorry," Sharice said, "but you are not going to school. It's inappropriate." Shaking her head, she reorganized the photo gallery, placing John's military portrait front and center, shifting photos of Noah and Madison to the background. "What would people think of that? Acting like you don't care about John."

"I do care!" Madison blurted out. "But what am I supposed to do, moping around here?"

"We know you loved him." Her dad was suddenly behind her, his hands on her shoulders. "It's hard. This is difficult for all of us."

No shit! And you're taking away the only thing that makes my life bearable, Madison thought as embarrassing tears formed in her eyes.

Without another word she went to her room and locked the door and cried, really cried, for the first time, with her sobs smothered in her pillow. Normally, it didn't bother her that she and her parents lived in totally different worlds. She could deal with it.

But it takes a crisis like this to point out how little your parents understand about you.

And now, she's stuck with nothing to do but watch her mother paint John as some sort of military saint. St. John of Arc. The Angel John. Hard to believe Mom is talking about the same guy who would hold her down and give her a wet willy.

She circles the kitchen again, then goes to the coffeemaker, the only thing in the room showing any sign of life, its red burner glowing. She fills a mug halfway, then peers out to the living room, where cameras are rolling. Dad sits upright, back ramrod straight as Mom speaks earnestly to the camera's cold eye.

"The loss is difficult," Sharice says sadly. "Unspeakable. But we are consoled by the fact that our son's life mattered. John made a difference in this world."

"We are proud to have been his parents," her dad adds, his voice strained with emotion.

"We know your son left a promising career in the NFL to fight the war against terrorism," says the reporter who sits out of Madison's view. "Did he find satisfaction in his work in Iraq?"

"Absolutely. John's dedication is clear from his own letters."

Sharice lifts an e-mail printout, now set in a frame that used to contain a photo of Madison's grandmother. " 'Life here is challenging, but we are accomplishing our mission, and that's something that I think will be a source of personal pride for me the rest of my life. The Iraqi people need us desperately. They need us to be diplomats, traffic cops, listeners, humanitarians, and defenders, and every day, I pray to God that I might fulfill those roles.' "

Tears glisten in Sharice's eyes as she lowers the framed letter in pensive silence.

A poignant moment—or, at least, it would be if Sharice hadn't acted out the exact same scenario half an hour ago for another television interview. Not to mention a similar performance before that. The tears, the quote from the letter, the silent pause, it was all executed on cue, perfectly timed.

Jesus Christ, my mother should have gone into show business, Madison thinks, backing away from the doorway. All the emoting and posthumous praise . . . John would not want that.

As Sharice and Jim field another question, Madison opens the cabinet beside the stove and feasts her eyes on the array of shiny bottlenecks until she locates the most delicious: Baileys Irish Cream. The bottle makes a "glug" sound as she turns it upright, filling her coffee mug to the brim.

Mmm. The alcohol part burns slightly, but the cream part isn't so bad.

Carefully, she replaces the bottle, closes up the cupboard, and goes to the window to watch a hummingbird alight on one of the feeders John used to delight in filling with sugar water. The lime-green bird broadcasts its color brilliantly, a beacon against the summer blue sky.

"Did you know that a hummingbird's heart can beat more than twelve hundred times a minute?" John used to say, and she would remind him that she knew because he'd told her, like, a bazillion times.

As the liqueur begins to warm her from the inside out, she promises to make sure all the feeders stay full. John would want that.

Chapter 21

New York City
Abby

On the plane, Abby unzips her backpack and takes out the red jersey before stuffing her belongings under the seat in front of her. Lovingly, she opens the shirt for a quick glimpse of the number "19" before folding it neatly and pressing it to the side of her face, a reassuring pillow. It smells of soap and citrus. It smells of John.

She settles against the window, unable to believe she is on her way to claim her husband's body.

Abby is seated on the left side of the plane, which takes off and circles south, allowing a prime view of Manhattan as it rises into the silken blue sky. Her eyes scan the green rectangle of Central Park, over the skyscrapers that once held her in awe, the Chrysler Building with its widgets and twirled ornamentation, the stoic Empire State Building, and others with curled or asymmetrical rooftops, boxes of glass and chrome. She holds her breath as the vista widens to South Ferry and the gaping hole that once held the two towers of the World Trade Center. Without the Twin Towers, the city's skyline seems broken, like a prizefighter missing his front teeth.

Sometimes it seems her life could be divided by the fall of those towers—divided into the girl who lived before that time, without a grave concern or world consciousness, and the woman who emerged in the aftermath.

She was in her junior year at Wagner College, a small private school on Staten Island, when the attacks happened. Her dormitory, a fourteen-story building aptly named Harbor View, overlooked New York Harbor from Grymes Hill, where students could study in suburban splendor while observing the frenzied energy of the city from a distance. The morning of September 11, 2001, Abby was toweling off her hair and going over notes for a quiz on Shakespeare's sonnets when she noticed the black smoke billowing out of the tower across the expanse of blue water. A fire in one of the Twin Towers.

When Abby turned the television on and learned that there had reports that a plane had crashed into the North Tower, she couldn't believe it. On such a clear, sunny day, how could that happen?

Within minutes, students were sweeping down the corridor, knocking randomly on doors, moving from television sets to wide windows as the massive tragedy unfolded before their eyes. Abby never had a chance to dry her hair but sat on the windowsill of her dorm room as Hitch hunched down on the bed and Flint paced the floor, uncharacteristically quiet. Abby called John and got his voice mail, which was no surprise, as he had a mandatory football practice each morning.

When the second plane hit the South Tower, Flint stopped pacing and fell to his knees in front of the small television set. "No!"

Abby slid from her perch and stood behind Flint, her hands on his shoulders little consolation for either of them as the news network switched over to other reporters, none of them able to confirm or clarify much of anything.

"Are we under attack?" Abby asked, feeling suddenly vulnerable on the thirteenth floor of a tall building.

"Who the hell knows," Flint muttered under his breath.

"Fannie! Oh, Lord!" Hitch bolted up and fished in his pocket for his cell phone. "She's on her way from the U.K. Not arriving till late this afternoon, but she's probably in the air already." He checked the time, pacing the room feverishly as he tried to reach his girlfriend.

At one point Abby looked at the clock and realized she'd

just missed her Shakespeare test, which suddenly didn't seem to matter. If any classes were going on. If this floor of the dorm were any indication, most students were glued to the events across the harbor.

Hitch reached Fanteen's parents and learned that she was, indeed, in the air over the Atlantic. With all air traffic currently shut off, no one could say what would happen to those flights headed this way.

Abby remained on that windowsill most of the afternoon, unable to watch but unable to look away as the huge white tower crumbled into a cloud of dust. When her cell phone rang, she almost didn't answer, but it was John.

"John—I've been trying to reach you. Are you okay?"

"I can't believe what we just saw. The South Tower went down."

"I know," she answered quietly. She closed her eyes against the images, but they persisted. A commercial jet plunging into a fireball. People hanging out open windows, smoke billowing out around them. And the ones who jumped . . .

"I feel like such a jerk," John said. "I'm off running a football and people are dying a few miles away. Right now I know what my father's been working toward all these years, serving our country. I get it. Those buildings were attacked, and I'm going in there. I'll walk if I have to."

"John, no!" Fear shot through her at the prospect. "Don't be a fool. They're trying to get everyone out of there." She wanted to tell him to slow down, to stop jumping to conclusions, but the day's events had thrown her so far off balance she couldn't form the words.

"That was no accident, Abs. America is under attack, and we can't sit back and let it happen."

"What can we do?" Abby asked him.

"Fight back," John said. "Fight for the U.S.A."

Abby shook her head. In her mind, war was not the answer, particularly when it was not clear who the enemy was. "You're losing me. But please, promise me you won't go into the city."

"If they put out a call for help, I'll be there. I'm going to give blood now. Look, I'm losing you, too. The cell connections are overloaded, I think. I'll call you later, okay?"

"Okay," she said, not bothering to tell him that more was lost than a cell phone connection.

They rode out the storm together, Abby, Flint, and Hitch.

"Do you think we're safe here?" Hitch asked.

"Probably not. I don't think we'll ever be safe again," Flint answered without taking his eyes off the television. "Then again, who ever heard of attacking Staten Island?"

Abby shook her head. "You are so not funny."

"I wasn't trying to be."

Late that night a call came through from Fanteen, whose plane had landed somewhere in Canada. "Some rather pastoral airport. They loaded us all onto buses and brought us to this church, and we're to sleep in the pews. Someone is bringing us blankets and hot food shortly. Seems there are no hotels nearby, and the closest ones are booked."

"You . . . in a church?" Abby teased. "That's got to be interesting."

"Indeed. So what's happened there? They've only told us that all the airports are closed."

Quietly Abby shared what she knew of the horrific events, feeling as if she'd fallen into some surreal nightmare.

"It's the end of the world as we know it," Flint said the next day when they were back at the television, sharing coffee Hitch had made from his secret stash usually reserved for finals week all-nighters. "From here on, everything changes."

Flint with his uncanny knack for unraveling truths, proved to be right once again, as the following weeks brought about the beginnings of a metamorphosis in the city and the mind. So many families, lives, and dreams would never be the same. Everyone knew someone. A friend traveling on one of the flights. A father who worked in one of the towers. A neighbor who'd been attending an early-morning meeting there. And beyond the personal toll, there were so many questions about the future. Were the fires burning at Ground Zero hazardous?

Would the downtown district ever recover? What would the next terrorist target be? Was it safe to fly? Was *anything* safe? Student life at Wagner resumed, but the tone was somber, all things shadowed by the devastation viewed daily from every harborside window.

As Abby grieved in her own quiet way, she was unable to track John's reaction—the volatile anger he felt over the attack, and the compulsion to serve his country. It was as if a bell had begun ringing with the attacks, an alarm that was getting louder and louder with each passing day.

"I don't know how long I can sit back and let the next guy do our country's dirty work," he told Abby one day as they stared across the harbor at the empty hole, now called Ground Zero. "If there's going to be a war on terrorism, I want to be on the front lines."

The conversation always made Abby's throat tighten, and lately John was so hot on the topic that her throat was getting sore. "But you've spent so much time building a career in football," Abby said, joining him at the windowsill of her room. "This is your senior year, your time to shine. I don't know that much about football, but I can read, and everyone's saying you'll be one of the top NFL draft picks this year."

He nodded. "So I'm good at the game. Doesn't that seem utterly meaningless in light of everything that's happened?"

"It's a huge accomplishment. It's everything you've worked for, John. Don't sell yourself short."

"Football used to mean the world to me," he said. "But the world changed when those four planes were hijacked, Abs. This country is under siege, and I'm going to focus all my time and energy on running a football?" He tugged on her hand, pulling her into his arms. "That is pretty lame."

And then he kissed her, a kiss that drew the breath from her body and sparked life in her heart. She loved this man. She had loved him before the world grew complicated and bleak, and now, his sudden desire to serve bowled her over with a mixture of strong feelings.

He was so bold and selfless. A true hero.

But wasn't it foolish to think he could make a difference by joining the army? Did guns and bombs ever solve anything?

Abby slides the windowshade of the plane down, closing off the memories. She had fallen in love with a brash boy, a charming football star, and the fall was an endless tumble, head over heels with such momentum that she could only succumb and enjoy the ride.

But what happens when the person you love evolves into someone else? When he makes choices that are hard for you to swallow, puts you into a position you never wanted to be in . . . an officer's wife.

A widow.

You still love him, of course. But Abby hopes it's okay to hate some of his decisions. She hugs the jersey in the crook of her neck, inhaling his scent, which will fade and disappear all too soon, just like her husband.

Chapter 22

"The next sand I see had better be somewhere tropical, like in the Caribbean or the Hawaiian Islands." Flint holds on to his sunglasses, a shield against the blowing sand as he jogs across the compound alongside Captain Jump.

"Right now, I'd settle for Atlantic City," Jump says from beneath a hood he's thrown over his helmet.

Flint would agree if he could talk without getting a mouthful of sand. Even Atlantic City would be better than working as an embed in Iraq. Last night he bunked with Alpha Company, sharing a room with five other men, and that was deluxe accommodations compared to his past few months here. In his time with the 121st Division, he's slept in the back of Humvees, outside on sand, dust, and dirt, or inside a cramped vehicle where his restless dreams were punctuated by explosions and the grind of the turret turning to search out threats on the horizon.

His time is up here, and his body longs for a smooth, clean bed and clear running water . . . just as soon as he gets some answers for Abby.

He shifts the packages in his arms to block the sandstorm and follows Charles Jump into one of the many nondescript bungalows of this Forward Operating Base in Fallujah. Since his arrival he has attended John Stanton's send-off, talked with Emjay Brown, and even had a few minutes to interview Stanton's brother, Noah, who was not the most forthcoming subject. Like squeezing water from a stone. From Alpha Company he learned that John Stanton was a stand-up guy. "What we knew of him," most guys said, as they aren't in the same company.

As his last task, Flint is helping Dr. Charles Jump, Bravo Company's resident mental health officer, deliver packages to his guys. The platoon has some free time right now, his opportunity to ask and observe.

"They're really feeling the loss right now," Jump says as they both bend into the wind, "but when people are grieving it's good to get them talking, and sometimes it's easier to open up to an outside party."

Stepping into the bungalow used as quarters, Flint is reminded of a pitch he once made for a script he wrote in college: *Animal House* meets *Platoon*. Eight beds crowd into the small space strewn with Christmas lights. The walls display a fine selection of centerfolds, as well as the obligatory maps, military codes, and a chart explaining body language in Iraqi culture.

"We got mail!" Jump announces in a big voice, a notch too cheerful for the men stretched out on bunks or hunched against the wall in an attempt to relax. Flint notices that all the men have their boots on and their M-16s close—a reminder that attacks don't always occur on the other side of the wire. "And if you haven't already met him, this is Dave Flint, a media guy from the states. Did you say L.A.?"

"Seattle," says Flint, scanning the room. From his bunk, where he's tuned in to an iPod, Emjay's dark eyes shine in the shadows, and Flint gets it.

Don't acknowledge me, those eyes are saying. *Don't tell them we talked.*

"Doc told us you were coming," says a soldier whose shirt reads LASSITER. He is stretched out on his cot, leafing through a magazine. "We're not supposed to cuss, and he wanted the pictures of the girls down, but he was overruled."

"Good thing," Flint says. "I like the pictures." He had hoped to keep things casual, wing it. It wasn't as if he was going to start whipping off the questions to these guys. They thought he was here to research a piece about the life of John Stanton, not, specifically, John Stanton's death. On his way here he decided not to mention that he knew John, that he is trying to gather information for John's wife, a former college roommate. Sometimes personal involvement muddies the waters.

A buff soldier with a squarish face relieves Flint of his packages. "These are probably for me," he says. "They always are."

"Hilliard's wife keeps us stocked with snacks," Jump says.

"And sheets." Hilliard slits open one box with a penknife. "When she found out how hot it was here and that we were sleeping on wool blankets, she got half of Little Rock to pitch in and send us sheets."

"We got like, a hundred. We gave the extras to Alpha Company," says a short, boyish soldier who introduces himself as Gunnar McGee from Mount Carmel, Pennsylvania. He braces a box between his palms and holds it out to Hilliard. "Want me to open it for you?"

"Yeah, sure." Hilliard pulls a container of peanut brittle from his open box.

Besides food, Hilliard's wife has sent a DVD containing *Scrubs, Lost,* and *Desperate Housewives.*

"Isn't that a chick show?" Flint asks, but no one seems embarrassed by the question.

"Eva Longoria is hot," insists Lassiter, a soldier with a shelf of hot sauces and a string of chili pepper lights over his bunk. Yeah, he seems to be an expert on hot.

"Spinelli?" Dr. Jump announces, reading the name on one package, and a scrawny kid pops up from one top bunk. "Looks like your mama remembered you." The kid, who looks like he's fourteen, catches the package in the air, then settles back into the mattress, worlds away from the rest of them.

"You're welcome," Doc says sarcastically, and Spinelli's head reappears.

"I said thank you." The boy glowers, then retreats again, and Flint wonders what his life would have been like if he'd been sent to a place like this when he was eighteen.

"I also got us a copy of yesterday's *Today* show from the Armed Services Network," Doc says, holding up a videotape.

A few of the guys seem interested, but Lassiter moans. "No news is good news."

"Have a seat," Doc offers, indicating a plastic chair next to an empty bunk. Did it belong to John and Noah Stanton? Last night, when he was looking for a place to bunk, he was told he could come here, but when Flint realized he'd be bunking in John or Noah's spot, he declined and went over to another platoon. Flint figured it might offend some of the guys if he assumed too much.

"And this is *Today* on NBC," Ann Curry announces.

"McGee, it's your girlfriend," Lassiter jokes.

"Shut up," McGee growls.

"John slept right up there, in that bunk beside you," Doc tells Flint, turning his back to the small television. "He'll be sorely missed here. He was one of the rare guys that got along with everybody. Partnered with Emjay over there. Both Stantons, good people. John used to play poker with Lassiter and McGee. And John and I go way back. We played football together in college."

"Is that right?" Flint says casually, not wanting Doc to dominate his time here. "You were on the Scarlet Knights?"

"Defensive end. I injured my knee senior year, which ended my football career. I realized I'd need a real job, so I detoured to med school instead." As he talks, Doc plucks a gold metal piece from the mesh of his helmet. "My Purple Heart," he says, flashing the medal at Flint. "Actually, this is just a replica of the real medal, which you don't wear in combat, of course. I got it in Afghanistan. You ever been there?"

"I haven't," Flint admits. "You were injured."

Doc frowns. "Heavy combat. Not a good scene. But that's another story. After you finish this thing on Stanton, you get in touch and I'll give you an exclusive on the Doc Jump story."

"Sounds like a plan," Flint says. "So you met John at Rutgers?"

Doc goes on to describe the different paths he and John took after college, how they'd remained friends but landed in the same platoon by chance.

Flint listens but also tries to tune in to conversations around him, about the peanut brittle Hilliard's wife made herself, about the tightest women in a new issue of *Playboy*, about Spinelli's mysterious care packages from home always containing tooth-paste. "How many teeth do you have in your head?" Lassiter jokes.

On the *Today* show, a chef from a New York restaurant stirs a sauce for filet mignon, and Lassiter talks of his plans to grill a "big-ass Texas steak," when he gets home.

"Did you want to get some quotes from us about your arti-cle?" Doc asks, drawing attention to Flint. "Our memories of John."

"That'd be great," Flint says, "but I don't want to force anything. If there's something anecdotal you want to share . . ."

"Well, Brown over there was John's partner whenever we were paired up in missions. Emjay, what would you say about John?"

Emjay turns toward them slowly, reluctant to be drawn in. "He was a good man," he says slowly. "A good friend."

"A friend to everybody," McGee adds. "He kept us going here, kept our spirits up."

"Every week he'd give out these bogus awards." Lassiter points to a ribbon hanging over his cot. "Mine's for Best Boner Move, when I nearly stepped on a land mine. Scared the shit out of me, but John knew how to turn everything around. He could make you laugh at yourself."

Doc hands Flint a pen. "You want to write this down?"

Act like a reporter, Flint thinks. "I got it covered." He takes a pen and pad from inside his camouflage jacket and scribbles a few notes. "Did John leave anything behind that was signifi-cant? A book he loved, or a photograph?"

"It's all gone." Gunnar McGee frowns at the empty bunk. "He used to write in a journal every day. Three notebooks full of stuff, but the MPs came in and took it all away. It was sent back to the States, for investigation."

"Really?" Flint scribbles again. "So there's going to be an inquiry into his death?"

Heads nod. "There always is," Doc said.

"Who do you think killed John Stanton?" Flint lobs the question up casually, like a coach warming his team up.

But the response is awkward—pursed lips, reticent stares. All peripheral conversation stops.

"Didn't you hear the whole story?" Doc asks. "There was an insurgent in the warehouse. We had him cornered, but he came out of his hiding place shooting, and John was the first one in the line of fire."

"Is that how it happened?" Flint asks the others, but no one volunteers. "Wow . . . from reading the report, you get a very different picture. I guess it pays to go to the source, right?"

"I just wish we got the sniper," Lassiter says. "Insurgent bastard."

Flint nods at the television. "They're showing John. Looks like they did a report on him."

The television screen was filled with images of John racing down the football field, breaking tackles, scoring, first for the Scarlet Knights, then for the Seattle Seahawks. Lassiter turns up the volume as the voice-over about John's life ends. The studio camera pans back to reveal a uniformed soldier and a petite woman sitting in the studio with Ann, who introduces John Stanton's father, Ret. Capt. Jim Stanton, and John's mother, Sharice Stanton.

"I never imagined John having a family," Gunnar McGee says wistfully. "He fit in so well here. It was like he belonged to us."

In his peripheral vision, Flint sees Emjay sit up to watch. Spinelli leans his head on the edge of the bed, quiet, attentive.

Flint recognizes John's mother from the wedding, but Jim Stanton looks like every other man in uniform. John's parents express their pride over their son's desire to serve his country, the example he set, the courage and selflessness that made him leave his career in the NFL to enlist in a combat unit.

The interview wraps up, the light shifts on the men's faces, sad and poignant.

"It's weird to know someone famous who died," Gunnar says. "It sort of makes us famous, too."

"I wish I could go on the *Today* show," Doc says balefully. "Nothing personal, Flint, but television's a lot sexier than newsprint." He chuckles, and Flint raises his hands, as if in surrender.

The sudden movement behind Flint sets off an internal alarm, until he hears Doc order the men to be at ease. The door has opened behind Flint, and he turns to see a lieutenant standing there—the name on his shirt is CHENOWITH.

That would be the name of the 1st Lieutenant of this platoon, the man Flint was supposed to get clearance from before he interviewed these men. Oops.

Chenowith takes in the dynamic of the moment quickly, then wheels. "Who the hell are you?" he asks.

"Dave Flint. I'm an embed."

"With this platoon?"

"With the 121st Airborne."

"Outside Baghdad? You're a little far from your assignment. Are you lost?"

"I'm here for the story of an American hero," Flint says, ready to banter all night if the lieutenant so desires. What's the worst Chenowith can do, ask him to leave? He's hoping to get out of Iraq in the next day or so, anyway. "It's not every day we lose an All-American football star to the enemy."

"True." Chenowith nods. "Can I get you to step outside, Mr. Flint?"

Outside the bungalow, the buffeting winds are full of sand. Chenowith presses against the side of the building that provides the most shelter.

"I don't know what you're thinking, talking to my men without clearance from the Public Affairs Unit," says Chenowith. Flint has his number. A recent college graduate of West Point. A by-the-book leader. "At the very least, you should have come to me first."

"It wasn't convenient." After three months here, Flint is beyond apologizing. "You've got some men in there who need help, Lieutenant."

"The army has provided us with a field therapist, who happens to be assigned to that platoon. And I won't have my authority undermined by some pop psychologist reporter scrambling for an easy story. I'll make sure you're provided transportation on the next convoy out of here. Is that *convenient* enough for you?"

"I'm just saying, you lose one or two of those guys to suicide, it won't look good for you."

"In case you haven't noticed, there's a war going on out here, and I don't have time to baby a soldier because he misses home or he's afraid of getting killed."

Flint puts his hands up in a gesture of surrender. "Nobody said it was easy. And I imagine you're already under scrutiny over Stanton's death."

The young lieutenant pulls protective goggles over his eyes, effectively shielding his reactions from Flint. "Why would that be?"

"Isn't his death under investigation?" Flint asks.

"That's standard procedure."

"But there's been the suggestion of friendly fire."

"It's my understanding that the investigation will rule out friendly fire."

"But was that what happened? Was Stanton's death an accident?" Flint suggests. "A weapon discharging by accident? That would be your bad luck, one of your guys taking out a famous hero like Stanton by accident. The Great American Hero, loved by all."

"Spare me the accolades. You can save them for your article."

"Not a fan?"

"John Stanton was a rebel bordering on anarchist. He was telling those men in there that this war is illegal, that it's a travesty. And that's your Great American Hero?"

A bead of sand whips into Flint's left eye, and he recoils in pain.

"I'll let you know when that convoy is ready," Chenowith says, moving away from the bungalow into a cloud of dust.

Chapter 23

Dover Air Force Base
Abby

"**A**re you the woman the MP called about from the gate?" The corporal rises from her desk chair and pulls a sweater close over her well-pressed uniform shirt, warding off the overactive air-conditioning.

"I'm Abby Fitzgerald. My husband is here. Or . . . his remains are." Having argued her way past the Military Police at the gate of Dover Air Force Base and into the mortuary without security clearance, Abby now wonders if the battle was worth the effort. Now that she's here, the whole thing seems a little morbid. She journeyed here, for what? To be here for John. Is she the only distraught widow who has come to the morgue driven by some crazy, protective instinct?

A sign over the door catches her eye. ALWAYS WITH HONOR. It gives her goose bumps, realizing that John is not the only fallen soldier to come through this facility. From the Iraq invasion alone, there are now more than two thousand dead. The staff here has done this before.

The other cubicles are surprisingly empty, but then Abby suspects it's probably lunchtime and this woman was the unlucky worker who had to stay behind and answer phones.

"We don't get many widows here," the woman says as she drags an office chair from another cubicle. She pats the seat of the chair, and Abby sits. "To be honest, we're a mortuary. This is just a stopping place for the soldiers' remains. We don't conduct any ceremonies or public events here. Formal services are held at the final destination, usually the hometown of the service member. But ma'am, you should have been counseled on this by someone in the field. Our public relations work is left to local casualty assistance officers. Weren't you contacted by someone at home?"

Sgt. Palumbo . . . Abby can still see the consternation in his brow when she told him she'd be coming here. "I met with a CAO, but I chose to come here. I wanted to be here, for my husband."

"I'm sorry for your loss, ma'am, I truly am." Behind the woman's gray glasses with designer "Bs" on the frames, Abby detects a flicker of sympathy. "But I'm not sure how I can help you today."

"I'm not sure, either." Abby pulls her purse onto her lap, feeling as if she's swimming through a surreal dream. "I guess I came here because I couldn't stand the idea of my husband arriving back in the States all alone. I know that probably sounds crazy, but I feel like, like I'm his only advocate here and . . ." Tears streak down her cheeks now, but she's determined to see this through.

"Ma'am?" The woman hands Abby a box of tissues. "I am so sorry about your husband. Was he over in Iraq?" When Abby nods, the woman sighs. "How can I help you? First, let me tell you that we take our work seriously here. Our mission is to work with dignity and precision and sensitivity. Each day begins with a prayer from our chaplain, and we know what we have to do here, and that's get the remains of our troops home."

Abby nods. "I appreciate that. Can I . . . can I see him?"

Instead of answering, the woman wheels her chair around to the computer. "How about I give you an update on what stage of processing has been completed? What was his name?"

"John Stanton."

As the woman taps the keyboard with fingernails that remind Abby of a saxophone reed, Abby searches the desk for a nameplate, but the office is not set up to receive visitors.

"Okay, yes. I found him. His remains have arrived and are

being processed, but we're not ready to release just yet. Let me see something." More clicking of nails. "The thing is, we have a few extra steps to go through that wouldn't happen in, say, a normal funeral home. I see here that he has already been scanned, which they do to all the remains to make sure no unexploded ordinance is present. His personal effects have been secured and inventoried."

Abby thought of John's journals. He loved to write. "It's the best therapy," he always said. She saved every letter he wrote. There were three boxes of them in their closet at home. "Can I pick up his journals today?"

"I'm not authorized to release his possessions, ma'am. But everything will go to you with his remains. The thing is, we have a very detailed process here, and for the protection of the family and the fallen service member, we follow it to the letter." She nodded at the monitor. "I see that the remains have already been identified."

"That's something I thought I could do," Abby says, her voice hoarse with emotion. "I guess I thought I could help identify him. For closure, for me."

"I can understand you thinking that way, ma'am, but we use other sources, digital X-rays, dental records. DNA if need be. And it says here that your husband's ID was positive. They were able to use his fingerprints."

His fingerprints . . .

More tears sting Abby's eyes. He was left with his hands intact, unlike so many troop fatalities she'd read about. His hands . . . the palms that used to run up her bare arms over her shoulders, the fingertip that would lodge in the cleft of her neck. She grabs a fresh handful of tissues and presses the white mass to her face.

"Okay." There's more tapping on the keyboard and clicking of the mouse. "Ma'am? Your husband's autopsy has already been done. It looks like they'll be embalming the body today, and then sometime tomorrow it will be ready for shipment wherever you choose. Which is Arlington, Virginia. I see you're to have burial in Arlington National Cemetery."

Abby shakes her head. "It's been suggested, but I . . ." She leans forward, wishing she could see the information on the monitor. "No, I didn't make that decision yet. It must have been his mother and . . . he wanted to be cremated."

"That's an option, if you wish," the woman says. "We take care of that here, and an engraved urn will be carried to the place of interment."

Abby straightens, galvanized by Sharice's interference. "I want him to be cremated," she says. "How can I make that happen?"

"I'll get the paperwork done for you right now. If you're his next of kin, all we need is your signature."

"Let's do it." Abby stands and steps behind the woman to view the computer screen. "And I'd like a copy of all the records you have on him." She wants to see what other requests Sharice has made. A twenty-one-gun salute? The U.S. Army Marching Band?

The woman shoots a look of alarm over her shoulder and minimizes the file. "I'm sorry, ma'am, but this is classified information. I can't release it to anyone."

"Not even my mother-in-law?" Abby asks.

"Ma'am, unless she's employed here at the mortuary, she's not going to see this file."

"I guess that's some consolation." Abby returns to the chair and asks the woman her name. Cpl. Heighter pulls her sweater close, taking a moment to look Abby in the eye, which she's been avoiding through most of their conversation.

For the first time Abby sees compassion in the woman's eyes and recognizes the caring soul of a patriot, a daughter, a sister . . . a human being. "Thank you, Corporal Heighter."

The corporal nods and excuses herself to expedite the paperwork.

When she's gone, Abby gets up to pace. She checks the terminal, but John's file isn't even listed there anymore. Damn. She checks over her shoulder—no sign of Heighter—and moves the mouse to click on an icon. A file opens, but to get any further she needs to put in a password. Damn.

Abby closes the file and paces again. Her jaw clenches at the thought of Sharice making plans for John without consulting her. Okay, she did ask for Sharice's guidance, but she didn't expect to be bowled over on major decisions.

Keep your perspective, she tells herself. What would John want?

John wanted to be cremated, his ashes spread in the River Seine.

"This is where I want to be when I'm gone." She hears his voice, a memory clear as a bell, and suddenly the scent of flowers is strong. She stops pacing, the bare wall before her blurring into an explosion of color—the flowers in the marketplace at Montmartre.

You wanted Paris, and your mother wants a hero's funeral, Arlington Cemetery.

How could Abby deter her in-laws?

Just then a small machine on a credenza against the wall hums to life, and papers roll out. A printer. Abby checks the other cubicles. No one in sight. She picks up a page and sees "JOHN STANTON" across the running head.

It's John's file.

Her fingers fumble for the pages, collecting and stacking them with lightning speed. Her eyes skim photographs of the body—a little sickening, but she'll go over it all later when there's time. Quickly she folds the papers and tucks them into her purse before Cpl. Heighter returns.

She signs off on the request for cremation and thanks Cpl. Heighter for her assistance. Outside, a cool breeze breaks the heat of the September sun, and she rolls down the windows of her car and stares at the folded papers in her purse.

There will be time to go through them later, when she's not so rattled.

For now, she has a call to make, albeit reluctantly.

"I thought we all agreed on Arlington Cemetery," Sharice says. "I've already booked our flights out there, and Sergeant Palumbo says he can organize a ceremony just about any day next week."

Next week? Of course. Abby winces, wondering how things could have moved so far without her input.

"What are the other options?" Sharice asks. "None, really."

"He wanted to have his ashes spread in Paris."

"You can't do that. It's illegal."

Abby squeezes her eyes shut in frustration. John's adventurous nature must have been a reaction to his mother's cautious approach to life. "All right. We'll bury him at Arlington Cemetery, but I'm having him cremated. I just signed the paperwork for it." On this point Abby will not defer. Granted, John's mother understands military culture, but Abby is beginning to gain confidence in the negotiation of her husband's last ceremony.

"But I already ordered a horse-drawn caisson to carry the casket," Sharice says. "It's really quite lovely."

Abby sighs. "So it will carry the urn."

The silence on the line makes Abby wonder if the call has been dropped. "Are you still there?"

"I'm here." Resignation gives new weight to Sharice's voice. "I'll have to make some adjustments. Jim and I have been looking at cemetery maps, and we've narrowed down the plot."

"His ashes won't need a plot," Abby says. "Look, my parents aren't far from Arlington. I'll take care of choosing the spot from this end."

"Fine. I'll handle the rest with Sergeant Palumbo. Call me if you need any other advice?"

Abby ends the call, dropping her cell phone onto the console of her mother's car and sinking down into her seat in defeat. "But he wanted his ashes spread in Paris," she says, annoyed at her mother-in-law.

"It's okay."

That voice . . . she glances around, but there's no one there. Weird, but it sounded like John.

"He's haunting you," she says aloud as she starts the car.

The song playing on XM Radio, "Paris Through a Window," is about seeing Paris for the first time. "From an obscure Broadway musical," the deejay explains.

As she passes by the MP booth and pulls onto the highway, Abby thinks back over the strange events: the strong scent of flowers, the printer coming alive and spitting out John's file, the voice. She wonders if John really is haunting her. Why? Certainly not to terrify her, like the ghosts of horror flicks. She has read that sometimes the dead remain on earth in some incarnation until something important to them is resolved. What might that issue be for John?

During the trip back to Virginia, she imagines that John is with her, asleep in the backseat.

And somehow, his presence so close in the car does not seem morbid at all.

Chapter 24

Abby's e-mail directions contain far more detail than any navigation system, and she seems to have forgotten that Flint visited her parents' house in northern Virginia twice while they were in college. The first time was Thanksgiving weekend of freshman year when, in his lovelorn stupor, he didn't realize that Abby's invitation was motivated by pity that his parents would be in Europe for the vacation, rather than unbridled adoration. Duh. The second time was the week Abby married John, when Flint flew in a few days before the ceremony and they played out their own rendition of *My Best Friend's Wedding* with Flint, most unfortunately, playing the Julia Roberts role.

Back then, Flint couldn't have imagined he'd ever be driving down this lane of nouveau colonials, past a subdued shopping center with a Subway and a pizza place and a Home Depot, to help Abby make funeral arrangements for John and piece together the details of her husband's death.

Flint follows the printout, smiling as he turns down Abby's street. There were times in the past few months when he thought he might not live to see suburbia again, and despite the traffic and the huge, gas-guzzling SUVs hogging the roads, he's tempted to fall to his knees outside the car and kiss the leaf-strewn sidewalk. He's glad to be back in the land of the free and drinkable tap water, home of the brave and multiple take-out shops. You don't know how good you have it till it's gone. It will take him awhile, he knows, to be able to venture out without the fear of rocket-propelled grenades or random explosive devices. But at least he made it back.

He parks the rental car in front of the Fitzgeralds' home and sees Abby standing in the doorway, a shimmering vision of dark hair and creamy skin beyond the beveled glass storm door.

Oh, it is good to be back.

He has to restrain himself from skipping up the paving stones of the front path lined by symmetrical box hedges or dancing up the stairs to the brick colonial house.

Abby pushes the door open as he approaches. "We've been ignoring the media parked out front," she says, "but for you, I'll make an exception." The years that have passed between them have changed Abby's appearance, softening the fresh-faced girl into a woman, but the Abby he crushed on is still there—the wide smile, the sprinkling of freckles that are impossible to cover, the round green eyes as changeable as sunlight on a pond.

As soon as he steps over the threshold, her arms reach up to his shoulders and he closes his eyes, savoring the momentary embrace after so long a drought.

This is how a woman feels. This is the touch of a friend.

"I'm sorry about John," he says.

She squeezes him harder, then steps back. "Thank you for going to Fallujah. You probably gave up a headline news story to do that for me."

"Actually, my assignment was up. And in the end I got a story out of it."

"I saw it," she says, nodding. "The piece about Hero Flights. The *Post* picked it up. It was beautifully done."

"Thanks." He had spun the story based on John's send-off from Camp Despair, but fashioned it to demonstrate the honor afforded every soldier killed in Iraq. His way of squeezing a story out without capitalizing on John's death.

"It must have taken great restraint to be on the scene and not write about John," she says. "Or is that something that's coming later? The unauthorized biography?"

"Only with your permission which I suppose would make it authorized," he says as she motions him into the living room, a tasteful slice of the upper middle class with polished wood floors, a Chinese rug, and brocade sofas under two large Japanese block prints. Nothing has changed since the day he sat here with Abby, two days before her wedding, and listened as she expanded on her worries over becoming a military wife. Although Flint always prided himself on being a good listener— an important quality for any journalist—he'd had to bite his tongue that day to keep from interjecting leading questions.

Are you sure the role of a soldier's wife is right for you?

Is this guy asking you to be someone you're not?

Are you sure you want to marry John Stanton?

Have you ever considered spending your life with me?

He shakes off the memory as he takes a seat on the sofa.

"Noah is meeting us at Arlington Cemetery," Abby says. "I think he's coming right from the airport."

Just my luck, I get to spend an afternoon skipping through a graveyard with Stoneface. When Flint tried to speak with John's brother back in Iraq, Noah had clammed up. Flint mentioned his relationship with John and Abby, but Noah had put up a hand and walked away.

Abby sits on the loveseat to his right. Her dark hair tumbles forward, a silken chestnut swath over her white T-shirt as she reaches for a folder on the coffee table. "I got this from the morgue at Dover Air Force Base," she says, handing it to Flint. "It's John's records. I'm not supposed to see it, but I got a copy through some magical mistake. Honestly, I haven't been able to read through all of it. There are some photos from the coroner and . . ." Her voice, now hoarse, trails off.

"That's awful."

She takes a deep breath. "Seeing them . . . it did give me some closure. I kept hoping they had the wrong guy, but . . . no. That's my John."

He frowns, holding the file respectfully. This might prove helpful, in light of what he had to tell Abby. "Good work, Abby. You just fought bureaucracy and won."

"Somehow, it's a hollow victory, but I just felt like I needed to connect somehow, I needed to know more." She folds her arms, hugs herself as if warding off a chill, though it's sunny and seventy degrees outside.

He nods. "And the army hasn't officially explained anything about the shooting?"

"Just that they were doing some sort of warehouse raid and John was hit by a sniper. Two bullets." She points at the folder. "I did read enough to know there were two rounds. One in the chest, another in the neck. I think the second one went into his head but . . ."

"They didn't mention that the sniper was one of our guys?"

Abby straightens, her hands dropping to the sofa cushions under her thighs. "What are you talking about?"

"John was killed by another U.S. soldier. So-called friendly fire."

Her brows rise, her freckles standing out over her pale face. "Is this fact or speculation?"

"I had a long interview with John's partner, Emjay Brown, who was beside John when he was shot. He says John yelled at the shooter that he was a friendly, meaning, they were on the same side, and John seemed to recognize the gunman."

Abby presses a hand over her mouth. "How could that happen?"

"It was dark. Maybe there was some confusion about strategic location of team members in the raid."

"So it was an accident?" She winces. "Why isn't the army telling me this?"

"To save face, and to save John's reputation as the patron saint of soldiers. If his death was the result of some soldier's blunder, it's hard to hold him up as the greatest crusader of the twenty-first century."

"Oh, God." She squeezes her eyes shut in frustration. "I hate being lied to."

"Then you should know there's one other possibility," Flint says, measuring his words carefully. He doesn't want to say this, he doesn't want to be the one to bring her any more pain, but she seems to be holding her breath, bracing for the impact, and he's always been a believer in the cold, hard truth. "It may not have been an accident," he says gently. "The shooter might have targeted John, shot him deliberately. It could have been an ambush, Abby."

Her breath breaks in a sob as her eyes glaze with tears. "Why? Why would anyone want to kill John?"

He opens the folder and braces himself against the cold, raw details of his friend's death. "That's up to us to find out."

Chapter 25

Abby remembers touring Arlington Cemetery during a fifth-grade class trip. The sweeping hills of green are punctuated by pillars of white that stagger away in lines as far as the eye can see. She has always been fascinated by the way those grave markers are lined up so perfectly. It's as if some giant had set up for a game of dominoes with white sugar cubes.

After John's ashes are placed here, will he become part of the attraction? A stop on the tour? Will school kids peer toward his sepulcher curiously? Will tourists imagine him as a bigger-than-life hero, buried here among presidents?

"I really don't want John to end up here," she tells Flint as he cuts into the parking lot a little too sharply, gravel flying under his rental car.

"So why are we here?" he asks. "Didn't you choose this?"

"John's parents insisted on burying him here, and I'm trying to compromise," she explains. "But I'm struggling with the choice. I'm going to appeal to Noah. Maybe he can talk his parents out of all the fanfare that Sharice is planning."

"Good luck with that." He turns off the engine, removes the key and tosses the ring into the air, dropping it between the seats. "Oops."

Abby finds herself smiling for the first time in days. When Flint told her he was stopping over in D.C., she felt grateful, of course, but now, after a quick refresher of his poor driving skills, snap judgment, and sardonic humor, Abby realizes that a shot of Flint is exactly what she needs. "You don't think Noah will be on my side?" she asks.

"When I spoke with Noah Stanton in Iraq, he was not forthcoming with information. The guy barely said two words."

"I'm sure he was in shock."

"No doubt suffering post-traumatic stress. I felt for him. But I wouldn't expect too much from him by way of support. The poor guy's in bad shape."

"But I think he'll help," Abby says as she gets out of the car. "He and John were close. I'm sure Noah will want to do the right thing for his brother."

They are parked near small one-story buildings that contain a Visitors' Center, gift shop, and the cemetery's administrative offices.

"I've never been here," Flint tells her. "While we're waiting, I'm going to have a look around."

Abby crosses to the small wooden sign that says WHERE VALOR PROUDLY SLEEPS, the designated spot where they are supposed to connect with Noah and the cemetery's public relations representative, Sgt. Kenneth Tremaine.

Overhead, an American flag trembles in the breeze, and Abby lifts her face to the sun, trying to sense whether or not John would want to be buried here. A strong sense of history, purpose, and honor emanate from these hallowed grounds, and yet, the lines of gravestones, so straight and stark white and orderly, give her pause. Orders and rules were never John's thing, which was one of the reasons his enlistment surprised some people. He used to say that he subscribed to "organized chaos."

When she looks down, her eyes meet a soldier in desert khakis. He is standing against the building, staring at her. His hollowed-out eyes and the slight growth of beard are incongruent with the uniform, giving him the look of an indigent in stolen clothes.

She flinches when he comes toward her, then catches herself.

"Noah . . ." Abby closes the distance between them, but when she reaches up to hug him, his shoulders are stiff, his demeanor vacant. She closes her eyes and embraces him, trying to infuse life through her palms on his back. "I'd ask how you are, but you look awful," she says, deciding to keep things honest. "I can't imagine what you've been through, losing him that way." She releases from the embrace to make eye contact, but his head is lowered, his eyes on the ground. "Noah?"

He shakes his head. "I can't . . . I can't talk about it."

"It must be difficult." She bites her lip.

Noah lifts one hand, as if to make a point. It quivers like the flag overhead. "I can't go there." He turns away, his broad shoulders a barrier.

She doesn't know what she expected of John's brother, but this wounded shell of a man comes as a shock. Although Noah was always the quiet, thoughtful brother, he possessed an easy smile and a good nature. Today the old Noah is barely recognizable.

All hope of asking Noah to clarify the events at Camp Desert Mission fades.

Abby holds up a hand to stop Flint as he approaches, but then nothing stops Flint.

"Hey, Noah. It's good to have you back." Flint extends a hand.

Noah shakes his hand, zombielike, then walks off, around the side of the building.

Flint frowns. "That went well."

"I'm worried about him." Abby begins to follow Noah, but just then a man in uniform steps around an elderly couple and cocks his head at her. "Excuse me—Abby Stanton?" When she nods, he introduces himself.

Sgt. Tremaine is a hand holder. He clings to Abby's hand while he speaks, long after any social handshaker would have let go. But somehow, Abby finds his clasp charming, even reassuring. She wonders if he'll hold Noah's hand this long, and if Noah will even notice. "It's a pleasure to meet you, though I'm sorry it's under such tragic circumstances," Sgt. Tremaine says in a voice that carefully balances warmth and reverence. "Now, I've been speaking with Sharice Stanton. That's John's mother, correct?"

"Right."

"I explained to her our policy on cremation, which allows cremated remains of a service member who dies in active duty to be placed in the columbarium, a crypt, where the remains will be given an engraved niche cover. Sharice Stanton wasn't happy with that; she wants a regular plot with a headstone."

Abby restrains herself from gnashing her teeth. Of course, an unmarked grave wouldn't suit Sharice at all. "Sharice has . . . certain expectations," Abby says.

The sergeant nods. "Yes, yes. Unfortunately, we can't assign an entire plot to an urn."

"I understand," Abby tells him.

"I knew you would." He pats her hand. "Now, I'd be happy to show you the columbarium where we will place the ashes. He'll get a niche cover with his name engraved, just like a tombstone, but smaller."

"That sounds fine," Abby says.

"But we have one more," Flint says. "John's brother Noah just flew in from Iraq. If you two want to wait here, I'll run and grab him."

Flint makes it sound way too easy, Abby thinks, though she doesn't want to let on to the chatty sergeant that Noah is out of his mind with grief and trauma. But two minutes later Flint returns with a broken Noah by his side. They climb into Flint's rental car and, guided by the sergeant, drive slowly uphill along one of the paved roads that meander casually over the green landscape.

"Now if you'll turn right here, young man, onto Roosevelt Drive, we'll go right past one of the most famous stops in the cemetery," Sgt. Tremaine says.

Flint maneuvers around a line of cars waiting by the side of the road—a funeral procession, Abby realizes. Although the cemetery bristles with the activity of visitors and the occasional tour bus, an aura of peace and dignity resides here.

They follow the curving road to a hillock. People crowd the path leading up the rise.

"Just follow that path and you're at JFK's grave," Sgt. Tremaine explains. "The memorial design is very distinctive—the Eternal Flame."

Abby nods, trying to take it all in and keep an eye on Noah at the same time. He has been moving along with the group, but he remains silent and withdrawn.

"Next time you visit, take a look at the quote etched in the stone there. 'And the glow from that fire can truly light the world.' Do you know what that's from?"

"Kennedy's Inaugural Address," Flint answers.

"So you've been there?" Sgt. Tremaine asks.

"I've just got a sick mind for detail. Don't ever challenge me to Trivial Pursuit."

"JFK's grave site is our most visited memorial," he says, confiding, "Everyone wants to be near the Kennedys."

"Except Republicans," Flint mutters.

Abby smiles, but Noah, in the backseat beside her, doesn't even acknowledge the joke. Sinking against the door, Abby wonders how Noah will cope. Although one of the first rules of psychological counseling is that you don't diagnose your family, her education and training in psychology is ringing an alarm. Noah needs help. Does he have to go back to Iraq? How long will the army give him for bereavement? Are there psychological services available to him in Fallujah? Counseling, therapy? How will he function in such a stressful environment in this overwrought state?

Flint parks along the roadside, and the group ventures along a path toward a low marble vault.

"The nice thing about the columbarium is that it's set back, away from the road and the more popular monuments," says Sgt. Tremaine. "I like the quiet."

Just then an explosion cracks the air.

Fear knifes through Abby's chest before she realizes that it's the report of a rifle.

Flint pivots on one foot, turning back toward her as Noah dives to the ground and rolls behind a white gravestone.

At the lead of the group, Sgt. Tremaine doesn't even break stride. "Not to worry," he says. "It's just the three-rifle volley, part of our ceremonial honors. There must be a funeral service going on nearby."

But Noah is beyond worried. Hunched behind the tombstone, he has fallen into another world.

Of course, he is flashing back. The explosion must take him right back to Iraq, to the scene of John's death or some other horrific event he's experienced.

"Noah?" Abby steps toward him, then crouches down so that her face is level with his. "That startled me," she admits, pressing a hand to her chest. "My heart is still racing."

Unmoving, he presses against the stone, one side of his jaw to the cool stone.

"Do you want to go back to the car?" she asks.

Without answering, he springs to his feet and takes off running, staying low, ready to dive for cover.

"Noah . . ." Abby calls after him as Flint and Sgt. Tremaine join her. But Noah doesn't slow or turn back. He keeps running, a single khaki figure disappearing in a mouth of white granite teeth.

Chapter 26

Arlington National Cemetery
Noah

In every pristine tombstone emerging from the rolling green fields, Noah sees a different incarnation of death.

The torso of a soldier whose legs were removed in the field to extract him from debris.

Flesh blackened from mortar fire and smoke.

A baby with shrapnel peppered through its body.

A soldier, his body looking deceptively whole but for the blood draining from a mortal bullet hole.

Death . . . it's everywhere.

And he's running, not because he thinks he can escape, but because he simply cannot rest.

During his first deployment to Iraq, Noah was assigned to Baghdad General, where army doctors treated wounded members of the armed services, as well as injured Iraqi soldiers and civilians. A registered nurse, Noah had just taken his state licensing exam when John talked him into enlisting.

"We can't sit back and let this happen to America," John had said. "It's our job to stop terrorism at its source, and I'm going to go over there and do it. Our country needs us now, Noah. Good people, the people on those planes, innocent victims. Children. Americans should have an expectation of safety, and it falls on the shoulders of the military to make that happen." As John lifted his beer, Noah glanced beyond him to

Elliot Bay. Noah remembered that moment so vividly these days, he could almost taste the beer—a porter. He could feel the smooth glossed table under his fingertips. And the heated passion burning through his brother singed like a broiler.

It had started with John's free Sonics tickets. Noah was bucking for a celebration after finishing his nursing boards, and John suggested he drive into Seattle to catch some basketball. Noah had expected beer and bonding, but then John had hit him with this . . . this crevice in the road.

They sat at a table by a window in the Pyramid Alehouse, and Noah recalled looking out at the water, realizing how dark and bleak it became at night. An abyss. A few steps off the dock under their window would be like falling off the edge of the earth.

Just as his brother was proposing.

Noah didn't want to go. He had no intention of fighting in a war. "Why would I sign up to shoot people?" he asked his brother.

"Is that what you think Dad does?" John asked.

"Not anymore, but yeah, he did. And it's not for me. I made the choice to try to help people. I'm into healing, man."

"And here's the irony," John said quietly. "Because we want the same thing, but the only way to heal this nation, the only way to help, in the wake of worldwide terrorism, is to stop the killing." He sat back and sipped his beer. John always had perfect timing, knowing when to shut up and let those silent spaces eat away at you. "And you are not really doing your part to heal this nation by staying in your cushy bubble, tapping the air out of some old codger's IV line."

Noah braced himself against the table, his fingernails digging into the laminate of the wood. The challenge was well-precedented. He'd spent his life proving himself, answering the call, prompted by: "I can throw stones farther than you." Or, "I'll bet you can't run to the mailbox and back in less than thirty seconds." Or, "You can't jump from the roof of the shed—you're too little."

This time, Noah wasn't going to jump. "You need to do

what you have to do," he told his brother. "I just invested two years in nursing school, and I'm going to put it to use." And nurses do more than tap air out of an IV line, he wanted to add.

"What if you can use your nursing skills to serve your country?" John lifted two fingers to the waiter, ordering another round. "You can enlist and serve in a medical unit."

And that was the point where Noah started to lose the argument. Two beers later, they were brothers-in-arms.

Noah had been so green and earnest, fresh out of nursing school and wanting to help, thinking he could make a difference . . . until he was assigned to the hospital in Baghdad.

It was so different from nursing school, where patients were somewhat sanitized and other nurses and aides were readily available to consult about a patient's needs or bitch about pulling a double shift. Here, gruesome victims were airlifted in every day, and "Stat" was called so often, Noah dreamed he was stuck doing triage on an endless line of soldiers.

When Noah had read about tourniquets and amputations in nursing school, he'd assumed that sort of medicine had ended with the Civil War. And yet in his first shift in the Baghdad ER, he'd watched in horror as a surgeon used a saw to remove a patient's arm—a sickening procedure that converted him to vegetarianism and made him vow never to enter a butcher shop again. He soon learned that amputation was not uncommon. When a knee had been shattered into jelly, the leg bone draping, there was no talk of knee replacement or orthopedic surgeons. The term "cutting losses" began to have new meaning.

"This war is unusual in that we're able to save ninety percent of the wounded who come through our doors," one of the doctors explained in a morning conference one day. "But in order to do that, we have to amputate limbs. There's just no other way around it."

How many times had he woken up shrieking in the middle of the night, reaching for his leg or his arm or his foot, sure that he'd walked into an IED and lost a limb while he was unconscious?

Yes, his stint at Baghdad General had cured him of all confidence in the medical profession, all hope in humanity. To think that people created these bombs, that they sat by the roadside for weeks waiting for the right time to detonate, disturbed him deeply. Or the suicide bombers with backpacks or vests loaded with enough explosives to turn their own bodies to a bloody mist. What had happened in their lives to bring them to such a depraved, brutal place?

The worst part was seeing kids in pain, and there was plenty of that in the hospital where they treated American soldiers, Iraqi soldiers, and civilians. It tears at you to see a baby with shrapnel in her tiny body, a small bundle so still you know it's over.

Little girls with fat tears rolling down their cheeks because some of their fingers have been blown off.

He still hears the screams, gut-wrenching screams, and hopeless moans of pain.

He sees himself walking down the hospital corridor at the end of his shift, his body limp from physical and mental exhaustion. And there, on the floor of the waiting room, which is blessedly quiet and empty, sits a child's pair of sandals, tiny shoes with a cartoon character printed on the straps, caked in blood. They've been abandoned, their owner obviously having been rushed inside to a curtained bay for treatment.

Noah left those shoes on top of the reception desk that night, but they were still there when he returned for work the next day, and the next day, until he tossed them into the Lost and Found and tried not to think about what happened to the child they belonged to.

It occurred to him then that, while a soldier chose to go to battle, a child had no choice. The war came to these children, driving bullets into their homes, pounding through familiar streets and marketplaces.

But he and John, they chose to go to Iraq. They enlisted in the Rangers with that very intention—to go where the terrorists were, to stop the siege.

In the beginning, Noah had enjoyed working side by side

with his brother. Basic training was like extended Boy Scout camp, pushing to the limit, sparring, sleeping in tents. He remembers sparring with his brother, defending himself against John's mean right hook. John had a skill for boxing, but Noah was the superior swordsman. God help him, he'd actually enjoyed bayonet training, stabbing the dummies.

It's all fun and games until the dummies become real bodies.

And now he's stuck in the middle. He'd rather die than return to the bloodbath and terror in the Middle East. He can't turn back time and return to the scarred old oak dining table, sitting across from John, who'd instigate a secret kick fight under the table. John would find a way to crack everyone up, and Noah had, on more than one occasion, spewed milk from his nose.

This got him in a heap of trouble. Of course, Noah was the one who got in trouble. Always Noah.

Like in basic training when Noah stabbed the dummy and a swarm of angry bees emerged. Apparently they'd been nesting inside the dummy, building their fortress in the stuffing, and they did not appreciate the interruption of the bayonet slicing through.

Noah got stung, causing an anaphylactic reaction. He'd always been allergic, but somehow the adrenaline rush of basic training, getting pumped and feeling mightier than a gladiator, gave him false confidence that he could overcome a little bee sting.

He ignored the swelling. At least, he tried to until his throat began to close up and he went down. John grabbed an Epi-Pen from the unit's first aid kit and stabbed him in the thigh with it. Later, over beers, they'd had a good laugh about it, how Noah had almost been eliminated by a yellow jacket. "Taken down by a mighty bee," John teased.

Now, Noah thinks of the bee allergy and wonders if maybe it's a way out.

Bees. Bees might be his salvation.

Chapter 27

Al Fallujah, Iraq

Where is the media now?
He hands the Ping-Pong paddle over to another guy and slams out into the deserted compound, a scattering of bungalows not much bigger than those plastic houses on a Monopoly board. This place is a ghost town without his posse—the paparazzi.

Stanton's death brought them out in droves: big-name reporters, aloof photographers, cameramen from all the major networks. They came with a million questions, and he played host, ready and willing to answer. A role model. A rising star.

And man, the spotlight is sweet. The taste of power makes his blood surge, liquid steel in his veins. Energy radiates when the camera is on him, the eye of the world watching in awe. The camera loves him, and he's happy to deliver a good show.

But in just a few days' time, the media attention to the platoon has dried up. The journalists and photographers and cameramen packed their gear and headed off to hotels with showers in Kuwait.

And he's left boomeranging back to the life of a drone in Camp Despair.

Withdrawal from the limelight is tough when you've got to go cold turkey. Although some of the other guys in the platoon seem relieved to have the cameras gone, he feels let down. None of this is worth the fucking effort if all those people back home can't see the sacrifices he's making. There's nothing worse than working without getting credit. When he was a kid, his older brother used to bamboozle him into back-breaking work, trick him into doing all his chores, and then that bastard would take all the credit when the old man got home.

And he promised himself he won't be taken advantage of anymore. Never again.

He wants the media back. Now.

And the quickest way to get the media sniffing around is action.

It'll be hard to match the media buzz of Stanton's death, but you got to work with what you got.

He pulls the door to the platoon's bungalow open and finds it empty but for Gunnar McGee snoring away on his cot. That man can drop off in seconds—a true gift, the ability to nap on cue and block out the world so completely.

The soles of his boots tread lightly on the floor as he walks the length of the small room, pondering how to make it happen. Nothing too obvious. Nothing that could be traced back to him.

So far, no one has drawn the line to him as a suspect in Stanton's murder, and he doesn't think anyone is the wiser, except maybe Emjay Brown, who's been nuttier than a fruitcake since the shooting. He would be worried that Brown saw him, if he hadn't disabled Brown's NOD himself.

In the end, the whole warehouse scenario had worked out perfectly, especially since that pussy Spinelli had cut his knee outside and needed the medic to bandage his boo-boo. That made two fewer people in the warehouse to see him, and two fewer soldiers to help John.

He paces past the rack of bunks, climbing up to see what Spinelli is reading. *MAD* magazine. The goddamned nose picker. He doesn't belong in this man's army.

Checking the door to make sure no one is coming, he reaches for the NOD beside Spinelli's bunk and dislodges a part of the device. Not that he wishes anyone harm, but if something happens to Spinelli, he won't be shedding any tears. The platoon can go on without Spinelli.

He is the weakest link.

Chapter 28

Fort Lewis
Sharice

When Sgt. Palumbo tears a blueberry muffin apart over the paperwork, Sharice has to look away. It probably doesn't matter if the papers get stained with crumbs, but she doesn't want to see it. She wants the funeral to go off without a hitch, and messy means mistakes.

Of course, it would have helped a great deal if Abby had handled some of these arrangements when she visited Arlington National Cemetery, but . . . oh, well. This is no time to push the girl beyond her stress limit.

"Does the family have any religious affiliations?" the sergeant asks.

Sharice wants to laugh, thinking of the answer her father used to give. "We believe in army," he used to say.

Indeed, the U.S. Army was the superpower that gave measure and meaning to their lives throughout her childhood. She still remembers climbing out of the swimming pool at Fort Hollabird just before sundown each summer evening to face the flagpole while the flag was lowered and a soldier played taps on a bugle. There were the moves every two to three years, watching her mother pack her room into boxes, or, when she was older, carefully wrapping and stowing her own mementos and diaries. She remembered those notorious first days at a new school in Colorado, or Panama, or Georgia. The army brat label fit like a glove.

Her sister envied the kids who could stay and graduate from the school next door to their kindergarten, but Sharice knew she would be bored with that life, that she'd be leaning on the fence every day, looking and longing for change.

The army was in her blood; from her father she learned fierce patriotism, and from her mother she inherited the household equivalent of combat readiness.

When she met Jim while attending an Officers' Club function with her father, she couldn't deny his good looks, but it was his conviction to "make a career of it" that sealed their future together.

"Sharice? You must have some religious preference." Sgt. Palumbo wipes his hands with a napkin. "Not that it's necessary, but it sounds a bit cold to say no preference."

"Methodist," she answers, "but I'd like to have the religious service conducted by the staff chaplain at Arlington Cemetery."

He nods, filling in the form.

"And can you check on the caisson? Make sure it will work for the urn. I thought we'd have a casket to carry when I ordered it."

"We'll handle that. One thing I have to ask you about is media coverage. We've had several inquiries from news agencies wanting to cover the funeral, but what is your feeling about it? We will, of course, respect the family's wishes, but I know there's been at least one request to televise the service at Arlington Cemetery."

"Television coverage . . ." Goose bumps rise on her upper arms at the suggestion. John's funeral is to be a nationwide event. A historic moment.

"It would be handled respectfully, of course," he says quickly. "With the telephoto lenses and all the technology available, the cameras would be kept a discreet distance from the mourners, and—"

"Yes, yes, it's fine." Sharice may sound a bit too enthusiastic, but she can't deny that this request warms her heart. America has embraced her son's heroism—people want a chance to honor him and say their good-byes. This is all that a mother could ask for.

As Sgt. Palumbo goes on to describe the various components of the military honor service, Sharice bites her lip, restraining a twinge of emotion over the many ways her son John had made Jim and her proud.

She still remembers the day John and Noah came to her, together, to tell her that they'd enlisted in the army. "I know you and Dad were disappointed when I decided not to attend West Point," John told her. "But I'm going to make it up to you, I promise."

He had more than made it up to her, but then John was not one to disappoint. He realized nothing could please her more than knowing her sons were walking in their father's and grandfather's footsteps, serving their country.

John had understood these things, but Noah . . . there was a boy who marched to a different drummer.

And now, refusing to come home before the funeral . . . it niggles at the back of her brain. Sharice wants to know more than a phone call will reveal. What's going on with him, really? Of course, he's grieving over John's death, everyone is feeling the loss. But shouldn't he be home, mourning with his family?

Noah was always the quiet child, the one who would rather hole up in his room with a book than play football or tag out in the yard with the neighborhood kids. Quiet is one thing, but he needs to communicate with his family at a time like this. Sharice vows to pull him in line when she sees him back east before the funeral.

Chapter 29

"Ihate this shit . . . night patrol." Antoine Hilliard turns the Humvee onto the main highway, a dangerous stretch of road.

"You hate everything here," Emjay says, never taking his eyes off the road ahead. Although Hilliard is driving, you need every set of eyes watching out for bombs tucked into oil drums or suitcases or cars abandoned by the roadside. Out here, day or night, every object is suspicious, every man a suspect.

In the patches of light from tall street lamps you can see rubble where IEDs, improvised explosive devices, have blown up the concrete divider. Emjay subconsciously begins to count the scars from bombs that have torn up the median, then stops himself. He can't afford to lose focus.

The Humvee moves away from a housing development on the outskirts of Fallujah, plunging into a stretch of unlit highway. Emjay straps on his NOD, which allows him to see details in the darkness, though it's all through a greenish haze.

"Guys—" From the back of the Humvee, Spinelli taps on Emjay's seat to get his attention. "We have to go back to the FOB. My NOD's not working."

"Fucking Spinelli," Hilliard grumbles.

Spinelli has been so quiet, Emjay almost forgot he was back there. Usually, night patrols are carried out by a team of four, but everything got shifted around when John went down. Emjay now has to partner with the kid, and with Noah stateside on leave, Chenowith is pushing Hilliard, "blurred vision or not," to get his ass out on patrols and take Noah's place as field medic. "Your guys need you out there," Chenowith told Hilliard, pulling the buddy card on him. The platoon is all messed up now, guys jockeying to form teams, with John dead and Noah home on leave. But it's all in a day's work at Camp Despair.

"We're not going back," Hilliard says.

"But my NOD's broken. I can't see anything."

"Let me take a look," Emjay offers, twisting around to take the device from the kid, who reminded him of a teen who'd just blown a homework assignment. Christ, the army was really sinking low, recruiting snot-nosed boys and sending them here, to the fifth level of hell.

"If we go back now, Chenowith will send us out, make us start patrolling at the first checkpoint again," Hilliard complains. "I am not driving back to camp."

"Sorry, man," Spinelli says. "It's not my fault."

"See, that's where you're wrong, because you should have checked the fucking equipment before we left the fucking FOB." As he talks, Hilliard's head tilts from side to side on his large square body, and Emjay is reminded how much he looks like one of those giant tortoises. Teenage Mutant Ninja Turtles. Of all the guys in the platoon, Hilliard is the one who spends the most time lifting weights, and the most time in front of the mirror. Lassiter sometimes calls him "Hans und Franz," which really pisses Hilliard off, but when you live in close quarters with eight guys, everybody gets some ribbing.

Spinelli's NOD is definitely not working, but Emjay quickly homes in on the problem. "It's been disabled. There's a piece missing," Emjay says. "I had the same problem with mine. I don't know how it got screwed up." *It looks like someone messed with it, just like mine,* Emjay thinks, but he doesn't say that aloud.

"Can you fix it?" Spinelli asks.

"Back at the base, sure. I don't know about right now."

Emjay turns the night-vision device over in his hands. "You gotta stay on top of this stuff, Spinelli."

"I checked it last week."

"Christ, Spinelli. A week in the desert is a fucking eternity." Hilliard slows the Humvee and begins to pull over.

"What you got?" Twenty yards ahead, a compact car stands with its hood open. Emjay can see one man leaning over the hood.

"Somebody breaking curfew." Hilliard puts the Humvee in park and straps on his own NOD.

"Hold up," Emjay tells him as he shoves the NOD back toward Spinelli and reaches for his M-16.

In the seconds that Emjay makes those adjustments, Hilliard opens his door, climbs out. "Stay where you are!" he shouts to the man leaning over the disabled car.

The rest happens in slow motion . . . the viscous pace of a nightmare.

Hilliard steps forward, yelling. "Stay where you are!"

But the man behind the disabled car straightens and bolts, lunging toward them.

Through the windshield of the Humvee, in the green light of his NOD, Emjay can make out the vest—the thick contraption strapped over the man's torso.

A suicide vest.

The man hurtles himself toward them, head bent, on his toes like a track runner.

Hilliard digs in his heels, about to back off, when there is a flash of white.

A percussive jolt that obliterates all sound but a loud ringing in the head, a tremor in the bones.

And suddenly it's raining, black, sticky dirt and dust and gravel.

And blood.

Emjay is trying to get out of the Humvee and get to Hilliard, but at the same time he realizes he's not moving. He's frozen in the wake of the explosion, frozen and stunned.

"Oh, God," Spinelli whimpers behind him. "Oh, God. You okay?"

"I think so." Emjay's body is shaking all over, but at least he can feel. He can move, goddammit. He throws himself into the door to push it open and nearly falls out. The dust is thick and gritty, hard to see, but he needs to get to Hilliard.

"Hilliard!" He rounds the front of the Humvee and pauses. Hilliard's body lies face down, his square torso and head covered in blood . . . the rest of him gone.

"Oh, God!" Spinelli sobs behind him. "My head. I'm bleeding!"

Emjay stumbles out of the helicopter and starts to walk across the roof of the army hospital in Baghdad, but two medics grab him under the arms and lead him to a wheelchair.

"I can do it," Emjay shouts back at the medic pushing him, but his voice is lost in the thrum of engine and whirring blades.

The wheelchair is pushed up to the elevator, and the medic walks into his line of vision and presses the button. The medic is a small mountain of a woman in scrubs—navy blue scrubs. Her hair is dark, cut short, her eyes are soulful and languid as honey, and her chocolate skin reminds him of home. How long has it been since he's seen a woman who isn't hidden in a black abaya, one he can actually look at without stirring up disgrace and scorn?

"It's okay, now," she tells him. "Your C.O. wanted us to check you out, and he's right. You're not looking so good."

He lifts a hand to his head, not sure if the blood on his hand is his own. Still, he rests his cheek against his blood-spattered hand and sobs, so relieved to be in someone else's hands, at least for the time being.

"It's okay to cry, honey." Her hand touches his shoulder, and at that moment he's sure she's not a flesh-and-blood woman but an angel. "We're going to take good care of you," she says, and to his surprise, now that the moment of danger has passed he begins to tremble and sob.

*   *   *

The men and women of the ER are exceedingly kind to him, wiping the blood and black char off with damp cloths, telling him when and where they will probe. A tall, rangy doctor with a cue-ball head and quick hands removes a piece of shrapnel from Emjay's neck.

"We're lucky this is just on the surface," he says, peering through a magnifying glass strapped to his head that makes him resemble a Cyclops. "Looks like you got lucky this time."

"No, sir." Emjay wants to tell the doctor that if he possessed real luck he'd be stateside right now with a beer and tickets to the Redskins game, but conversation is not something he can access anymore in this stunned, stone world. He braces as the nurse swabs his neck with iodine wash, but all he can feel now is the cold.

While Emjay should be able to return to duty in a day or two, Spinelli's wound is a bit more complicated. An MRI reveals that a piece of shrapnel penetrated his left eye, hence the blood and blurred vision. The ER physician feels confident that Spinelli's sight can be restored, but the procedure is too specialized for the facility here. They'll close up the laceration here, then send Spinelli back to the U.S. for further surgery at Walter Reed Hospital.

"You got the golden ticket," Emjay tells Spinelli, who is seated on the bed across from him.

"Yeah. And all this time I was aiming for my foot." Spinelli leans back against the pillow and lets out a sob. "Oh, God. I'm still seeing him."

"Me, too." But for Emjay, the image of Hilliard's shredded torso is imposed over the memory of John splayed on the floor, bleeding out in seconds. And his heart is beating fast and furious, like a fire racing through dry brush, out of control. He can't slow it down, can't find calm anymore, and the pulsing in his ears is nearly deafening.

"I appreciate what you did for me out there," Spinelli tells him. "I'm so sorry I fucked up. I didn't know the night device was broken . . . I didn't." His cheeks are wet, whether from tears or eye wash, Emjay is not sure.

"Your broken NOD probably saved my life," Emjay says. The Humvee shielded them from most of the blast, and because of Spinelli he stayed in the vehicle a few extra seconds.

"Hilliard was so pissed at me," Spinelli sniffs. "Hilliard. I can't believe it."

Emjay closes his eyes, but the image of Hilliard's truncated torso is there, haunting him, the sickening sight throbbing like his pulse.

Oh, God, that's not how Emjay wants to remember this man.

He braces his eyes open and tries to imagine the faces of the people who will miss Antoine Hilliard, his kids and his wife, who sent care packages every week loaded up with nuts and candy and copies of *Body Builder* magazine. There was a mother; Emjay remembers hearing Hilliard talk about her, that she still lived back in Arkansas. And Hilliard used to talk about his friends, a core group in Little Rock, where he'd spent his childhood and attended high school.

"I can't believe he's gone," Spinelli says.

"I know."

As Spinelli succumbs to another sob, Emjay stares up at the speckled ceiling tile and realizes that, for all their differences, he and Spinelli suddenly have way too much in common.

"It's okay to cry, man," Emjay says over the clamor of his heartbeat, a drum that bangs on and on, out of control. A tear runs down his own cheek, a selfish tear not so much for the lives lost as the ruination of his own life. Never again will he be able to close his eyes without seeing them . . . the dead. But today was the kid's first visit to hell and, with that eye injury, it will probably be his last.

Maybe there's hope for Spinelli. If he leaves here and never comes back, maybe he can forget.

"It's okay," he tells Spinelli, spinning a lie. "You're gonna be all right now."

Chapter 30

Arlington National Cemetery
Madison

Who knew a funeral could be like a day at Disney World? The air resonates with the music of a full marching band, soaring strains of trumpets, instruments mingling with the low thrum of bass brass and rumbling drums. Dozens of soldiers in dress blues parade below a towering brown stone archway, the gold stripe down the sides of their trousers bending and straightening in perfect unison. It is a sea of blue punctuated by shiny gold buttons, flat gold-trimmed caps, and silver-bayoneted rifles tipped toward heaven. Sun glints off the bayonets and the cone of the tuba as a gentle autumn breeze teases the flags born by the color guard.

And at the rear of the parade rolls a cart with silver, broad-spoked wheels. The cart is lined with shiny, fringed satin and drawn by two white steeds that make her think of white knights and fairytales. You wouldn't be at all surprised to see this cart pull up in front of Cinderella's castle.

Of course, they're calling the parade a funeral procession, and the costumes are army dress uniforms. And the cart is not a princess's carriage but a caisson bearing her brother's ashes.

Oh, God.

That limo ride up the twisty hills of the cemetery was not a ride on Big Thunder Railroad.

The whole funeral is unfurling like a well-planned wedding,

and it's no wonder, after the way her mother massaged every detail.

Mom actually called it the funeral of the century—she's that into the whole status thing.

Today Mom is working closely with the cemetery's funeral director, signaling with a nod or a whisper when it's time to move to the next phase.

Dad is playing the colonel, buttoned into his dress uniform and standing at attention, ready to salute any general who might pass by.

Abby is surrounded by Suz and her college friends, Fanteen and Hitch, who flew in from England, and that reporter guy who was actually embedded in Iraq the same time as John. Suz is great and the college friends are kind of interesting. The British woman, Fanteen, looks sort of goth, with jet black hair and a nose ring. Hard to believe she's got two kids. Fanteen's husband is this skinny, very mellow dude and the reporter guy, Flint, seems okay, but surprisingly quiet. She expected him to be bold and pushy, asking lots of questions, but mostly he watches everything. They're a nice group but they're Abby's friends, and none of her friends were able to make the trip all the way out here just to watch her brother get his ashes stowed near some famous presidents.

Noah and Madison seem to be the only outcasts: Noah by choice and Maddy by bad luck. Noah is still in no-talking mode, wild-eyed and weird, so people steer clear of him, and Madison, well, there just aren't any other sixteen-year-olds in sight. She's too old to be indulged like a kid and too young for total inclusion in the adult world.

It would be great if she and Noah could hang together, but Noah-Balboa is not himself. Not at all. Besides looking awful, sort of haunted and bony and pale, he's acting like he's drunk or stoned on drugs. Drugs were never his thing, and she's been with him all morning and he hasn't touched a drop of liquor, so his whacked-out appearance is that much more of a mystery.

And a concern.

When all of this sinks in, when the awful, cold truth really hits her after the fanfare dies down, she and Noah could maybe help each other.

Maybe . . . if the real Noah shows up.

Chapter 31

The Columbarium
Abby

By the time the funeral procession reaches the columbarium, Abby is in a panic. Her heart races, her throat has gone dry, and her palms are moist with sweat.

Her heels scrape over the paving stones, grinding the truth through her marrow. This is all wrong, and it's all her fault. Why didn't she stand up for what John would have wanted? Why did she let Sharice have her way?

It's not that there's anything wrong with the columbarium itself. In fact, it's lovely and dignified. An open array of walls form angled courtyards that open to stone arches and fountains and trees. Not a dark musty crypt, but a charming, serene structure.

Which makes her utter revulsion that much more surprising.

This place is majestic—a very dignified place of rest.

So why does it seem so wrong to leave her husband's ashes here?

Why does she feel the impulse to snatch that urn from the caisson, kick off her shoes, and run like crazy over the grassy lawns, away from this pomp and circumstance, away from all these people who very kindly came to show their respects but did not really know John at all?

The impulse to flee with her husband's remains is strong because he does not belong here. John loved his country, yes, but he lived so many lives before he was a soldier. He was a kid who loved to build things, a Boy Scout, a football player, friend, humanitarian. The definition of John was evolving and ever-changing—a work in progress—and it pains her to see him defined in death solely as a soldier.

Silence shivers through the huge group of mourners as the honor guards face the back of the caisson. One of the white horses nickers softly, tossing its head.

The soldier lifts his arms and reaches his white-gloved hands toward the urn.

"Wait!" The word puffs out despite the lack of air in her lungs. Abby staggers forward and touches the urn. "I . . . I need a minute alone. One last good-bye."

The soldier's face remains stoically set but Abby detects a flicker of movement in his eyes beneath the shiny visor of his cap. He has probably never encountered an insane widow before. Maybe he's wondering if he should hold fast to the urn. Defend the ashes! Have distraught family members ever dropped them?

A small gasp cuts the air, and Sharice's face looms into Abby's line of vision. "Abby? It's time to let go, dear."

But the honor guard does not seem to notice Sharice; his acute attention is on Abby. "Of course, Mrs. Stanton," he says quietly. He grasps the urn with one hand, then offers Abby the crook of his other arm, which she accepts, sure that it is the kindest gesture anyone has made toward her.

The soldier escorts her around a wide stone wall to another world where green vines curl up to the edge of the red-and-gray stone path and green shrubs provide a modicum of privacy.

He places the urn on a low wall. "Take all the time you need." He sounds sincere, as if it really doesn't matter that a hundred or so people are waiting on the other side of the wall.

She bows her head, her eyes transmitting thanks as he takes two steps back, then cuts a sharp about-face and disappears beyond the wall.

"Abby?" Suz's eyes are wide with concern as she peers around the corner.

"Come, quick!" Abby motions wildly and her friend scurries over. "I can't go through with this," she whispers tearfully. "I can't leave him here. Not because I can't let go, but because I don't think this is the right place for him." She covers her mouth with one hand, as if to censure her own words. "I didn't have the heart to steal Sharice's thunder, but now I just can't do this!"

"It's okay! We talked about this." Suz's voice is soothing, her hands in motion as she places her big black handbag on the ledge and unzips it.

"What am I going to do?" Abby gasps. "There are a hundred people on the other side of that wall, all of them waiting for me to give him up."

"Not to worry." Suz reaches into her bag and holds up a Ziploc bag filled with . . . gray ashes?

"What's that?"

"We'll do a switch. You'll take John's ashes home with you and we'll leave these inside."

"But what . . . is that Scott?"

"No, just what I could scrape out of my vacuum at home."

"You brought those from home?" Abby cannot believe the premeditation that has gone into this exchange, but Suz is a woman of action, and she discussed Abby's concerns with her more than once.

Suz opens the urn. "Okay, there's supposed to be a liner in this thing. And I've heard there'll be bone chunks . . . not just dust." As she talks, she sticks a pen inside, trying to separate the liner from the urn. "Am I grossing you out?"

Abby shakes her head. "You're going to make me laugh."

"Easy peasy," Suz says, jabbing the pen down deep. It slips, sending a small cloud of white dust up between them.

"Oh!" Abby bites back a laugh. "Maybe we should just ask the honor guard to shove the Ziploc bag in the vault."

"Wise-ass." Suz manages to extract the liner, which she quickly seals into a plastic bag and tucks into her purse. Seconds later, she plunks the vacuum dust into the urn and closes the lid. "There." She brushes her hands against each other. "And I thought this trip would give me a break from dusting. What do I know?"

"Hey . . ." A voice calls from behind them.

Abby's head snaps up, but it's just Madison, who crosses the flagstones and joins them.

"What are you guys doing? Rolling joints or something?"

"Joints?" Suz's brows rise. "Do people still use that terminology?"

"We had one last thing to do for John," Abby says, "but we're all finished." She squeezes Madison's hand. "I'll tell you all about it later."

Abby lifts the urn, takes a deep breath, and heads back to the waiting crowd, flanked by Madison and Suz.

"You did the right thing," Suz says, patting her big purse.

Moments later, after the urn is stowed and a lone bugler plays taps, Abby knows that Suz is right.

She did the right thing.

Abby lets her eyes soften, and the dark silhouette of the bugler against the pale wall of niches seems poetic. She recalls the words to this song, which she sang as a girl in scout camp while the color guards lowered the flag at the end of the day.

"All is well, safely rest, God is nigh."

Wherever his ashes end up resting, she prays his spirit is in a better place.

"Go with God," she whispers. "Safely rest."

Chapter 32

Washington, D.C.
Sharice

From her station near the door of the reception hall in this historic old wing of the Smithsonian, Sharice feels surprisingly nauseated. Isn't that the sign of all her planning coming to fruition? She's read that film directors often take sick after they complete production on a movie; it's as if the body succumbs to the necessary demands of a grueling shooting schedule, and then, the minute the dream has been fulfilled, the body hollers for fair compensation.

Her hands are moist and tacky as clay, having squeezed the palms of half of Washington, her feet are raw from standing in heels, and her jaw is frozen from forming the regretful smile of the mother of the deceased.

"So kind of you to come."

"John thought so much of you."

"Thanks for being so thoughtful."

Good Lord, she's a walking Hallmark card.

Now that the demands of planning John's funerals are at bay, Sharice will be forced to think about the reality, that her oldest son is really gone, and that's too painful.

Activity at the reception has waned, though the hall is still half full of friends, military personnel, and media. Off in one corner she recognizes a group of John's friends from Rutgers—Spike Montessa and Marco Arechiga among them. Both boys seem to have found success, wives, suburban homes. The guys from the Seahawks have already departed. As they said their good-byes, Sharice nearly lost all composure at the sight of tears in Killer Kelly's eyes. To see a hulking, grown man like that break down . . . it's too much to bear, especially knowing what a good friend he was to John.

And where is her family? She hasn't seen Noah for quite some time, and she hopes he hasn't departed without saying good-bye. Abby sits at a table with her parents and friends, and she spies Madison sitting on a bench near the mirrored wall, talking with a young woman. Is that a friend of Abby's? The woman looks familiar but Sharice can't place her.

She spots Jim at a table by the window, talking with friends. When she joins him, their friends, Lt. and Mrs. Briggins, are saying their good-byes. Sharice hugs Laurel Briggins, then collapses into a chair. Under the long tablecloth, she pushes off her shoes and winces over the pain. The nerves on the bottom of her feet feel like they've been pounded into a pulp.

"My feet are killing me."

Jim cocks an eyebrow. "I won't say it."

"Please, don't," she says, not wanting to hear "I told you so."

They had an argument that morning over her choice of shoes—dramatic black heels that elongated her legs. She tossed off the comment that women's shoes had to be designed by men as torture devices, and Jim had pointed out that she might want to wear something more practical, as it was going to be a long day. And she had lashed out that she was not going to go down in history as the hero's mother who sported old grandma shoes. Then she burst into tears, and Jim had approached her from behind, kissed her cheek, then escaped into the shower.

Of course, the argument wasn't really about shoes. Their arguments never were about the matter being discussed—mundane things like who left the car without gas or why they were eating crackers that contained trans fats. The thing that was eating away at them was always a few levels beneath the surface, the hideous beast of the deep that could not be broached because you would run out of breath and the pressure would crush you.

Today, it was about John . . . everything is about John now. She and Jim had both awakened before the alarm went off in that strange hotel room, with a feeling of foreboding. Sharice herself would have given anything not to have to play out this day.

But sometimes you don't have a choice.

"I'm glad Madison finally found someone to talk to," Sharice says. "She's really been a crab on this trip."

"It's got to be hard for her, too," Jim says, defending her. "She was close to John, and she's still a kid. Sixteen. I can't imagine going through something like this at her age."

"You almost did," Sharice reminds him. "Weren't you just seventeen when you signed up? Half of the guys from your neighborhood had already been to Vietnam, and some of them didn't come back."

"That was different. Different times." He picks at the edge of the label on his bottle of beer. "Maddy's under a lot of stress." He glances up. "We all are, darlin'. You're going to be mad at me, but I let her have a drink. A Harvey Wallbanger."

"Jim!"

"I figure it's better she goes through me than sneaking around."

"If she got one drink from you she probably charmed the bartender out of two." Sharice rubs her feet together under the table and sighs. She can only hope that no one noticed Jim slipping an alcoholic drink to their daughter.

"She's a good kid." He defends her, again.

"A good kid who just tied one on at her brother's funeral."

"Sharice, honey . . ." He leans over the table. "Take a deep breath and let yourself relax a little. You've probably had the roughest day of anyone here." He squeezes her hand. "Want a Harvey Wallbanger?"

She lets out a breath, a pitiful attempt at a laugh.

She senses a change behind her—a few guests departing— and she glances up to see Abby joining them.

"Sharice." Abby's head tilts. "I wanted to thank you for everything you've done."

Jim rises and slides a chair over for Abby. "Sit, please. Join us."

As Abby smoothes the skirt of her new black dress to sit,

Sharice notices a run coming up the heel of her daughter-in-law's dark pantyhose. Girls today, they just don't know how to dress up anymore. When she was in her twenties you didn't go anywhere without clear nail polish in your bag to fix a run.

"Everything went so smoothly because of you. It was obvious you thought through every small detail," Abby says, drawing Sharice's attention back. "I don't know how you did it, but I'll always be grateful." She pops out of her chair and leans down to hug Sharice.

"No one can multitask details quite like Sharice," Jim says.

"I was happy to do it. You know I always have to keep busy." Sharice pats Abby's shoulder. "Thank you for letting me be involved."

"It worked out well, I think," Abby says, moving back to her seat. "I can't believe the level of media attention John attracted. Did you see all the cameras there today? It's hard to believe people care so much."

"If there's any silver lining here, it's that John was recognized as a hero." When Abby puts a hand up to stop her, Sharice just smiles. "I know, you're uncomfortable seeing him put on a pedestal, but that boy always followed his convictions. Having known him, you've got to admit he was as stubborn as they come."

"Yes, yes, John did have a mind of his own. That's not it." Abby presses her hands to her lips in prayer position. "It's the hero thing. There are some details of his death you need to know."

Sharice's teeth clamp tight, bracing herself. She can listen to what Abby has learned.

"Abby?" Jim scratches his jaw, inquisitive. "What is it?"

"It seems that John's death was not combat related. Someone in his own unit shot him, maybe by accident, maybe deliberately. My friend Flint has been helping me track down the whole story."

At first, Sharice does not comprehend. Abby's words are just non sequiturs tossed in the air, unstrung and lacking in meaning.

"Wait a second," Jim says. "Where did you get this information?"

"Flint was embedded in Iraq. When John was killed, he visited John's company for a while at Camp Despair. He spoke at length with the soldier who was with John when he was shot."

"Fratricide?" Jim's eyes narrow; he is skeptical. "That would have to be reported."

"Or deliberately overlooked," Abby says, a frightened look in her eyes.

Sharice is still wading through the viscous news. Does this mean John's death was unnecessary? His life taken because somebody aimed their rifle in the wrong direction? A foolish mistake. Not an act of heroism.

And now that he's gone, is it worth muckraking? No amount of investigation will bring him back, but it might harm his reputation. Will they strip him of his medals? His Purple Heart, Medal of Valor?

Abby sighs. "I'm sorry. I know this is upsetting, but I wanted you to know before I started to pursue things. I want some answers from the army, some sort of investigation."

"Why would you want to do that?" Sharice asks, her voice surprisingly void of emotion. "Why tarnish John's reputation now, when you don't even know what happened? You don't have the facts yet, do you?"

"No," Abby admits cautiously.

"And you may never know what happened over there," Jim says wistfully, his eyes distant. "You really can't know, unless you're there."

"True, there are things we'll never know," Abby says, "but right now the most difficult task is getting the army to give me a detailed account of what happened that day in the warehouse." She rubs her temples, then lifts her head, resolved. "I know John would want the truth to be known, and I'm not going to stop until I get to the heart of this. He would want me to pursue the investigation."

Abby rises, resolute. "I'm going to start making calls tomorrow."

And ruin everything, Sharice thinks. *Everything my son lived for will be gone . . .*

"Sharice . . . Jim, listen. I'm sorry if this causes you further distress." Abby squeezes her eyes shut. "Believe me, I'd like nothing more than to pretend I never heard this and just let it go. I want peace, for all of us. But I keep grappling with it in my mind, and the only answer is that I have to find the truth. It's what John would have wanted."

She steps forward and touches Sharice's shoulder. "I'm so sorry."

In that moment, Sharice sees her own reality warping in that rare distortion that happens once or twice in a lifetime. It happened when she was a kid, the day JFK was shot, and a stranger flagged her mother down in the parking lot at the commissary to ask if it was true. All of the shows she watched on television were cancelled for days. A neighbor ran out of her house in curlers, tears streaming down her face, wanting to talk, looking for consolation because suddenly, the world was not as it was supposed to be.

Reality wrinkled again the day that terrorists hijacked four commercial flights and crashed them on U.S. soil. That September morning, she'd slept through the first attacks and awakened at 9:30 West Coast time to a world in crisis, TV journalists with more questions than answers, and skies empty except for the fighter jets circling from McChord Air Force Base.

And now, again . . . three times in one lifetime, reality shimmers and bends like fired glass. Her son is no longer a hero; he is reduced to a victim, a life lost in a costly error.

A mistake.

She looks across the table for help, but Jim is already gone, curled inside. Here is another topic to be added to the list of things that will not be discussed.

"I can't believe it," she says.

"Well, I can." He stands, the action tugging slightly at the tablecloth as he heads off to the bar, leaving Sharice alone.

"Why didn't you tell us?" Sharice asks, trying to keep the blame and disappointment from her voice. "Your father and I had no idea that John's death was suspicious."

"What do you want me to say? Because my head is so over-loaded with everything, I swear, it's going to explode." Noah presses back against a marble column on the patio and shakes his head, as if he could shake it all off.

Poor Noah. She's been so caught up in the funeral arrange-ments, she didn't realize he was this bad off. At first Sharice worried that he had left the reception without saying good-bye. It was a relief to find that he had simply fled the noise in-side for this quiet garden. The dozen or so tables out here are nearly empty now, much to Sharice's relief. She's not ready to share this troubling turn of events with her friends. Not yet.

"It's always suspicious, Ma," he says. "And John . . . I wasn't there when it happened. I was outside the building and they carried him out in a panic and put him in front of me and . . ." He presses his eyes shut, but not before she sees the glaze of pain.

"Because you're the company medic," Sharice says, putting the scenario together for the first time. "Was there a doctor there?"

He shakes his head. "Everyone thought I could fix him. Stop the bleeding, sew him up, make him new again. They wanted me to be some kind of miracle worker, and I couldn't do it. I tried, but I couldn't save him." He presses his face into one arm, wiping the tears on his sleeve.

The sleeve of a dress shirt.

"Noah, where is your dress uniform?" she asks. Did he ap-pear at the funeral in a suit? With all the photographers there, the television coverage . . .

"Would you stop obsessing over stupid details and listen to me?" Fury flashes to the surface as he points off toward the setting sun. "We just stowed your son's ashes. My brother. He's gone, and no amount of pomp and circumstance is going to get him back." His eyes are ablaze with anger as he smacks the pillar, then turns away from her.

"You're right. I'm sorry." She touches his back, and the an-gular shoulder blade under her fingers seems so foreign. This man, her son. "I'm just so rattled by the things Abby told me.

After all this, she's going to demand some sort of investigation, and I just want to know if it's a wild goose chase. Honestly, I wish she'd just keep it to herself."

"Leave Abby alone," he says quietly. "She's trying to do the right thing."

"But as you said, none of this is going to bring John back. And in the worst-case scenario, it will diminish your brother's reputation."

"Not for me. Whether he died in combat or by accident, he'll still be John. His reasons for being in Iraq were altruistic and pure." He turns back to face her. "But in the past few months, that all changed. John realized it was a huge mistake: the invasion, the killing, our being there at all."

"No . . . he was so gung ho."

"He wanted to be part of the solution, not the problem." Noah sighs. "John felt disenfranchised, alienated from the mission. A lot of the guys over there feel that way now. There's no clear course, no reason to be there."

"I can't believe I'm hearing this. Nobody forced you boys to sign up. You did it willingly, with a desire to serve. And now you want to give up because you've hit some obstacles? Think again. I know it's not easy, but Stantons don't take the easy path. You'd better work on that attitude before you return to Iraq."

"I signed up because I followed my older brother every-where, like a lost puppy. And don't worry about me going back to my unit with a bad attitude, because that's not going to happen. I'm not going back, Ma. I'm not going back to Iraq."

Pain pierces her heart. Closing her eyes, Sharice can see it, long and shiny as a bayonet.

"Don't freak out," he says. "God, I thought you'd be happy. You already lost one son."

"Are you being reassigned?" she asks, trying not to transmit her utter disappointment as she opens her eyes.

"No. I'm leaving the army. Going to Canada."

No! Noah, you can't! She can't help the gasp that leaves her throat, but before she can recover and form new words, a commotion by the doors draws their attention.

"Are you going to put music with this?" Madison's voice projects from inside, where she is talking to a reporter behind a videocam. She walks backward, her heels clomping heavily on the wood floor as she heads their way. From the way she teeters with each step, Sharice can tell she's had too much to drink. "If you do, make it something cool and not that old army oompah band stuff. Maybe something from Green Day. Oh, I know, I know. 'When September Ends'! I loved that song when it first came out. Or is that too obvious? You know, it's not really 'bout September eleventh . . ."

Sharice's despair deepens. Her daughter is giving an interview? No doubt Madison has already broadcasted her antiwar slogans. With any luck, the interview is not live.

Madison trips on the door saddle and starts to fall onto the patio.

Noah rushes over and grabs her by the shoulders. "Maddy . . . you okay?"

"It's the other brother!" she says cheerily, leaning against him for a moment. "Noah, Noah-Balboa, banana-fana foe-foah . . ."

"Hi, Noah." The reporter, a petite man who looks too young to be out on a school day, has the fake smile of a bully in on a huge joke.

Behind his camera, the photographer grins.

"And here we have John's mother, Mrs. Retired-Captain Shir-fleece Stanton." Madison hiccups and covers her mother. "Shir-lease. Shir-please." She hiccups again, her face contorting.

"Maddy . . . that's enough." Sharice steps forward in an attempt to intervene.

Madison meets her eyes, holding up a finger as if to say, give me a minute. The girl turns toward the garden, as if she's just spotted something in the shrubs, and vomits.

"Okay." The reporter calls, in resignation. "Thanks, Madison." The camera lights cut off, and the two men step inside, interview over.

"Oh, Maddy." Sharice pulls off her shoes and drops them on the patio. Then, standing at her daughter's side, she pulls Madison's hair back, a humbled witness as, after so many years spent weaving values and characters into her children, the fabric of her family is disintegrating.

Chapter 33

Union Station, Washington, D.C.
Noah

The blue jeans feel surprisingly comfortable for new clothes, already washed and distressed so that they fold like a flag over his limbs as he moves through the station and pauses under the giant board listing departing Amtrak trains. Noah Stanton is traveling light, having left his dress uniform standing on a hanger in Beaver's closet like a ghost of the man he used to be. Beaver, a friend from nursing school who relocated to northern Virginia, didn't mind him leaving his gear behind.

"Just shove it into the back of the closet under the stairs," Beaver said when Noah was on his way out this morning. "No one ever looks in there. But don't you want to take some of the stuff along? Like, socks, and shit? It gets cold up in Canada."

"I'm good," Noah insisted, and for the first time in a long time, he wondered if that might be true.

He's grateful to Beaver, and he feels lighter without his army gear, lighter now that he's passed John's letters on.

When he logged on to Beaver's computer that morning, he hesitated. Only one document was clearly marked: In the event of my death, please forward this to Abby Fitzgerald. That one definitely had to go, but what about the others? He'd anguished over the decision since that night he'd first read those files on the computer in Fallujah. John's writing contained personal observations and bitter ruminations, uncensored material. What had John intended to do with these documents? Was it just a way to vent, or did he want to share his observations with the world? In the end, Noah decided to let Abby decide. She was John's partner and best friend; she would be a conscientious caretaker of his intellectual properties.

After Noah sent Abby the e-mail with John's attachments, the relief came as a surprise. It was as if he were shedding layers, unburdening himself of old skins.

Moving down the aisle of a newsstand, he adjusts the large knapsack strapped to his back and wonders if she'll come. He doesn't blame her if she doesn't.

The knapsack makes him feel like a mountain man, which is probably how he'll look in six months—bearded and thin, sporting flannel shirts, boots, and a down parka. Hell, he might even break down and buy a hat. He pauses in the wide entrance to a sports store, eyeing the wool caps with "Redskins" woven into the brim. The fabric looks thick and warm, but he doesn't want anything that shouts USA. For now, he's on the run.

"Now announcing the arrival of the Acela Express to New York on track eleven . . ." The man's voice is so bold and theatrical, it reminds him of a ringmaster at the circus. "The Acela Express on track eleven. All aboard!"

That's his train. Less than three hours to New York, then just ten hours and fifteen minutes to Montreal. Half a day, and you could be in another country. It's a miracle of sorts.

Fourteen hours to freedom. His heart soars at the prospect.

Pausing at the archway, Noah scans the vast waiting room. No familiar faces. He reaches into his jacket to check his ticket for the fifth time, as if it might have vanished into desert sand in his pocket. The train to Canada is called the Adirondack #69. Adirondack makes Noah think of those laid-back resort chairs made of wood, and, of course, there's sixty-nine, which he hasn't ever had the good fortune to try. Well, maybe someday.

Someday sounds good. The future holds a promise of hope, now that he won't have to live with scars on his soul, the bad karma of having killed someone. In his mind, it's better to be a fugitive, AWOL from the army, than to live with the blood of another human being on his conscience.

As he locates the sign for Track 11 and joins the end of the queue, he soaks up the atmosphere: the bored faces of commuters, the forced cool of college kids. This may be one of his last glimpses of America, and he wants to remember its diversity, its beauty, its flaws. He is watching a young mother chase her toddler past a bench when he sees her rush past a coffee kiosk, nearly toppling a man stirring his drink. His mother has always struck him as a woman of poise and social aplomb, but now, watching her try to run in sandals with both hands gripping her big purse, he is reminded that she's human.

He waves, catching her attention.

Relieved, she waves back and hurries over to join him.

Up close, she averts her gaze, unable to really look him in the eye. "The Metro took longer than I thought. I was afraid I missed you."

"I'm glad you made it."

She is bent over her purse, where she is digging for something. "Here." She pulls out a fistful of twenties and presses it into his palm. "It's all I could get from the ATM."

Noah pushes the money into his pocket. It will help pay for food and a place to stay until he can find work. "Thank you," he says, knowing how difficult this is for her to accept, how embarrassing it will prove in her everyday life when word gets out around the base that her second son is a deserter.

He doesn't tell her that Madison already gave him every cent she could get her hands on. In fact, his little sister took him shopping yesterday and outfitted him in this shirt and these prewashed jeans. He had to rein her in when she tried to dress him in cashmere sweaters and white shirts that reminded him of Prince, but Madison was determined to get him started with a civilian wardrobe, all paid for with their parents' credit cards. Somehow, he knows she will not appreciate Madison's collusion.

"What will you do up there? How will you survive?" his mother asks.

"I'll get a job."

"You can't work as a nurse up there, can you?"

"Nah. My license is no good up there, but I'd like to try something different for a change. Something with less stress." He would like to find somewhere to work out in the open spaces, somewhere he could get his hands in the soil. Maybe grow something. As a kid, he'd loved to plant seeds and pull weeds in the garden, but somewhere along the way he'd given it up, given up on himself. "I'll be fine," he assures her.

She frowns. "You don't sound worried, but I am."

Looking down at her, he notices that the frown lines around her mouth don't disappear anymore; they're a permanent part of her face, a historical road map. "I won't be the first soldier to cross the border. There's a whole resistance movement going on, and it's pretty well organized. Personal statements from the AWOL soldiers are listed on their Web site. It's not clear whether the Canadian government will grant them asylum, but I figure I've got a few years before I have to make a move. I've e-mailed a few of the guys. When I get there, I'll connect."

"I'll still be worried."

"Okay, you can worry. That's your job, but I really will be fine."

The stationmaster announces the last call for Noah's train to New York. "That's me." He leans down to place a kiss on her cheek, and she throws her arms around him and envelops him in a hug.

When she pulls back, tears sparkle in her eyes. "Don't ever tell your father I was in on this," she says. "He'd never forgive me."

He squeezes her shoulder, which seems so small in his hand. Suddenly, he feels like the parent consoling the child. "No worries," he says. "I can keep a secret."

Chapter 34

Jim Stanton watches them from behind a rack of paperbacks at the opening to one of those gift shops that sell everything from the morning paper to candy bars and earplugs for your trip.

He didn't have to follow Sharice here, dogging her from a block back like a detective in a TV show. When he saw the departure time written beside the words UNION STATION on the hotel notepad next to the bed, he knew.

He just knew.

When you live with someone for thirty years, when you share the same bed and toothpaste, split the yard chores, and rub her feet when they're sore, you begin to know these things. Sharice complains about lack of communication, about the walls he constructs to hide behind. But he sees and feels far too much. No one should have to suffer from his personal shit.

For Jim, the world would be a better place if more walls were erected, if people could deal with their own discontent instead of taking it out on others, if the touchy-feely types weren't always trying to extricate people's feelings and broadcast them like loud, painful, red captions. Whoever said feelings were rational or worth anything at all? For God's sake, whatever happened to sucking it up?

And right now, Jim is relieved that Sharice doesn't know he's come to the train station; she'll never have to know, thank

God. If he told her, she would want to discuss Noah's decision. She would probe and prod Jim for his *feelings* about their son going AWOL, pulling Jim through a grinder over the monumental crisis of his life.

Leaning to the side of the rack of paperbacks, Jim assesses his second son, the follower. Birth order always seemed to be Noah's curse, especially growing up in the shadow of a strong-willed boy like John. "If your brother jumps off a cliff, are you going to follow?" Jim would ask Noah, and the boy would nod, proud of his allegiance to his older brother. It seems like Jim has devoted his entire relationship with Noah to trying to teach that boy to have a mind of his own. And now . . . this is his decision? His son has finally made a choice of his own, and this is it . . . to run from military service?

AWOL? A deserter.

With a grunt of pain, Jim turns away from the sight of his wife and son caught in a farewell embrace. "Sounds like an ulcer," the doctor said when Jim told him of the pain in his gut. "But you'd better come in and we'll run some tests." An ulcer—sign of a worrier. Jim had never considered himself to be such a weak link, and now, after surviving combat wounds and two tours in Vietnam, his body was betraying him with an ulcer.

He purchases a packet of antacids from the uninterested clerk at the register and returns to his vantage point behind the book rack. Sharice is patting Noah's back, but she seems so small in his arms. The boy swallows her up, though Jim remembers a time when he could hold Noah in one arm. When they're babies, when they need everything from you, you lull yourself into thinking it will be that way forever.

There's an announcement—all aboard for a train—and people say their last good-byes at the track entrance while a late passenger bolts the length of the waiting room.

Jim steps out from behind the rack of books and drinks in the sight of Noah, the square Stanton jaw, shoulders that seem impossibly wide in the gray T-shirt. This will be his last moment with his son, a view from thirty yards away, and that realization intensifies the burning in his gut. To lose two sons in the course of a week . . .

Bitterness curdles in his stomach at the unfairness of it, though he chastises himself for expecting anything to be fair. He's seen life and death spin in random circles long enough to know that the arrow that misses you now will veer closer on its return orbit.

Noah hugs his mother one last time, then turns and walks to the track entrance with a hiker's swagger, a large pack on his back. At the threshold he turns back to his mother and almost smiles. Almost. Then, he disappears into the future.

Jim screws his mouth to one side, swallowing back the spit that wants to rise to his eyes. His son is deserting. It seems ludicrous, impossible that any son of his would run from his military duty.

At the same time, part of Jim knows that it's the only rational thing to do. Not that he approves. Not that he'll ever be able to acknowledge his second son again.

But somewhere, beyond the border, his son will be alive, with a chance at having a full, healthy life, and despite his code of honor and allegiances, Jim recognizes the good in that choice.

Canada is Noah's saving grace. Maybe he can find a safe haven, a niche where he can live without ever thinking of Weapons of Mass Destruction and Nuclear Armaments.

Wouldn't that be nice.

"Go, son," Jim says under his breath. "Run hard. Run fast."

Chapter 35

Sterling, Virginia
Abby

Noah's e-mail stops Abby in her tracks.
She is killing time at her parents' house, unable to concentrate enough to get lost in a book but sick of the prattle on television. She logs on to the computer in the guest room and sees the e-mail from her brother-in-law.

His message is brief: "I thought you should see these."

When she opens the attachment and finds John's letters—electronic journal entries—a small sigh escapes her throat. His voice comes through so clearly in his writing that it hurts her to read on.

And yet, she can't resist at least skimming his accounts of conversations with the locals, exotic birds and cloth in markets, observations of architecture and Islamic customs, visits to the local orphanage, where he knew the workers and many of the children. When John wrote about Iraqi people he had met, he mentioned many of them by name, revealing their personalities and some of the differences in culture he had observed. There were comedic accounts of the guys in his platoon with loving descriptions of some of the "kids" he served with.

"Doc is a natural leader, and I suppose you could do worse than Chenowith, although some of the guys have taken to calling him 'Cadet' behind his back because he never lets you forget the fact that he attended West Point. Personally, I like to seek out the underdogs, the quiet ones. Emjay Brown, son of a chicken farmer from the Maryland shore, is good people.

Whenever we go out on missions, I try to get hooked up with him. And I'm trying to look out for the new kid, Spinelli, who appears to have bitten off more than he can chew by enlisting. Sometimes at night I hear him crying in his bunk, and it breaks my heart. I wish I had the power to send the kid back home."

John loved people. How did she forget that? He would have been thrilled by the thousand-plus people who attended his funeral, as long as they had a good time.

But as she reads on, his journals voice concerns about U.S. involvement in Iraq. "Does U.S. intervention contribute to the greater good of this country?" he wrote. "The U.S. likes to call these eruptions of violence insurgencies, but really we are in the midst of an age-old civil war."

These concerns had begun to come through in his e-mails, though Abby sensed that sometimes he censored himself due to the lack of security over the Internet. It was all disturbing and somehow reassuring. John's letters reminded her so much of the man he was: steadfast, conscientious, committed to ending the hatred that sparked 9/11.

> I am not too popular here among my own guys these days. The jealousy is so palpable you could cut it with a knife. When they ask me about my football career, I try to hold back, knowing that some people are incited by my success. It's that entitlement thing that's going on in America. They think: "If you've got something good going on, then I want it, I <u>deserve</u> it." When they don't see that achievements are richer when you've worked for them.
>
> Some guys don't like it when I question the decisions of our government, but isn't America all about asking the difficult questions? I enjoy the political debates, but some of the guys get riled up. But no matter how long we argue, no one has been able to explain why our country has sent us here, involved in a war in Iraq.
>
> We have our own McCarthy right in this platoon. I have been called an anarchist and a traitor.
>
> That's okay. Popularity is overrated.

She scrolls ahead, finding an entry John wrote a week before he was shot.

> I went into this thinking I was defending my country, fighting terrorism, but now I have to ask myself who the enemy really is. The lines grow fuzzier every day.
>
> One of the guys here has actual notches on his belt, one for each killing. He's got a bloodlust, a desire to kill, whether it's insurgents or just some locals who might cross him. Yesterday, as we were heading out to the vehicles, two of the guys in my unit smacked fists and told each other: "Happy hunting." It makes me sick, seeing a situation that gives these animals license to kill.
>
> I came into this blinded by patriotism. I thought I was doing the right thing, signing up with Noah, but am I doing any good here? Who the hell is the enemy when my own guys fantasize about killing?
>
> When all is said and done, will there be more peace in the world than when we started this invasion?

John never revealed this level of disenfranchisement to her. She pictures him on patrol in Fallujah, rife with alienation and guilt and a feeling of responsibility for his fellow soldiers who abused their power.

And who is this soldier with notches on his belt? It's hard to believe this behavior is tolerated in this day and age. It's unsettling to think of John in his last days, in the company of men lacking in moral fiber and integrity. John did not suffer fools gladly, and she suspects he gave these men hell, though that's little consolation.

She closes the file, then notices something else in the attachment—a file called: JUST IN CASE. When she clicks it open, the headline at the top steals the breath from her body:

> Abs, just in case something happens to me, this is for you. Please, please don't read it unless I don't get out of here alive.

Oh, God.

For the first time since John's death eeriness creeps over her, and goose bumps form on her upper arms. Why did John write this? Did he have a feeling of foreboding, some kind of warning that someone in his platoon was about to ambush him? In his journals, he wrote that he wasn't popular with the guys, but a difference of opinion was hardly enough motivation to kill someone.

Her hand hovers over the mouse, suspended in the knowledge that once she scrolls down and reads on, it will be the final gesture, confirmation that he is gone.

> Abs,
>
> I'm not sure why I'm writing this except that I've been getting some weird feelings lately, and it would be so wrong if something happened to me and I didn't tell you one last time how much you mean to me.
>
> First, you are a beautiful person, through and through. I miss you, but the truth is that I'm always missing you. My bad. No one seemed more surprised than you when I decided to enlist, and though you've always been supportive I realize that many aspects of military life have pushed you out of your comfort zone. Sorry for that. But still, you stick by me. You must really like me. ;-)
>
> The luckiest day of my life was—no, not the Superbowl. It was the night I met you. Snow delay at JFK. Abs, I want our life together to go on and on, but if you're reading this . . .
>
> On a clear night, look up and count the stars and hold onto that number and know that I love you more. I will always love you.
>
> John

By the time Abby finishes reading, the tears in her eyes blur the words, but she dashes them away, wanting this last connection to her husband.

This last good-bye.

Chapter 36

Canadian Border
Noah

North.
Images of snow-covered hills and tall evergreens crowd Noah's mind. He's been hearing the "Snow" song from the movie *White Christmas* play in his head ever since the train passed into the state of Maine. That corny movie is one of his mother's favorites, with all the troops coming up to the inn to support the general in the end.

Good God, it's only September, but the temperature does seem to be dropping with the sun as the train travels north, shooting through banks of opaque mist and towns where street lights flash from red to green, and warm, yellow-lit windows welcome people home to dinner. These small-town streets, these modest houses—this is the America John wanted to protect when he took that wrong turn into the army. Good people trying to do the right thing without fear of terrorism. It all started with the best of intentions.

Noah wants to think that he's doing the right thing now, that his escape to Canada is not an act of cowardice, as his father will surely see it, but an act of courage, a move toward saving other people's lives, if not just his own.

He wants to think that, for him, north is the answer.

Right now, it's his only choice.

When he booked his ticket, the Amtrak agent warned that there might be delays at the border crossing. Since 9/11 both the U.S. and Canada had stepped up customs and immigration procedures. But when the train stops at the border, the crossing seems uneventful. Seated in the two rows of seats that face each other at the end of the car, Noah is one of the first to go. He feels a slight buzz of nerves as he hands his driver's license and passport to the Immigration officer, but he reminds himself that he's not doing anything illegal. Not yet, at least. He's not AWOL until his leave officially ends.

"Enjoy your stay." The agent hands back Noah's passport and license, then moves down the aisle to the next passenger.

Noah tucks the ID away, anxious for the train to keep moving north. He read somewhere that of all people surveyed, the ones who lived in colder climates reported a higher level of happiness.

After the train departs the border stop, Noah stands, stretches, and takes the down jacket from his duffle bag. Balled up and wedged against the cold window, it makes a great pillow. He stretches out his leg, glad for the half-empty train, since he didn't think it was wise to blow his cash on a sleeper car.

His head sinks into the plush pile of the jacket. He closes his eyes and falls into the most relaxing state he's known in months. In a light sleep, he's still conscious of the rocking train, the whoosh of covered tunnels.

Soon the rhythmic sound of the train is the beat of a bass drum from the school band on the football field. The lights bounce off helmets and illuminate the players' white jerseys as he waves them down field, down, way down.

His right hand grips the ball as he dances right, left, trying to steer clear of the defensive tackles. His arm sings, loose and strong, ready to shoot the ball down the field. But where the hell is his receiver?

John! John? Where are you?

He squints against the lights, and number 19 darts out from behind a dark jersey and runs backward into the end zone. John . . . he's open.

Noah snaps the ball, hard, and it launches through the air in a clean, wide arc. A rocket to the end zone, it smacks into John's chest. John palms the ball in the air—a touchdown!

A moment so sweet, Noah smiles in his sleep.

But someone across the aisle is kicking him, nudging him from the dream.

He pulls himself from sleep to see his brother sitting across from him, kicking him the way he used to under the dining room table. John's white number 19 jersey glows, just as it did in the dream.

"Nice move, bro," John said, nodding in approval. "Nice move."

Noah smiles, and when he takes a breath, a weight has lifted from his chest. He closes his eyes and falls back to sleep dreaming of tall pines on snow-covered hills.

Chapter 37

Fort Lewis
Flint

Flint is glad to see Abby eating, pleased that she is serious about holding the army accountable, and, on top of all that, he's relieved to have a chance to see Abby at all. He had worried that once they returned to the Seattle area they would fall back into their previous roles, distant and disconnected. So when Abby called him to ask for help investigating John's death, he got behind the wheel of his Prius for the first time in months and pulled into the extended parking lot that is I-5.

He scoops in a mouthful of rice, having passed on the spicy stuff. Since his return to the States he's suffered major heartburn, probably from all the excess after months of eating granola bars and jerky. His transition back to the land of the all-night burrito stand and the drive-through window is taking a bit longer than he expected. Most nights he still wakes up at least once, panicked over the ominous silence.

"Isn't it ironic that the guys you serve with, your best friends and blood brothers, can't attend your funeral? I mean, here this poor solider is killed—Hilliard?"

He nods. "Antoine Hilliard."

"Killed by a suicide bomber," Abby says as she closes a white paper container of Szechuan spicy scallops. "That had to be awful, for all of them."

"It's one of the exigencies of military service, I guess."

"But I feel sorry for them," Abby says. "They don't get a chance to grieve or mourn. No time to celebrate a person's life. Where's the closure?"

"They have a memorial service, sometimes it's combined with the Hero Flights, but there's no time spared for bereavement." He puts the rice aside, wondering if Abby has given herself a chance to grieve. She looks great, but you never know what's churning inside a person.

"It's good that they make an effort," she says, "but a ten-minute service is hardly enough to destress."

Flint swipes a pen from Abby's kitchen counter. "Let's make a list of avenues for you to pursue, since I don't think your contacts in the army are going to grant you an impartial investigation unless you put some pressure on them. First . . ." He clicks the pen and writes *Emjay Brown*.

"You'll want to connect with the guys in John's platoon. When their deployment ends, you've got to meet them. Especially the guy who was right beside him when the bullets hit, Emjay Brown. That guy knows something."

"Something he's holding back?" Abby asks.

"It might even be something in his subconscious right now, but troubling memories like that have a bad habit of sneaking to the surface."

"And psychology is supposed to be my specialty."

"Just be sure you find a way to get with these guys when they return . . . when?"

"December."

"There's usually some reception on base. Make sure you go, and see what you can find out from his fellow soldiers. I can probably help you when you get to that point."

"I think I can handle it," she says. "This degree is giving me a lot of practice with my interview skills."

"Ah, yes, the shrink thing. How's that coming along?"

"I won't be a full-fledged head shrinker, just a licensed counselor. If I make up the assignments I missed, I'll finish my classwork this semester and begin full-time clinicals in January."

He whistles. "Close enough. If you can say ADHD to parents with second-grade boys, you'll pay for your leather sofa in no time."

"I won't be able to prescribe drugs," she says. "And to be honest, it's been a helpful distraction. I could have taken the rest of the semester off, but then I would have gone crazy focusing only on this." She points to the notepad.

"And nobody wants a crazy therapist, right?" He's grateful for the rapport they still have; the teasing banter is safe and somehow reassuring.

Abby points her chopsticks at him. "Okay, enough picking on me. I need a game plan that extends beyond the homecoming of Bravo Company." She slides a yellow-ruled notepad over and flips through the top pages. "This is a list of my phone contacts for the U.S. Army, a big dead end. My inquiries sort of lead back to where I began, at Sergeant Palumbo, the casualty assistance officer. All they can tell me is that John's personal belongings will be shipped back to me—nobody knows when. And I'll be getting a letter from John's commander, Colonel Billy Waters, but that sounds like it will be more of a protocol condolence thing than an explanation of what happened."

He nods. "I've seen a few letters to widows. They're personal, sometimes poignant, but it's a formality."

"If I hadn't gone to Dover and, by some magic, extracted a copy of John's file, I wouldn't even know there were two bullet wounds." She puts down her chopsticks and presses a napkin to her mouth. "It's not easy being Nancy Drew in the U.S. Army."

"Tell me about it. So the army isn't forthcoming. What exactly do we know?"

"That he was hit by two bullets. Two rounds from an M-16 were recovered."

"And that's the type of gun carried by his platoon," Flint says.

She nods. "And there's the soldier you talked with—Emjay Brown. How reliable a source is he?"

"The guy was pretty broken up, a suicide risk. But that doesn't make him an unreliable source."

"So . . ." Abby folds her hands on the table, reluctant to go on. "So you think it was friendly fire."

"Did they find a sniper in the warehouse? An Iraqi insurgent?" he asks, already knowing the answer.

Abby closes her eyes. "No, they did not."

"So I'd say he was shot by one of our guys. Strictly speculation, of course, but if I were writing the story, I would certainly hint at that possibility."

"How could the army do that to him?" she asks, her voice quavering. "How could they let that happen?"

Flint sucks in a breath, feeling at a loss. He'd like to hug Abby and tell her that it's all going to be okay and that John probably had no idea what hit him, but none of that would be true.

She plucks a napkin from the holder on the table and presses it to each eye. "I'm sorry. I know you didn't come here to see me blubber."

"It's okay to cry, Abby." *Though it kills me to watch.*

He turns away to give her space, and picks up her list of army personnel. Some of the names have notes and slogans beside them, like "Hear No Evil, Speak No Evil" by Sgt. Palumbo's name, and "You Can't Handle the Truth" penciled in beside the name of a colonel at the Pentagon. One thing is for sure, Abby is conducting a very cute investigation.

"I have some of my own contacts in the army," he says. "If you want, I'll see what I can find out from them. But rumor has it that this one's being played very close to the vest. The army never released a combat incident report. That tells me that something is fishy."

Abby is nodding vigorously. "Ask away. I am so sick of cold-calling these people, explaining my sad story, and getting past all their condolences to the heart of the matter. I probably sound ruthless on the phone, but no one is giving me the answers I need."

"I can do ruthless," he says. "Let me make some calls. In

the meantime, there's one other avenue you might want to consider."

The way her dark hair tumbles over one shoulder when she tilts her head, those green eyes so wide and inquisitive . . . he has to look away.

"What's that?"

He clears his voice. *Focus, you idiot.* "You could play the celebrity card. It seems to me a lot of reporters would jump at this story—" His fingers form quotation marks. "'Hero struck down in his prime, but what's the real story, and why isn't the Pentagon telling?'"

Her frown is the same, that funny way her mouth scrunches over to one side. "I could do it," she says, "but Sharice and Jim would freak. As it is, they're not happy that I'm pursuing this at all, even in my quiet way."

"Just keep it in mind as an option." He stacks some empty paper containers and brings their glasses to the sink. When he and Abby shared a suite in college, Flint was the Felix Unger of the group, clearing away drinking glasses before people were finished, making visitors slip off their shoes at the door. He'd worked through some of his fanatical neatness; the remainder of it had been stripped from him when he became an embed in Iraq. You don't wear the same armored vest for three straight months without learning to live with your own stink.

When he turned back, she was still sitting, gripping the kitchen table pensively. Her freckles stood out in stark contrast to her pale skin.

"What?" he asks, leaning back against the kitchen sink. "What's wrong . . . other than the obvious, that you just lost your husband and all that."

She sucks in a breath. "There's something I want to show you, but first . . . I need you to promise me that all this will stay between you and me."

"As in, don't tell Mrs. Niedermeyer down the block?"

"As in, this can never be published. This has got to be more than off the record. It's so secret, I was even afraid to e-mail it to you and have it out there on the Internet."

"Abby, come on! Have I ever crossed the line, or even come close to it with personal stuff involving you?"

"No, but . . . this is so sensitive, and John's not here to defend himself anymore. It's up to me to do it for him."

"I would never take advantage that way. Never." He pushes away from the sink and throws his arms into the air. "Is that what you think?"

This is the part where the irate reporter is supposed to rail over the indignity of having his integrity questioned, storm out the door, and never return. And the Flint of a few years ago would have done just that. Hell, a few months ago he would have walked.

But Abby is his friend. She needs help navigating the waters that he's been sailing for years. Of course, there is another reason to stay, but that is something Flint can't name. Best not to go there right now.

"Don't be offended." She picks up a manila folder from beside her computer and hands it over. "Noah e-mailed them to me. Apparently, John was keeping an electronic journal, besides the written ones. I printed out a copy of everything for you. Just take these home and read them over when you get a chance. Then you can tell me whether something was going on in John's platoon, or if I'm just being paranoid."

He pulls the envelope open, but she whips it out of his hands.

"What are you doing?" she asks sternly. "You can't read them here."

"Why the hell not?"

"It's . . . it's too personal. I'd have to go in the closet and shrivel up."

"Okay, then." He tucks it under his arm and grabs his jacket from the chair by the door. "Lest you shrivel . . . I'll take these to go."

Rain. Flint never thought he would miss Seattle's weather, but in the desert of Iraq, when he felt his body broiling in the 130-degree sun, he'd longed for the cool, wet drops on his face.

He leans on the rail of the balcony facing Lake Union, where one of the last prop planes of the day is landing on the water. The one-bedroom condo behind him was his trophy when he purchased it two years ago, but, like anything material, its importance has diminished as other issues—like staying alive in the desert—swelled.

He'd passed that hurdle and survived, though it was still hard to sleep here, where the occasional rumble of a passing bus or whir of a landing seaplane could jar him awake in alarm. Then there'd been the task of ending his relationship with Delilah, which had loomed large for so long that when they actually met and decided to part, the finale was anticlimactic.

And now . . . Abby.

His original plan was to read through the files tonight and call Abby in the morning, so that she wouldn't smell his overeagerness and construe it as interest. Which it was. His lack of focus on anything else was proof of his renewed attraction to Abby, but he was trying to keep it all in the friendly category right now. Having written pieces about obsessive stalkers, he had learned what a complete put-off the obsessive type could be.

But now that he's read John's journals, he can't put off calling.

Flint steps in out of the rain, peels off his damp socks, and wipes his face on the sleeve of his shirt. The way he reads the whole situation, Abby isn't paranoid. John's platoon had been a volatile mix of borderline sociopathic cowboys and misguided patriots. He flips through his notes to locate the names of the men in John's platoon. He'd seen the dynamic before. Cowboys like Lassiter. The unwitting followers like Gunnar McGee. Cocky know-it-alls like Doc, and narcissists like Hilliard. What a crew.

There was dissension among the guys, heated arguments, jealousy. In that milieu, what was the likelihood of one of these guys turning on John?

Very likely.

And Stanton saw it coming. He sensed trouble brewing.

Did they kill him because of his opinions? Because he no longer believed in the war? Flint itches to get at the moral center of this story.

Right now they have only a handful of pieces of the puzzle. A grainy outline of the true picture, but Flint senses a substantial story here, a tale that needs to be revealed.

Of course, he will never be able to write it.

That's killing him. But in the course of a lifetime, he figures you have to crash and burn a thousand times before you get it right. What's that myth? He's like the phoenix rising from the ashes.

By the time he flips open his phone and calls Abby's number, he has already put it behind him. It's a bitter pill that went down hard, but the worst is over now.

Well, almost.

Chapter 38

Seattle
Abby

At five a.m. the Seattle studio of the morning show affiliate is an assault of cold air and blinding lights. Abby feels like a phony, propped in an upholstered chair on a platform in front of a blue screen. She has never been on television before, but if this is the typical experience, she's glad to be pursuing a degree in psychology.

The segment producer, who has an unusual name that Abby can't make out, like Micah or Micko, looks like he's fourteen and talks superfast like an auctioneer. He explains that they'll project the skyline of Seattle on the screen behind her. She's not to touch her microphone or leave this chair during the interview. She needs to wear an earpiece to hear Carly Michaels, the host of *American Morning*.

Yesterday, by phone, Abby went over salient points to be touched on in the interview, and yet, when Micah starts counting down to when the feed comes to them, nerves whip her heartbeat up to double time. She hates this. It's very uncomfortable to speak to a voice in your ear, a face on a screen.

Honestly, Abby is a little afraid of Carly Michaels. The host of *American Morning* has a reputation for getting to the heart of the matter with a minimum of time wasted in chit-chat. If Abby can make her points without sounding like a whiny widow, she's confident Carly will get it.

While Carly introduces her, Abby takes a minute to let her

shoulders relax, her heart rate slow closer to normal. This is not fun, but it's important.

I'm doing this for John, she keeps telling herself. But really, she would rather be home reading the driest of psychology texts. She would rather role-play as a therapist utilizing cognitive behavior therapy. She would rather scrub the toilet or scrape the bird droppings off the porch than put herself out there on national television and demand answers from the military.

After offering condolences, Carly digs right in. "Thank you for speaking with us. I understand you've been trying to get information regarding the circumstances of your husband's death. What have you learned?"

"It's been frustrating, to say the least, Carly. I've made dozens of calls to military personnel, trying to get some answers, but I'm left with the same questions. If there was an insurgent sniper in the building the day my husband was killed, why wasn't he found? Why was I not told that my husband was killed by two rounds from an M-16?"

"An M-16 being the type of rifle our troops use in Iraq," Carly interjects.

"Exactly. I'm trying to piece things together, at a loss without reliable information. However, there's been a report that the soldier who was by John's side when he was shot actually saw a U.S. soldier retreating from the scene."

There . . . she got that in. Before the show she and Flint had gone through a list of critical points she wanted to make, and Carly was giving her the perfect leads to share important items.

Carly is shaking her head in disbelief. "With so many signs pointing to fratricide, one soldier killing another, why isn't the government investigating this incident?"

"I wish I knew," Abby says. "John Stanton has been held up as a great American hero, and yet there's been no action taken to explain his death, which does not seem to be combat related at all."

"We think you deserve some answers from the United States Army, Abby," Carly says. "So we've asked Colonel Witt Hollister to speak with us from our news bureau in Washington, D.C."

An army representative? This is a surprise for Abby, but she's hopeful that she can make some headway right here and now.

"Good morning, Colonel Hollister," Carly says sweetly.

His name reminds Abby of an old-fashioned book series she stumbled upon in third grade called the Happy Hollisters in which a large family encounters and solves mysteries in their travels. An only child, Abby had always loved the way the kids turned to each other for resources and ideas. Besides, they were always so happy.

As is Colonel Hollister. The man on the monitor has a halo of snow-white hair matched by his brilliant smile. "Good morning, Carly. And Mrs. Stanton, I'm so sorry for your loss."

"Colonel, what can you tell us about John Stanton's death?" Carly asks.

"The loss of Specialist John Stanton was a true tragedy, Carly," he says, all pearly teeth and halo hair. "I'm not at liberty to discuss the details or the circumstances."

"Colonel, Abby Stanton just lost her husband." Carly tilts her head with that flinty I'm-not-giving-up-so-you'd-better-answer look. "Don't you agree she should have access to this very personal information?"

Abby feels a flash of momentary satisfaction that Carly is on her side.

"I would love to be able to offer John Stanton's family information to help with closure. However, Specialist Stanton was assigned to a Forward Operating Base in Fallujah, a dangerous area, a very active combat zone. The army cannot disclose information regarding operations or missions in a highly volatile area such as—"

"But Colonel," Abby interrupts, running over his words, "how top secret is the activity in this area if there are news teams embedded there? If they can report what's going on, why can't I have a few simple details about a mission that cost my husband his life?"

"I wish it were that simple, Mrs. Stanton," he says with a forlorn expression, and Abby wishes he were in the same studio so she could smack that condescension right off his face.

"Colonel—" Carly takes another shot. "Is there or is there not an investigation being conducted regarding the details of John Stanton's death?"

"Absolutely," he answers. "I can assure you that every casualty is thoroughly investigated."

"And in the army's investigation is there any mention of friendly fire?" Abby asks.

"I have not heard that term used in connection with John Stanton." Colonel Hollister is now void of emotion, a flat affect.

He's lying, Abby realizes. Part of her training is learning to read body language and demeanor, and Hollister's sudden shift in attitude is telling.

Anger burns through her, a flash fire. It's a good thing the colonel is thousands of miles away; if they had to share the same studio, *American Morning* would have a new wrestling segment.

"Here's a question I'm sure you can answer, Colonel," Abby says. "If you were me, if you'd just lost, say, your wife while she was serving in Iraq, how would you piece together what happened to her? How would you assemble the pieces to relive her last day in your mind, to calculate what her last thought might have been, to determine that, though she is dead, that death was not a result of foul play or unfair advantage?"

Tears sting Abby's eyes but she refuses to blot at them. They are tears of anger, she tells herself, a reaction to the bright lights. She will not cry in front of this stuffed shirt who would love to see her reduced to tears.

"If, in the end, all that was left of your wife was an urn full of ashes, how would you reconcile her death, Colonel?"

"Mrs. Stanton," he says, "losing a loved one is a—"

"Don't patronize me!" she snaps. "My name is Abby Fitzgerald and my husband John is dead and I want to know what happened to cause that death while he was serving his country in Iraq. That is what I am asking; that is what I demand to know."

But of course, Colonel Hollister cannot give her any real answers; most likely he doesn't know much more about John's death than what he has read in news stories.

When the whitewashed burn of the studio lights dims at the end of the interview, Abby expects a cold reception from Micah. It's not like her to be brusque and argumentative, but then again she's never been pushed into a situation like this before.

"That was great!" Micah calls, rushing over to her as she waits for the mike pack to be removed. "I like the way you refused to stand down."

Abby lets out a breath of relief. "I don't think the colonel liked it too much."

"Ah, screw him!" Micah grins. "We wanted to give the army a chance to respond, and though they gave us a spokesperson, he really didn't have a response." He shrugs, his jacket lifting on his bony shoulders. "Their loss!"

Abby climbs down from the small stage with mixed feelings. "We'll see about that," she says, "because if they continue to shut me out, I'm lost, too."

"You'll do fine," Micah insists. "Just stay on them. And thanks for a great interview. I had you pegged as a shrinking violet, but you've got guts, kid." He extends his hand and Abby shakes it firmly. "Good luck to you, Abby Fitzgerald."

I'll take it, Abby thinks. Having hit the stone wall of the U.S. Army, Abby knows she's going to need luck, lots of it.

PART II
December 2006

Chapter 39

Tacoma, Washington
Suz

"This place is packed," Suz says, circling the long line of cars that extends all the way out to I-5. "You'd think they were giving the stuff away."

"Dis place is packed, Mommy," Sofia parrots from the backseat.

"You got that right." Suz glimpses her daughter in the rearview mirror and smiles. Her own little chatterbox.

"Do you see Santa, Mommy?" Sofia asks.

"Not yet, but we'll find him." Suz has circled the parking lot three times in search of an empty spot, but then it is Christmastime, and this is a popular shopping center, built to resemble a quaint village, its central streets of inviting shop windows open only to pedestrian traffic. Scott used to call it a movie set when they came here, joking that he was always expecting Steven Spielberg to be lowered down on a crane to talk the actors through another take.

Up ahead, two red lights emerge out of nowhere and Suz slams on the brakes. "Finally!" she says, waving her thanks as the car takes off and she slips into the spot.

"Finally, Mommy," Sofia echoes. She climbs out of her car seat and grabs this week's favorite shopping bag. Christmas trees sway on the bag, which contains a shoebox with an unnamed doll wrapped inside—Fia's odd fixation. Last week, seeing how grungy the box had become, Suz insisted that Sofia open it so that she could rewrap it in shiny new Christmas paper. Sofia's eyes shone as she tore into the paper; the process of unwrapping tickled her with delight. She couldn't care less about the doll, so Suz rewrapped it and—voilà!—a new gift.

"Hold on to Mommy," she warns, pulling her daughter close as they cross the crowded parking lot. Sofia squeezes her hand fiercely, as if to keep her mother anchored on the earth, and Suz doesn't have the heart to explain that Mommy is not flying off into the clouds but that they're watching for cars. Suz cannot resist her daughter's ferocious love, though she imagines Sofia's separation anxiety has everything to do with Scott's death.

What can you do? She can only try her best to be twice as loving.

They make their way down the Disneyesque Main Street to a plaza with a gazebo, fountain, play structure, and a three-story Christmas tree, a real Douglas fir. On the opposite side of the tree is a small cottage—gingerbread, trimmed with giant gumdrops and peppermint swirls.

Catching her first glimpse of Santa's house, Sofia stops skipping and blinks. "Mommy," she says, pointing to the house, "it's a cookie house!"

"That's Santa's office," Suz explains. Sofia already got the lesson that Santa lives at the North Pole, and Sofia is also making the adjustment to Suz having an office where she goes a few days a week. "That's where he meets good girls and boys to find out what they want for Christmas."

Sofia loops a finger into a buttonhole of her coat and sways gently as she confides, "Sofia is good."

"Sofia?" Suz hears Abby behind her. As she turns, Sofia is already running into Abby's arms.

"How's my favorite girl?" Abby asks, shifting a large shopping bag so that she can lift Sofia into her arms.

"I'm fine, thanks," Suz jokes, reaching over to hug Abby's free shoulder. "You're looking pretty darned good for a widow."

"Same," Abby returns, shaking her head.

It's a running joke between them, and though Suz is very good at making light of everything, she is acutely aware of the pain underneath. Truth and pain—isn't that supposed to be the root of all comedy?

"I brought you a Christmas gift," Abby tells Sofia, "and you don't have to wait until Christmas to open it. Unless you want to, of course."

"Do you want to wait?" Suz asks.

Sofia presses her hands to her cheeks. "No, Mommy. No."

Abby lowers her to the ground, then removes a flat, rectangular package wrapped in green paper covered with cartoon penguins leaping through wreaths. Sofia tears into the paper and uncovers a talking alphabet book that sings Sofia's favorite song and pronounces each letter.

Sofia's eyes go round with delight as she presses the book against her little body.

"What do you say?" Suz prods.

"Thank you, Abby." She presses the button to start the alphabet song.

"Are you going to hate me for buying that?" Abby winces. "I couldn't resist. It's her favorite song and it's educational . . ."

"Yeah, yeah, I'll just be singing it in my sleep."

As Abby holds the book, Sofia points out all the letters.

"She's fairly advanced for three. I studied early childhood development last semester," Abby says. "The kid knows her phonics already?"

Suz nods, misting over with pride. "They grow so fast. But the teachers at her preschool are fantastic."

"And her mom's not so bad, either." Abby slips an arm around Suz's shoulders and gives her a gentle shake. "You're my hero. You really do it all. Single parent. Good friend. And now event planner."

"Not like I have a choice." Suz swipes one eye dry. "Which reminds me, I'm having a will drawn up. Scott and I never had one, which was young and stupid. But I wanted to ask you if you'd consider being Sofia's guardian if anything happens."

"Wow." It's Abby's turn to mist over. "Of course. I'm flattered. You know I love this kid." She rubs Sofia's shoulder, but the child is too engrossed in an alphabet game to notice.

"Okay, then, who's ready to visit with Santa?" Suz asks.

Abby picks up her shopping bag and takes Sofia's small hand. "I can't wait, and I know Sofia's been good this year."

The child hands her new book to her mother and skips off with Abby, adding, "Sofia is very good."

A sanguine smile tugs at Suz. This is the first year her three-year-old daughter is aware of Santa's Christmas tradition, and she feels a twinge of sadness that Scott isn't here to share in the joy. He always talked about the day when he'd be staying up all night to assemble a bicycle or a giant dollhouse. Suz has been worrying about making the holiday special for Sofia, who will only have one parent this Christmas morning, but she has decided to wrap one gift from Scott. Maybe it can be a tradition in years to come—a sweet memory of the father who loved her with all his heart.

"So tell me about the new job," Abby says as they join the line behind a grandma pushing a double stroller. "Everyone misses you at Java Joe's."

"And I miss those triple-shot lattes. There are some mornings when I could really use an infusion of energy, but once I get to work, the day just flies by."

"An event planner . . . sounds like the perfect job for a former party girl. Do you help people plan their weddings?" Abby asks.

"Actually, my specialty is becoming business conferences and workshops. You know how small companies or professional associations take over an entire hotel for a few days and sponsor meetings and refresher courses for their memberships? Well, when it comes to the venue, the meals, the lodging and conference materials, I'm your girl."

"Fantastic. I've never seen anyone launch themselves back into the professional world with such aplomb," says Abby.

"Necessity is a great motivator. Although I like the work. Sure beats selling tractors back in Nebraska, and I'm glad I can afford to stay near my brother and his family in Seattle. Which reminds me. Wiley and Trina are supposed to spend Christmas in Hawaii this year. They booked the trip a year ago, something they've been saving for forever, and now they're talking about cancelling just for me. The thing is, I was wondering if you were going to be around for Christmas. No pressure, but if you are, Sofia and I would love to hook up with you. Then Wiley's crew could go off to the tropical paradise they deserve without having to worry about me."

"Hawaii? Are you sure you don't want to join them?"

"I can't afford it." Suz lowers her voice, conscious that the woman in front of them with the stroller seems to be listening in. "And right now, it just seems too festive for me. I don't want to be a killjoy for them, but . . . it just doesn't feel right." As Suz speaks, her hand absently reaches down and strokes the downy blond hair at the nape of Sofia's neck. "This was where Scott spent his last Christmas, so I want to stay here. A few years down the road I might feel differently, but Washington has been our home for two years now, and right now it offers stability for Sofia and memories of Scott for us both. But . . . oh, I've put you on the spot! I don't mean that you have to spend Christmas with us. Were you planning to go home to your folks?"

"Actually, I was thinking I'd stay here. I was just back east in September and . . . I guess I realized my home is here now, with or without John." Abby sucks in a breath. "What I'm trying to say is, I'd love to celebrate Christmas with the Wollenberg women. You can stay with me at Fort Lewis, and we'll go caroling on Christmas Eve, just like last year."

Suz pulls her daughter closer so that the new book Sofia is holding doesn't poke the woman in front of them in line. "Remember how Sofia slept through every song, bundled in her stroller?" But Scott had insisted they wheel the baby along.

"I recall Scott trying to give the base commander's wife a peek at her, and Sofia woke up howling," Abby says with a grin.

"That's my girl," Suz says, and to her surprise the woman in front of them turns back and flashes them a smile.

For the first time this season, Suz allows herself to fantasize placing her daughter's gifts under the tree and waking up in a house on the old fir-lined lane where they used to live. They'll go caroling and bake gingerbread cookies, drink soy eggnog and watch *Mr. Magoo's Christmas Carol*—Scott's favorite. Yes, Christmas with Abby will be perfect. The garden apartment she's renting in Tacoma is close to work and the Montessori school, but it lacks the sense of community she had in Fort Lewis.

"I promise we won't impose," Suz says. "We'll get out of your hair if you've got some papers to write for school."

"I'm good to go till January. E-mailed my final paper in this morning. Exams ended last week, and now I'm just hoping to get the placement I want when clinicals start after the first of the year. I'm trying to work with soldiers and their families. I think John would like that—my way of helping the troops."

"He'd be very proud of you," Suz assures her. "Somewhere up there, you know John's giving you a salute and grinning that cocky smile of his." She smacks her forehead. "Do I sound way too corny?"

"Are you ladies military wives?" asks the woman in front of them. A fringe of graying hair curls out around her fleece headband, and from the way she's been indulging the kids in the stroller, Suz figures she's the grandmother.

"We were," Suz answers as Abby looks away. "We lost our husbands in Iraq."

"I'm so sorry," the woman says, pressing her eyes closed momentarily. "My husband was a marine. Retired, now. But he lost his brother in Vietnam. He still calls him his angel. Whenever he has a close call, pulls the car out of a skid or whatnot, he says, 'My angel came through for me.'"

"That's a nice way to honor his brother," Abby says, moving closer to the woman to gaze into the stroller. "And who are these little cherubs?"

"My grandchildren. Two and three months."

Suz shifts to observe the children. The toddler is asleep, but the infant squirms gently, working a chubby fist into her mouth. "Adorable."

"They keep me busy," the woman says, tweaking one of the infant's blue booties. "Let me tell you, I never had much patience as a mother, but now that I'm a grandmother, I have the time to really enjoy them." As she spoke, she wheeled the double stroller to the front of the line, where a photographer dressed in a green tunic and felt cap with a jingle bell on the tassel handed her a brochure.

"Welcome to Santaland. Getting some photos of the kids with Santa today?"

Tuning the sales pitch out, Suz turned back to Abby, who was showing Sofia how three letters formed the word "dog."

"You haven't told me the latest on your battle with Uncle Sam," Suz says. In the weeks after John's death, Suz shared Abby's shock upon learning that he might have been killed by a man in his own platoon. "Has the army agreed to conduct an unbiased investigation yet?"

"So far, no success. I got a few phone calls from officers with important-sounding titles after I went on *American Morning*, but they just promised to do what they could and asked me to keep mum for a while. It's frustrating. Flint is trying to work his contacts in the military, but shortly after the funeral he was sent down to Georgia to follow the trial of a suspected Ku Klux Klan leader."

"From one battlefront to another," Suz observes. "By the way, I enjoyed your college friends. Fanteen is a very unconventional mom, and Flint is the voice of calm in the eye of a storm."

"Flint wasn't always that way. Back in college he was a wild man, no sense of responsibility, always spinning off in a dozen different directions."

"Did you guys date?" asks Suz.

"Sort of. But his lack of commitment drove me nuts. Then I met John, and Flint fell in with Delilah. He still hasn't committed, but that's just Flint. He'll probably be with Delilah forever."

Seeing that they're next in line for Santa, Suz smooths her daughter's flaxen curls. "And you still haven't been able to get any details from Noah?" she asks. It seems odd that John's brother, who was assigned to the same platoon as John, hasn't come forward to share what he knows about the shooting. At the very least, Suz would expect him to talk with the family, but Noah disappeared shortly after the funeral.

"No one has spoken with Noah since the day after John's funeral," Abby says. "He's officially AWOL now."

"Do you think he knows something about John's death?" Suz covers Sofia's ears with her hands, and her daughter swats them away. Not that her daughter really understands any of this, but Sofia is quite observant for a three-year-old. "You don't think he's involved in some way?"

"Honestly, I don't know what to think. He and John had a sort of sibling rivalry going, with Noah always competing to win validation from John." Abby presses a hand over her mouth. "Did I say that? Oh, dear. I'm already sounding like a therapist. Anyway, I'd like Noah to know that I'm not judging him for deserting. It's just that . . ." She sucks in a breath, tentative. "With so many unanswered questions about John's death, I'd really like to talk with someone who was there."

"Well, you'll get your chance soon. I hear the company is returning as scheduled in two weeks." Suz has mixed feelings about the return of Scott's unit. Part of her is happy for all the other soldiers, but another part feels hollow, as if there will never be closure for the families whose loved ones won't be returning from Iraq.

"Welcome to Santaland," the photographer in the elf outfit says, her candy-cane scepter pointing the way to the doorway to Santa's workshop. "I see you're all set for the deluxe photo package."

"No, thanks." Suz shakes her head. "We just want to visit with Santa, right, pumpkin?" She takes Sofia's hand and leads her forward.

"But it's all taken care of," the elf insists, checking her clipboard. "You're getting two copies of the portrait, two portraits printed on ornaments, and the locket. All paid for."

"There must be some mistake," Abby says. "We haven't paid for anything."

"It was all taken care of by the woman in front of you." The photographer shows the clipboard to Suz. "She's not with you?"

Shaking her head, Suz scans the order. The elf is right. Down at the bottom of the invoice, just above the signature, she sees the note: *Merry Christmas from your angel.*

"It's from the grandma in front of us," she tells Abby, feeling goose bumps at the base of her neck. "She wants to be our Christmas angel."

"Mommy, can she be my angel?" Sofia tugs on Suz's wrists, wanting to be lifted up.

Suz pulls her into her arms, savoring the sweet smell of her baby skin. "Sweetie, you have so many angels, I can't even count them."

"Thank you, Mommy." Sofia squeezes her, so hard for such a little thing.

"Speaking of angels . . ." Suz smiles at Abby. "Have you heard anything from yours lately? Any rumbling houses in the night? Hot spots in the bed? Printers coming to life and sending you messages?"

The two women exchange a grin as the elf ushers them through the peppermint-trimmed doorway of Santa's workshop.

"My angel has been pretty quiet lately," Abby admits. "But that's the thing about guardian angels: they're very quiet until you need them."

Chapter 40

Fort Lewis
Sharice

The first Christmas without my sons.
Sharice presses a needle through the red cloth that forms a holly berry on the quilt and gasps. Beneath the quilt, the needle has pierced her fingertip.

She jerks her hand back and sucks her fingertip.

Foolish of her, forgetting her thimbles when she knew the women at the Family Readiness Group were going to be quilting. Usually the methodical, slow work soothed her nerves and opened the window to light conversation about children and plans, but today, the room is tense, the talk having turned to politics.

Always dangerous in a quilting circle.

"Need a Band-Aid, Sharice?" Rachel Maynard hasn't lifted her eyes from her sewing but somehow she knows Sharice's finger is bleeding.

"I'm fine," Sharice shoots back, hoping to interrupt the diatribe, but Jenn Hausner is still going on about a teacher at the school who's been sharing stories about the effects of American occupation on the children of Iraq. Jenn has been dominating the quilting circle of late, though Sharice keeps telling herself that this quilt had better get finished soon or they're going to miss the Christmas season completely and ruin their mission. The quilt is being auctioned at a Christmas bazaar to raise money for care packages for the troops in Iraq and Afghanistan. The

FRG is always focused on some task to make life more bearable for the armed service members, and while Sharice has always been proud to be a part of the group, lately she's felt a cool undercurrent running through some of the meetings.

"First, I told him I can't believe he's talking about Iraq with fourth-grade students," Jenn says. "I mean, when I went to fourth grade my teacher didn't talk about things that could give us nightmares."

"That may well be," Eva Capeci says, "but the world was a different place when I was in fourth grade." Like Sharice, Eva is more of an old-timer. In fact, they met years ago at Fort Drum when Sharice's boys were little, but they were both so busy caring for their own families at the time that they hadn't really become friends until both husbands landed at Fort Lewis some twenty-five years later.

"Oh, Eva, now you're making me feel old." Chessie Johnston presses her lips together to suppress a giggle. "When I was in fourth grade, they taught the American Revolution as current events."

Eva and Sharice laugh along with her, but the other women don't seem to get the joke.

Jenn's needle moves adeptly, though her cheeks hold twin squares of scarlet, evidence of her high agitation. "Anyway, I told Mr. Minetta not to make it sound like we were the bad guys. Those Iraqi children are much better off with American GIs walking through their neighborhood; even if our soldiers look like the Incredible Hulk to the kids, they're safer now than they've ever been."

Sharice tucks her needle into her patch of the quilt and rises. "Maybe I'll take a Band-Aid after all and switch over to folding flyers. Without my thimbles I'm all thumbs."

"And you definitely don't want to bleed on the quilt," Chessie says. "Though we could certainly say that we made the quilt with blood, sweat, and tears."

Again, the three women enjoy a laugh, but the others withdraw, as if dusted by a cold frost. As Sharice goes over to the sink to wash her hands and put on the Band-Aid, she does a mental count of the frost brigade. There's Rachel, Jenn, Suki, Janet, and Britt, to Eva, Chessie, and her. Is it the age difference between the two groups? Whatever the case, her group is clearly outnumbered.

"So what happened with the teacher?" Janet asks as she pulls the thread taut. "Is he changing the curriculum?"

"Please! We really got into it after that. He started this anti-war crap, and I told him our president was right to send our soldiers over there." Despite her ire, Jenn works steadily, methodically, which Sharice finds a little unsettling. She can taste the metallic sheath of repression, cold and sharp in the back of her throat.

"And did he argue with you?" asks Britt.

"He started to. He went off on the president for a minute, then he did a tirade on free speech. So predictable."

Predictable? Sharice thinks. *Well, thank God for that.* She rues the day when free speech is no longer part of our Constitutional rights.

"But he backed down?" Janet puts an arm on Jenn's shoulder. "You know he did. No one crosses Jenn Hausner and lives to tell the tale."

"I just played my ace in the hole. Told him that my husband is deployed to Iraq. That shut him up pretty fast."

It's the younger wives' turn to snicker now, and Sharice wonders if she and Eva and Chessie sounded that offensive. She stands beside the sink in the corner, thinking that it's time to leave.

"In your face, Mr. Liberal Schoolteacher," Janet says.

"But before I left, I made my point." Jenn nods. "People can talk, and everyone is quick to criticize, but when you're in something as deep as we are, you just know what's right. You and I know we're doing the right thing over there."

Do we? Sharice wonders. She is beginning to doubt the usefulness of American troops in Iraq, but she can't say that aloud. The woman who's lost one son to violence and the other to cowardice is in no position to question the mission of the other deployed soldiers. Bad enough that people know of her shame. She can't go anywhere on base—not to the PX or the commissary—without generating stares and muffled whispers. Why do they bother to whisper, when she knows what they're saying: *There's the woman who had two sons, one a hero, the other a deserter.*

Those who are better-informed know that her son's hero status may soon be in question, but Abby's quest for an investigation hasn't spread as rapidly as the white-hot news that Noah did not return to duty when his bereavement leave ended.

How did this happen; this total reversal in role, from conservative military wife to controversial victim?

She remembers how she used to feel when people would criticize the presence of the military in a place where her sons or husband were deployed. She would bristle and sometimes snap back a rebuttal. "How can you speculate from your living room couch when our men are over there in the thick of it?" Ooh, that used to fire her up.

And now . . . she's questioning in her heart, but she can't step out and play that role in public. Not yet, maybe not ever.

"Our guys belong over there," Jenn says, "and anyone who questions that doesn't have the right to call themselves an American."

"Easy there, Jenn." Chessie arches one brow. "Let's keep politics out of this quilt. Nobody wants to be sleeping with a blanket of controversy over their head."

Head down like a bull ready to charge, Jenn defends herself. "It's not about politics, Chessie. It's about our men putting their lives on the line for this country, and they need our support. If you don't support the president, you're stabbing our own guys in the back. You gotta support the leadership or you're just plain unpatriotic."

"Seems to me our country was founded on the expectation of freedom," Chessie says, "and that would include the freedom to disagree with our president. Freedom to hold opinions. Freedom to argue and debate. That's all I'm saying."

"Come on, Chessie. Are you really going to sit here and say that you don't support our guys over in Iraq and Afghanistan?"

"See? You're putting words in my mouth," Chessie said. "I knew we should've dropped this."

Jenn shakes her head. "I don't see why. Our guys are all soldiers. If we don't support them, who will?"

There were a few murmurs of agreement, but Britt stops sewing. "But what if you just don't feel that way?" she asks in a plaintive voice as she rubs her fingers over a gold star on the quilt. "I love my husband and my country, but I really don't see the merit in this war, if that's what they're still calling it. I mean, I'm all for ending terrorism, but I think our guys really don't belong in Iraq right now."

"I hear you," Chessie chimes in.

Sharice grips the sink behind her, trying to tamp down the arguments swelling within. "It's a complex issue," she says aloud, as if realizing it for the first time. "And Britt makes a good point. Sometimes your gut feeling doesn't match the things you want to believe in."

"Well, I don't rely much on feelings," Jenn says. "Sometimes I don't *feel* like getting out of bed in the morning, but I don't give in to that, do I? You can't put stock in feelings. You just need to do what's right."

Is that a shot at me? Sharice wonders as she sucks in a breath. Or is Jenn so smug that she doesn't see the different circumstances and beliefs of the women in this room?

"Must be nice to have all the answers, to know what's right," Eva says in a voice so low it's almost a snarl. "To be so darned sure of yourself."

"I have always had a strong moral compass," Jenn says. "I just know."

"Well I hope that damned moral compass will help you find your way if you get lost in the woods." Repressed fury quavers through Eva's voice as she lifts her needle and rips the thread off with her hand. "Because that's about all it's good for." She grabs her purse and cuts toward the door.

"Where are you going?" Janet asks. "We're supposed to finish today. The auction is this weekend."

"You'll be fine without me," Eva calls as she flies out the door.

Seeing the clear line of escape, Sharice follows her.

"And where are *you* going?" someone calls after her.

She does not answer, does not look back. Right now she needs to put distance between herself and Jenn Hausner.

Outside the community center Eva is weeping into a laurel hedge, her head tipped into her hands.

"Oh, Eva . . . let me get you a tissue." Sharice rubs her friend between the shoulder blades and finds that Eva's soft red jacket is padded, like a cozy sleeping bag.

"I'm sorry." Eva swipes at her eyes with the back of one hand. "I don't know what came over me, except that when Jenn Hausner sinks her teeth in like a bulldog, I can't stand it!" She laughs through her tears.

"She's just young and stupid." Generally Sharice tries not to be so judgmental, but there it is.

"Stupid and insensitive. I usually don't let her get to me, but we just heard, Kevin . . . he's going back to Iraq. His unit in One Hundred Palms is being deployed again." Kevin, Eva's youngest son, always seemed to be the softest of the three. As a child, he was always crying over skinned knees and bruises.

But they grow up to be marines, Sharice thinks, and they march off to battle.

"I don't know why it upsets me so much," Eva says apologetically. "I guess I thought it would be over by now, everything in Iraq. I mean, he made it through the invasion of Baghdad in one piece. He leaves in January. He'll be fine, right?"

Somehow, the question make Sharice want to cry. Should she answer honestly or give the pat answer to give Eva some comfort?

Eva adds, "I don't know why, but I've never been this worried. Not even when Tony was deployed for Desert Storm."

Sharice rubs her friend's shoulder. On the other side of the laurel hedge is the community center flagpole, which isn't battened down correctly. Both women stare blankly as the rope flaps in the wind, making pinging noises on the pole.

"You tell Kevin to be careful over there," Sharice says quietly. "He's to wear his flak jacket and helmet. And we'll pray for him. Once he's over there, we'll get the girls to send him a care package." She gestures toward the women inside the community center.

"I'll send my own care packages. Anything to avoid Jenn Hausner."

"Are you quitting the FRG?" Sharice asks.

"At the moment I'm not sure whether I'll go back to a meeting next week or next year. Right now it's not worth the aggravation." She points inside. "Did you hear them?"

"Loud and clear." Sharice heard more than the words that were spoken; reading between the lines, it's clear that Jenn and her friends want to limit the group to their own definition of patriots. "You know, the FRG meetings have always left me with a sense of usefulness and well-being, a sense that I was engaged in a charitable, philanthropic act, but today . . . today was a disaster."

"I'm so sorry!" Eva squeezes her upper arm. "With everything you've gone through, John and now Noah . . . and here I'm crying because one of my sons is being deployed."

"It's okay to cry." This is something Sharice has been learning the hard way, something she wishes she could share with her husband.

"Oh! You're so sweet." In one quick move Eva throws her arms around Sharice and envelops her in an embrace.

At first Sharice is taken by surprise, but she lets herself lean into Eva's padded shoulder, lets herself relax in the circle of compassion.

Eva takes a deep breath, easing her grip. "And I almost forgot to tell you the most important thing! Some of the wives are organizing a support group for people who don't support the war." She steps back, standing taller. "The idea came up by accident. I was working with some gals on the Toys for Tots drive and we got to talking. We're thinking of calling ourselves WAW, for Women Against War. Right now the group is in the planning stages, but you're welcome to join."

"An antiwar group?" Sharice presses a hand to one cheek. "Jim would have a heart attack."

"I think Jim would be fine about you meeting with people of like mind and discussing peaceful solutions," Eva says. "Right to free assembly does apply to military wives, you know. And it's not like we're talking anarchy or free love or any of that stuff that pitted society against the military back in the sixties. We just want a chance to discuss our concern over our government's military actions with other concerned, informed people."

Although Eva makes it sound harmless, Sharice senses that this thing has teeth.

Besides, her husband would be appalled, and right now, the last thing she wants to do is burden him with controversial political behavior. Although he's retired, he still works in a military organization in a world that values security, restraint, respect.

"I'm afraid I'll have to pass on WAW," Sharice says. "With everything that's gone on lately . . . I'm still overwhelmed."

"Promise me you'll think about it. It would be good for you."

It's out of the question, but Sharice can't reject it flatly, not when her friend is feeling so vulnerable. "But I don't have any medallions or love beads," she says.

"I don't know what you're talking about," Eva says. "But I like the sound of the love beads."

Chapter 41

Fort Lewis
Abby

This was the last thing she wanted to do on a Saturday afternoon.

There was college football, Christmas shopping at the mall, cookies to bake and send back east. Right now even laundry would be preferable to coming face-to-face with the men her husband had spent the last months of his life with.

The invitation specified that the event was open to all families, friends, and neighbors of the soldiers in the 32nd Infantry Division, and since that encompassed a large group of people, event organizers decided to use the gym of Lewis High School for the afternoon event that promised a visit from Santa for the kids. With a mixture of dread and optimism, Abby heads toward the gymnasium, passing tables offering hot cider, cocoa, soda pop, and refreshments. Why does this feel like her first school dance?

She crosses under a string of blinking colored lights into the party scene of fat round tables surrounded by chairs and people. Children skirt around the edges, chasing each other and rolling on some gym mats that have been left against the wall. More lights are strung over doorways, 3-D snowmen sculptures decorate the stage. The music is loud, the conversations louder, and everywhere, everywhere you look, are men in uniform.

Her purse buzzes, and she extracts her cell phone. Suz.

"Okay, I'm swimming in hot cider, and I've just learned that my husband was the best shot in his platoon. Which is pretty scary, because I don't think Scott could hit a target unless the bull's-eye was the size of a lunar crater. Where the hell are you?"

"I just walked into the gym. Where are you?"

"By the Christmas tree decked with miniature cannons and guns, but stay there—I see you now."

As Abby slides her cell phone back into her bag, Suz emerges from the landscape of tables. She is wearing a fawn-brown suit that matches her hair. The jacket's leopard-print collar and cuffs add a touch of playfulness—very Suz.

Abby nods in approval. "Don't you look professional."

"This, my dear—" Suz gestures down the lines of the suit like a model on *The Price Is Right*—"is the uniform of an event planner."

"Sweet. You decided not to bring Sofia?"

"She's on a play date. She would have liked seeing Santa again, but all the soldiers here would have been overwhelming for her. Every time she sees a man in uniform, she's sure it's her daddy for the first few seconds. I won't put her through an afternoon of disappointment."

"She would probably be bored here, anyway." Abby nervously pushes her hair over one shoulder as a wave of stress splashes in her face. "It seems wrong to come to a party like this when you're not feeling at all festive."

"Don't forget what Flint said. This might be your only chance to talk with the guys in John's platoon," Suz points out. "And see what I brought? I printed it out just before I left the house. It's the names of all the guys that were in Bravo Company with Scott and John. Let's see if we can connect with them and find out what happened that day."

"Okay." Abby squeezes her friend's arm in thanks, then takes the list as they head over to the door together. "Thank God you're here to keep me on track." She scans the names of the nine original members of the platoon John and Scott were assigned to: Brown, Hilliard, Jump, Lassiter, McGee, Roland. Two

Stantons and Scott Wollenberg. "Brown is the one Flint wants me to meet. Emjay Brown. He was with John when he was shot."

Suz nods. "Got it."

The woman at the reception table shakes her head. "Specialist Brown isn't here, though he is on the list. That means we expect him, but he hasn't checked in."

When Suz asks her about some of the other guys in the platoon, the woman, whose name tag reads CHER SAWICKI, scans the faces beyond them. "Doc Jump was the platoon leader, but I don't see him around anymore. Hold on . . . there's Ty Lassiter."

Cher hurries around the table and catches the attention of a tall, gangly soldier who strikes Abby as being way out of proportion. Ears too big for his head, eyes too close together, torso too short, legs too long. Maybe that's why his belt seems to be up to his armpits, although that's more an optical illusion than a reality.

"Ty, these ladies have been looking for members of your platoon," Cher explains, motioning to Abby and Suz.

"Hey—" He gets an eyeful of Suz and grins, but as he swings further and sees Abby, he freezes. "Uh . . . hi. I know your face. John had a photo, but you were in the news at his funeral. You're the king's wife, right?"

Abby starts to nod, then lets out a snort. "The king? Wow, I haven't heard that since John was in college."

"Yeah, well, John's rep was huge. I'm sure you know your husband was a legend. We've got a lot of John stories."

Abby gestures to Suz. "And this is Suz Wollenberg. Scott's widow."

He sucks in a deep breath. "Wow. I didn't recognize you. I really liked Scott. That guy could make you laugh. He had some great stories. A total crackup."

"Yup," Suz agrees. "That was Scott."

Lassiter taps the arm of a short but solid man in desert khaki, who turns toward them to reveal a round baby face. "About-face, McGee. Say hello to your buddies' wives." When

McGee's face puckers in confusion, Lassiter adds: "Or widows, I guess. I'm sorry, ladies. This part is new to me."

"That's okay. We're not big on protocol," Suz assures him as she shakes Gunnar McGee's hand.

"I'm sorry about your husbands," Gunnar says, his eyes flashing with pain. "They were good guys. Great men. I'm sorry for your loss. That Scott, he would be so quiet a lot of the time, but when he said something he cracked everyone up. And John was a natural leader. He kept us sane. Kept us focused." His blue eyes go hollow and cold. "I don't know what you've heard about Iraq, but it's not a good place to be right now. I hope I never go back."

Lassiter smacks his shoulder. "You got three more years of enlistment. Of course you're going back."

"I sure don't want to."

"Well, you're here now, and that's a good thing. Welcome home," says Abby. "I'm glad you guys made it back in time for the holidays."

"I wish all of us could have made it back." Lassiter crosses his lanky arms against his chest. "We lost four men during this deployment. That's a huge loss for a platoon our size. Roland was the first, then your husbands. And I don't know if you heard, but Antoine Hilliard was taken out by a suicide bomber, just after John was killed."

Abby nods sympathetically. "It must be hard on guys like you, losing people you lived and worked with."

"Yeah, it ain't easy," Lassiter agrees.

They chat for a while, sticking to mundane topics to keep the conversation going: the unusual inch of snow they had the previous week, the traffic that chokes the greater Seattle area, the foods the men missed most while deployed in Iraq. Once the ice is broken, Suz digs in.

"You probably don't realize it, but Abby here has had a lot of trouble getting answers from the military," Suz says. "They've never been able to tell her what really happened to John that day in the warehouse."

"I heard about this." Lassiter nods. "You went on *American Morning*, right?"

Abby sighs. "I did, but it didn't seem to help. I'm trying to piece things together, get details. I just want to know the truth."

Gunnar squints at Abby, as if surprised. "Really? It was a sniper. John got shot."

This she knows, but she doesn't think it wise to tell these soldiers that she magically copped a classified file. "Did you get a look at the sniper?" Abby asks him.

"Nah. I'm sorry we didn't take him out, but he gave us the slip," says Gunnar.

Suz turns to Lassiter. "Did you see the shooter?"

"It was dark. An old warehouse. I didn't see diddly, but who was partnered up with John that day?" He squints at Gunnar McGee. "Brown, right? Emjay Brown was working with him, ma'am."

"Please, call me Abby."

"That's right," Gunnar agrees. "You really want to talk to Emjay Brown, but I haven't seen him here tonight. He's kept a really low profile since we got back. Sulking, I think, 'cause his girl dumped him."

"That's awful!" Suz says.

"Yeah, well, it happens," Lassiter mutters, suggesting that he's had some experience in this area.

"I'll tell you, I was glad to have the wife and kids to come back to." McGee already has his wallet open, photos of a girl and boy cascading out in clear sleeves. "My wife is inside somewhere, but these guys are off with Grandma today. They make it all worthwhile."

Abby is admiring the photos when she hears a woman calling her name. Who could that be? She turns and catches Sharice stuffing the belt of a raincoat into her pockets as she crosses the hall to hug Abby.

"Sharice?" She blinks, surprised to see not only her mother-in-law but also Jim Stanton in dress uniform caught in conversation with another group by the door, trailed by Madison, who could only be described as seething beneath her black velveteen tunic with matching nail polish.

"I know." Sharice frowns, her demeanor lacking its usual vibrance. "You're wondering why we're here," she says in a low voice. "I'd like to know myself, but when the invitation came in the mail, Jim got a bee in his bonnet. He seems to think this will give us all some kind of closure, but honestly, I've been dreading it all week." She lifts her chin and forces a smile for the two soldiers. "Hello. Have we met?"

While Suz introduces Sharice to the men, Abby joins Madison, who paces in front of the refreshment tables like a shark circling its prey.

"Maddy, hey. I almost didn't recognize you. Going goth tonight?"

"I didn't want to come, so I decided to dress as the anticonservative. Do you like my nails? I didn't have time to dye my hair green."

"You know," Abby admits, "I really didn't want to come either. I don't think I'll be up for a celebration for a very long time. But . . . here I am." Should she tell Madison she's here to do some digging? She's always been honest with Madison, but the goth getup is a little alienating.

Madison looks over Abby's shoulder, frowning. "They're *selling* beer? I thought it would be free." She walks past the trophy case, then leans into the nook behind it.

Trying to maintain a conversation, Abby follows, glad when Madison waves her closer.

"Could you hook me up, Abby?" she whispers. "Buy a few for me?"

"Beer?" Abby tries not to reveal her surprise. "I don't think that would be a good idea." She gives Madison's shoulder a friendly shove. "And you need a couple? Ever heard of binge drinking, kiddo?"

"They're not all for me. My friends are meeting me here." When Madison smiles, Abby's eyes are drawn to her black lipstick, stark against the pale powder of her face.

244 Rosalind Noonan

Creepy, but Abby won't acknowledge that. She doesn't want to be one of them—the enemy, parental authority—but she would like Madison to keep thinking of her as an ally. "I'd like to help you out," Abby says, "but I don't think that's going to happen right now."

"No worries." Madison flicks her golden hair over one shoulder, clearly annoyed.

Abby moves into the nook beside her, trying to think of a way to make amends, or at least find something else to talk about, but Madison doesn't seem interested in either. On the other side of the trophy case, two people move closer, their figures watery globs through the glass.

"I'm sure they don't realize how awful they make us all feel," one of them says. A woman's voice.

"Who invited them, anyway?" another woman answers.

"I think the invitation went out to every soldier in the division, and every soldier's family. There must be a list."

"But how long do you think they keep widows on the list? I mean, a couple of months and they have to move out of base housing."

Widows. Abby's back stiffens at the mention of the word. Beside her, Madison doesn't notice; her gaze cruises down the corridor, searching for escape.

"I don't think they get it. But really, they should know that it's a huge downer for people to see widows at an event that should be pure happiness for the men who made it back in one piece."

Abby presses her eyes closed. Pure happiness . . . would she ever experience that sensation again?

Instead, she's left holding anger for these inconsiderate women, and a daunting pain in her chest because they see her as a pariah. Granted, she understands their feeling that it will never happen to them. If you truly believed that he would be killed, you wouldn't be able to let your husband leave your arms when it was time to deploy. It's a pattern of denial everyone employs, a coping mechanism that allows people to take calculated risks. No, I'm not going to refrain from driving for fear of dying in a car crash. No, I won't deny myself this chocolate eclair on the chance that it will clog my arteries.

No, my husband isn't going to die in a desert on the other side of the world.

Chapter 42

There is no reason for her to be here.
    None of these soldiers want to meet her. The married ones
avert their eyes as if their wives will scold them for talking to
her, and the single ones salivate until they learn that she is the
sister of Spec. John Stanton, who was killed in action. When
that realization hits them, they skulk away, afraid to defile the
legacy of a hero.
    Which makes for a deadly dull party.
    Thank God her friends agreed to meet her here. She steps
into the dark, mildewed chamber of the girls' locker room, her
fingers crawling over the wall for a light switch. There. Light
bounces off the gray lockers, the wooden benches so worn
down you could get splinters in your butt.
    As she passes through the rows of lockers and past the
glass-walled office used by P.E. teachers, she wonders about
the ghosts that might haunt this locker room. People say that a
gym teacher keeled over and died of a heart attack in the boys'
locker room back in the sixties, and that his ghost rattles the
locker doors whenever bullies pick on a puny kid.
    Or maybe that's, like, the wind blowing?
    Under the red glow of the EXIT sign, she pushes into the
metal bar of the outside door and steps into a puff of cool, damp
air. It's barely four-thirty but it's dark already, mists clinging to
the empty football field where a handful of joggers circle on the

track. To her left, she sees two dark figures leaning against the brick of the building.

Two slackers. Her friends.

Madison lets the door fall against one hip as she leans out to yell, "Get me something to prop this thing open!"

Sienna leans back against the wall and sucks a red glow into the dark, as if it's all too much work, but Ziggy scrambles off toward the baseball field. A steel trash barrel proves too heavy to budge, as does a rock half buried beside the backstop, but he emerges from the dugout with the solution—an old sneaker someone left behind.

"Weird," Madison says as he jogs closer.

By this time, Sienna has swaggered along the length of the building, taking her good old time. "Any luck in there?" she asks.

"Nah. They're selling beer, but nobody's going to serve me."

"Shit." Ziggy lodges the sneaker in the open door. "We'll have to recruit a buyer."

They go to the front of the school, where people spill out of the party to take a smoke. Madison hangs back, afraid that one of her parents' friends will breeze by and figure out that she's with the kids trying to cop some booze. She's seen Ziggy try to score alcohol or weed before, but she's never been a part of it. Not like this.

I used to be a good kid, she thinks, as the black enamel of her nails winks up at her. That was then, this is Madison A.D.

After Death.

After a few false starts, Ziggy seems to have hooked a young soldier who wants to talk. Madison hangs back with Sienna, two shadows against the wall, watching Ziggy perfect the art of the deal.

"I go to school with your younger brother," Ziggy says. "Clayton, right? Plays JV basketball, right? I know him. Wears that thick white headband."

"That's him." The soldier sucks on his cigarette stub, then plucks it out and pitches it into the wet dirt.

"He's good." Ziggy pats his ankle-length black coat and finds a package of cigarettes, which he offers to the soldier boy.

"He's good, but I was better," the soldier says, taking a cigarette. Madison notices that his hand shakes as he leans into Ziggy's lighter. "I was good, but nobody picked me up for college play. My grades weren't so hot. So. I had to go. Nothing to do but enlist, and they pulled me right in." He makes a sucking noise.

"Hey, man, how was Iraq?" Ziggy asks.

A moment of hesitation, and Madison is sure Ziggy has blown it with this guy. He doesn't want to talk about the war. Nobody wants to talk about it.

The soldier doesn't blink as smoke curls into his face. "I'm glad it's over."

"Did you get shot at and shit?"

"Yeah, it's dangerous over there. One of my buddies lost his leg from an IED." He says this last part over his shoulder, as if he didn't mean to open up but the words had just spilled out.

"That's crazy shit over there." Ziggy dances from foot to foot, the keep-warm dance. "Hey, you think you can do me a favor? Get us a couple of brewskis inside?"

"That's baby shit, man," the soldier says, but he holds out his hand for the cash. "You got somewhere to put them?"

Ziggy grips the lapels of his black coat and opens it wide, a small bat stretching its wings into a graceful glider. "Man, I got pockets in my pockets."

The soldier holds the crimped twenty-dollar bill like a paper airplane and points it toward the entrance of the school. "Giddyup."

Chapter 43

Fort Lewis
Emjay

Something is twitching in his left eye, inside the eyeball, an alien in his eye. It's in there tugging ever so gently, pulling his string. Sometimes it pulses while he's on duty, and he's sure Lt. Chenowith is going to rip him a new one and send him to the infirmary, but so far that hasn't happened.

He pauses in the doorway of the high school. Does anyone here see it? Has anyone noticed?

The squeak of his heel on the linoleum floor of the corridor seems loud as a shot as he steps forward again—careful, metered steps. He feels brittle and frail, like he is walking on eggshells, but Doc says that's just the medication doing its job. Keeping him sane.

He studies the faces of people passing by on their way to or from the gymnasium.

The tug on his eye is invisible. No one knows he's being yanked.

Or is he invisible? The two women seated at the check-in table are locked into each other, caught in a story. They act like it's okay for him to be alone, although he's having trouble with his aloneness. After months of being part of a platoon, and before that, being part of a couple, Emjay has been suddenly set adrift. Alone. Even when he is surrounded by people, he is alone.

Ironic, but he used to lie on his bunk and wish for solitude, close his eyes and pretend that no one was there.

"How are you doing?" the woman is suddenly asking him.

His throat chokes on an answer. The truth is, he's not doing well, but he's not sure how to say this, or that she really wants to hear the truth.

"How can I help you?" she asks before he can form an answer. Her gaze flicks to his uniform, then she smiles knowingly. "Corporal Brown? Did you RSVP?" She flips through a list. "Let's see, we've got a couple of Browns."

"Emjay Brown."

"There you are! I've got you on my list. Welcome back, sir."

He nods, thinking that he doesn't feel as if he really has come back. He's having trouble making adjustments. Leaving his gun behind feels so wrong, like a missing appendage. Yeah, he's seen way too much of that. But you're not allowed to take it with you everywhere you go, as you've been trained. People get scared. The police will arrest you. He knows all those things, and yet, he wants the gun with him, wishes he had it right now for peace of mind.

"Oh, see here? I've got a special note for you. You seem to be a popular guy tonight. People have been looking for you."

Who?

For a glimmer of a second he thinks it's Cheryl who's come for him, that maybe she didn't mean it about breaking up and she wants to be with him tonight. But that's not real. She already moved down to Sacramento. He saw the empty apartment.

His therapist told him not to come tonight. Christ, could it be Doc looking for him? Ready to come down hard on him for breaking with the plan.

As the woman smiles up at him and hands him a piece of paper, he wonders how she can be so happy about everything. "Now refreshments are down the hall that way, and there's music and plenty of places to sit inside the gymnasium. Oh, and here's your name tag. You have a good time, okay?"

Knowing that's his cue to leave the table, he presses the

name tag to the note and starts down the corridor, away from the gymnasium. He can't take the noise, the chaos, the squirming, unpredictable people, and all the soldiers, healthy and laughing now, but soon to be missing an arm or leg. Here today, blown into a bloody mist within a strange maze of streets in Biblical Mesopotamia tomorrow.

So why is he here? The pulse in his eye beats faster. He came here for a reason.

Once he's out of sight of the ladies at the table, he presses against the cool glass and unfolds the note.

> Corporal Brown:
> I don't think we've met, but I would really like to talk with you about my husband, John Stanton, who always wrote nice things about you. Please don't leave before we connect.
> Thanks,
> Abby Fitzgerald (Stanton)

Not Cheryl, but Abby.

Of course, she is the reason he's here. He knew there was a reason. There are things he must tell her, things John would want her to know because she's trying to find out. She's trying to figure out who did it. The army doesn't want to know, but Abby wants to see it clearly. She even went on television to ask for help, and he wanted to help, but he was too far away, in another world, viewing a delayed broadcast on the Armed Forces Television Network.

"Corporal Brown?"

His hands jerk the letter down, startled by the voice.

Down the hall, two silhouettes loom against the light. Two women.

"That's him," says the woman whose voice he recognizes as the table lady.

"Emjay Brown?" The other woman steps into the gray fuzz as he begins to shrink back. "I'm Abby, John's wife."

Abby . . . Abby . . .

He wants to talk to her, but he feels himself imploding. He is the groundhog poised at the top of his hole, blinded by the light, stumbling back into the ground until another day.

His hand palms the cool glass of the window, bracing, trying to find foundation.

"Do you mind if I ask you a few questions?"

He waves her forward, not trusting his voice.

"Hey, Emjay." She steps forward, her big round eyes alighting on him, peering inside him. "How are you handling all this?"

He lets out the breath he's been holding. "Not too well."

"It must be hard for you," she says. "When John was killed, I had my friends around me. Time off from work. The funeral, so many people wishing me well. But you didn't have that luxury. You just had to keep moving."

He nods. "It got to me. Losing John, right beside me and . . . and Hilliard." He clenches his jaw. "One minute you're talking to them, the next minute they're gone. You close your eyes, but you never stop seeing them, their faces."

Abby nods. "It's good to talk about it. Have you reached out for professional help at all?"

"I got a therapist in the army."

"Good."

"But I wanted to talk to you about what happened to John, because I told them, I told the C.O.'s what happened, but they didn't believe me." He glances into the shadows. The noise echoing from the gym seems hollow and mocking.

Abby is shaking her head. "I can't believe they're not investigating." She sighs. "But that's my battle to fight. What did you see, Emjay?"

He stands tall, sucking in a breath. "First, the muzzle flash. It was dark, and my night-vision device was all screwed up, but I saw the first shot. I think that one hit him in the chest. He went down, but he was still talking. Yelling, really. 'Don't shoot. I'm a friendly,' he told them. And then he said his name. 'I'm John Stanton, U.S. Army. I'm in *your* army,' he said. Yelling from the ground. That's when the second shot came, from closer range. That one hit his neck, maybe his head. It was dark, but there was blood everywhere. Shit, I was already pressing on his chest wound. That second shot whirred right past my head."

His heart is hammering in his chest and he is sweating, his back drenched with perspiration as it ripples through him again—the panic, the chaos.

He sinks down, down to stop the blood, down to stay low, out of the line of fire.

"Who did that? Got to be someone John knows, the way he's yelling. My NOD . . . Why aren't these goddamned night goggles working?"

He reaches over, grabs John's NOD that's tipped off his head onto the floor, and pulls it over his eyes, searching for movement.

There he is . . .

An American soldier jumping over a wooden crate, running away. Dodging behind a scaffold of shelves.

"Medic!" Emjay screams. He presses his hands to John's shoulder, but they slip down, bloodied, sticky. "Man down!"

"Come on, John! Come on, man. You're gonna make it," Emjay whispers, desperately trying to gain purchase on the wound so that he can apply pressure. "Keep breathing, John. Stay with me, man. John?"

But John does not answer.

Chapter 44

"So how does that work in terms of operations?" Jim Stanton asks the young doctor who so graciously offered to buy him a drink. Jim is intrigued by the army's new policy of placing field officers with psychology training in each combat unit in an attempt to eliminate suicides in combat zones.

"It's a relatively new protocol," Jump explains. "Overall, I was just one of the guys, expected to stand guard, accomplish missions, secure perimeters. Occasionally, I would confer with company commanders on the mental state of our troops."

"A soldier and a head shrinker?" Jim pinches the square point of his chin. "When I was in 'Nam, we didn't have field clinicians. Not even close."

Dr. Charles Jump, whom everyone calls "Doc," grins like a cowboy, half smile, half bemusement. "From what I've read, you guys could've used some help back then. A lot of self-medicating going on?"

"You could say that. Personally, I stayed away from drugs, but you can't avoid the mind-bending experience of a war like that. How many years has it been? Decades later, and I still have nightmares." Jim doesn't usually open up like this—not even with his own wife—but he has warmed to Dr. Jump, one of John's friends in Bravo Company and apparently one of John's football buddies from Rutgers. Not that Jim remembers him from those days; back then John did his own thing, traveling in his own packs without input from his parents, and that was okay with Jim. If you can't let go of your kids in college, when are you going to do it?

"Recurrent nightmares . . . after all these years. It's amazing how our subconscious speaks to us through dreams. You've discussed these nightmares with a therapist?"

"Naw. I've never seen a shrink. Back in the Stone Age, when I grew up, therapists were for the wealthy and those touchy-feely types who didn't have the guts to be real men." Jim squints at Doc. "You trying to recruit me?"

Doc laughs. "To be honest, I've got more than my share of patients in my new capacity at Lakeside Hospital. I'm just saying, everyone needs a way to vent, let it all out. A destresser."

"Honestly, my wife's been trying to get me into family therapy for the past few years."

"Family therapy is a little different," Jump says. "For family, I try to get the couple in along with any children living in the home."

Jim shrugs. "Not interested, but if I were, I have to say I'd want to work with someone like you. I like your attitude, Jump. No nonsense. Where did you train?"

"I did my graduate work at Harvard, undergrad at Rutgers, of course."

"Harvard must have been a hefty bill."

"Hence I am a minion of the U.S. Army for the next few years. At least until my tuition is paid off. I wasn't one of those pampered scholarship students. I played football in undergrad—that's where I met John—but I had to give it up senior year because of a knee injury."

"That's a shame. I know how the leg injuries can be. My legs have more stitches than Frankenstein, but I still like to go for a run when I can."

Across the gymnasium, Madison looks tired, bored, and a bit soggy. Jim raises his hand, trying to get her attention.

"Dr. Jump, I'd like you to meet my daughter," Jim says as Madison joins them. He introduces Madison to the shrink.

"Nice to meet you." Jump holds her hand until she meets his eyes. Clearly, Jim observes, this is a man who knows how to deal with kids. "I knew John had a younger sister, but I thought you were much younger. Grammar school."

When Madison grins, the smile reaches her eyes for the first time in a long time. "You knew 'im? John?"

"I was in his platoon in Iraq," he says. "But we've been friends forever. We played football together at Rutgers."

Madison moves from one foot to the other, teetering on the heels of her boots.

"You okay, honey?" he asks, touching her lightly on the shoulder.

"Fine. I jess . . ." She shrinks away from his touch. "I'm getting a ride home with Ziggy, okay?"

"Ziggy's here?" he calls after her, but she is already striding back toward the door. She bumps into a woman on the way but doesn't stop to apologize.

"Has she been abusing alcohol for a while now?" Jump asks.

Jim's eyebrows rise. "Alcohol? You think she's been drinking?" When Jump doesn't answer, he sighs. "It wasn't a real issue until John died. Then . . . well, add to that her brother Noah is AWOL, completely cut off from us. It's all been hard on Madison. Certainly more than any girl her age should have to deal with."

"Have you found family arguments accelerating at home?" the therapist asks. When Jim takes a moment to consider his answer, Jump touches his shoulder. "I'm sorry. I don't mean to pry, but since you mentioned your wife wanting family therapy, well . . ." He takes a breath, gazing toward the door where Madison exited. "Family therapy might be an effective way to resolve some long-term issues for Madison. As well as for you and your wife."

"And here I thought you were overbooked," Jim says with a grin.

"I am." Jump removes a card from a silver holder and hands it over. "But I could get you some referrals. Hey, we both work for Uncle Sam. You might as well take advantage of services available to you. When you get a toothache, you see a dentist, right?"

Jim nods.

"So think of me as the mechanic for the family minivan. I'll keep your wheels from falling off."

"Do they teach you marketing at Harvard?" Jim asks.

"That's just what I bring to the mix." Dr. Jump smiles. "See you around, Captain."

Jim tucks the card safely into his wallet. Not that he'll ever call, but if he did need a therapist someday, Jump would be at the top of his list.

Chapter 45

“Take some deep breaths. Keep breathing. It's okay, Emjay.” Abby tries to speak calmly as she kneels beside the panicked soldier, who presses his hands into the tiled floor, calling for John. “You're not in Iraq anymore. You're back in the States and you're okay.”

From his hands and knees Emjay Brown stretches up toward her, his eyes wide open but unseeing. “I can't make it stop!” he hisses in desperation. “He's bleeding out.”

“Emjay . . .” she says firmly, “you need to come back.” Abby is trying to maintain a steady, firm tone, but inside her heart is racing, her nerves singing with adrenaline.

He's having a flashback! Although she's studied aspects of post-traumatic stress disorder, she's never witnessed anything like this firsthand, an episode of past trauma so horrific that it's spilling into Emjay's present world. Is she doing the right thing? She remembers that it's okay to wake up a sleepwalker, so her gut instinct tells her that it's advisable to talk Emjay back into the present.

“Can't stop the bleeding!” he cries, his voice cracking in anguish.

“It's okay. You did your best, Emjay, but he's gone now. Do you understand?”

He swings his head back and forth in a jerky motion, then looks down at his open palms.

"It's over, Emjay," she says reassuringly. "That horrible day is gone. You don't have to be there anymore."

He sucks in a deep quivering breath, and suddenly tears glisten in his eyes—eyes that now see her clearly.

"Oh God." His face crumples in pain as he nervously takes in his surroundings. "Abby? I'm so sorry, Abby. I tried, but I couldn't save him."

"I know, Emjay." She sits on the floor beside the huddled man and rubs his back between the shoulder blades. "I know."

They remain that way for a while, Emjay sobbing and Abby trying to comfort him. She is thankful that this end of the corridor is somewhat secluded, and the few people who notice them look away quickly, affording them some privacy.

"I know this has been very difficult for you." Abby speaks softly, trying to reassure him. "I really appreciate your honesty, and I'm grateful for your help. You know, John cared a great deal about you."

"I know," he says, sobbing.

Her throat is suddenly tight, knotted with emotion. Now that the episode has passed, other questions plague her. Was this Emjay's first flashback? What if it happens to him again, in a dangerous location? Does the army recognize that he's suffering from PTSD? And beyond all that, who is looking out for this frazzled man?

His face is wet with tears, and she reaches into her purse for tissues, hoping he won't find them too effeminate.

He's fine with it, accepts the tissues and takes a deep breath.

"I'd better go," he says, pushing away from the floor. "This isn't my scene and, anyway, I came here to talk with you."

She rises, wiping her palms on her hips. "I appreciate that. Do you need a ride home?" She's not sure he should be driving.

"I'll take the bus." He takes a deep, calming breath, and she sees beauty in his dark, round face. A stormy beauty. If only the turmoil lingering there could pass. "It drops me right at the barracks."

"I thought you weren't coming," someone calls down the hall.

Emjay darts a nervous look over Abby's shoulder, his dark eyes stricken. "My therapist," he whispers, confiding to Abby. "I'm not supposed to be here."

"What?" Was Emjay restricted to quarters? Abby wheels to see a tall soldier swaggering toward them. "We were just heading out," she calls casually, trying to cover for Emjay, though she's not sure what he's so afraid of. To Emjay, she says, "I'll walk you to the door."

The tall therapist walks like a cowboy, Abby thinks as he heads their way.

"Whoa-hoa!" he bellows. Definitely a cowboy. "I know you."

The three of them meet under a cold fluorescent light that fairly beams on the tall man's shiny, shaved head. *He would be the cowboy they call Curly,* she thinks perversely.

"You're John's wife. I'm so sorry for your loss." He extends a hand. "Staff Sergeant Charles Jump. We've met before, many years ago. I was one of John's teammates back in college." She studies his face, piercing blue eyes, wide lips, and an overall demeanor of authority. Maybe he looked different back when he had hair? She honestly doesn't remember him. She takes his hand, but his attention has already moved to Emjay. "You okay?"

"Yes, sir. I was just . . . I mean—"

"He's on his way out," Abby says, curious as to why Emjay is so nervous around Charles Jump. Effective therapy is usually based on trust, but Emjay Brown seems to fear this man.

"Heading home, Doc," Emjay says as they make their way to the door.

"I can see that." Doc walks alongside them with ease. "I guess I'm just surprised to see you here after our conversation. An event like this can pack an emotional wallop."

"Bye, Abby," Emjay says at the door.

"You take care." She reaches for his hands and gives them a squeeze. They tremble slightly in her grip, and then he turns and heads into the damp night.

"Poor man." Jump folds his arms, peering out through the slit of window in the high-school door. "There's one patient I really feel for. He saw a lot of action over in Iraq, and it's not over for him. He'll probably be deployed again."

"Can I ask why he wasn't supposed to come tonight?" Abby says.

"That's part of his treatment plan, and I've probably already said too much."

"You're right, I shouldn't have asked. I'm finishing up a degree in counseling, and I should have known better than to ask."

He turns to her and smiles. "Can we start over? Hi, I'm Dr. Charles Jump. The guys in my platoon call me Doc, but before I got my degree friends called me Jump."

"So . . . Jump, I have to ask you the same question I've been throwing out to your fellow soldiers all night. Do you know any details about the way John died?"

"I heard that he was shot," he says slowly, "but honestly, I didn't see anything. I was on the other side of the warehouse, and it was pitch-black in there. I heard the bang of the rifle, but the next thing I saw was John outside on a stretcher." He tilts his head, studying her face. "You're disappointed. I guess that doesn't help much."

"I'm just searching for some answers. Answers I might never find." She takes a breath, trying to focus on the here and now. "So what's a psychologist doing in a combat platoon?"

"Actually, I'm a psychiatrist. While your husband was running the pigskin, I was busting my butt in a medical program."

"Wow. That makes my question even more pertinent. What *are* you doing in the army?"

"Ever heard of the GI Bill? I didn't have the bucks to pay for med school, but military service was one option that let me earn my way. Since the Iraq invasion, the army has been trying to have someone like me in their forward divisions. If you've been studying psych, I'm sure you can imagine the psychological fallout these guys experience."

She could now say she'd seen it firsthand. "Are you going back to Iraq?"

"I've been reassigned to the hospital here at Fort Lewis for now. But, knowing the army, I try not to get too used to any one place." He points a thumb toward the refreshments. "Can I buy you a beer? I'd be remiss if I didn't spend a few minutes checking on how you're doing."

"I'm not drinking these days," she says, worrying a button on her jacket. "I haven't been in much of a party mood."

"Then how about a spiced hot cider? Cocoa?"

Abby closes up her jacket. "No, thanks. I'm about ready to head home." His offer is kind, but she doesn't think she can hold up her end of a conversation having watched Emjay Brown relive the moments of terror surrounding John's death. To watch him cower on the floor and apply pressure to what he remembered as her husband's wounds . . . it was traumatic for her. She hadn't expected to relive the moment with him.

"Abby . . ." He tilts his head, as if trying to get into her line of vision. "You're a million miles away, girl. And I'm not sure I can let you go yet. You see, John and I had a pact. We promised each other we'd take care of family if one of us didn't make it out of Iraq."

Abby spares him a smile. It sounds like something John would do, though she's surprised he never mentioned it to her. In fact, he never really mentioned being on friendly terms with Charles Jump.

"So you see, it's part of my commitment to John to make sure you're okay."

"I'm okay." She holds out her arms for inspection. "I'm a walking, talking, functioning member of society."

He cradles his chin in one hand and squints at her. "I'm afraid I'll need more than one session to make that assessment. Really, I feel I owe it to John. Maybe we could get together for coffee sometime."

She has to admit, Jump is one of the most lighthearted individuals she's spoken with today. "If we have coffee, then you're off the hook with your promise to my husband?"

"Just as long as I can make sure you're okay." The corner of his lips curls in a grin. "Okay being the clinical term, of course."

"All right, then." She gives him her number and he programs it right into his cell phone.

"I'll call you in the next week or so," he promises.

"Okay." And for the first time in a long time, Abby realizes she's got something to look forward to.

"So let's recap," Suz says as they cross the parking lot. The mist has turned to sprinkling rain, the kind that swirls like glitter under street lamps. "You talked a war veteran through a flashback. God love you, Abby. He's lucky he was with someone who has some training for crazies."

"He's not crazy," Abby defended.

"Sorry, he's got PMS. Or PTA. No, wait, that's what I'm going to be suffering once Sofia starts school."

"You are so cruel. Post-traumatic stress disorder," Abby corrects her. "PTSD."

"Whatever. I'm very glad he came tonight, because Corporal Brown does not sound like the kind of person you would want to meet in a dark alley. Lassiter and McGee were charming and sweet and remembered our guys fondly. There were a few surprise guests, though we should have expected your in-laws. Sharice doesn't miss a military function."

"Although you'd think she and Jim might be a little embarrassed to show their faces with Noah being AWOL."

"But no one mentioned him tonight," says Suz, "and they're still basking in the glow of John's heroism. Nice that they brought along little Madison, who came in costume as Morticia Addams."

Abby grins as she unlocks the car. "Ruthless."

"And let's not forget the man who wins the Razzie for worst impersonation of a commanding officer, Lieutenant Chenowith."

"Did you happen to pick up that he attended West Point?" Abby slides behind the wheel and closes the door.

"I almost missed it until he said it, like, the *eighth* time. I'm sorry, but that guy is a piece of work. Were you there when he almost forgot Scott's name? Grrr."

Lt. Chenowith was easy to read. The slight man with the

monkish patch of hair atop his head nearly squirmed with discomfort when Abby asked him about the investigation into
John's death.

"We followed protocol," he told her. "Everything, by the
book. But you have to understand, we don't make the decision
to launch an investigation. That comes from our commanders.
When you're running a mission on a Forward Operating Base
like Fallujah, you make sure your soldiers follow orders."

Abby had smelled a lie.

"I don't trust Chenowith," Abby tells Suz as the windshield
wipers scrape the blur away. "Did you see the way he was
yanking on his earlobe while he talked to us?"

"Yanking on his chain?" Suz says with a giggle. "Or yanking our chains?"

Abby puts the car in gear and pulls out of the spot. "You're
in fine form tonight."

"I'm so incredibly relieved." Suz lets her head loll back
against the car seat. "Seeing all those soldiers and military
wives tonight, it brought me right back to when Scott and I
lived in the thick of it, and to be honest, I'm glad that phase of
my life is over. Don't get me wrong, I loved my husband. But
the U.S. Army was not a love match for me. I'm so glad to be
free of it all. Free at last!"

As the car travels into the night, Abby realizes the irony of
Suz struggling to free herself of the military while she is trying
to submerge herself in the culture, counseling soldiers and
their wives. Two roads diverged in a wood . . .

When she pulls in front of the house, the yellow glow of the
porch light illuminates a dark bulk in the front chair . . . a body?
Stepping out of the car, she recognizes the long blond hair and
black leather jacket.

"Madison?" Abby hustles up the walkway, wondering how
long the girl has been waiting in the cold rain. "Are you okay?"

Madison sits up straight, leans over the railing to her left,
and throws up into the bushes.

"Oh, honey."

The flash of memory of how it feels to be sixteen, heartbroken, misunderstood, and barfing in the bushes shoves aside Abby's long-term worries. For now, it's enough to be helping the girl inside to the sink, finding a clean washcloth, splashing a pot of warm water over the porch.

Abby finds an extra blanket and pillow in the closet but doesn't bother to open up the couch when she finds Madison already nestled into the crook beside the overstuffed arm, her black fingernails curled under her chin.

As Abby tucks the soft fleece around Madison's shoulders, she stirs and lets out a tiny moan. "I'm sorry."

"It happens," Abby says, knowing this is not the time for a lecture or a discussion of Madison's pattern of alcohol abuse. Right now Madison doesn't need her to be a therapist or a parent; she needs a friend. "Get some sleep," she says, but Madison is already off and dreaming.

Inside the bedroom, she closes the door and dials Sharice and Jim's number. When Sharice answers, the worried tone in her voice overrides Abby's annoyance at having to intervene.

"Sharice, it's Abby. I'm calling to let you know that Madison is here, and she's safe. She's been drinking and I'd say she's down for the night."

"Oh, dear." Silence, while Sharice does what? Dries her tears? Unloads the dishwasher? Pounds the wall with her fist? Despite the fact that she's known Sharice for more than five years now, Abby realizes she doesn't really *know* her mother-in-law.

"I . . . Maybe I should come get her. You shouldn't have to deal with this."

"It's okay. In fact, I think it will be better if you come in the morning."

"If you don't mind. I . . ." Sharice lets out a breath. "I'm just so relieved that she's all right." Her voice quavers, and if she closes her eyes Abby can see the tears. "Jim is already asleep, and I'd hate to wake him. He gets that insomnia in the early morning."

"She's welcome to stay the night, though I might try and talk to her about teenage drinking in the morning. Most kids experiment, but there seems to be a pattern here."

"Look, I'm aware that there's a problem, and I suspect it's not just that my daughter likes to have a cocktail now and again."

"It's good that you recognize the big picture."

"I've been trying to get Jim to go into family therapy with us, but you know how stubborn he can be. He's big on toughing things out. That may work for him, but it's clear that Madison is her own person, and I'm not going to stand idly by while she's in pain."

"I'm glad you're intervening, Sharice. Would you like me to get you some names? I can ask around at Lakeside, see who might be the best match."

"We'll need to go through the army medical services, but if you can find some candidates, I'd appreciate it. I've . . ." her voice grows strained. "I've never had to 'shop' for a psychologist before. It's very nerve-wracking."

"You'll do fine," Abby assures her. "You're taking a very positive step here. Let me know any way I can help, okay?"

"Okay. And Abby? Thank you."

Abby blinks, wondering if she's ever heard those words said with such sincerity before. She may not understand Sharice, but here is one small connection.

"You're welcome."

Chapter 46

The King

He clicks on the color pot and adds a bit of color to her lips, bringing them to a shade closer to cherry red. Mmm. Much better. The photograph is from the funeral, and she's pale and a bit washed out, but with a little Photoshop he can fix that. By the time he prints it out he'll have a regular centerfold spread hanging over his bed.

Abby Fitzgerald's lips are most enticing, thick and voluptuous. John must have loved the feel of those fat lips against his body.

Well, John isn't feeling anymore.

And he's determined to be next in line to plunder the pleasures of Abby's succulent lips.

Let it be a lesson to older brothers everywhere that they can't bulldoze over their siblings, stealing all the glory from the younger ones. Badgering and bullying. The firstborn gets all the credit. The firstborn gets away with murder. Well, in the end, John got the punishment he deserved.

The clothes Abby is wearing in the photo are a bit grim. He has already experimented with superimposing a naked body over her dark dress, but somehow that cheapens her whole appearance. The clothes will stay on for now, and his imagination can wander over her supple white skin, the curve of her waist, the round fullness of her breasts.

For now, he will imagine the seductive woman beneath the dark dress.

Soon enough, she will peel away the layers for him, tear off her dress and panties and bra to press her flesh against him.

Yes, she will go crazy for him, seduce him, serve him.

In the end, she will become his wife, his possession, his arm candy.

Just one trophy from the king's collection.

And once Abby is in place, he'll penetrate the rest of the family. Dad will want to show his support. Sharice can bake and sew for them. And little sister Maddy . . .

A girl on the brink of womanhood . . . tender, tormented and nubile. Probably a virgin. He sucks in a lusty breath. Oh, yes. He will enjoy having her, too.

All part of the king's collection.

Chapter 47

Fort Lewis
Abby

Abby is typing the last line of an e-mail to Flint summing up last night's party when the doorbell rings. Flint was eager to hear her impressions of the guys in the platoon, and she wants to share her experience with Emjay Brown, as well as her annoyance with the lack of cooperation from Lt. Cheno-with.

She types the last sentence and quickly scans what she wrote. Again, the doorbell chimes.

"Hold on!" she calls, clicking on the SEND button.

Bounding to the door, she trips and stubs her baby toe on one of three boxes on the living room floor—John's things.

"Eeow!" She winces, hopping to the door.

At last, the army has released his possessions, but now that everything is finally in her hands, she's lost momentum. That's another reason she is writing to Flint: to ask for his help going through this stuff with an investigative reporter's eye. If she does it alone, Abby is afraid she'll be reduced to tears, making it a painful, unproductive process.

Peeking through the smoked glass of the sidelight, she can make out a man in uniform holding a box wrapped in silver foil paper and dripping with scarlet curled ribbon. A Christmas gift. For her?

She opens the door to find the gift box in the arms of Charles Jump.

"Hey, I took a chance that you'd be home. How's it going?" His eyes fairly twinkle with concern, but she is not a fan of unexpected visits.

"I'm doing okay." She rubs her sore toe against the other leg. Good thing she was wearing socks or she might have lost a toe. "What's up?"

"I brought you a gift." He holds the package up proudly. "I got to thinking that the holidays are getting close, and I thought of something that would make the perfect gift for you."

"That's very thoughtful of you." She reaches for the package, hesitant. Right now presents have little appeal for her, but her mother taught her well. Accept a gift and say thank you. "Thank you, but it's really not necessary."

"You need to have something under your tree, right?"

Abby turns her gaze to the gift, the fat bow made of red ribbon imprinted with white velveteen holly leaves. "Actually, I'm not doing a tree this year."

"Not doing a tree? Why, that's positively un-American!"

She hugs the package close, shrugging in her fleece overshirt. "I've been busy with school, and, without John here, it seems pointless to decorate."

"But you've got to have a tree." Jump checks his watch. "There's still time. Put the gift inside and grab some shoes. We're going to get you a tree."

"I don't think so—" She begins to argue, but Jump is adamant. "Quick, before you turn into Scroogetta."

Abby slips on her clogs, wraps a scarf around her neck, and grabs her black gloves. "This is silly," she says as she locks the door behind her.

"Stop fighting it. This is exactly the sort of thing John wanted me to handle for you, so you might as well get used to it. I am going to be your new guardian angel."

Jump drives to a local nursery, where they walk among the rows of fresh-cut fir trees, their steps muted by fallen needles underfoot.

"Don't you love that smell?" Abby closes her eyes and is immediately transported to Christmases past—the morass of gift wrap underfoot after a present-opening frenzy with her cousins, the tradition of reading *The Night Before Christmas* with her dad, and the late nights spent with John kissing beneath the bejeweled tree.

"How about this one?" Jump holds up a tree that is easily a foot taller than he is—a seven footer.

"That would work—for a family of giants. I need something small this year. Easy to manage."

He releases the tree and leans down to pick up a two-inch sprig that fell from it. "Is that small enough?"

She smacks his shoulder with her gloves and turns toward the interior of the nursery. "Wise guy."

They settle on a live tree, a three-foot grand fir that can sit on Abby's end table and then be planted outside after the holidays.

"John would have liked it," Abby says as Jump lifts it from the backseat of his car. "He did a lot of landscaping in the yard here. Always looking out for the birds, trying to keep things green."

"You can let me know when you want to plant it after the holidays," Jump says in a strained voice as he lugs the tree up the porch step. "I'll give you a hand with that. This thing is too heavy for you to lift."

Abby unlocks the door and warns him to watch out for the boxes. He seems to strain as he navigates around them and sets the potted fir down on the end table in Abby's living room.

John would have carried the small tree with ease, Abby thinks, her mind making the comparison before she can catch herself.

"What's in the boxes?" Flint drops his coat on a chair.

When Abby explains that they're full of John's possessions from Iraq, he offers to go through them with her, acknowledging how emotionally trying that sort of thing can be.

"One of my friends has already offered," she says. "And you're doing so much already."

"Okay, then. Do you have any wine?" Jump asks as he plugs in the string of lights to test them.

Abby hesitates. This is not a date.

"I like to unwind with a glass at the end of the day," he says.

"I probably have something." In the kitchen, Abby finds a bottle of red wine someone brought to their house for a party once. She opens it and pours a glass for Jump.

Wait a minute, she tells herself. Why are you reading into this? Just sip some wine and relax. A little red wine is a great destresser and a good source of antioxidants.

Jump thanks her for the wine, and while he strings the lights she goes into her closet to dig for Christmas ornaments. It's not hard to find them with half of her walk-in closet empty now. Sharice has spent two days helping her go through John's things, determining what should be donated and what the family might want to hold on to as keepsakes. Since then, the empty half of her closet has been symbolic of her half-empty heart, incomplete without John.

Abby takes a deep sip of wine for fortification, then chooses a small box of wooden ornaments that have been in her family for three generations.

It doesn't take long to fill the small tree, and soon the corner of Abby's living room is aglow with light and tiny bits of nostalgia.

Sipping the last of her wine, Abby takes a moment to admire the small bit of magic. "It's lovely, Jump. Thank you so much."

"I'd say it's just what you needed." He moves up behind her, slips an arm over her shoulders and squeezes the top of her arm.

His move takes Abby by surprise and she feels herself tense. His touch is soothing, but she's not completely clear on his intentions.

"It's nice of you to look out for me." She steps away, out of his reach. "I appreciate all your help, Jump, but I'm not comfortable with this." She swirls her fingers in the air, as if drawing a lasso around the two of them.

"Hmm . . . the swirling, invisible *this*. Don't worry." He grins, that reckless cowboy look as he cocks one eyebrow and loops his thumbs into his belt. "I just want to be your friend. Sorry if I gave you the wrong impression."

She shrugs. "Just as long as we're square." Between the wine and the warm glow of color from her tree, Abby is beginning to feel relaxed and more festive.

"Why don't we go for a walk, get some fresh air?" he suggests. "Bundle up and we can walk around and check out the Christmas light displays."

"Now that sounds like fun," Abby says, feeling more at ease with the notion of the cool night air and the safety of being in public to cool any attraction between them.

They stroll along the small streets of the base, where the twenty-five-mile-per-hour speed limit keeps things more laid-back and quiet. With the A-frames of houses outlined in dripping icicle lights, the base reminds Abby of a Nordic village. In the stretch of unattached homes known as Officers' Row, every house is decked out with lights or an interesting display of characters, from a blow-up Tigger in a Santa cap to a detailed gingerbread house large enough for children to walk through. For Abby, the evening seems infused with charm as a group of carolers passes by and serenades them, puffs of white forming in the cool air in front of their mouths.

"This was a great idea," she tells Jump when they arrive back at her house.

"I'm glad you enjoyed yourself." He unlocks the trunk of his car and pulls out a white canvas sack. "You need a break now and then, Abby. Don't be so hard on yourself," he says as he hoists the sack onto his shoulder.

"What is that? Going off to play Santa Claus?" she teases.

"It's my laundry," he admits with a sheepish grin. "I was hoping I could do it at your place sometime. The laundry facility in the BOQ is the pits, always crowded."

Abby lets out a laugh. "You're kidding, right?"

"It would be a huge favor to me. Look, can I just leave it

here in your laundry room? I can come back and work on it some other day. I'll do it when you're not around if you want to give me a key."

The whole idea makes Abby a little uncomfortable, but isn't it a small favor after everything Jump has done for her this afternoon? "You can leave it in the laundry room," she tells him. "We'll figure out a time for you to get it done."

He stows the laundry sack, takes one last look at the little twinkling tree, then heads out, promising to call her.

Abby stands at the threshold and watches him go, all the while telling herself to just chill out. Don't read into things. Don't let your mind run rampant.

It's okay to accept someone's help, she tells herself.

And it's okay if that someone is a man.

Chapter 48

"That's the last one." Flint shoves the box into the tiny attic crawlspace over Abby's bedroom closet, then flips up the ladder and slides the hatch closed. "All taken care of."

"Until I have to move in a few months," Abby says, scowling up at the attic space. "And then, come March or April, I'll have to decide again what to keep and what to let go and . . ." Tears glaze over her green eyes. "It's stupid to hold on to some of those things. What am I going to do with a key chain Madison glued gems on when she was five?" She sucks in a shaky breath. "It's not like we had any kids to pass this stuff on to."

Flint folds her into his arms, closing his eyes as she sobs into the shoulder of his cotton sweater. "I know," he says softly, rubbing her shoulder blades, which seem so delicate and compact beneath her gray Rutgers sweatshirt. "It really sucks."

"And they stole his journals," she says raggedly. "How can they do that? Claiming that they include sensitive intelligence. That they need to be held until the investigation is complete." She pushes away from Flint and throws her arms up, her grief flipping into fury. "What investigation? If that isn't a crock."

Much better, Flint thinks. This is the Abby he fell in love with.

"Chenowith told me there *was no* investigation." She stabs a finger in the air to drive home the point. "They're lying through their teeth, and I'm sick to death of it."

"So let's nail them to the wall on it. The military told a blatant lie and if you stay on them, keep hammering away, you're going to chisel it down to the truth eventually, Abby."

She shakes her head as she marches out of the closet. "I thought I could do this on my own, but talking to Emjay, seeing him break down, I realize I am in way over my head."

He follows her out to the bedroom where she whips two tissues out of a box and presses them to her eyes.

"Way over my head."

"Don't say that. You've made a lot of progress. You reached out to people who were at the scene and you asked the tough questions. That's more than anyone else has done."

"But it's not enough. I thought, somehow, if I asked the right questions and I studied John's journals, I'd figure out who did it. Who did it and *why*. Why would anyone want to kill him . . . murder him?"

"And no one is saying you won't get to the truth. Sometimes it's a circuitous route, but you can't give up now." He paces to the bureau and nearly smacks into a wedding photo of John and Abby, John in his dress uniform and Abby in that veil that had tiny sprigs of baby's breath quivering against her red-streaked hair. "The truth exists. Like a gemstone that's buried, Abby, it just needs to be uncovered."

"I'm so tired of fighting for it." She collapses onto the bed, her head resting on her knees. "I'm sick of being the shrill widow. The lunatic fringe."

He sits beside her, wary when his hands sink into the brushed corduroy of the quilt, so soft and pliant. Good God, they're sitting on a bed together. It's dangerous territory for him, but apparently a safe haven for Abby.

Which is what he wants her to have right now. It's too soon for things to go any further between them, he knows that. But this . . . this close proximity is torture for him.

He leans back on the bed, elbows folded beneath his head. There . . . that should remind him to behave. "You have always been a lunatic," he says. "But you can never be shrill."

She lifts her head and scowls at him. "Thanks, Flint. You always had a flair for the backhanded compliment." Despite her rebuke, she stretches out beside him, pressing her face to his chest. Her hands curl beneath her chin, her legs tucked in a fetal position, and it requires all the strength he can muster to keep from turning on his side and pulling her into his arms.

They remain silent for a while, Flint focusing on the sound of her breath and the scent of her hair so close—a mixture of citrus and lavender. Is the citrus from the oranges in the salad?

In exchange for his help she had made him dinner—vegetable quiche and orange-spinach salad. A good thing, because he was famished after the five hours they spent sorting through the boxes, dividing items destined for trash, Goodwill, and storage in the attic. During the short break they took, sitting on the couch in the warm glow of Abby's little Christmas tree to eat and drink some of the Chardonnay he'd brought, he steered the conversation away from John to more upbeat topics. Abby's upcoming internship, nightlife in Seattle, the civil rights issues in the trial he's covering in Atlanta. With Abby, conversation expanded exponentially. That woman was never at a loss for words, never more so than when topics included controversy. God, he loved that about her.

Now that they are finished going through the boxes, he's tired, but Abby is totally wiped from dealing with the emotional attachment to John's possessions and from the sheer volume of items—dozens of books, khaki T-shirts, and socks. His worn desert combat boots, even a bar of used soap and a can of shaving cream, which she lifted to her nostrils, sniffed, and burst into tears at the familiar scent of him.

Abby breaks the silence with a sigh. "So what do I do next?" she asks quietly. "That is, if I can pull myself together to make one more strike?"

"Write up everything you know: the facts, the theories, the conjectures. Put it all in writing. I'll help you if you want. I can be your editor. So you get it down on paper and send it to the army. All the chiefs and generals on your list. Send it to any name and address you can get your hands on."

"I've got a very long list." When she speaks he can feel her breath warm the right side of his shirt. Torture.

"So you exploit any military connection you have," he goes on, focusing on the pattern of dots and bumps textured on the ceiling. "You see if you can hook someone on trying to take the investigation to the end."

"A bigwig at the Pentagon or a politician?"

"Either of those would work. At the same time, we'll try to get your opinion published, too. Probably as an editorial, I'm thinking. I'll put in a plug for you at the paper in Seattle, and I've got a few contacts around the country I can e-mail it to." He lifts his head to look down at her. "What say you?"

"I say . . . it sounds like a plan."

"Now you're talking. I'll do what I can to help you."

"I'd better get cracking on it soon," she says, stifling a yawn. "Come January, I'll be working full-time in my psych clinical. I'm looking forward to it, though other students warn you that it's all-consuming."

"I wish like hell this trial would wrap up, but looking at the witness list, I have a feeling I'll be camping out in Atlanta for a few more weeks."

"I can't believe they've got you living out of a suitcase when you were embedded in Iraq all those months. Don't they reward you for your hard work?"

"Abby, this story *is* the reward. A prominent man on trial for homicide in his role as Klan leader? They don't give these assignments to the newbies. Besides, living out of a suitcase at the Hilton definitely beats sleeping in an armored vehicle. The Hilton has better martinis. Correction. It *has* martinis."

When she is quiet, he adds, "But I do wish I was closer to Seattle right now. I'd like to help you more."

"And you must miss Delilah. I'll bet she wants you here, too."

"Delilah and I . . ." He searches for the right terminology. *Breakup* sounds so juvenile for anyone past eighteen. "We're not seeing each other anymore."

"Oh, Flint . . . I thought she was the one for you."

"Apparently, she thought the same. I'm the one who balked."

"Oh, no, Flint . . ." She presses her palm to his chest and

jostles him. "After all these years, you're still running from commitment?"

"I'm not going to grace that question with a response," he says, very aware of her hand splayed on his chest.

"Chicken." She digs a finger into his ribs, tickling.

He sucks in a breath and smacks her hand lightly. "Okay, I am. I'm ready to commit, but Delilah just wasn't the right girl."

"That's too bad, because I really, really, really thought you'd found it. I always wanted you to fall in love, maybe because you were such a tough nut to crack. But you know what? I'm not giving up on you."

"Gee, thanks."

"I mean it, wise guy." She nudges his rib cage again. "That's my wish for you. That someday, soon, you'll find that amazing, knock-your-socks-off, once-in-a-lifetime love," Abby says drowsily. "The kind of love John and I had. That's my wish for you."

I already found it. Flint thinks as Abby's hand slides off his chest to the mattress. He glances down at her smooth brow, the bridge of her nose sprinkled with freckles. She is asleep.

I found that love. Flint mouths the words silently as he watches her shoulders rise and fall with each breath. *But she's grieving for someone else.*

Chapter 49

Fort Lewis
Abby

"**M**erry Christmas, Abby!" Swiping the sleeve of her sweatshirt over her nose to scratch an itch, Abby looks up from the birdfeeder she's filling with black sunflower seeds to see Jump jogging toward her. In his gray sweat pants, navy Nike jacket, and black leather gloves, Charles Jump has become a familiar sight along neighborhood running paths. It's the third or fourth time he's stopped by this week.

"Merry Christmas," she calls. "I can't believe it's already Christmas Eve."

"Indeed." He takes the feeder she just filled and, reaching up beside the stepladder she needs to use, hangs it on its hook. "The holidays go so quickly. Hey, is my laundry done yet?"

She scoffs. "Like that's ever going to happen. I told you, I've got enough on my plate right now, and washerwoman isn't part of my career aspirations."

"Ooh." He plants his feet wide over the clear cylinder she's filling with seed. "Have I hit a sore spot here?"

"Nope. I'm just being honest. You're welcome to go on in and pick up your laundry bag right now if you want."

"How about if I get a load of wash started? I'll start the washer, go for my run, then double back and put it in the dryer."

She shakes her head. What was he not getting about the

word no? "I gotta ask, why is it so important for you to do your laundry in my house?"

He sucks in a breath through his teeth. "Okay . . . now you've hit my soft spot. It's about more than clean clothes."

"So I suspected."

"The thing is, I miss having a home. I hate living single. Life in the BOQ can be dog-eat-dog, as you can imagine. It's worse than dorm living, because these are grown men who are tossing your wet clothes onto the floor if you don't get to the machines fast enough."

"Sounds like you need a place of your own," she says. And on a doctor's salary, an apartment in the area should be no problem.

"I'm working on that. But in the meantime, can you help me out?"

She looks down at the paper parcel of black seeds. "Jump, please don't beg. It's so awkward."

"Okay, here's the deal. I was married before my first deployment to Iraq. Did you know that?" He lets out a breath, rubbing the stubble of his new-grown hair with one of the black leather gloves he always wears while jogging. "It's not something I like to talk about. Suffice it to say, I got back to find my wife AWOL and my home gone . . . in the wind. God, that was devastating."

"I'm sorry," she says earnestly, tipping her head up to meet his gaze. "I didn't know." She feels like a jerk, not recognizing that Jump, like anyone else, has a history with difficulties he's struggling to overcome. Has she been so wrapped up in her own grief, her own battles, that she's unable to pick up on the needs of people around her?

"If you don't mind, I'll just go in and get the bag, then I'll be out of your hair," he says.

"No, don't do that." Abby rolls back on her heels and rises. "Why don't you go in and start a load of laundry. Just push my basket aside if it's in the way."

"Thanks!" He takes a few strides forward, then stops, turns back. "Hey, do you have plans tonight? I'd be happy to take you for dinner at the Officers' Club. Nobody should be alone on Christmas Eve."

"Actually, I have people coming over. Friends and John's family." She pours sugar solution into the hummingbird feeder, thinking. *Oh, what the hell.* "You met John's family, right? Would you like to join us?"

"That would be great." This time his broad smile reaches his blue eyes, dazzling. He grabs Abby's shoulders and plants a kiss on her cheek. "You're a lifesaver!"

As he lopes along the patio and into the house, Abby wonders if she did the right thing. She needs to stay open to people, to keep her heart from folding up upon itself like an origami crescent. She's well aware of that, but right now she feels far too vulnerable, too exposed.

"Eventually, I'll get this all in balance," she tells a gaggle of bushtits who have already overrun a seed cake. "It's all about balance."

Chapter 50

The young soldier carving the roast, his necktie tucked into his shirt, has won Sharice's heart. Watching him serve, Sharice would swear there's a halo emanating from his cordial, confident smile. Sometimes, when you're feeling overwhelmed and cannot see a clear way out, fate intervenes with a ray of sunshine, a godsend like Dr. Charles Jump.

Or Captain Jump. The man has earned so many titles, she's not sure what to call him, though he has suggested Doc, since he'll be treating the family in therapy. Sharice takes a deep breath, the air thick with smells of roast beef, garlic, baked potatoes, and vanilla from the glorious centerpiece of white candles at the center of Abby and John's table . . .

Abby's table now.

"Can you cut hers into small pieces?" Abby's friend Suz asks.

Down by Dr. Jump's hip, Sofia stands with a china plate pressed to her tiny face. "Roast beast, please."

"Hold the plate flat, sweetie," Abby instructs, helping the little girl lower the plate.

"I'll make special Sofia-sized bites." Jump smiles down at her as he drops small squares of beef onto her plate. "How's that?"

"Thank you, Dr. Jump!" She hops in the air as she says his name—almost tossing the meat.

"Okay, okay, we know you like his name, pumpkin," Suz says, guiding her to a chair at the table.

Madison sits opposite Sofia, scraping tracks into a mound of mashed potatoes with her fork.

"Madison." Sharice projects her annoyance as her daughter eases the fork into her mouth. "Please, wait for the rest of us to be seated. Where are your manners?"

"Whatever," Madison says over a mouthful as she rests the fork on the edge of the plate.

"Everything okay?" Jim comes up behind Sharice.

His hand on her shoulder reassures her, so warm and solid. Where has he been these past few years when she needed him? Where has her head been? Distance encouraged by routine wedged them further and further apart, but now that chasm seems to be closing. By necessity, they are finding each other again, a touch here, a few words of support there.

They have reached across the vast space that opened up with the loss of their son and found a tight if tenuous handhold.

"We're fine," she says, handing him a white china plate, then taking one for herself. "Everything looks lovely, Abby. And Suz, you must give me the recipe for that crab dip."

"It's so easy," Suz says, tucking a Velcro bib around Sofia's neck to cover her red velvet dress. "Once you get it down, you'll make it all the time."

"Who else needs roast beef?" Jump asks. "Sharice? Rare or medium well?"

"Somewhere in between," Sharice says, holding out her plate. The white candles ablaze in their silver candelabra are so bright her eyes glaze with tears. "Thanks so much. You know, looking at this fabulous feast, I realize we have so much to be thankful for."

"Ma, wrong holiday," Madison mutters. "This isn't Thanksgiving."

"Still . . ." Sharice carries her plate to the table and sits down beside Abby. "I'm grateful that we're all here together."

Abby squeezes her wrist warmly. "Me, too. I'm glad we're all here together tonight."

She puts her hand over Abby's momentarily, thinking of the list of therapists Abby gave her. A great help for Sharice, who freezes at the proposition of calling health care professionals and setting up interviews. Sharice and Abby had their differences, but at her core Abby was a good person with the best of intentions.

This Christmas will be the most difficult of her lifetime, and yet she expels a sigh of relief that there's hope for the remainder of her family. She and Jim will get Madison into therapy with Dr. Jump. Maybe Jim will even agree to family therapy, having confided to her that he relates to Dr. Jump, feeling a unique kinship because this man, like Jim, has experienced the pain and grit of combat.

And maybe Sharice will even find a modicum of relief through therapy. Not that she puts any stock in it. God knows, she has friends she can talk to. Of late, she's taken to having tea with Eva and Britt, who feel compelled to voice their opinions about the need to pull our troops out of Iraq. Sharice is not sure she agrees, wondering if it's fair to let that country implode after our boys have invested so much in trying to infuse structure there. What about the Iraqi police departments they're trying to train? And the bridges and schools our troops are building? It would be such a shame to just leave, and abandon the entire mission. But mostly, when she's with Eva and Britt, it's all just conversation, now that John and Noah are no longer deployed there. She's happy to listen while the ladies vent, knowing that they do not judge her for Noah's actions. Besides, Britt makes the best cranberry scones.

"I'd like to make a toast," Dr. Jump says, raising a glass of ruby-red wine. "To the men and women who serve our country: past—" he nods to Jim, "present, and future. That we might keep America safe for our families. That we might protect our freedom to enjoy times like this." He raises his glass.

"I'll second that, sir." Jim lifts his glass, a glaze of unshed tears in his dark eyes.

Emotion forms a knot in Sharice's throat as glasses are raised. Her eagle eye double-checks Madison—just sparkling cider. Sharice sips a Diet Coke, her new drink of choice so that Madison can see you don't need alcohol to have a good time. Reinforcing behavior by example, not by lecture. She's determined not to screw this up, not to let her last child slip through her fingers.

"And Merry Christmas, one and all!" Dr. Jump adds, beaming a grin from the head of the table. Now that his hair is growing in he looks younger, more like one of John's contemporaries, though Sharice still cannot place him from her memories of John's years at Rutgers. As soon as the holidays are over, she's going to dig in the attic for John's yearbooks and sneak a peak at the younger version of Dr. Jump.

For her part, Sharice is reassured just knowing that this man was a friend of John's, that Charles Jump stood by her eldest boy on the football field as well as the open desert battlefield. Basking in this knowledge, she feels that her son would approve of their embarking on the very personal, very trusting therapeutic relationship with Dr. Jump.

John, honey, wherever you are, thanks for sending us this savior.

Chapter 51

This was not the way she planned to spend Christmas Eve—
building a tricycle while Abby and her friend sat back and
sipped wine. In fact, she didn't even know Abby was friends
with Charles Jump, the company field therapist, until he appeared at dinner tonight with a box of chocolates and a look
of lust in his eyes.

Or was she imagining that? Maybe it was the mutual "I got
your back" deal she had going with Abby that made her so
protective of her friend. Over dishes in the kitchen, Abby
whispered that he was just a lonely soldier at Christmastime,
but if that were the case, why didn't he stay for dinner and
then get the hell out to a bar or the Officers' Club or his couch,
where all the other lonely soldiers were spending their Christmas
Eves. Not to be selfish or anything, but Jump was going to go
home and sleep in while her kid was going to wake up in six
hours fully anticipating toys and presents under the tree. Toys
with "some assembly required." And it's nearly midnight and
Suz has just removed the metal rivets from the box housing the
ninety-nine pieces of Sofia's tricycle.

Sucking on the finger that got scraped while opening the
box, Suz settles on the floor in a yoga child's pose and spreads
the nuts and bolts out on the rug. "Oh, this is going to be
fun," she says, squinting at the diagram.

"Oh, wow. Let me help you." Abby sets her wineglass on a

table and slides to the floor beside her. "I'm pretty good at this stuff. As a kid I always loved puzzles."

"Well, good, because Scott was the assembly-line foreman of our family. I was Director of Purchasing and Acquisitions." Suz starts lining up nuts and bolts by size, while Abby unfolds the directions.

"Last time I was here, your living room was full of boxes," Jump says, leaning back and folding his long legs. "What did you do with them?"

"They're stashed in the attic now. My friend Flint and I went through them, but the army confiscated most of the things I really valued, like John's journals. I was so eager to read them. I guess I thought they might reveal who killed him."

"Really?" Jump seems surprised. "Do you think he knew the insurgent?"

"I think the sniper was someone in your platoon. In fact, I know it was. The question is, who?" Abby rises and, stepping over loose screws, tiptoes toward the kitchen. "We're going to need the tool kit."

"*Really?* Well, that's scary," Jump says thoughtfully.

"Two, four, six, eight . . ." Suz counts the bolts. "Oh, good. At least we've got all the pieces we're supposed to have. Let's see if they fit together." She reaches into the box, lifts out the shiny silver handlebars with pink streamers hanging from the handgrips, and pretends to drive. "So cute!"

"Excuse me, ma'am, but do you a license to drive that?" Abby teases Suz, kneeling beside her with a red toolbox. "You know, Jump, I realize you didn't see anything in that warehouse, but you must have had a sense of the dynamics at play in that platoon."

"I did my best. It was a big part of my job."

"So if you were profiling John's killer, what would you say?" Abby presses him as she finds two pink metal pieces and starts to attach them.

"Well . . ." Jump clears his throat, and Suz glances up at him as he recrosses his legs. "I can't reveal anything the troops shared with me in confidence."

"Of course." Abby spins a nut. "I wouldn't expect that. My question is why? Why would someone want to kill John?"

He sucks in a deep breath. "Hmm. Jealousy? Not to name names, but John was quite the celebrity when he joined our little platoon. When the media was around, the journalists wanted to shadow John—anyone else in the platoon was second-rate. Some of the guys may have resented that."

"Resentment is one thing," Suz says, handing Abby a bolt. "But motive enough to kill a guy?"

"Not to mention the fact that John's celebrity status put extra pressure on our commanding officers to do the right thing. And, I'm sure you noticed that our esteemed lieutenant is fairly cocky. A West Point graduate with a Napoleon complex."

"Honestly, Chenowith does give me a very bad vibe," Abby says. "If it was a matter of trusting my instincts, I'd pursue him as the prime suspect."

Suz hands Abby a screwdriver. "That would be so awful if he was the one."

"All this assumes that your theory is correct, Abby," Jump says. "And to be honest, I'm not convinced you're right."

"But I—"

He holds up his hands to stop her. "Please, save me the details. Professionally, I've moved into another area and I'm trying to leave that last assignment behind me. Iraq took its toll on me, too, and it's difficult for me to revisit. You forget, I lost my best friend there."

"I'm so sorry," Abby says. "Of course, you suffered first-hand."

"It's okay to ask. You know I want to help." He leans forward on the sofa, his hands pressed together in prayer position. "Maybe it's good for me to vent. I'm going to get going. But while we're on this subject, there was another unusual dynamic in that platoon."

Abby and Suz both stop what they're doing and gaze up at him.

"There was also an extreme case of sibling rivalry. The

younger brother seemed to think that his older brother led a charmed life. Their relationship was a constant competition. Not unusual for siblings so close in age, but rife with possibility."

"Noah would never hurt John," Abby says, her hands twisting the screwdriver. "I think his love for John was what sent him off the deep end after John died. I'll never forget that day he ran from us at Arlington Cemetery. Just ran like the wind. He was so distraught."

"They enlisted together, right?" Suz takes the large wheel from the box. "That sounds pretty close to me."

"Statistically, most homicides are committed by someone who knows the victim well." Jump's eyes are cool as ice—his intellectual persona? Suz hands Abby a wheel, her eyes riveted on the shrink. "Husbands kill wives, gangs take out one of their members, lovers kill their exes. I'm not saying this is the case with the Stanton brothers but you can't ignore statistics." He stands. "And on that note . . ."

"Merry Christmas," Suz says, rolling back on her heels and turning toward the clock in the dining area.. "I guess it's officially Christmas Day."

Abby stands up, leaving the screwdriver on the rug. "I'm glad you joined us," she says, walking him to the door.

Suz grabs the screwdriver and grits her teeth as she tightens the screws. Abby's almost got this thing waxed! She reaches under the seat to tighten a bolt and scrapes her hand in the process.

"Dammit." Tears sting her eyes, not so much from the cut as from the sting of not having Scott here to assemble his daughter's first tricycle. A line of blood drips down the back of her hand. She'd better wash up before she turns the pink trike red.

While Abby and Jump chat on the threshold, she ducks into the bathroom. When she returns, Jump is gone, and Abby is on the floor finishing off the assembly job.

"I thought he would never leave," Suz says quietly as she tiptoes down the hall, passing Abby's prized family photos.

She gazes past a photo of John in uniform, then does a double take. Beneath the glass frame, fat dots of liquid cling to the photograph under John's eyes, like tears on his cheeks.

"This is weird." Suz stares. "Did someone try to do 3-D art here?"

"What?" Abby joins Suz, leaning into the portrait. "What is that?" She removes it from the wall and holds it under the lamp for a better view. "Oh, God, it's like he's crying."

Suz nods. "Tears on his cheeks."

Abby shivers. "Very creepy." She drops to the floor and pries off the clamps on the back of the frame to get inside. "How do you think it happened?"

"I don't know, but none of the other photos have moisture under the frame. It's very strange."

Gently, Abby presses a tissue to the drops of moisture on the portrait. Fortunately, it absorbs the drops without affecting the surface of the photo. "I've never seen that happen before. Maybe it's from the steam of the radiator."

"Or maybe it's a supernatural occurrence," Suz says. "Crazy as that sounds, I gotta admit." This one she feels deep in her gut. Drops of moisture did not randomly appear on the cheeks of dead men in photos.

"The thing that really creeps me out is that I just had to extract myself from Jump at the door," Abby says, wincing. "He was trying to kiss me goodnight. I don't know whether it was too much wine or just the spirit of the season but . . . I told him it's way too soon." She shivers. "And now this . . ."

"It's a message from the next world, Abby." Suz rubs her arms, warding off goose bumps. "He's trying to tell you something. Wherever he is, John is crying."

Chapter 52

Fort Lewis
Abby

Abby flips over onto her right side, stuffs the pillow under her neck, and clamps her eyes closed. As if that's going to work.

After a tense moment spent willing herself asleep, she sits up and turns on the light. Maybe it's because she's trying to sleep on the couch, having given her bed to Sofia and Suz. Maybe it's because it's her first Christmas in so many years without John. Maybe it's the teardrops on John's photo, a sad reminder of him even if it was a sheer coincidence.

Or maybe it's Charles Jump.

After the weird occurrence with the drops of moisture on John's picture, she didn't share all the details with Suz. In truth, Jump didn't want to leave tonight. He played the "I'm alone at Christmas" sympathy card. And much to her surprise, Abby was sorely tempted to let him stay. When he pressed close to kiss her cheek, she imagined him beside her in the sofabed, blankets between them, of course, but his long, warm body stretched out just inches away made her skin tingle with awareness. Just having a warm body beside her would have been reassuring.

But crazy. She's not ready for a relationship, even if her body craves the physical reassurance. It's wrong to lead Jump on, especially since he's a genuinely nice guy, John's friend. If she could just place him from Rutgers . . . She'd searched John's letters and electronic journal entries for any mention of Charles Jump, but his name never came up. Which is weird. John had mentioned Emjay as a friend. He'd mentioned Noah a few times, and had talked about wanting to take "the kid" Spinelli under his wing. But nothing about Charles Jump.

Wouldn't your best friend appear in your written thoughts?

She tosses the covers back and goes into the kitchen to make some herbal tea. While the water heats she pulls a blanket over her shoulders and paces from the kitchen to the tiny dining area. As she tries to connect John and Charles, something Jump said earlier tonight hits her.

You forget, I lost my best friend . . .

Not just a good friend, but a best friend? Something is off balance there. Abby is convinced she would have known about anyone John considered a best friend. There'd been a few at the funeral . . . Spike Montessa from Rutgers, Kevin "Killer" Kelly from the Seahawks. Good guys, close friends. Even though John wasn't able to be with them often, he spoke of them, e-mailed them, made plans for reunion weekends.

As she dunks a chamomile tea bag, Abby lowers her head and presses on with the debate.

If she knew John's friends, why didn't she know anything about Charles Jump before now?

It appears that Jump's attachment to John was somewhat one-sided. So . . . was Charles exaggerating the relationship, or did he have a distorted view of himself?

She thinks of the people who, over the years, wanted a piece of John's glory. The fans, the groupies, the players, the media, the girls. Before she and John were married, the girls were a worry. Beautiful blondes with kick-ass bodies. Cheerleaders in short skirts and go-go boots prancing across the football field. "Boobs to beat the band," John used to say. But he'd also called them eye candy. "They're fine to look at," he whispered, pressing his thumb into that sensitive spot at the nape of her neck. "But I'm in love with you."

A small cry jumps from her throat, and she presses the blanket to her eyes to wipe the sudden tears. God, she misses him.

The tea warms her inside, and she falls asleep remembering John's words.

But I'm in love with you.

Sometime during the night she rolls over into a warm nook in the bed. Awakening, she touches the sheet, her palm smoothing over the glow there. The clean smell of his shaving cream, clove and soap, makes her smile.

He's back . . . his ghost is back. She doesn't know why, but for now, this Christmas morning, she finds it reassuring. Abby plants her body in the warm groove of the mattress and slides into a deep, sound sleep.

PART III

January–May 2007

Chapter 53

Washington
Flint

As he drives through a sheath of gray rain on I-5, Flint re-hearses the speech for the eighth or ninth time. "The thing is, Abby, I've been crazy about you ever since college. And in all the years since, what people perceived as failure to commit was really just lack of satisfaction; I was holding out for a real connection with a woman. Something I had with you . . ."

The windshield wipers swipe the splatter clear for a second, changing his line of thought.

Or something you thought you had with Abby, says the dark voice of his cynical self. What if she hadn't felt that same spark back in college?

Attraction has got to be mutual to make it work, and he doesn't know if Abby thinks of him as anything more than a friend. *Does she like me?* The question tugs at him like a band stretched tight in his gut, which makes it all seem totally adolescent.

It's infantile relationship stuff, but he can't seem to make it go away.

And so he's driving to her place, straight from the airport, to straighten a few things out. The trial concluded in Atlanta this morning, and though he'll return for the sentencing hearing in a few weeks, for now he's done with the assignment. When the wheels of the plane ground into the runway, he felt nudged by relief. Christmas had been a bitch without her, despite the fact that his nieces and nephews in Chicago could be quite entertaining. His months in the desert had forced him to take a look at the things that last, the stones that remain after you sift everything through a sieve. In the shakedown of his life, Abby was essential.

He downshifts and takes the exit for Fort Lewis. In his beat-up leather laptop case is a marked-up copy of Abby's account of what she believes happened to John Stanton in that dark Fallujah warehouse, and he figures it's as good a reason as any to be driving down to Fort Lewis to see her.

The lights are burning gold inside her living room when he pulls up. Good, because he didn't want to jinx things by calling ahead.

The wiper blades straddle the middle of the windshield when he kills the engine. He grabs his laptop, shoulders the door open, and steps into the rain. Abby answers the door with a pair of men's khaki boxers in her hands.

"I thought you were in Atlanta!" Her face brightens at the sight of him, her hands working to fold the shorts.

"The trial is over. I just got back." He ducks in out of the rain and finds a wadded lump of clothes on the sofa next to a stack of T-shirts and shorts. "Is this more of John's stuff? Wow, I thought we took care of all that before Christmas."

"We did. This is just . . ." She folds the boxers into a small square and adds them to a stack of clothes. "A favor for a friend. So . . . did you get my editorial piece?"

"That's why I'm here." He eases his computer case onto the dining room table beside a nest of bundled men's socks. "I thought we could go over some changes and get it submitted before you begin your internship. When do you start at the hospital?"

"Next Monday, so I really want to get the editorial squared away." As Abby talks, she pulls back her silky hair, twists it at the nape of her neck, and arranges the twist on one shoulder.

The gesture is so lovely he has to bite his bottom lip to keep from saying something poetically adoring. Christ, he's such a sucker for her. He hands her a marked-up copy of the editorial.

"I was thinking you could start with something more immediate." He moves behind her, looking over her shoulder as she
reads. "An image, like the shot exploding in the darkness, and
then go on from—"

Just then the bathroom door pops open, startling Flint. He
turns on his heel just in time to see a cloud of steam emerge,
along with a tall, angular man clad only in a yellow towel at
his waist. Drops of moisture bead over his chest and along his
muscular shoulders. His dog tags dangle at his throat, along
with a gold heart-shaped medal.

Flint's gaping mouth curls into a snarl.

"Hey," the stranger says, "how's it going?" He moves off
down the hallway toward the bedroom.

Flint's heart freezes in his chest. Abby is already seeing
someone.

Doing his laundry. Shacking up. And here he'd been holding
back, trying to give her time to heal . . .

Abby presses the edited papers to her chest, wincing. "Do
you remember Charles Jump? He was in John's platoon."

Flint shakes his head. "Actually, I don't. Or maybe I just
don't recognize him naked. Christ, Abby. You don't waste any
time."

"It's not how it looks! I know it's weird, but he was really
good friends with John." She points to a framed photo on the
wall. "He gave me this as a Christmas gift, and, well . . ." She
lowers her voice. "I guess I felt a little guilty because I didn't
even realize that Jump and John were friends."

In the photo, two men in desert khakis stand side-by-side, a
helicopter perched on the sand behind them. John is grinning,
his arm slung around the other man's shoulders, hugging
Dr. Charles Jump.

"Him? That's the one they called Doc. Mr. Personality."
Flint scowls. Something about the photo is off, artless. "You
know, one photo op does not make a friendship."

"I know, but Charles went to Rutgers with John," she says,
worrying the corner of the papers. "They played football together for a while."

"Not really a sufficient answer for why the man is in your bathroom, Abby. John had a lot of friends. I don't see you doing their laundry." Using his keys, he lifts one corner of a pair of black, low-rise briefs on the table.

Abby slaps his hand away. "The laundry is a favor, just a one-time thing," she insists. "And he's showering here because there's no hot water in the BOQ, the bachelors quarters where he lives."

"Ah! The old 'no hot water' ruse." Flint forces himself to grin, as if it doesn't matter one lick. As if his entire speech about reevaluating his life priorities and wanting Abby to be among them didn't just go down the drain along with Doc's shower suds.

"Anyway . . ." Abby smooths out the edited papers on the table. "I like the idea of a new opening. Actually, all your changes look good. If I incorporate this stuff, do you think it will be ready?"

"Yeah, sure." He digs his hands into the back pockets of his jeans, struggling to shift his focus from the dick in the bathroom to Abby's editorial. "I've already got a green light at my paper, and I've gotten a few nibbles from e-mail pitches. With a little polish it should fly."

"That's a relief." She smooths the papers onto the table and turns to Flint. "You know, Jump has helped me profile the guys in the platoon."

"Really? Maybe I should interview him. I have a talent for dragging out the truth. Journalism tricks."

"It's difficult for him to go there," Abby says. "But he's managed to sift through his memories to help me understand the dynamic of that platoon."

"Really? Let me have it."

"Well, in his capacity as a field psychiatrist, Dr. Jump observed that a few men had intense rivalries with John. He observed friction between John and Lieutenant Chenowith—the West Point grad. Chenowith seemed intimidated by John's fame, and maybe a little jealous."

"I get it," he says, thinking of the way Chenowith ordered him off the forward base. Was it because he didn't want Flint to sniff around and find incriminating evidence? "No love lost there."

"Jump also said that Antoine Hilliard despised John."

"Hilliard?" Flint scratches the stubble on his chin, two days' growth. Flint hates shaving. He liked to think that the stubble made him look intellectual, but at Christmas his mother told him it was "downright seedy." "I didn't pick up on any friction there. But you know, Hilliard was killed by a bomb."

"Yes, I heard that, so if he had something to do with John's death, the trail ends there." Abby rubs her hands together. "Jump also noted that John and Noah had an intense sibling rivalry, something I was aware of but never considered a factor in John's death. I find it hard to believe that Noah would ever hurt his brother, let alone kill him, but Jump thinks it highly suspect that Noah fled after John died. He believes that Noah ran off to escape prosecution."

"Oh, come on." Flint smacks his forehead. A few weeks out of town and this nincompoop steps in and fills Abby's head with asinine theories like this. "Noah isn't the first war resister to go AWOL and flee to Canada. Granted, the guy had a total meltdown after his brother died, but can you blame him? And honestly, if my boss told me I had to go back to Iraq right now, I think I'd run off to Canada, too."

"I understand that, Flint." Abby pulls the sleeves of her sweatshirt over her hands and folds her arms across her chest. "I want to believe in Noah, too, but often, in homicides, the killer is someone you know well."

"Don't you think I know that?" Anger sluices through his veins, cold and steely. He rubs his cold hands together, not wanting to lash out at Abby, despite the fact that this conversation has gone from bizarre to ridiculous. "I've covered crime beats. I've quoted statistics."

"Then you have to agree, Noah is a loaded suspect."

He shakes his head. "Every soldier in goddamned Fallujah

at that time is a goddamned suspect. Pardon my French." He blows on his hands, and his breath forms a puff in the air. "It's cold in here."

"Freezing, again." Abby rubs her hands over her arms as she marches to the thermostat on the wall in the hallway. "I don't know what's wrong with the furnace. Look, it's set at sixty-eight, but it's fifty-two degrees in here."

"Fifty-two? Sounds like a thermostat problem." He joins her at the wall, noticing that the thermostat hangs just a few inches from that photograph of John and Dr. Dickhead. "It wasn't that cold when I came in a minute ago."

Abby shakes her head. "This keeps happening when Charles is here. I wonder if he turns it down when I'm not looking."

"Part Eskimo, is he?"

"I was thinking it's a reaction to being so hot in Iraq. Over-compensating," she says in a quiet voice so the idiot in the bedroom can't hear. "You know, those hundred-and-thirty-degree days you have in the desert?"

"If that isn't a load of psycho-crap."

"Pardon your French." She jiggles the thermostat and sighs. "I give up! Suz keeps saying that John's ghost is turning the heat off."

"His ghost?" He grins, watching as Abby crosses to the couch and bundles the fleece throw over her shoulders. Somehow the notion of John's ghost, like Topper, messing with the furnace lightens things up and almost lets him forget about the jerk getting dressed in Abby's bedroom. Almost. "You gotta love Suz. So is the ghost trying to save you money on heating bills, or just trying to piss you off?"

"Something tells me you're not taking this seriously, but it's odd. I've had a furnace specialist out here and he tells me it's working fine, which it was while he was here."

"Wait!" He blows on his hands for warmth. "Didn't you say the temperature drops only when Jump is here? I'm thinking Suz is right. John's ghost is trying to freeze the guy out." He lets out a laugh, though it lacks heart.

But Abby is not amused. "Okay, that's it." She whirled around, blanket trailing her down the hall.

"Where are you going?" he asks.

"To confront Jump about changing the thermostat," she calls over her shoulder.

He plants one hand on the wall and leans in over the small square box housing the brains of the heating system. Maybe it's a faulty wire? He is jiggling the switch when something moves in his peripheral vision. A crashing bang follows.

He turns to see that one of Abby's framed portraits has fallen off the wall—the picture of John and Jump.

"What kind of guy gives a girl a photo of himself with her dead husband as a Christmas gift?" he mutters under his breath as he bends down to pick up the photo. As he reaches for it he sees that it's cracked, the glass splintered in small shards. Not only that, but the polished pewter frame is cold to the touch, as if it's been in a freezer.

Upon holding it closer for examination, Flint sees the glass fog up before his eyes. Ice crystals blossom in separate patches then spread until the entire panel of glass is painted white with . . . frost?

And the frame is so cold, he worries that his fingers might adhere to its surface, frozen together. He releases it, letting it drop the last inch or so to the floor as he straightens.

"What are you doing?" Abby asks, coming up behind him. "Flint! Did you just toss my picture on the floor?"

"I didn't break it. It fell off the wall, shattered. I just picked it up and . . ."

"I can't believe you." She kneels and picks it up. The moment she sees the smashed glass, her face crumples, her lips puckering in a pout that takes a good twenty years away. "You didn't have to break it."

"I didn't! Abby . . ."

"You don't have to like Jump," she says in a quavering voice, "but please, have some respect for John's memory."

"Abby . . ." He gets accused of having no respect, but the guy getting dressed in Abby's bedroom, wearing the clean clothes she laundered, is a good guy? Frustrated, Flint wheels away from her, not wanting to say anything that will further inflame the situation, knowing that nothing he says or does in this moment will be construed the right way.

"I gotta go." He grabs his laptop and strides to the door, expecting Abby to try and stop him. To apologize. To maintain the peace. To beg him to stay.

But she is conspicuously silent as he pushes out the door into the driving rain.

My mistake, he thinks. *My mistake from the beginning. I was wrong to e-mail her when I learned about John. Wrong to try and help her. Wrong to come here. Wrong to fall for her.*

Opening up to Abby was like sticking a knife in his own gut and twisting it around a few times. *I am the king of schmucks.*

Chapter 54

Outside Fort Lewis
Emjay

When you're on guard duty, every dark doorway might open to an insurgent with a rifle. Every person walking on the street might be your murderer.

Emjay Brown did not want to venture out alone.

He would have preferred to stay in the apartment, keeping watch at the window.

But he needed to ease the pain, dull the fear. He ran out of pills from Doc, burned through the beers and whiskey he bought with his last pay check.

And the only way he knows to self-medicate in a pinch is whiskey.

So here he is, creeping along the street in the middle of the night, a moving target as he passes under the yellow gloom of streetlights.

Not a good hood to be out in at night without a partner, without a second pair of eyes to cover you.

But he has his rifle.

"A soldier never goes anywhere without his rifle."

"Sir, yes, sir!"

His trench coat covers the weapon just fine, so people don't freak out. Of course, he walks with a limp, the rifle swinging against his leg when he moves. That's okay. Better to be bruised and alive.

In the distance, two white lights pop out of nowhere, and he breaks into a run.

The lights are coming at him, closing on him, faster, faster . . .

He lunges toward a bus shelter and swings inside for cover just before the lights of a car try to sweep over him. They miss, but too close for comfort.

His breath is a raspy hiss in the hollow shell of the bus stop.

Damn, but they shouldn't send him out here alone. A one-man mission is suicide in the desert.

The pumping, slamming, jamming in his chest has got to stop. Goddamn, it's so fast. But it will only slow when he gets a drink.

And where are the reinforcements?

His mission objective is two blocks away.

Two long blocks.

Heart racing. Erratic. It's going to pop before he gets there.

This is the dark stretch of road, no light here by the park.

Like you need a park here in the middle of nowhere, here where green surrounds you.

He crouches low as he moves along the park's perimeters. It's a relief to be out of the light, but there are too many shrubs and trees in the park where insurgents could hide.

Stay low.

Keep away from them.

Suicide bombers.

Roadside bombs.

Rocket-propelled grenades, missiles that will scorch your soul.

He scurries quickly past a hunk of stone the size of a tractor, then crouches behind a bench. If his heart would stop thudding, clamoring, it would be easier to get there. With his sleeve, he wipes the sweat from his brow and stares into the park, looking for them.

Fear flares in his chest at the thought of moving on. How will he get there alive with all these obstacles coming at him? Oh, God.

Another set of white lights floats toward him . . . and another. And one in the distance. A convoy.

Our guys? Friendlies? And can they be trusted?

He squints into the light, hopeful, until it happens.

The explosion from one of the cars, a shot that cracks the night.

"Eerrr!" Belly in the dirt, he fires his weapon, bracing his finger on the trigger. But the familiar jolt of rapid-fire rounds never comes. There is only one shot, a single bullet that skitters off harmlessly into the dark abyss.

What the hell?

What is this piece of shit in his arms?

He looks down and sees, not his familiar M-16, but an old hunting rifle.

What nightmare is this?

He combat-crawls under the park bench and curls up there, shivering. Something skitters over his head and he scratches his scalp feverishly to scrape off the itch. If he stays here, low and quiet, maybe they won't come. Maybe the convoy will move past him and the night will become quiet again. Squeezed into the compact space, he thinks himself safe.

Safe as the hill beyond the chicken coops on a balmy summer night.

Chapter 55

Lakeside Hospital
Madison

"So . . . do you think I'm crazy?" Madison asks as she goes through the books on the shelf of the shrink's office. Mostly dusty, fat textbooks. Snooze.

"I think crazy means different things to different people," he answers. "The question is, would you like to have more psychological stability? Would you like to feel more grounded?"

"Yes . . . and no." She takes a deep breath, thinking about it. "I'd like to feel safe, like it's okay to stand still for a minute. But then, I wouldn't want to give up the ability to fly." She turns back to face him, the man in the navy doctor's coat who now sits straddling his wheely desk chair like a cowboy in a saloon. He's cute—a buff body lingers under that lab coat—but way too military for her taste. Something about him seems so anal. Probably washes his soap dish. "The thing is," she goes on, pacing over to the wall where a bunch of degrees are mounted, "if you're going to keep flying, sometimes you're going to crash and burn."

"And you don't mind that? The moments when you're crashing?"

"Of course I do." She reads the first diploma from Rutgers. That's right. She remembers he went to school with John. "Charles D. Jump." She turns back to him and crosses her arms. "What's the D. stand for, Chucky?"

He winces. "I usually don't tell, but I will if you promise not to call me that again?"

"Hit a soft spot, did I?" She grins. "So what should I call you?"

"Doc would be fine."

"As in, 'What's up, Doc?'" When he doesn't laugh, she shrugs. "Yeah, I guess you heard that one before."

"Only a hundred times."

She can feel him watching her as she crosses to the closed door, where two fresh navy lab coats are hanging on a hook. "What's with the lab coats?" she asks, pulling one jacket off its hook and slipping it on. The fabric feels crisp under her fingers. "Do you need a degree to wear one of these ugly things?"

"Yes, you do. That ugly coat actually costs about a hundred thousand dollars in student loans."

"Ouch. That's fickle fashion for you." The sleeves dangle down to her knees and she's getting the soft scent of fabric softener. Suddenly, the act of trying on the coat seems sort of sexy, like she was jumping into his bathrobe or something. Quickly, she sheds the jacket, hangs it up and goes to the window.

She didn't want to come here. It's nerves that are making her blabber on like this, nerves and a streak of rebellion that flared when she learned Dr. Charles Jump was going to be her therapist. When she agreed to see someone, she pictured a kind, nonintimidating woman like Abby.

Not a rangy man with eyes like glue. Not a shrink with a hot bod under his lab coat. Definitely not someone so army.

Aren't you supposed to be able to pick your own therapist?

Madison didn't like her mother hooking up with a doctor who carved the roast at Christmas Eve dinner. "Geez, Ma, you really beat the bushes to find someone for me," she had complained to her mother.

But, hey, it could be worse. What if she complained and they switched her to a warty old lech? Or a brittle birdwoman? Or one of those foreign doctors you can't understand? Sienna had to see this Asian gynecologist who cracked a joke about burned eggs, and Sienna freaked, thinking that the eggs in her ovaries were scorched. Scary.

"You know, you're welcome to have a seat," he says.

"Do you want me to lie on the couch?"

"You can if you want to."

"Do other people come in and flake out there?"

"Many people find it freeing. Relax the body, free the mind."

"I think it's weird." She goes to the leather couch and perches on its square arm. The leather feels slippery under the seat of her jeans. "Does somebody clean it, like the seats on a commercial jet?"

"It's very clean," he says. "As is the fish tank, which we'll discuss next session. I'd like to spend part of my time hearing about you, Madison."

"What do you want me to say?" She shrugs. "Honestly, my life is boring. School. Homework. Text messaging. Hanging out. Only I'm not allowed to do that anymore because my parents are sure my friends are a bad influence."

"Are they?"

Madison takes a breath, not sure how much of the truth she wants to share. "They don't influence me," she says curtly. "Although I wish they did. My life would be so much more interesting."

He leans his chin on the back of the chair, a listening posture. "In what ways? How are your friends so outlandish?"

Now there's an open question. And the ironic part is that there's nothing outlandish to reveal. What is she supposed to say, that Sienna likes to be with Ziggy when she's feeling slutty? That Ziggy has a weakness for weed?

Boring.

"If I tell you, it's confidential, right?" she asks.

He nods. "Doctor-patient privilege."

"You know all those fires that were started in state parks, all around the Seattle area?" She bites her lower lip, improvising. "My friend Ziggy started them. He likes to go out on weekends and play pyro."

"Does he? And how do you feel about that?"

She shrugs. "Sometimes I get nervous that he's going to get caught. I mean, he's seventeen. They would try him as an adult now, right?"

"Probably."

Madison turns away and stares into the fish tank, conjuring her next story. "And Sienna? My BFF. She's got her issues, too."

"What's up with her?"

"It's awful." As an angelfish flutters by she considers telling Doc that Sienna is a nympho who sleeps with all the male teachers at the high school, but that seems so stale. "Sienna has a problem with . . ."

Quick! Fill in the blank, she thinks.

". . . cutting," she says, going on to tell him how Sienna has scars up and down her arms. All self-inflicted cuts from a razor blade. Winging it, she tells him that Sienna carved Ziggy's name into her arm. But as soon as she says it, she realizes how stupid she sounds. Nobody would ever do that, would they?

"Cutting is a problem we're seeing more and more of these days," Doc says.

"Not such a big problem in this part of the world," she says wryly, "since we never get enough sun to wear a short-sleeved shirt."

She turns away from the fish tank to catch his eye, but he's not laughing.

But at least he's not pissed off, either.

"Forget Ziggy and Sienna for now." He straightens, his pale blue eyes zapping her. "How about Madison? What does Madison like to do for fun?"

She folds her arms across her chest. "For fun, I send e-mails to my brother," she says.

"To Noah? Or John."

Madison grins. "Both."

Now he smiles, but it's just a little trickle of a grin, as if he's trying not to laugh at a funeral.

But still, it's a smile, she thinks, letting her gaze slide down his buff body down to the cool green clogs. His scrubs are navy blue, and the color suits him well. You can see the chain of his dog tags at his neck, and he likes to grab hold of this gold medal that also hangs there and run it over the chain. She just bets that medal is hot to the touch, and she can't help but wonder if he's wearing boxers or briefs under those scrubs.

Not that she would ever do anything to find out. She's in enough trouble without getting into an older man's pants, especially an older man who's her therapist. Ick. It's just that sometimes her mind goes to weird places.

"Do you miss your brothers?" Doc asks.

"Well, duh."

"I'll take that as a yes," he says casually.

Madison turns back to the fish and begins to think that therapy might not be so bad after all. In fact, hanging with Doc is going to be okay.

Chapter 56

Lakeside Hospital
Abby

"**N**ow before we go upstairs for a tour of the psych ward, let's just go over our expectations of you as a student intern here at Lakeside so's you don't overstep your bounds and I don't get pissed off at you." When she lectures her new brood, Rhonda Hobart has the wily charm of a grandmother chastising her charges for breaking curfew. The harsh fluorescent lights of the conference room cast a bluish sheen on her dark skin, which is not at all unattractive. With the blue glow, her oversized earrings, and her exotic hairstyle, a complicated weave atop her head crowned by a braid of hair, Rhonda has the makings of a superhero: Rhonda, Queen of Orientation.

Abby finds Rhonda reassuring. For the time she's been in this conference room filling out forms and listening to other guest speakers from Human Resources, the college, and the Emergency Room, she's forgotten her worries about this internship at Lakeside.

"The focus of your five-month joy ride here will be therapeutic communication," Rhonda says. "Good ol' TC. You're going to get very sick of hearing those two letters, but you will learn how to execute this form of therapy effectively while you're under my wing. Now, I know you haven't seen the ward yet, but can anyone tell me where it's appropriate to meet with a patient to practice therapeutic communication?"

A girl in the front, with flat dark hair and owlish brown

glasses raises her hand. "In the Day Room, or in group, or in the dining hall."

"Excellent. And your name is . . . ?"

"Cilla."

"And tell me, Cilla, where is the one place where you will not linger with the patient?"

"Their room?" For a mousey-looking woman, Cilla possesses a low, gruff voice.

"Exactly. Our approach is to encourage interaction, and that means getting the patients out of their rooms, drawing them out of themselves. That's why each patient must attend group therapy at least twice a day, as well as a twelve-step program meeting. Meal and snack times are also a social occasion, an opportunity to get patients talking and sharing. You are going to say 'How does that make you feel?' so many times, you'll be saying it in your sleep."

A few student interns chuckle. Rhonda, who paces among the desks as she speaks, grins. Abby senses that Rhonda enjoys playing the hard-ass instructor, but she senses a big heart and a good sense of humor beneath that psychedelic scrub shirt.

"Now, we are not allowed to post a patient roster on the Web site for reasons of confidentiality, but you will find rosters and case notes available upstairs. It's your responsibility to apprise yourself of patients' backgrounds and diagnoses. You must know which patients are flight risks or suicide risks. You must know who is on a special diet and why.

"Most of our patients upstairs are substance abusers, and that usually means alcoholism. We currently have a young female patient suffering from body dysmorphic disorder. She has a distorted view of herself, thinks she looks hideous." She wags a finger at the group. "I'm only pointing this out because it's rare. Something you might never come across again. We also have our share of patients in treatment for chemical dependency, but you'll see that our overall treatment program is the same. Every patient—bipolar, eating disorder, chemical dependency—must attend group and the twelve-step meeting.

"I'm assuming you all downloaded the article on therapeutic communication that I posted on the Web site for you. You will need this article. I repeat, keep this article. Since this is your main approach throughout your internship, let's go over the main points."

Although Abby flips her notes open to the article, her gaze slips to the door, her mind wondering what will happen when they go upstairs to the ward. Dr. Charles Jump is one of the directors of psychological services, and it's inevitable that they will run into each other here in the hospital from time to time. She counts herself lucky that she managed to slip in this morning for her first day without an encounter with him.

Shifting in her chair, she smooths her brand-new purple scrub shirt around her neck and wonders if Jump has gotten over their last encounter. Such an ugly scene.

She should have been more cautious, more true to herself. She didn't get it the day that Flint dropped by, found Jump showering at her place, and flipped out. At the time, she thought Flint was overreacting. Granted, Jump was an imposition at times, but she tried to put up with him, keeping in mind that he'd been a friend to John.

But Abby's annoyance progressed as Jump pushed and pushed. He made himself comfortable on her couch. He made himself a copy of her key so that he wouldn't have to bother her to do laundry. A week or so later, when Jump was there showering once again due to lack of hot water in his housing quarters, Abby started to feel that he was invading her personal space. She was choking, feeling strangled by Jump, who didn't seem to understand personal limits.

Galvanized by the need to be free, Abby tugged a basket of clean clothes into the living room and started folding. She hadn't been planning to finish his laundry for him, but while he was in the shower she realized that if she sent the clothes home with him, he would no longer have that excuse to stop by.

Of course, they would have to have "the talk." Although they were never really an item, Abby would have to end this relationship that had sort of crept into her house. But for today, she figured getting Jump and his laundry out of her house would be a good start.

"You can take your laundry with you when you go today," she called when she heard the bathroom door open. She tucked stacks of clothes into his canvas bag.

"No rush," he said, emerging from the bathroom with a towel slung low over his hips. He paused in the hallway, as if modeling Cannon bath towels. "I'll come back for it tomorrow."

"No problem, it's all ready now." She leaned into the bag to stuff in a bundle of socks. When she straightened, he was standing so close she could see the beads of water on his neck.

"Or, we could take the laundry into the bedroom and just unpack," he said. "Why should I bring it back and forth when I spend all of my time here?"

"You know, we need to talk about that." Abby checked her temper as a million angry responses bubbled in her brain. "I think it would be best if we took a break for a while."

"You can't abandon me. I won't let you." In one step he swallowed the space between them and slid his arms around her waist.

She was not going to kiss him. This was going to stop now. "Please, don't make this difficult. I thought—"

"Sometimes you think too much," he said, pressing himself against her, clamping his mouth over hers. She could feel his erection against her pelvis.

So wrong.

"No," she gasped, breaking free of the liplock. Her hands slid over his slick shoulders as she tried to push him away. "Jump, stop it."

"You know you want it." Taking her by surprise, he gripped her by the waist and pushed her until her back was against the wall.

"No. Get off me." It was a struggle, but she managed to wriggle away, scraping her elbow in the process. She turned away and tightened the drawstring on his laundry bag, thinking she'd give him a moment to calm down. "I really want you to get dressed and leave. Now." She expected him to go quietly.

"You can't dismiss me just like that. I've grown very attached to you, Abby. You know that. And I'm not going to just take my stuff and walk out on what could be something very satisfying between the two of us."

She felt his hands on her shoulders again, his pelvis pressing into her backside. "Mutually satisfying."

"Okay, that's the last time you're going to touch me." She wheeled, breaking free of his grip. Her hands quivered as she reached for her cell phone on the kitchen counter. "Move toward me again, and I'm calling the Military Police. Their response time is pretty damned good, and I think they'll be pretty quick to toss you on your face when they hear that you're trying to assault John Stanton's widow."

"Oh, come on! You're going to bring John into this now? Play the old celebrity card, like he's some kind of god. Is that your plan? Well, news flash: that well has run dry. Your celebrity husband is dead. His name and status aren't going to play around here anymore."

"I can't believe I just heard that." Abby flipped her cell phone open, finger at the ready. "You'd better go. Right now, or I swear, I'll call the MP."

"Save your cell phone minutes. I'm going." He went to the bathroom to retrieve his clothes and returned clothed, then dragged the laundry bag to the door and tossed it to the porch, before turning back to scowl at her. "There are lots of other whores out there who'd love to ball a doctor like me."

On that sour note he finally walked out, leaving Abby feeling scared and a little cheapened from having known him.

She wonders why she didn't cut off their relationship sooner. Maybe if she'd acted differently, told him no a few times when he was creeping into her life, if she'd made so many choices differently, this wouldn't have happened.

Maybe if . . . what if . . .

Of course, intellectually, she knows better.

It wasn't her fault.

Abby hasn't seen Charles Jump since that unpleasant day. When she reported to the hospital this morning and found that Rhonda Hobart would be her adviser, she started to think that she could work through her internship with a minimum of awkwardness. Granted, Jump is one of the head honchos—her boss's boss—but Abby doesn't think they'll ever cross paths professionally. She should be all right here at Lakeside.

Abby is going to pretend it never happened and hope that it goes away. She is going to be one of the best damned psych interns this hospital has ever seen and hope that she never crosses paths with Dr. Charles Jump once she leaves here.

That afternoon, she called a locksmith and had the tumblers changed on every door. She checked the window locks, told her new neighbors Ed and Marilyn that Jump was no longer welcome at her home, and so far it hadn't been a problem.

Until today.

The atmosphere in the conference room has changed now; the meeting is winding down. People flip their notes closed, get up, toss empty coffee cups into the trash bin. Half the group heads off to HR, while the other half will go upstairs for the tour of the ward on the thirteenth floor. Rhonda has explained that they cannot bring more than a handful of interns through the ward at one time, as the patients find it intimidating.

Upstairs, Nurse Hobart shows the five interns how to use their ID cards to unlock the door to the psych ward. The group files into the open nurses' station, where Rhonda shows them how to access patient files on the computer.

Standing in the nurses' station, Abby observes that the Day Room, the largest meeting area, designed to be a combination living room, den, TV room, and craft station, reminds her a lot of the movie *One Flew Over the Cuckoo's Nest.* An attempt at a cheerful mural of daisies has been painted on the widest wall. The chairs are either plastic or upholstered in vinyl.

"All the furniture is bolted down," Rhonda says, "so don't go trying to be moving a chair around. Most of the patients are in group therapy right now, which is why it's so quiet out here."

Rhonda moves to a patient in the corner, snoring loudly, in what appears to be an easy chair on wheels. "How you doing, honey?" She pats his hands, folded at his waist, and he shivers in reaction but does not open his eyes.

"That poor man is heavily sedated." Rhonda shakes her head as she leads the group away from him. "Haven't seen the whites of his eyes for days."

Rhonda shows them one of the empty patient rooms, which is small and bare bones—no mirrors, windows, or art work on the walls. There is no bathroom door, and the doors to the patient rooms are kept locked open unless they're in lockdown.

"Not much privacy," Cilla comments.

"None at all," Rhonda agrees. "Patients are here to interact. They want privacy, they can check into the Ritz. Probably costs the same amount." They move down the hall, pausing outside a meeting room. "The rooms for the group meetings are equally spartan," Rhonda says in a lowered voice. "Take a quick look, but don't interrupt."

From her vantage point Abby sees the therapist, a short man with thick blond hair and skinny round glasses. He appears to be listening while a woman with her knees tucked under her chin speaks. There's a heavyset man with an eyepatch, a woman slumped to the side, a man who has the straight posture and shaved head of a well-trained soldier.

"Come along, little chicks." Rhonda calls Abby and the other student away.

Back at the nurses' station, Rhonda steps up to the computer. "Each of you has been assigned three or four patients. You can start meeting with them this afternoon, start writing up your notes on how you are drawing them out through TC."

The interns take their patient lists and eagerly begin to read.

"I got the dysmorphic!" Alicia's eyebrows wiggle.

"Pyromania . . ." someone else says.

"Hush, children," Rhonda says.

Abby skims her list and falters on the second name. "Emjay Brown? It can't be." She skims through Emjay's case history, which shows his assignment in Iraq with John's squad. A chill shivers down her spine when she sees that he is assigned to Dr. Charles Jump.

Of course, it is the same person. Abby kicks herself. *You should have done something for him that day; you saw him suffer through that flashback.*

"You got a problem?" Rhonda asks.

"I know this man. I never expected to see him here."

Rhonda frowns at the list. "Is he a friend?"

"More like an acquaintance. Shouldn't I be taken off his case?"

"Well, with this patient, he wouldn't recognize you if you were his mama." She nods toward the Day Room. "He's the patient snoring out there. I wouldn't worry about compromising treatment because of a personal connection. He's not waking up anytime soon."

"Shouldn't the dosage of the sedative be reduced?"

"It probably should, but then nurses don't prescribe, and neither do interns. And Dr. Jump does not take kindly to having his orders questioned." She looks over her shoulder to make sure no one was listening in. "Most of the docs in this ward are sweethearts. They'll work with you. But Dr. Jump, he's okay sometimes, but when he's got one of his funks on, no amount of sweet-talking is going to sway him. He'll rip you a new one, just like that." She snaps her fingers.

In the Day Room, Abby sits beside Emjay and rubs the back of his hand. "Hey, Emjay. Can you wake up? It's Abby, John's wife. Do you remember John? John Stanton. You worked together. You guys were buddies in Iraq."

There is no response.

Discouraged, she meets another patient on her list, a young woman named Tara who is fighting an addiction to crystal meth. Only twenty-three, Tara has a little girl, who is currently staying with Tara's mother. Together they make colored flowers out of tissue paper, while Tara talks about why it makes her uncomfortable to leave Amber with her mother.

After that, the patients head into group therapy and Abby

returns to Emjay's side. He is still sleeping but restless now, writhing in his seat, pressing against the cloth bindings on his wrists. She feels for him, knowing that just a few months ago he was a healthy, active man.

She talks to him, telling him how she misses John. "Did you know he set up half a dozen bird feeders around our house? And guess who has to keep them filled with seeds and sugar water for the hummingbirds?" She talks about Suz and Sofia, what they did for Christmas, how they're adjusting to their new home. She asks him where he would like to go when he's finished with the army. "Where is home for you, Emjay?"

His breathing is the steady drone of narcotic.

"Emjay? I'm Abby. Do you remember me?"

He opens his eyes, his lids twittering. It seems a struggle for him to focus, but when his gaze meets hers there's no sign of recognition.

Emjay Brown is so heavily sedated, it's a wonder he can still breathe.

Spotting a physician in a navy lab coat, Abby pats Emjay's hand and goes over to the doctor. "Excuse me? I was wondering if you could look at the medications my patient is on? He has no record of voluntary movement for the past three days, since he was admitted, actually."

The woman, an older physician with ginger-colored hair tied back and a black mole beside her mouth, frowns. "Whose patient is he?"

"Dr. Jump."

The woman—Dr. Holland, her name tag says—holds up a hand. "You really need to contact him."

"Please, Dr. Holland." Abby holds up Emjay's chart, concocting a quick lie. "I tried to page him, but he's out of town for a few days. And it would be a shame to keep this patient sedated that long."

Sighing, Dr. Holland flips through the chart. "The levels are high . . . but this patient has a history of violence."

"Post-traumatic stress," Abby says quickly. "He served in Iraq."

"I appreciate that. However, we're responsible for making sure he doesn't hurt himself or anyone else."

"But he can't receive effective therapy if he remains in a vegetative state." Abby can barely believe her own nerve, the hubris to talk back to a doctor.

But Dr. Holland doesn't appear to be offended as she flips through the chart once again, shaking her head. "That *is* a high dosage of Ativan." She flips back to the front page and scribbles something. "I'm adjusting his meds. But make sure Dr. Jump is apprised of this as soon as he returns."

"Absolutely. Thank you." Abby takes the chart back with a mixture of relief and horror.

Her first day on the job and she's intervened in a patient's care.

She just lied to a doctor.

And she's planning to lie again, for as long as it takes to give Emjay Brown a chance to become himself again.

Chapter 57

The last time Sharice dropped in on Jim's office at I-Corp was . . . well, never. At least, not that he can remember.

So it's natural that her visit today is causing a ripple of surprise among his coworkers.

"Well, hey, Sharice. How's everything going?" Grady Bullard swings by the door on his way back from the coffeemaker, his mug in hand.

"I'm fine, Grady," Sharice says as her fingers flicker a wave to Jim, who's trying to coax a few last copies from a printer with a dying ink cartridge. "How are the kids?"

"Good. Playing traveling basketball. That's my life, one gym to another."

"You look fabulous!" Teresa says, peeking over the top of her cubicle. "Took me a minute to recognize you."

Sharice's brows shoot up. "Thanks, I guess."

"No, no!" Teresa throws her arms in the air and runs around the cubicle to join Sharice. "I just meant that we so rarely see you here, I couldn't place your face. And you do look terrific. Did you change your hair?"

Sharice loosens the scarf around her neck. "Must be my new shade of lipstick."

Jim glances up from the copier. Did she really change lipsticks? He didn't notice that, although he has been aware of Sharice in new ways of late. The smell of violet emanating from her hair. The way she tucks the covers so neatly under her chin. The way her jeans hug her hips, still curvy and trim after all these years.

In these moments of revelation he sometimes feels that he is married to a stranger, a woman with traits and habits he ought to recognize after nearly thirty years, but somehow, they are new to him. Discoveries. Eye-openers.

But then, he's been rediscovering many things in the past few weeks.

"Did you take lunch yet?" Sharice asks him. "I was hoping we could go for a walk."

"Jim never takes lunch," Grady calls from his desk. "He's a workaholic."

"Then today can be the first." Sharice smiles at him with lips so silvery pink he'd like to glide right over them like a speed skater. Maybe she did get some new lipstick. "Why don't you get your jacket? We can split a quesadilla at Madigan Café."

Jim holds the door for Sharice, who chooses this time to tell him about how her ladies' group is working on a list of recommended treats for soldiers in Iraq. "Since people want to help, we want them to know what foods can and cannot survive the trip," she says.

While she shares an anecdote about chocolates that were shipped over with calamitous results, Jim latches onto the sights around him. Gardeners blowing leaves from a median strip with a statue of Meriwether Lewis, two women pushing strollers, joggers, a UPS delivery truck.

The walk from Jim's office to the café takes them across a picturesque part of the base past the green fields of a park and tidy rows of brick houses with dormer windows, all set off by white picket fences. With the twenty-five-mile-per-hour speed limit and the bold white clouds framing Mount Rainier in the distance, the base could be any small American town fifty years ago. Just beyond the park was a shot of blue—American Lake. On the Fourth of July, this park would be packed with people awaiting the fireworks display.

Jim sucks it all in, a breath of America.

There was a time in his life when he thought he wouldn't live to enjoy a sight like this again. Desperate days and nights. He's trying to let those memories recede. Not that they'll ever go away completely, but Dr. Jump says they can draw back.

The sea at low tide.

"I just came from the pharmacy," Sharice says as they cross the street to the walkway along the lake. "Madison needed a refill on her medication from Dr. Jump, and . . . I don't know why, but I had a moment of panic in the store. As I checked the medication and glanced at the printout listing all the possible side effects, I got frightened. Really scared, Jim. I mean, we've lost the boys, and now our baby needs therapy and serious medication for depression?"

"She's under a doctor's care. Dr. Jump is the best."

"But she's so young. Still a kid, with very adult problems."

"Madison has been through a lot for a kid her age. We all have, Sharice, but can you imagine dealing with all this at her age?"

Old-fashioned lampposts line the waterfront walkway along with benches that face out to American Lake, which today is a sea of dark blue. When the sun moves from behind the clouds, diamonds of light dance in a line on its surface. Jim moves to the left to skirt one of the benches, thinking of how, last week when he was jogging, he ran right over one, up then down, never breaking stride, like Gene Kelly in one of those old-time movies. It's a testament to the way he's been feeling since the new year, an affirmation of hope.

For the first time in months, he's sleeping again. Peaceful sleep, most of the time. Though the nightmares still rattle his cage on occasion, they are rare, and not quite so vivid. Sleep can cure a world of ills, though nothing can bring back a son.

He turns toward Sharice, thinking of the things they have survived together. It's a wonder that any marriage survives the twisted road two people must endure. "It's a beautiful day," he says. "But you don't ever join me for lunch. What's on your mind?"

She connects with his gaze, her brown eyes full of rue. "Jim, what's Lexapro for?"

A wave of sickness washes over him with the question.

She knows. Dammit, she found out.

"It's used to treat depression and anxiety."

She nods. "And you didn't think to tell me you were going to start taking antidepressants?"

"How did you find out?"

"The pharmacy. When I went to pick up Madison's refill, they handed me yours, too. Why didn't you tell me, Jim? Am I that unapproachable?"

"It's not you," he says. "It's not even the Lexapro that embarrasses me. It's therapy. I started seeing Dr. Jump back in December, after the battalion reunion party."

Sharice squints at him. "When did you find the time?"

"He fit me in during my lunch hour so no one would know. Dr. Jump is a good guy, a great soldier, and the Harvard credential doesn't hurt. The soldiering bond helped me relate, really trust him. He diagnosed me with post-traumatic stress disorder. I know, I know, I've always thought that was just a sissy's excuse to get out of serving. It stems from my tours in 'Nam, and the nightmares and insomnia, it's all tied in. Do you know that post-traumatic stress can occur years later?"

"This is good," Sharice says. "You have to know I would have been supportive. But why didn't you tell me?" Her voice is thick with emotion. "Oh my God, Jim, how many years have we been married, and you keep something like this a secret?"

"It's my own hangup." Jim wants to kick himself a few dozen times. He never wanted to hurt Sharice this way. "I never believed in all that crap about getting in touch with your feelings. But then I got to the point where my feelings tainted everything I did."

"Set off by John's death, wasn't it?" she asks. "All the bad feelings, the insomnia . . ."

He nods. "John's death was the catalyst to bring that stuff to the surface, and it also didn't hurt to lose Noah." He turns away, not able to go there, not even sure why he mentioned the name that's never spoken between them. "Anyhow, Dr. Jump says it probably would have been set off by something else at a later time. Good to work it all out now."

"I guess." Sharice takes his hand, lifts it, presses it to her cheek. "I've been so worried about you."

"I know." He leans forward and kisses her on the lips, lightly. When was the last time he kissed her in public? It feels scandalous, and downright sexy for a man pushing sixty.

"When they handed me the prescription, I was so worried. I thought, maybe something was wrong with you. Then . . . I was just blindsided. In the past few weeks, you've been sleeping better, laughing more. You seem, well, maybe happy is pushing it for a surly crust like you, but you seem more at peace."

He smiles. Sharice started calling him a surly crust when he was in his twenties; the nickname suited him then, as it still does today.

"Do you think that's the Lexapro working?" she asks.

"Could be. I've been on it for more than a month now. That and the therapy. Dr. Jump has gotten a lot of stuff out of me, things I thought I'd forgotten."

She lifts both their hands in the air, stepping back in awe. "Look at you! You're a success story for therapy."

"Grudgingly. I still think there are a lot of quacks out there. But Dr. Jump is good people. That's why I feel completely confident having Madison under his care."

"You really trust him?"

"One hundred percent."

Chapter 58

Lakeside Hospital
Abby

Three days after the dosage of sedative is reduced, Emjay Brown once again manages to speak. "What day is it?"

"Wednesday."

He motions for water, and Abby brings the cup's straw to his lips. But now, for the first time, he takes it from her and drinks.

Abby watches him attentively, resisting the urge to jump up and do a happy dance in the middle of the Day Room. She has been by his side for many hours during the past three days. At times he asked for a drink, and once he even had her change the channel on the television until she hit on a basketball game. But this is the first time he's strung words together.

He braces his arms in the chair to take in the surroundings, the plant hanging from the ceiling in the corner, the mural of flowers on the far wall. "I really fucked up this time. I made it to the Cuckoo's Nest."

"You're in Lakeside Hospital, in the psych ward. Do you know why you're here, Emjay?"

He takes another sip, thinking. "I was under attack." He closes his eyes. "A convoy. A whole mess of armored vehicles. And my gun . . . it wasn't my gun. I looked down and all I had for firepower was some lame hunting rifle."

"Is that what you remember?"

"I think so. Or maybe that part's a dream. I don't know." His chin lolls to his chest. "Do you know what happened?"

"You were found on Mason Boulevard with a rifle in the middle of the night," Abby says.

"Jesus Christ." He rubs his knuckles over the growth on his cheek. "Did I hurt anyone?"

"A shot was fired from the rifle, but it jammed after that. The police found a slug lodged in a tree by the road." Abby knows this because she has researched that night, checked news accounts and police reports. She thought Emjay would want to know.

"A small mercy." He sighs and scratches his upper arms.

"How do you feel now?"

"Like somebody turned the world on slow motion. Like I'm trying to run underwater with lead shoes. Everything is slow."

"You're on medication to stabilize you. Dr. Jump has you on Ativan to relax you, and Wellbutrin for depression."

"Well, that explains it." He scratches his arms vigorously, then falls back in the chair as if the itching has exhausted him. "That explains why I feel so dead."

"You feel dead," she says. "That feeling probably isn't completely caused by the medications. Have you ever heard of post-traumatic stress disorder?"

He closes his eyes and nods.

"Very often, episodes like the one you just had occur months after a stressful incident, a stressor, like an accident, an attack, a violent war experience."

He nods again, but this time his dark brown cheeks are streaked with tears. "What's going to happen to me?" he asks in a whisper.

"You can work toward recovery."

He shakes his head. "Yeah. Sure."

"Emjay, your episode is a reaction to horrific memories, things you have endured that are difficult for any of us to understand or explain. If you take positive action, one day your reaction to those memories will be less intense. You can improve your ability to cope."

"Can you make it all stop?" he asks.

She's not sure if he's talking about life or his memories. "Do certain images replay in your head?" she asks.

"Over and over. I close my eyes but they're still there. I just want them to stop."

"You know, Emjay, you'll never forget your war experiences. We can't erase them, and we can't completely remove the emotional pain you feel when you remember them."

"Then what's the point?" He leans back in the chair and presses his eyes closed. "What's the point?"

"The point is that we're here to help you if you want to make an attempt at feeling better. And I'm not talking about the fuzzy world of medications. We can come up with a recovery plan together. But you have to be ready to make that commitment." She closes his chart and stands, noticing that his eyes are still closed. He must be exhausted. "You think about what we discussed, okay?"

She returns to the nurses' station and grabs the chart for her new patient, a military wife with a history of alcoholism. Bernadette asked to be admitted after she went on a drinking spree and left her six-month-old with a sitter for three days. Her husband, now deployed in Iraq, is not here to offer emotional support and probably doesn't even know of his wife's meltdown yet.

Abby is reading through Bernadette's chart, composing "therapeutic" questions in her mind, when she hears someone buzz through the door to the ward. Although she's become so accustomed to the buzzer she barely notices, this time something is different. The air seems to chill twenty degrees, and without looking up, she knows it's him.

Dr. Charles Jump.

She has managed to avoid him in her three days on duty, and she was hoping for a fourth until now. A little research, and she learned he was on the evening shift this week. She suspected that he was covering for another doctor at the moment.

Don't let him smell your fear. Don't back down. Just act normal.

He doesn't acknowledge her as he enters the nurses' station and brushes past her, edging her out of the space where the charts are stored.

"Who's been messing with my patients' charts?" He rifles through the open file then turns to her. "Do you have the charts for Dryer and Brown?"

She shakes her head, tying to remain void of expression. "I have Bernadette Conseco." *Not your patient, thank God.*

"Where the hell are my patient charts? Nurse Hobart? Where's Rhonda Hobart?" he calls, swiping past her again. The metal part of his clipboard scrapes her elbow, stinging. Deliberate? Probably, the bastard.

But she refuses to look up and acknowledge the pain.

So much for worrying about any sexual harassment at work. Jump is acting as if he's never met her, which is chilling in a different way.

What kind of person swings to such radical extremes? First, he insists on being a part of her life, helping her in any way he can—his promise to John. Then, he refuses to let their relationship end. "You can't abandon me, I won't let you," he said, first pathetic, then angry. And now, he's cold, slightly hostile, estranged.

Those mood swings, the fear of abandonment . . . Could it be that he suffers from borderline personality disorder? Fluctuating emotions, inappropriate anger . . .

My first week as an intern, and I'm diagnosing the director of psych services.

If that isn't typical of an overenthusiastic student. For now, she will apply her knowledge of the field to the patients she's assigned to work with.

Once she hears his barking voice fade down the hall, she runs her index finger over the tabs of the files until she comes to "E." There in the front of the file is the chart for Emjay Brown. Jump didn't think to look there, and when he asked her if she had it, she was honest when she said no.

Abby glances out at the Day Room where Emjay seems to have drifted off to sleep between a handful of patients involved in an animated card game and Oprah chatting with some author about near-death experiences.

It's been a day of landmarks.

Emjay Brown returned to the land of the living.

She survived a face-to-face with Dr. Jump.

And it looks like she's got Brown's chart concealed from Jump for at least one more day. Of course, all this information will have to go into the hospital databases eventually, but electronic charts are only updated once a week.

She's still got time to help Emjay. Time to solicit another doctor to look at the case. Time to figure out why Charles Jump is determined to either seduce her or hurt her.

Chapter 59

Canada
Noah

Noah Stanton breaks open a fresh bale of hay and loosens it with a pitchfork. Lipsy and Pearl need fresh hay in their stalls. He stabs the pitchfork in and begins tossing the fresh hay into Lipsy's stall. Stab, toss. Stab, toss. The rhythmic motion that once made the muscles in his shoulders and back ache now feels like a soothing song. Work on the Delacroixs' small mixed farm is physical and very tiring, but at the end of the day, sleep is welcome and peaceful.

Lipsy's round, sleepy eye watches him as he corrals her into the cleaned stall. Edna and Collette have had her for many years and she's proven to be an excellent milking cow. He'd been impressed and surprised to meet these women who milked the cows themselves; he didn't think anyone did that anymore.

When he asked where the milking machines were, the old woman clapped her hands to her cheeks dramatically and exclaimed, *"Mon Dieu! Vous êtes ridicule!"* He later figured out she thought he was speaking nonsense, but her disapproval was obvious in that moment.

"We do the milking," Collette explained. A solid young woman with hair the color of caramel cascading from a high ponytail and a mouth that curved in a permanent smile, she had the patience to explain so many things to him. "My mother will continue to milk the cows, but she is growing old and needs help lifting buckets and bales of hay and whatnot."

Heavy lifting he could do.

In exchange for his work, they provided him with meals and the use of a small cottage behind the farm. The one-room cottage with its fireplace, simple kitchen, and shower stall suit him well. This is a place where a man can live and be safe.

Finished with Lipsy's stall, he hangs the pitchfork and gloves on the wall and heads back to the cottage for a cup of tea. Nestled amid tall pines, the cottage is a tiny gem, its new windows glittering in the receding afternoon light.

When he first arrived, the windows of the cottage needed replacing, and he has begun that task. He accompanied Collette into the city when she made the drive back in December to purchase double-paned replacements from a wholesaler, then did the job himself, hammering and caulking, pressing insulation into the walls. After the first window was installed, he stood there for a good ten minutes, soaking it all up: the shock of golden light on a pasture, long purple shadows dwarfing towering evergreens.

By installing the window, he feels that he has opened up this beauty, somehow gained access to it.

So many windows here in the north.

Windows to look outside. Windows to gaze within.

He lights the fire under the kettle and opens his laptop, realizing that it's time. There's an outside chance that his story might reach someone who's trapped in the same place, someone else searching for a window. He's been told by the webmaster that his bio will be posted whenever he's ready. He's been putting this off, mostly waiting for the words to form, but now that his path is clear, his fingers fairly fly over the keyboard.

For a kid raised in a military family, going AWOL seemed to be the unthinkable. And yet, having served in Iraq, I have witnessed atrocities of this illegal war that are

far beyond my comprehension. Violence and bloodshed
without reason.

He takes his hands from the keyboard, wondering if he
should be more specific. The images of daily life at Baghdad
Hospital come to mind. The bodies brought in by soldiers desperate to save their buddies. The amputations, pulverized limbs
dropped into red plastic bags with the casualness of a housewife cleaning a roaster.

Is that necessary to reach people?

His mission is not to shock but to help the reader become
more aware.

> For the thinking man, blind service in war is a dilemma.
> Do what you're told, not what is right. I could no longer
> live that way. I feel fortunate to have escaped without
> blood on my hands, and I pray for the soldiers who live
> that ordeal every day and night.

To the brewed tea he adds a touch of milk, marveling at the
richness of fresh milk. Taking one of Edna's fresh-baked lemon
cookies from a tin, he decides to give more of his personal past
and writes:

> Canada has given me my second chance to live, and
> I have fallen in love with this beautiful countryside. The
> good people here remind me every day that I made the
> right decision not to be a tool of destruction.

That will put him back on the radar, although he suspects
the U.S. government could have found him if they really
wanted to track him down. So be it. The other war resisters
on the Web site had been left to live in peace. Granted, the
Canadian government had yet to grant them political asylum, but the war resisters movement was still in its infancy.
He clicks on the Web site to see their faces—Jeremy,

Brandon and Patrick, Darrell and Robin. He's never met any of them, but he enjoys seeing their faces, men living their lives. Living.

> I am sorry for the good people of Iraq who cannot "opt out" the way a war resister can escape to Canada. It is not enough for American soldiers to hand out candy and pencils to Iraqi schoolchildren. It's not enough to rebuild the schools and hospitals and bridges we destroyed. The solution may not be simple, but it exists simply in the end result of peace.

He sends the e-mail, then grabs his jacket to clean the horses' stalls before he brings them in for the night.

Down in the paddock, Collette is adjusting the saddle on Midnight, "Minuit" she calls him.

"Getting some exercise?" he calls through the cool evening air.

"I am always getting exercise." Her tone is matter-of-fact as she lifts herself easily onto the tall horse.

"I meant the horse," he says.

She shakes her head. "No, you meant to tease me." Collette has a solid grip on reality that's harsh and reassuring.

They have spent many evenings sitting by the fire in the big house, after a fine meal cooked by Edna, who doesn't even try to understand Noah when he speaks English. Collette is tutoring him in French, and somewhere in the process they have exchanged stories of their childhoods.

Collette has helped him remember the good times he had with John. The day Noah lost his boots in a snowdrift and John carried him all the way home—three blocks—on his back. The way John supported him when he played football with the older boys, picking Noah first for his team and letting him be quarterback. And John's generous manner when they were teenagers. That night when he lent Noah his car and gave him three condoms to take out Courtney Swanson. Noah, a virgin at the time, looked at the three packets and asked if you needed to wear all three at once.

Embarrassing, yes, but good memories. Noah is proud to have been John Stanton's brother. He is still angry at John for dying, but he is no longer angry at him for living.

Chapter 60

Washington
Abby

The "Secret Cupid" gift exchange is a tradition among the staff in the psych ward at Lakeside Hospital. Each year at the start of the second week in February, interested staff members put their names into a hat and select the name of a person they'll play Cupid to. Cupids are instructed to secretly deliver five small gifts to their person: pens, a Starbucks gift card, pantyhose, candy—anything under five dollars.

When Abby picks Rhonda Hobart, she's pleased to purchase small gifts for the tough but nurturing training supervisor. A personalized mug. A box of pens. Her favorite hazelnut-flavored coffee creamer. Abby looks forward to delivering Rhonda's gifts, one a day, until the brief staff meeting on February fourteenth when the Secret Cupids' identities will be revealed.

But the first day, Abby's satisfaction at seeing Rhonda squeal over her cute little Beanie Baby is diminished when she finds her own gift next to her locker in the staff room—a potted miniature rose bush with a note saying: I WILL NEVER STOP LOVING YOU.

Repulsive fear tingles down her spine as she sets the roses back on the ground. Her Cupid will not win any points for being PC.

Is it someone with a crush—or a moronic practical joke? She decides to wait for the second gift. Maybe she is overreacting. Maybe it's just someone's attempt at making her feel loved.

That first night she puts it out of her mind and focuses on her treatment plan for Emjay, who is progressing well, in her novice opinion. He's beginning to understand that there might be some value in talk therapy and has even started opening up a bit in group sessions.

The second day she tries to check in at her locker during the day, hoping to spy her Secret Cupid and confront him or her. Not only does she not catch Cupid, she does not receive a gift that day. Hmm. Maybe Cupid knows he/she blew it on the last note and is trying to rethink the plan.

Day three goes by without any sign of a gift. At the end of the day Abby closes her locker with a huge sigh of relief. She doesn't need a gift, though she did enjoy watching Rhonda enjoy a cup of coffee in her new "Rhonda" mug.

When Abby arrives home, there's a bouquet of black lilies on her front porch with a note that says: IF I CAN'T HAVE YOU, NO ONE ELSE CAN.

Oh, it's a sicko. It must be Jump.

Dread weighs her down as she brings the flowers in and puts them in water, unable to find any beauty in the swirling cone shapes of the dark calla lilies. Black flowers . . . rare and exotic, but not the most cheerful variety.

This has Jump written all over it.

How unlucky could she be to have Jump as her Secret Cupid? Or maybe he found out who picked her and forced a trade. Whatever the scenario, she will not falter. She won't let his sick attachment affect her job performance, end of story.

But that night, she finds she cannot sleep with the lilies in the house and tosses them onto the patio after dark, reminding herself to pick them up and put them in the compost bin in the morning.

When the fourth day also goes by without a gift, Abby begins to imagine what frightening symbol might be awaiting her at home. To offset her dread, she calls Suz, who agrees to meet at Abby's house, then go out to dinner from there.

But as Abby heads toward her car in the parking lot, she realizes that Cupid has struck unexpectedly once again. On the hood of her car sits a gift wrapped in pink paper with red foil hearts—so cheerful and sweet. She nudges it with her keys, feeling a strong desire to slide it to the ground then kick it over to the garbage can where it would remain, abandoned, until the hospital custodian removed it along with the trash.

But compulsion makes her tear into it. She needs to know what she's up against, what the enemy has tossed at her.

It's a framed photo of John. In the picture his soulful brown eyes exude knowledge and warmth, and she wants to reach into the landscape of the photograph and bury her face against his shoulder, bask like a cat curled in the sunshine in the wise aura that swirled around him. However the frame, a weave of silver bars, possesses a darker karma. Like Gothic latticework, it feels like sticky ice in her fingers. She wants to drop it and run, but how can she abandon a photo of John? Tossing it into the trash and running is no longer an option.

She pulls off the envelope taped to the wrapping and opens the note. VALENTINE, I WOULD DIE FOR YOU.

The sound that escapes her throat seems alien, the cry of a wounded bird. The sheer ruthlessness, the perversity behind all this—the impact is like a physical punch right to her chest.

Her blood ices over in her veins at the realization that this must be Jump. Who else in the psych ward even knows that she is John's widow? She still goes by her maiden name, Abby Fitzgerald, and she's never mentioned John to anyone but Emjay, preferring to keep her professional life separate, to keep the daily pangs of grief personal.

But now . . . now that she is sure Charles Jump is terrorizing her, a window of truth opens upon the scene of John's death. Truth bursts, bold and bright.

Charles Jump killed John.

It must have been him.

Although his motivation is not clear, she knows he had access, he had the means, and he has exhibited the sociopathic behavior that would make him capable of killing without guilt or conscience.

Frantic, she gathers up the wrapping, the framed photo, and

the note into her arms, then runs along the crosswalk of the parking lot and straight through the automatic double doors. She does not stop when a scrap of wrapping paper falls to the ground beside her. Only when she is on the elevator heading up to the ward does she even try to catch her breath and slow her racing pulse. When the doors open she bolts out and spots Rhonda Hobart heading down the corridor with two interns.

"Rhonda! We need to talk," she blurts out.

Annoyance fades from Rhonda's face when she catches sight of Abby. "Step into my office," she says, nodding toward the tiny kitchenette, a closet of a room containing a refrigerator, coffee-maker, and microwave. In a ward where many rooms do not have doors and privacy is nearly forbidden, it's not easy to find a place for two people to have a personal conference.

Abby presses into the room and pushes back boxes of cocoa mix and sweetener so that she can drop her armful of debris onto the counter.

"Honey, you look like you just got goosed by a ghost. What's all that?" Rhonda asks, nodding at the photo and torn gift wrap.

"A gift from my Secret Cupid." Abby explains how she was upset by the first two gifts of flowers with inappropriate notes. "And now this . . . I found it on my car just now. The photo—" Abby pauses in an attempt to control the tremor that's crept into her voice. "That's a picture of my husband, John. He was killed in Iraq last September."

Rhonda's lips purse in a pout. "Oh, Abby . . . How cruel is that? I can imagine how that makes you feel." She shakes her head, gazing down at the photograph. "A good-looking man he was. But do you think maybe someone thought you'd appreciate the photo?"

"Here's the note."

Rhonda winces as she reads the note. "'Valentine, I would die for you.' Now, that's just sick."

"I don't know what to do. I have a feeling I know who's giving me these things, but I can't prove it."

Rhonda nods encouragingly. "Tell me. Who do you think?"

"I . . ." She glances at the kitchenette's open doorway behind Rhonda, then says in a near whisper: "I think it's Dr. Jump."

"Really?" Rhonda's chocolate-brown eyes open wide. "I gotta say, that's the last name I expected to hear. Dr. Jump is pretty popular among the staff here and, frankly, with his busy schedule, I don't know where he'd find the time. What makes you think it was him?"

"We had a relationship. Well, I thought we were *friends* before I started my internship. It all ended badly, and I don't think he can put it behind him. I know he doesn't treat me fairly."

"Are you sure we're talking about the same guy? The other interns adore Dr. Jump. I just had two newbies beg me to let them trail him. Maybe it's the attractive, single-man thing but . . . I don't know quite what to say, Abby. People around here are fond of Charles Jump. I know the man has his moments, but even when he's bad, he's a hell of a lot more charming than some of the ogres I've worked for in the past."

"You don't know him," Abby says, pinching the bridge of her nose. She was considering telling Rhonda about her history with Jump, but now she'll have to take a different tack. "How long has he been a director here? Two months?"

"In this line of work, you get to know your coworkers pretty damned fast. But Abby, if you want to lodge a complaint against him, I'll get HR here faster than you can whistle. The only drawback of that is, just so you know, you'll have to go on record with your previous relationship with him."

Fear and humiliation stab through Abby's chest. "I'd be willing to do that if . . . if it would stop him from . . ."

"Abby . . ." Rhonda's hand between her shoulder blades is soothing, but it's also the note of compassion that brings Abby to tears. "I can't promise you anything, but someone is out of line here. The notes on those gifts are definitely inappropriate, and that last gift is downright cruel."

Tears sting Abby's eyes. "But we have no proof that Dr. Jump gave them to me."

"No, child, we don't."

Abby's face drops into her palms as tears run down her cheeks. What can she do?

"When you're ready to make the complaint, I'll be here for you," Rhonda says.

Abby nods as, down the corridor, the security door buzzes. Its irony is not lost on her.

We work so hard to keep the unstable people under lock and key, and the most menacing lunatic of all has all the freedom in the world. All the freedom and power to terrify.

"Valentine's Day is such a bitch," Suz says as she steps closer to the netting of the playland, keeping an eye on Sofia, who is collecting balls and tossing them back into the pit. "When you're single, you're a loser because you don't have a sweetheart. When you're a widow, your heart is cracked in two. Scott always said it was a holiday created by Hallmark to increase card sales, and now I'm starting to buy into his cynicism."

Abby nods glumly.

"Would you talk about it already?"

And so she tells her. Beginning with the way Jump started edging into her home and finishing with the Secret Cupid gift she received today, Abby tells Suz how Charles Jump has preyed on her, physically abused her, terrorized her. When she finishes, Suz is clutching Abby's hand, her eyes glittering with tears.

"That bastard! He probably killed your husband and . . . and nearly raped you. The monster!"

"Nearly being the operative word."

"The man tried to hump you like a dog," Suz growls between her teeth. "And don't you feel a wink of guilt, because he's an animal. Someone has got to stop him. Have you reported him?"

"I spoke with my supervisor about him, but she sort of warned me not to make any waves. He's a popular guy at work, and his position certainly trumps mine. With his power, his charisma, people are going to take his word over mine."

"I don't care if he founded the damned hospital and cured the blind. A psycho is a psycho. Where I come from, your father would be hunting him down with a shotgun and running his ass out of town."

Abby lets out a laugh. "My father doesn't own a gun. And do you really think violence is the answer?"

"With an animal like that? Absolutely!" Suz bends down to roll two balls over to her daughter. "There you go, pumpkin."

Abby scrapes back her hair, taking a breath. "I need to stay objective. I mean, I need to separate what I know and what I suspect."

"The police can figure this out. You need to report him, Abby."

"And what would they investigate? A few menacing notes left by an anonymous Cupid? Real-life police departments don't operate the way detectives do on television. No one is going to try and lift fingerprints from a couple of sick love notes. In real life, the police act after a clear-cut crime has been committed."

"Well, I don't want to wait until this psycho goes over the line. I'm very worried about you, Abby. You've got to get yourself out of that internship and away from him."

"But I can't leave the program now. Besides, I promised John I would finish."

"Yeah, well, I promised myself I'd never take my daughter to one of these indoor playgrounds." Suz squats down to shag some balls before they roll out of the play area. "And here I am."

"I'm being practical. I can't transfer at this point without losing major credits. Besides, I think I'm really helping my clients. Especially Emjay." It's not ethical to discuss the details of his therapy, but Abby worries over what would happen if she left and Dr. Jump reinstated the mind-numbing dosage of tranquilizers he's been on.

"So if you're not going to back off, we've got to find a way to take that sucker down." Suz tosses a squishy ball into the air and catches it with a snap of the wrist. "A monster like this doesn't just rear his ugly head out of nowhere. He's got to have a history. Let's get Flint on him, find out his background."

Abby bites her lower lip. "Flint and I aren't exactly talking. He came over a few weeks ago and we got a little short with each other. I think he was jealous of Jump. He blew a gasket when he saw Jump's laundry spread out in my living room."

"Good instincts. I always liked that guy."

"Then I got testy with him when he smashed a photo of Jump and John." Abby pauses. "At least I thought Flint smashed it. It was that weird period when the heat kept going off in the house."

"Oh, right around Christmas." Suz nods. "John showing his disapproval by freezing Jump out."

"I didn't believe that at the time, but if it's true, then John had some astute insights about Jump."

"Ya-ha. I say you mend your friggin' fences with Flint and get him investigating Jump's sorry ass."

Abby can tell Suz is mad because her language has gone to hell. "I can't call Flint. He's got a life of his own, a job that consumes him."

"Suit yourself. But you and I are going to get cracking on investigating the sordid past of Charles Jump."

At the informal staff meeting the next morning, laughter and wisecracks abound as people discover the identity of their Secret Cupid. When Rhonda opens the Beyoncé CD and discovers that her Secret Cupid is Abby, she throws her arms in the air and gives her a huge hug.

"How'd you know I liked Beyoncé and hazelnut coffee?" Rhonda demands.

"I'm a good listener."

"Thank you so much." Leaning close for another hug, Rhonda whispers: "He's not here, is he?"

Abby shakes her head. "The coast is clear."

"Well, I'm here when you need me. Here drinking my coffee and listening to Beyoncé. I'm going to have the whole Day Room singing along by lunchtime."

* * *

"Eighteen minutes till Getaway Friday." Lizzy double-checks her watch, scribbles something on a chart, then tosses her pen onto the counter. "Not that I'm counting or anything."

"Got plans?" Abby asks.

"That's why I switched shifts." An intern in the same program as Abby, Lizzy usually works evenings. "My boyfriend is taking me to Seattle for a fabulous dinner, then we're staying overnight in that hotel on the bay. The Edgewater Inn?"

"That's a famous one." Abby has never stayed there, but she's seen photographs. "You know, the Beatles stayed there when they visited Seattle."

Lizzy tucks her short blond hair behind one ear studded with half a dozen gems. "What are the Beatles?" When Abby pauses to explain, Lizzy nudges her shoulder. "Kidding. What are you up to this weekend?"

"I get to spend the weekend with the love of my life."

Lizzy grins. "Romantic dinner? Heading off on his seaplane to Vancouver?"

"We're sticking close to home. Lots of tea parties with Nilla wafers. Walks in the park and hours of *Sesame Street*." When Lizzy's freckled nose wrinkles, Abby adds: "I've got my friend's three-year-old for the weekend. Suz is flying off to Chicago for a wedding, so Sofia and I get to have a girls' night in."

Lizzy's attention switches to the hallway, where a group session is ending. "What's up, Doc?" she jokes, and Abby doesn't have to look up to know that she's talking to Dr. Jump. The icy shiver descending her spine indicates he's near.

"Like I've never heard that one before." Instead of heading straight out of the ward and into his office, his usual pattern, Jump stops into the nurses' station and steps up to the counter right between Lizzy and Abby. As he checks something on the computer, he fishes out his dog tags and fingers the gold medal there, the replica of the Purple Heart that he's so proud of.

It's a struggle to keep her breathing steady. The revulsion of having his body so close is tangible, a bad taste in her mouth.

Most days she manages to avoid major exchanges with him, scheduling herself for group sessions other doctors are leading. Once a week she sees him in evaluation meetings, but so far the only patient they share is Emjay, so most of her evaluations are from other doctors.

She hoped to avoid him completely today, but her luck has run out.

"So what are you doing this weekend, Doc?"

Is she flirting with him? Abby remembers a time when his lean frame and crystal-clear blue eyes held a tug of attraction—long before the beast within had reared its fierce head.

"No plans," Doc answers.

"But it's Valentine's Day." Lizzy crosses her legs and cocks her head so that her blond bangs fall seductively over one eye. "Everybody needs somebody on Valentine's Day."

Stupid, stupid girl.

Abby jerks her gaze back to her paperwork as Jump snaps a chart closed and steps back.

"I've got a lot of patients who need me," Jump says, folding his hands beneath his chin as if in prayer. "That's about the extent of attachment on my Valentine's Day."

Except for poisonous notes.

"Ms. Fitzgerald."

Abby freezes, her hand suspended over the file drawer.

"I have a special Valentine's Day gift for you."

Her mouth is suddenly dry, her tongue bunched in her throat as she forces herself to meet his icy blue gaze. "You shouldn't have."

His laughter pelts her in the gut, a helter-skelter spray of bullets. "But you don't even know the value of this gift." He steps toward her and casually rests a hip against the counter.

Fear burns through her with the awareness of his body, inches away. *He can't do anything to you here. He can't hurt you here, with all these people around.*

If only she could believe that.

"You have been chosen to work under my tutelage for the

next few weeks," he says proudly. "I am going to give you my undivided attention, and share with you . . ." his voice grows low, husky, "everything I have to give."

"Sounds like quite an honor," she says, pulling out a random chart as a diversion. "But I'm sure there are other interns far more deserving. Rhonda could recommend someone else."

"Ah, but she's the one who insisted I take you under my wing."

What? How could Rhonda do that to her, after Abby had confided in her?

"For starters, I'd like you to write up treatment plans on all my patients this weekend," he says. "Due Monday morning."

"Dr. Jump, that's two weeks' worth of work."

"But a talented student like you needs to be challenged. All that time on your hands. Of course, I can cancel the treatment plans if you could help me with my laundry. It's really backing up and—"

"What?"

"I'm kidding." He smiles, a glint of pure evil in his dove blue eyes. "Happy Valentine's Day."

Chapter 61

Surrounded by a mess so uncharacteristic of her organized nature, Sharice sits on the floor of the den beside the attic stairs and flips through the Rutgers University yearbook of 2000–2001. This time, she carefully combs each and every page so that she doesn't miss mention of him, the way she did before when she casually leafed through it and searched for his name in the alphabetized section.

Her perusal tugs at her heart as she comes across photos of both her sons. Football practice. Student government. Noah and a friend splashing in a fountain on a hot spring day. A photo of her sons lined up with other students waiting to give blood after 9/11. And there's a shot of John leading a meeting as the head of a political group he founded called "Peace Now." She snorts, recalling how that drove Jim crazy, that his son would rally to reduce the size of the U.S. Army.

But as she turns the last pages of the yearbook, her chest grows tight with the proof that there is no Charles Jump listed— in any grade-level list.

He said he went to school with John, so she has searched every one of John's yearbooks on the off chance that Jump is two or three years older or younger than John. He's not even listed under "not pictured."

Something is wrong here.

The sick pang in her stomach is back—the feeling of dread

that blackened her mood yesterday when the pharmacist called out of the blue to check on Madison.

"Your daughter is on a regimen that might require some supervision," Philip said. "Her physician has prescribed anti-depressants and tranquilizers, which we don't see often in teenagers. Sometimes kids that age don't understand that doubling up on medication or taking something ahead of schedule can be toxic. I just wanted to make sure Madison is vigilantly following prescribed dosages."

She assured Philip that Madison would be very careful, made a point of counseling her daughter about it after school, then called Dr. Jump's office to see if he might cut back Madison's dosage.

Thirty minutes later when the doctor called back, his voice bristled with annoyance. "Is Madison having an allergic reaction to anything?" he asked Sharice.

"No, it's just that . . . she's just sixteen and I worry about her being on such strong medications so young."

"Have you consulted another physician?" he asked in a low voice. "Because I have to tell you, I didn't spend three years at the Mayo Clinic to have my medical opinion undermined by a housewife."

"No, that's not my intent. I'm sorry . . ." She went on apologizing, and by the end of the conversation Charles Jump's tone lightened up, even to the point that he suggested she send him some of the delicious snickerdoodles like the ones he'd sampled at Christmas.

After that she tried to put the matter out of her mind. However, something occurred as she lay in bed last night going over things in her head.

The Mayo Clinic. That's where he said he went to med school. But he'd always been so proud about studying medicine at Harvard. It was one of the things about Dr. Jump that had impressed Jim so much.

That had planted the seed of suspicion, which compelled her out of bed this morning on a mission to find out what she could.

Sharice turns on the computer and tries to do an online search. Computers are not her thing, so she's not surprised when she can't get class lists online from Rutgers or Harvard, where Dr. Jump attended medical school.

So she picks up the phone and makes a call.

It takes two transfers to get to the right place, but the person she speaks with in the records department is very kind. "I can't give you a class list of graduates," the woman explains, "but if you give me a name, I can verify whether that person graduated from Rutgers University."

"Charles Jump," Sharice says, her stomach tensed in a tight knot. "But I'll need you to check a few years," she says, quickly fabricating a lie. "You see, we . . . had a fire in our office and we're trying to recreate personnel records."

The woman seems hesitant at first, but she checks for Charles's name in her data of matriculating students. "I'm sorry, but I don't see the name here," the woman says. "Maybe the dates are wrong? If you can give me his social security number, I can run him that way."

"I'll do that," Sharice says, thanking the woman for her time. She's still dazed as she ends the call and presses the phone to her chest.

Charles Jump did not attend Rutgers. Or if he did, he was not there during the years John attended.

The doctor lied.

Why?

She glances down at the yearbooks, class photos, pom-poms, mortarboards and tassels spread around her, mementoes of her sons' college years. If Dr. Jump lied about Rutgers, what about Harvard?

The call to Harvard University makes Sharice nervous, but she persists, knowing that this is about more than a little white lie. It was one thing for him to pretend to be John's friend; that lie was somewhat harmless. But Dr. Jump is now treating her daughter and her husband. If his credentials are fraudulent . . . and she was the one who pushed so hard to get them both in therapy . . .

Unfortunately, Harvard Medical School cannot verify Jump's matriculation unless she provides a social security number. A call to the Mayo Clinic is another dead end.

What to do next? Sharice isn't sure, but she knows she has to get to the bottom of this, has to make things right. She's the one who fixes things, mends them, holds the family together.

She's not usually the one making the mistake.

Chapter 62

Fort Lewis
Abby

"Elmo loves five! Give me five!" Elmo's furry red face fills the TV screen.

Two feet away, Sofia holds up five fingers and bobs her head in time to the music. "That's five!" Sofia sings.

"Not so close to the TV." Abby ushers Sofia back a few steps, then sits back down to her third treatment plan for Jump. She's enjoying having Sofia here, but struggles to balance her extra work from the hospital with the joys of childcare.

This treatment plan is for a man named Derek who's suffering from post-traumatic stress after deployment to Iraq. Derek, who went undiagnosed for a while, was nearly court-martialed after he barricaded himself in his apartment for three days. And right now, Dr. Jump has him on a high-dosage cocktail of antidepressants and tranquilizers.

That seems to be the pattern in terms of Jump's treatment plans—this doctor believes in drugs, and lots of them. Not that the other patients aren't on medications. It's just that Dr. Jump prescribes very high dosages, higher than any Abby has seen in the treatment plans of other doctors on the ward. Abby isn't all that familiar with dosages, and as a psychologist she will not be able to prescribe medications, but she worries that Dr. Jump's dosages might be toxic.

"Yay!" Sofia claps as Elmo's song ends. She skips around the coffee table, then pauses at her pink tricycle in the corner.

"My bike! Let's go to the park. Take my pink bike," she says, flicking the pink and silver streamers on the handlebars.

"We've already been there. Twice." But then, there's plenty of time to play when you wake up at six a.m. on a Saturday. Abby yawns over her open book. "I'm glad you like to step out, kiddo. Give me two minutes to finish with this plan and we'll head out again."

"Two minutes." Sofia holds up two fingers solemnly.

Abby pushes through the report, then helps Sofia ease her arms into her quilted white coat. "It's cold out there, so you need your hat again."

"Cold out there!" Sofia chimes as Abby ties the little pom-pom tassels under her chin. Under the puffy jacket, Sofia moves a bit like a penguin, and Abby has to stifle a laugh as she follows the little girl out the door. Abby lugs the pink bike over the front porch to the path, then they circle around the house and head toward the commons beyond the small backyard.

The sky has clouded over and, without the sun, the air seems colder. Abby pulls her hands into her sleeves, vowing not to keep Sofia out for too long. A few of the neighbors are out jogging or strolling with their dogs. Pedaling steadily, Sofia travels to the play structure where she parks beside the wood chips and runs to the purple slide.

Over on the lawn, a bunch of kids are playing football. When one of the kids breaks away and heads over, Abby realizes it's her neighbor Peri Corbett, her hair tucked under a watch cap.

"How are you, Abby? I saw you out with the little one earlier. Suz's daughter, is it?"

"Sofia. She loves the park." Abby nods toward the football players. "I take it some of those players are your kids?"

"They're all mine for the night. My son's ninth birthday."

"Tell him happy birthday for me."

They are joined by a couple, new neighbors—Cory and Jack—who are walking a red dog with floppy ears and a fluffy tail that beats the pavement when Sofia pets him.

"Sweet doggy," Sofia coos.

"Abby!" a man calls.

When Abby glances up at the smiling face of Charles Jump, her mouth goes dry. Defensive reflexes unwind like a mounting alarm: Protect Sofia. Tell everyone to run. Call the police . . .

"Hey. I saw you out here earlier when I was jogging by. Thought I'd bring a peace offering." He holds up a Thermos with two plastic cups on top. "Hot cider."

"Isn't that nice," Peri says, nodding approvingly. "Just the thing to take the edge off in this cold."

"I don't think that's a good idea right now," she says. "I'm baby-sitting, and I've got a ton of work to finish off. I need to keep a clear head."

"It's nonalcoholic, my grandma's recipe for hot apple cider. I know it's more traditional to break bread together, but I didn't think I could get you out to dinner."

"You were right about that."

Jump sets the Thermos on a nearby picnic table and divides the steaming liquid between the two cups. "We had a fight," he tells the others. "She's still mad at me. Can you tell?"

Abby turns away from him, infuriated, but she doesn't miss the knowing smiles of the others, who think they're about to see two people about to kiss and make up. Damn him! He's got them charmed.

Of course, because he's a sociopath. A textbook case.

Just a few minutes ago she had just been reading over the profile of a sociopath: a grandiose sense of self. A pathological liar who feels no shame or remorse. Manipulative and loaded with superficial charm—the charisma that was now tightening around her neighbors like a noose.

"You have to be careful with the clove," he tells the neighbors. "Too much clove and it will taste like soap." He lifts the cups and holds one out to Abby. "I wish you all could taste it, but I only brought two cups."

"We'll try it next time," Cory says, politely. "Abby should have it."

"No, go ahead," Abby says. "You take mine."

"It's a peace offering," Peri interjects. "It's sort of a ceremonial thing, right? So you have to drink it."

"Fine." Because everyone is watching her, Abby takes a cup and sniffs. The amber liquid smells of apples and cinnamon, and the cup is already warming the palm of her hand. "Smells good."

"Well, taste it already," Peri says. "I love the smell of hot cider in the house. I use that mix at Christmastime."

Under the neighbors' scrutiny, Abby takes a sip, allowing the cider's warmth to penetrate. "Delicious." She nods and extends the cup to Jump. "So we're cool." She sounds like a jerk, she knows that, but her neighbors don't know the big picture.

But Jump makes no move to accept the cup. "How is it? Too much clove?"

She sips again to appease him. "Nope. It's perfect."

He sits down at the picnic table and sets down the Thermos. "And who's this urchin?"

Sofia sits atop her tricycle, steering nowhere and mugging like a model for a car show.

"You remember Sofia? Suz's daughter." Abby turns to Sofia, hoping the edge of distress isn't obvious in her voice. "Honey, do you remember Dr. Jump?"

"Dr. Jump!" As she says it, Sofia does a little hop off the seat, her feet remaining on the pedals.

"Aren't you a cutie," Jump says.

"She's a doll," Peri says. "Sofia is in preschool with my son Zach."

As Peri points out her kids among the football players across the way, Abby places her half-empty cup on the picnic table behind them and steals protectively toward Sofia. How is she going to get rid of Jump now? The neighbors think he's her boyfriend.

Kneeling beside Sofia, she studies the back of Jump's hateful head. He would be furious once he found out the truth: that she and Suz are investigating him, checking out his background. Abby is convinced that they'll find something unseemly—enough to get him dismissed from his position at the hospital. And she's convinced that when they dig deeper, they'll discover that he is John's killer, that he's the man who was either jealous enough or angry enough or craven enough to take another man's life.

The only answer is to leave . . . now. "We need to get going," she says. "Say good-bye to everyone, Sofia." A cold pain slices down the back of her neck, causing her to momentarily lose focus. Is she coming down with the flu? She should have worn a scarf. She pushes the tricycle with Sofia on it to the pavement, wishing she could huddle on the back and ride along. Maybe she and Sofia can take a nap together.

Behind her, Jump is shouting: "Hold on! We didn't get a chance to talk."

"Sorry. Gotta go," she says, rubbing the back of her neck.

"Wait up. I'll walk you back."

She wants to shout back that she can make it on her own, but it takes all her energy just to focus on following the toddler on her tricycle. At the porch Sofia seems to move in slow motion, climbing off the tricycle, adjusting her hat, stepping up to the porch.

"Come on, honey," Abby sighs.

The warmth of the house hits her along with a sudden wave of dizziness. Abby drops into a chair, grateful that she didn't have far to walk.

"Are you okay?" Suddenly Jump's voice sounds like it's echoing down a hall.

"You have to go . . ."

"Abby, you need help. You're responsible for this child." His tone flips from concern to anger. "What the hell have you been doing?"

"Nothing." The word peels from her throat as the upholstered arm of the chair comes up under her head. She collapses into its nook

She wants to call 911. She wants to wrap Sofia in her arms and hold her there till this storm passes. She wants to run and ask Peri to watch Sofia for a while because the world is spinning out of control, making her so dizzy, her body so heavy.

But she is unable to lift her head or move her lips.

"You drunken whore." His words stretch from a distance. "If you won't take care of the kid, I'll do it for you." His voice streams over her, circling the warm cocoon around her.

She wills herself to get out of the chair—get up and stop him!—but her body is a mass of stone. *Don't take her! Don't you dare touch her! Stop, right now!*

"Come on, Sofia." In her mind's eye, malice curls the edges of his words like a parchment burning on the edges. Those flames burn in her head now, a fire raging out of control. "Dr. Jump will take care of you."

His footsteps are the last thing she hears.

Chapter 63

It's not until later in the afternoon, just before sunset, while Jim Stanton is loping along his usual jogging path, that he recalls the dream.

Some movement in the trees—a squirrel or a falling dead branch—brings the jungle imagery back to his mind, and suddenly it all comes back to him. The football game in the jungle, a tropical forest like Vietnam. Cut amid the trees and hillocks is a muddy football field, its grass surface and lime lines slightly clumped and ripped up by cleats but still holding.

Three men in combat fatigues occupy the field. On the twenty-yard line, Jim is poised, pumping the ball, deciding where to pass. In the end zone is John, ensconced in a wide white hospital bed, his head propped up, his body whole. His arms are open wide, and his smile—big and gregarious—is so John. He's too far away for Jim to consider lobbing the ball, but John looks so damned happy that Jim cannot take his eyes off him.

In the dream Noah keeps calling from midfield, "Dad! Throw it here! I'm open!" as he zigzags exuberantly over the field.

If you drew a line between their positions, you would have a triangle, with Jim standing at the skinny acute angle. That is, if Noah would stand still.

"I'm open, Dad!" he calls, somehow annoying Jim, who grips the ball, not sure what to do. A pass to John is like throwing the ball away, while Noah could easily catch the ball and run.

Still, Jim palms the ball, riddled with indecision, at the head of the triangle.

"Triangulation." Dr. Jump's voice peels in his head. "Triangulation occurs in family dynamics. For example, you have an issue with your wife but you cannot communicate with her directly, so you discuss it with Madison, who then is compelled to intercede and becomes part of the relationship."

Jim looks from Noah to John, unable to make his decision. But then the bushes move behind John, and heads appear in the brush beyond the end zone. Goddamn it, the Viet Cong, creeping up behind John.

Lit by panic, Jim drops the ball and tears down the field to his firstborn son. Got to push that bed off the field before the enemy gets to him. Move it, move it! Come on, man, run!

But the pain in his bad leg throbs.

And then he woke up.

After the dream, Jim didn't have too much trouble getting back to sleep, probably because of the medication. But now, as he lopes toward home, the ache in his bad leg steely from the cold, the dream tugs at the edges of his conscience, something minor to be attended to, something to straighten out, like a traffic ticket or an overdue electric bill.

Since he's been working with Dr. Jump, nothing really rattles his cage. It's all on the fringes. Surface level.

The streetlights are on when he turns onto the last block, yellow glows against the cobalt sky. Slowing his pace in front of the house, Jim winces at the pain in his leg. Man, it's a whopper.

Inside, the only light comes from the computer monitor in the dining room alcove, where Madison and Sharice sit together, faces lit by the screen.

"Oh . . ." Sharice gasps at the sight of him, as if he wasn't supposed to come in through the front door. Although she quickly turns back to the monitor, he does not miss the shimmer of tear streaks on her face.

"Mom . . ." Leaning in front of her mother, Madison usurps

the mouse and clicks a few pages closed. "Just close it out, okay?" she says, clearly annoyed with her mother. She is worlds ahead of her parents when it comes to navigating the Internet, a skill that frequently leaves Jim wary and wondering if she has too much cyber-freedom.

"But I . . ." Sharice shakes her head. "I'm not going to lie to him."

"What's going on?" Jim demands.

Madison is already on her feet, storming to the stairs. The tips of her hair sweep his shoulder as she hurries past him. "I'm done."

"Don't go anywhere." Jim reaches for her wrist, but she yanks it away, scowling at him. "What is it?" he asks his wife.

Sharice tips her head toward the computer. "We found Noah."

Those three words open up a wide chasm between them; it's as if Jim could separate his life into the minutes and hours spent on solid ground before this moment, and the marshland of the future riddled with mud holes that will suck his feet down into pits of guilt, puddles of disloyalty.

"Actually, Madison found him a few weeks ago. She's been e-mailing back and forth with him, and it sounds like he's doing well." Sharice speaks quickly, nervously. "His name and photo are posted on a Web site of war resisters who've fled to Canada, and we were just looking at the site. His personal statement is beautifully written. You should take a look."

Jim sits on the sofa, leans down and begins unlacing his running shoes. "You know I can't."

"Okay, *that* I don't get." Madison pounds up to the landing, then wheels. "He's your son, Dad. He survived, and he's just trying to stay alive. What is wrong with you? You act like he's dead, too. Is that what you want?"

"Of course not." Jim looks up at her, his heart racing to keep up with the emotions that can't seem to find a main artery to flow through in his body. He loves his son, of course he does. Then why can't he feel anything at this moment? Nothing but a stagnant numbness in his soul. "Noah is my son. You don't give up on one of your own. But I can't turn my back on my country to spare the life of one man. That goes against everything I believe in, everything I've sworn to protect."

"Oh, please!" Madison tosses her head defiantly. "Take a look around, Dad! This country you're protecting doesn't want soldiers overseas getting in people's faces and getting themselves killed. People want peace. No one wants to lose a son or brother or husband in a war where there isn't even a fucking enemy!"

Jim sucks air between his gritted teeth as Sharice springs to her feet at the computer desk. "Madison!" Sharice glares at her daughter.

"Watch your mouth, young lady." Jim's head is beginning to ache. Domestic strife is an alien thing in this household. He and Sharice have always kept their arguments on the level of debate, their disagreements tamped down.

"Don't shush me when you know it's true," Madison rails. "You can act like a patriot all you want, but at the end of the day Noah is out there somewhere, all alone." Her voice cracks with emotion. "And I for one am going to keep letting him know that someone loves him. And you can't stop me."

"Don't push us," Jim threatens.

"I—I hate you!" she shouts, then pounds up the stairs.

Jim is looking down at his hands when the door slams upstairs and a silence falls over the dark house. "Adolescence," he mutters. "How long does that go on?"

"Another thirty years or so?" Sharice's slippers tap the wood floor as she moves about, turning on lights. The red dragonfly Tiffany lamp in the living room, the orange glass cones that hang over the kitchen counter. The house is instantly warmed, a home. This, he realizes, is Sharice's gift—turning a building into a home, making a dark place warm and inviting and inhabitable.

"At least she's not drinking," Sharice says. "And you can understand why she's upset." She returns to the computer and clicks the mouse. "If I ask you a question, do you promise you won't snap at me?"

Jim sighs. "Ask away."

"Is it treasonous and illegal just for you to look?"

"That's not it." He paces past her, past the Web site behind her, into the kitchen where he grips the counter. "You know that's not it." The truth is, he's never had much of a tolerance for the war resisters. He remembers them from the sixties, their faces splashed on TV screens with their bold, black eyeglasses and picket signs. College kids spitting at cops, shapely girls in bell-bottom pants shoving peace signs at you, longhairs, freaks, lazy-ass kids who expect someone else to fight for their freedom.

"Then please." She pats the bench beside her. "Come look. For me?"

And there he is on the football field, palming the ball, quarterback in the clutch. Why doesn't he throw it to Noah? Why not give the boy a chance to run with it?

With a sick feeling in his gut, he puts his hands on his wife's shoulders and allows himself to take in the Web site. No longhairs or hippies, just boys, young men like the ones who served in his own platoon.

Boys like his son.

"He looks good, doesn't he?" Sharice asks.

Jim blinks back tears, unable to answer for the knot in his throat.

Chapter 64

Abby awakens in the dark, her mouth dry and fuzzy, her shoulder stiff from sleeping in such an unnatural position huddled in the chair. Trying to find comfort, she shifts positions and notices the digital clock on the TV cable box: 6:14.

a.m. or p.m.?

Through the haze of drowsiness she tries to orient herself. She's at home in her own living room, but—

Oh, God!

She bolts upright and nausea springs through her core. Sofia . . . where is she? And—

"No!" She curls up, face to her thighs and hands balled into fists as she remembers it all far too vividly.

Jump.

Oh, God! He took her.

"Sofia?" Maybe she's here. Maybe his threats were unfounded. "Sofia, honey?" Pushing out of the chair, she breathes over a wave of dizziness and stumbles over to turn on the light.

Palming the walls for support, she searches the apartment. Although there are signs of Sofia everywhere, from the sweet baby-powder scent of her hand wipes to the plastic booster seat strapped onto Abby's kitchen chair, the child is not here.

Being upright makes her dizzy, and she races into the bathroom, gagging. Afterward, she rinses her mouth with cold water. As she straightens and spies her own reflection in the mirror over the sink, the seriousness of the situation hits her once again. She has lost a child.

"Oh my God!" The words are almost a desperate prayer as she grabs the phone and searches her directory for Charles's number. He took her. He took Sofia away!

Did he think she wouldn't remember?

With shaking fingers, she presses in his number and waits, seconds ticking slowly, as the phone rings and rings.

"This is Dr. Jump." His voice sounds cordial, professional.

"You need to bring her back, right away," Abby says, swiping her sleeve over her face. Until now she didn't even notice that she was crying. "Bring her back to me."

"Who is this?" Now he sounds pompous.

"Bring Sofia back right now!" she rages.

"Abby? I don't know what you're talking about."

As the bottom drops out of her world, Abby collapses onto the dining room table. Her mind goes to the dark places where Jump might have taken the toddler . . . did he mistreat her? Was that part of his psychosis?

The table's surface, cool against her cheek, grounds her somehow, reminding her that her reality is not a hallucination. Jump took Sofia, but obviously the direct approach is not getting her anywhere. She needs to take a different tack. "You took her for a walk this afternoon," she says. "Remember? After we ran into you in the park and I . . ." She restrains her fury as the pieces fall into place. "I got sick."

From the cider you pressed me to drink. Poisoned. Laced with some drug.

Which one did he use on her? OxyContin? Morphine? Xanax? Percocet? Or a mixture of narcotics and tranquilizers?

A drugstore full of prescription medications lurks at Dr. Jump's fingertips.

That would explain the sudden illness, the cotton mouth, the nausea. But right now, her fury isn't going to play with Jump.

"Thanks for taking care of her," she says. At this point

she'll suck up to him, stroke his ego, anything to get Sofia back safely. "How about if I come pick her up?"

"Abby, I don't know what you're talking about. Has the stress of the internship gotten to you? Or perhaps it's latent grief from John's death. Grief does have a way of catching up with us."

"No! Stop twisting things around and tell me what you did with Sofia!" she demands. "Where is she?"

His sigh is dramatic, loaded with pity. "Again, I don't know what you're talking about. But if you've lost track of a young child, you'd better call the police . . . and not your internship director, who has better things to do on a Saturday night."

"You're lying!" she protests, but it's all in vain. With a click, he disconnects the call.

"Damn you!" Abby hangs up and pushes herself away from the table. Her head, still woozy from the drugs, is swimming with panic and adrenaline, but she has to organize her thoughts.

First priority: find Sofia.

She goes through the house once again, this time searching under the bed and inside closets. Where could she be? Abby's heart twists at the image of Sofia alone in the dark. "Where are you?"

She can't do this alone. Every minute counts when a child is missing.

Quickly, she calls 911 on her cell. While she talks to the dispatcher, she shrugs on her jacket and begins circling the house. The sight of the pink tricycle on the front porch makes her throat grow thick with emotion but she presses on, circling around the side, checking every shrub.

The dispatcher on the phone is removed but patient, and Abby tries to stay calm as she answers every question. Yes, a child is missing. A baby girl. No, not an infant, she's three, more a toddler. How long? It's been a few hours. Struggling to explain, Abby simply says that she dozed off while the child was playing and she's afraid the little girl let herself out of the house. She'll tell Suz the truth, of course, and once the police arrive she's going to tell them the entire story: the drugs, the lies . . . all of Jump's deceptions.

But, right now, Sofia is everything.

Panic overtakes her as she checks the park, searching in the tunnel slide, the sandbox, behind the picnic table. This was where it started with that damned hot cider. What a fool she was! Why did she drink it—just to avoid making a scene? So what if the neighbors thought she was rude and crazy.

Breathing is impossible, but she pushes on, her entire body trembling.

"Are you still there?" the dispatcher asks.

"Yes, yes, I'm here." She breaks into a run on the path until she reaches the back of her house.

"Please stay on the line," the woman says firmly. "The police will be there in two to four minutes."

"I'm here." Abby's jaw quivers as she cuts around the side of the house and begins to search the front. The light from the streetlamp bounces off the hood of her car, and she heads that way, wondering if she should wait to call Suz or phone her right now.

Two steps later, she sees the bulky quilted coat in the backseat. Sofia is strapped into her car seat, deathly still.

"Oh, honey!" In one forward movement Abby lunges toward the car and grabs the door handle.

The interior light of the car and the rush of cold air cause the child to stir, allaying Abby's worst fears. "Sofia, sweetie . . ." She leans into the car fumbling over the straps with one hand. "I found her," Abby tells the dispatcher breathlessly. "In her car seat. I'm hanging up now so I can get her out."

"The police are on their way. Should I dispatch an ambulance, too?"

"No, I don't think so. She's breathing and . . . I don't want to scare her."

As this conversation goes on, Sofia cracks open her eyes, then rubs her face with one fist. "Get out!" she whines, kicking her legs.

A very good sign. Abby tucks her cell phone into her jacket pocket and unbuckles the straps. "Here you go, pumpkin." She tries to lend a hand, but Sofia is already climbing down to the floor and reaching for Abby, who hoists her into her arms and hugs her thoroughly and gently. The downy feel of a child's hair against your cheek, the smell of baby powder and cherry No-More-Tears shampoo, the perfect combination of solid bone and pliant muscle and flesh—Abby savors it all, grateful for Sofia's safety.

"Abby?" Sofia pats her shoulder and Abby lifts her head. "Can I have french fries?" Her tone is so earnest Abby feels a pang in her heart.

"Are you hungry, sweetie?"

Sofia nods, yawning. "Do you have french fries?" she asks, tucking her tiny fingers into the collar of Abby's coat. "I hungry."

"We'll get you some french fries," Abby promises. She closes the car door and carries the little girl up the front walk and into the warm house.

When the police arrive two minutes later, Abby focuses on keeping things on an even keel for Sofia, who seems happy to lie on her back with her legs curled to her chest and watch *Dora the Explorer.*

When the police ask Sofia what happened that afternoon after Abby "got sick," she just shakes her head and answers, "I'm not allowed to tell."

Officer Thompson asks her, "Who says you're not allowed to tell? You can always tell the police."

But Sofia just shakes her head and smiles. Her lips are sealed.

Outside on the front porch, Abby keeps one eye on her charge inside as she quickly tells the police her account of the afternoon—that she was drugged and Sofia was abducted by Dr. Jump.

"Those are pretty heavy charges, ma'am." Officer Thompson shifts from one foot to the other.

"I know, but it's the truth. I . . . I would give you one of the cups he put the drugs in, but he took them away."

Officer Thompson nods. "Have you ever used illegal drugs before, ma'am?"

"No! Of course not." Abby covers her eyes with one hand then rakes her hair back from her forehead. Her head hurts and nausea still bubbles in her stomach, and, to top it all off, the police don't seem to believe her. "You need to go and arrest Dr. Charles Jump for kidnapping and . . . and whatever charge there is for drugging someone. He lives in the Bachelor Officers' Quarters on base."

"Ma'am . . . Mrs. Stanton . . ." the second cop speaks up now. An older man with bristly gray hair and a mustache, Officer Bigelow. "We deal with your situation a lot, and I can assure you that we don't take sides."

"My situation?" Abby's fists press to her hips. "What might that be?"

"Stay calm, ma'am." Bigelow's eyes are wide with condescension. "I'm just saying we handle lots of domestic disputes."

"This is not a domestic dispute!" Abby growls, keeping her voice low.

"Mrs. Stanton," Thompson intervenes, "we took a complaint earlier this afternoon, charging you with harassment and reckless endangerment of a minor."

"What?" Abby feels the earth shifting beneath her for the second time that day. She backs against the door, holding the knob for balance. "Who lodged a complaint against me?"

Officer Thompson's eyes glaze over; he's seen this a thousand times before. "Dr. Charles Jump."

After the police leave, Abby turns her total attention to Sofia.

French fries are delivered from one of the small restaurants on base.

The Wiggles expound the beauty of cold spaghetti and mashed bananas over John's sound system that used to be dedicated to Green Day and the Eagles.

A warm bath is drawn, and all the tub toys are allowed to float at one time while Abby and Sofia draw on the tiles with special tub crayons and talk about their day.

"If you get her talking, she'll tell you if something bad happened to her," Suz said when Abby reached her on her cell phone after the police left. "She might have been scared to talk to the police, but I know my daughter; she'll spill the beans to you."

Suz had been the eye of the storm, the voice of calm amid swirling chaos. When Abby apologized and berated herself for losing control of the situation, Suz told her to "Shut the hell up and stop blaming yourself."

As Abby wipes Sofia's back with a warm washcloth, she employs her interviewing skills to keep Sofia talking about the afternoon. At the same time, she unobtrusively examines the child's body for bruises or marks or signs of abuse. Thank God, there are none.

"You know," Abby says, a fluffy yellow towel huddled under her chin, "I think tomorrow is going to be a lot more fun than today." She's already decided that Jump can go to hell with his treatment plans; after this weekend, schoolwork is the least of her worries. "Maybe we can go visit Chuck E. Cheese's."

"Chuckle Cheese!" Sofia draws a huge orange swirl of excitement on the side of the tub. "Yay!"

After many questions and rambling conversations about their day, Abby's assessment is that Sofia wasn't harmed during her absence. But what did happen during those hours when Abby was unconscious? She knows she won't be able to sleep tonight, worrying about it.

They are stretched out on Abby's bed, pillows stacked behind them, just finishing their third book. "Goodnight, Moon," Abby says, turning to kiss Sofia on the forehead.

A tiny fist comes up to rub her nose.

"I thought you were already asleep," Abby says.

"No, Moon."

"Sofia? I want to ask you a question. Where did you go today? This afternoon when I got sick and fell asleep, what did you do?"

"I ride my bike," she says proudly.

Did she mean earlier in the afternoon? "You know you're not supposed to ride your bike without a grown-up."

"I know, silly." Sofia lifts her feet in the air and grabs her toes, knees to nose.

"Sofia, was there a grown-up with you?"

"Of course, horse." Sofia kicks her feet into the air excitedly. "Dr. Jump!"

Chapter 65

Tacoma
Suz

"**S**he's asleep." Suz closes the door to her daughter's bedroom, closes her eyes and mouths: "Thank you, Lord." Since Abby and Sofia picked her up at Sea-Tac, Suz has spent most of the time gobbling her daughter with hugs and kisses. You never can kiss your child enough, though you forget that when they piss you off by stealing a toy from another kid on the playground or plumbing their nose for boogers while sitting in a cart at the grocery store.

Thank God, Sofia is fine. Suz may not know a hell of a lot of things, but she knows her daughter, and her downy little fluff has not been ruffled by anything that happened this weekend. Thank you, God, a million times squared.

Though when it comes to ruffled feathers, she can't say the same for poor Abby. She studies her friend, who is stretched out on the couch, her hair rolled into a twist on one side. If that girl hasn't been to hell and back . . . "How're you feeling?"

"Better today." Abby rubs her eyes. "I don't know what Jump dosed me with. I'm hoping it wasn't something black-market like Ecstasy."

"Trying to make you his sex slave?"

Abby sighs. "It didn't make me horny, but I did feel like I was burning up at one point. I don't know what it was. He might have dissolved a morphine capsule, which would be consistent with the nausea and throwing up, or he could have mixed a few drugs. He's got access to all kinds of medications."

"You've been through the wringer, kid." Suz sits at the far end of the sofa and gives the toe of Abby's sock a squeeze. "You want to stay here tonight?"

"I think I'd sleep better here, and I can go to work directly from here in the morning."

"Mi coucha es su coucha. But do you really want to go to that loony bin and see him?"

"Of course I don't *want* to; but I need to. I'm starting to get the big picture with Jump, I think. I need to stand my ground, not let him bully me, and definitely not let him stab me in the back. This calls for vigilance and fortitude."

"And Luke friggin' Skywalker's light saber. Abby, you've got to defend yourself."

"You're right." Abby sits up and tucks her feet under her as Suz pulls down a throw blanket and spreads it over the two of them. "I've been piecing things together in my head, looking in my textbooks, trying to profile Jump, and my take is, he's a very dangerous man. I think he's a sociopath. The clinical term is antisocial personality disorder. A sociopath acts without remorse or guilt. He has no regard for the feelings or rights of others. He can be charming at times. He'll give the appearance of engaging others in relationships, but there's no depth or meaning. He has an innate ability to find the weakness in people, and he'll prey on that weakness and gain pleasure from doing it. He'll target a person and use that person for all they can give, whether it's sex, money, or power. He's manipulative, deceitful, intimidating. It's a chilling profile, really."

"You're describing every psycho killer from every movie that's kept me up late at night." Suz hugs a pillow. "How do you cure these monsters?"

"There is no known treatment for sociopaths, unless the disorder is caught before adolescence."

"Really? So these people are just fucking crazy?"

Abby lets out a breath. "Fucking crazy would be an accurate term. People use Charles Manson or Jeffrey Dahmer as examples, but there are an estimated two million sociopaths in North America, living with families, working in offices. Making people's lives a living hell. A sociopath isn't necessarily a murderer, but he might kill someone if he has something to gain by it and, most importantly, if he can get away with it. A sociopath doesn't want to be caught or punished, and it's the risk of punishment for a crime—not the guilt or realization that it's morally wrong—that prevents him from committing it."

"I'd say Jump fits that description."

"I wish I'd seen this earlier. I have a theory," Abby says.

"Lay it on me."

"Let's say my diagnosis is correct, that Charles Jump is a sociopath. He goes into the army and lands in the same platoon as this popular former football star, John Stanton. He's never met Stanton before, but when he sees that reporters follow him around and the bosses treat him with a certain measure of respect, Jump buddies up with the notion that some of John's celebrity glow will land on him."

"I can see it. But Charles Jump met John in college, right?"

"I think that was a lie." With a tired groan, Abby stretches down to the floor for her bag. She pulls out a folder and hands it to Suz. "Last night, after Sofia went to sleep, I pulled some of John's things out of the attic. Do you see the photo that Jump gave me showing John and him together? Well, when I was going through a scrapbook I came across this picture of John with his football buddy, Spike Montessa. Take a look at the photos side by side."

"Okay." Suz places the photograph next to the newspaper clipping. "Good Lord, it's the same photo!" In both photos John is on the left, with his arm slung around the shoulder of the other man whose uniform number is twenty-one. "One of these was doctored," Suz says, checking the lines, the face tones, the lighting. "Now see, there's a shadow on the left side of John and Spike's faces, but Jump is fully lit like a studio shot."

"Right. The photograph with Jump was Photoshop'd. I don't know why I didn't see that before."

"You had a few things on your mind," Suz says, sneering at the picture of Jump before flopping the folder onto the coffee table. "That weasel. So he faked a friendship with John to try and get into the limelight."

"It looks that way. Which would explain why John didn't mention him as a friend, didn't include him in the electronic journal entries I found. But you know John. He didn't suffer fools gladly, and he wasn't about to pretend to have a relationship he didn't feel."

"Which probably pissed Jump off."

"I'm sure it did. My theory is that Charles Jump targeted John. He was jealous of his success as a football player in college and high school. A little research would have told Jump that John has a wife, a supportive family, a father who got a Purple Heart in Vietnam. And the eyes of the world were on him because he walked away from big money and fame to serve his country. By contrast, I doubt that anyone paid much attention when Jump enlisted."

"So he hated John for his celebrity," Suz says.

"And his popularity among the other guys in the platoon. Jump was brought in as a psych officer, but from what Emjay tells me, John was the unofficial leader. Most of the guys liked John, though some of them weren't crazy about his politics."

"So . . . fast-forward to that day in the warehouse." Suz knows where this is going, but it seems that Abby needs to get it out.

"That day, Jump had it all planned. Sociopaths have no remorse, but they can be brilliant. Jump might have even rigged that warehouse mission, provided fake intelligence claiming an insurgent was spotted in the building. Also he just happened to be the person in the squad responsible for maintaining the night-vision goggles—NODs, they call them. And Emjay's didn't work, so he couldn't get a good look at the man who shot John."

"Oh, cripes. It was Jump, wasn't it." Suz punches the pillow in her arms. "But you'd think he'd steer clear of all you Stantons. Isn't he afraid of being found out?"

"He's gotten away with it so far, and coming after John's

family is part of the plan. In targeting John, Charles Jump wants to collect John's trophies: John's wife, his parents. He even tried to move into John's house."

"He's a monster, Abby. And can you imagine what he's doing to the people in therapy with him?"

"Oh, God! I recommended him for Madison!" Abby reaches down into her purse for her cell phone. "I have to call Sharice."

"And you'd better protect yourself, Abby. I don't like the idea of you ever having to see him again at that hospital."

"Believe me, I will be very careful. I always stay as far away from him as possible. Besides, in the psych ward, you're never alone with someone. There's a rule of three, so there will always be someone else around when I'm dealing with him."

"Better stick to that, girl," Suz warns, smacking Abby's knees to let her know she means business. While Abby talks with Sharice, she slips into her bedroom to begin unpacking and mull over a strategy to keep Abby safe from this prickly monster encased in a buff body.

Chapter 66

Fort Lewis
Charles

*Y*ou bitch.
You were supposed to be my arm candy, maybe even my little wife, if only to prove I could score every perk John had, but you fight me every step of the way. Ornery bitch . . .

With a growl he pushes the weight bar high, arms extended, muscles howling with resistance. He likes to push himself to the edge, until his muscles feel like they're going to snap like a rubber band. The edge gets his juices flowing, keeps him stoked.

Excitement lives on the edge.

Grunting, he brings the weight bar back and replaces it on the rack. There.

He sits up and shoots a look at Abby Fitzgerald stretched out on the bed, her pale, full breasts buoyant beneath their rosy pink nipples, a thin veil barely covering the fluff of hair at the juncture of her thighs. She wants him. She definitely wants him.

That's why she's being such a bitch, fighting him like this. Abby likes the fight.

He walks past her, strutting before the mirror. His biceps are so pumped you can see the veins that wrap through his arms. His skin is shiny and pink, the muscles flush with blood. He strikes a pose before her, seething at the wanton pout on her lips.

Yes, she wants him, but she's stuck in her own uppity bitchiness. Snubbing him.

He hates snubs. His old man used to treat him like a little

shit, like a poor relation. Always expected him to wear the old, pilly clothes from his brother, the broken Razor scooter, the dirty running shoes with the Nike swish peeling off. John got them new the year before, but Charles got stuck with hand-me-downs.

John always got everything new. John was the running back football star. John was the friggin' second coming of Christ.

That's why he had to take John down. Too full of himself, an egotistical blimp, hogging the camera, the interviews, the limelight. John had to die, and he'd taken care of that, right?

Then why did he get a Christmas card in December with a photo of his brother and his wife and kids sitting in red sweaters in front of the stone fireplace? Sweat beads on his upper lip, but he wipes it away, shakes off the confusion.

No, no, he took care of him. That was done.

And now was the time to reap the benefits. Cash in the chips.

If Abby wasn't going to play into his hand, he knew someone who would.

Someone nubile and naive. Another accessory of John's.

The blond woman-child would be putty in his hands . . . and he would savor sculpting her from raw clay.

Chapter 67

Madison stretches and wiggles into the comfortable nooks of the leather sofa in Dr. Jump's office. "Are you sure about this?" she asks him, craning her neck around to try and see him sitting behind her.

"How does it feel, lying down?" he asks.

"Weird." She crosses her legs. "Cozy, but I'm used to looking at someone when I talk to them." Besides, she thinks, I like to look at you. Dr. Jump is way older than any guy at school, but he's buff under that lab coat. Madison is sure he pumps iron. Over her last few sessions she's gotten a kick out of checking out his butt when he wasn't looking.

"It's more traditional in therapy for the client not to view the therapist," he says from behind her. "Let's try this today, see if it works for you."

"Okay. But if I fall asleep, don't blame me."

"I'll wake you when your session is over. So how's everything? What's up at school?"

"The usual. Normal kids striving to be popular. Popular kids worrying about being unseated. Geeks and nerds trying not to get bullied. Same-old same-old."

"And where does Madison fit into the grand scheme?"

She sighs. "I don't know." What she doesn't say is that she's beginning to care less and less about school and friends and grades. Is that from the medication? Is that depression?

She doesn't want to ask, because then Dr. Jump might cut off her happy pills. It was weird how easy it was to get the pills in the first place. Way too easy.

She said she was depressed and just like that he gives her a prescription for the cure. Well, sort of. The pills dull the pain for sure, but they dull everything else, too. They make her sluggish and slow, like her whole life is taking place underwater in a snow globe filled with viscous liquid. Very weird.

She gave a few to Sienna and Ziggy and they thought it was awesome. Go figure.

Sometimes she thinks that maybe she'll stop taking them, but Chucky—Doc—keeps reminding her that it takes the medication awhile to work. So, she sticks with it.

And that's why she's as relaxed as a jellyfish all the time. She yawns. Even right now, as Doc talks about something that happened to him in high school, she could drop right off to sleep.

But she's sort of in trouble with school. Junior year grades have a lot of weight for when you apply to college, and her four-point-oh is shot to hell right now. She's got a paper overdue in American history that she hasn't even started, and a big fat 54 percent in red ink on her last trig test.

Oh, well.

Doc is still hot, his voice a mellifluous charm in her ears. When all else fails, she's got this.

Unless Abby gets her way. She heard her mother talking on the phone last night, arguing with Abby about whether she should be in therapy with Doc. Mom had said something about cutting off the sessions.

What was that about?

Abby's all worried and bent out of shape about something, but Madison is sure she's overthinking it. Abby's good at heart, but now that she's almost finished with her psych master's, she thinks she knows everything about therapy.

If Abby really got the whole psychology thing, she would see how Doc helps Madison. She'd understand how good it feels to have an older, more mature guy listening to her problems. Doc is worlds apart from the guys at school. Skinny giraffes who trip over their own legs. The Emos and the Goths, ready to bleed black ink. Lazy jocks who think a good time is sitting home with an on-demand movie and cutting farts on the couch.

She folds her hands on her lap, suddenly wondering who's been on this couch before. Hopefully, nobody too gross.

Sometimes Madison daydreams that Doc Jump is really into her in a mature, sensitive-guy sort of way. That he falls in love with her, lifts her off this couch, and carries her out the door to a cool mansion where they can live happily ever after with cute little sons who will never have to move to another house and never have to fight in a war. Sort of like that scene in *An Officer and a Gentleman*, which her mother melts over every time it's on cable. Except, well, duh, in Madison's version, he's wearing scrubs instead of a U.S. Navy uniform.

"You're not talking much today," he says. "What else is going on at school? Made any new friends lately?"

"Girls or boys?" she asks.

"Either one. Whatever you want to tell me, although one of these days, when you really trust me, you'll start telling me about the boys you like at school."

"I'd tell you if there were any that didn't disgust me," she says.

The first time he asked her about her sex life, she laughed and nervously told him a few lies because there was nothing else to say. She told him that she and Sienna had gotten naked for Ziggy and touched each other. She got that idea from a porn show she saw on cable at Sienna's house.

He actually believed her . . . and he seemed to be interested.

Which made her a little nervous that he'd catch her in the lie, so she admitted that she was a virgin. And he seemed to like that, too.

Now, he asks her, "Have you had any more sexual experiences with your friend Sienna?"

"No," she answers, feeling too lethargic to dream up something new. "And it's not sex or anything. I mean, I'm not a lesbian."

"But you enjoyed touching another woman's breasts?"

"We just did it to get a rise out of Ziggy." She folds her arms protectively, then, realizing what she just said, laughs. "That's pretty funny. Get a rise out of him? Get it?"

"Yes." His voice is silky and dark, like chocolate fudge melting on her tongue. "You know, Madison, sexual needs and desires are a normal part of a healthy young woman's life."

"I know that." She senses him moving behind her. Moving a little closer? Whatever he's doing, she has this feeling that he's kind of into her, too.

"Do you ever think about having sex with a man, Madison?" From his voice she can tell that he's closer, almost leaning near her ear.

"Sometimes," she whispers, sure that he's going to lean close enough to touch her. She closes her eyes, a tingle of anticipation dancing over her skin as she waits for it to happen.

Instead, she gasps at the sharp jab of pain in her upper arm. What the crap was that?

Her eyes flutter open, a hypodermic needle filling her scope. A swelling wave tingles up into her head . . . and then the room swims over her, swirling her down the drain.

Chapter 68

Just looking at her lying there. Her small breasts poking up at him through her T-shirt makes him hard as a rock.

He checks the door behind him, fiddling around the knob for a lock. No! Son of a bitch! The goddamned door won't lock. Stupid safety feature for psycho patients.

But who would know if he jumped on top of the girl and humped her right here, right now? Nailed her on the couch?

He squeezes her breasts, firm little mounds. Damn, he wants to do her, but the risk of getting caught is too great.

What the hell was he thinking when he drugged her here? She's going to have to be admitted now, and that means there'll be lots of nurses and interns and staff around her, watching, watching all the time.

He kneels beside her, pounds his forehead in frustration.

Stupid, imbecile plan of his! He should have lured her somewhere else . . . his car or the park. He could have dragged her back into the thicket and had his way with her supple, lean body for hours. But no, he thought it would happen here. Idiot!

Rage burns through him, flaring up from his loins and firing through his soul. Damn!

Leaning close, her runs a finger over her fat lower lip, wishing her could dip inside that luscious mouth. His fingertips trail down, toying with her pert nipples once again, then framing her slightly rounded hips with both hands till his fingers sink into her tight little butt.

Did she realize how it had inflamed him when she wriggled that little butt on the couch, nestling into the pockets of the leather?

How he'd grown rock solid, eager to feel himself press against her tender flesh?

He would take her another time, another day. But he would definitely have her.

He goes to the phone and calls upstairs to the nursing staff in the psych ward. With any luck, he gave her the right dose of morphine, but the nurses could figure it out, hook her up on monitors, start fluids.

"This is Dr. Jump. I'm in my office in the office wing, and one of my patients just had a meltdown. Yes, Madison Stanton. She'll need to be admitted for observation."

Chapter 69

So far this Monday morning, Abby has managed to avoid Dr. Jump at the hospital. She spent the morning leading a twelve-step meeting monitored by Dr. Holland, then attended a group therapy session during which Emjay Brown was very articulate, sharing anecdotes and describing feelings, encouraging another soldier to "let it out."

Now, meeting with him for therapeutic communication in the Day Room, she flips through his chart as he shares a joke with Jake, a soldier who is also suffering from PTSD. Emjay Brown has progressed well since the first day she saw him, heavily medicated and sleeping, here in the Day Room.

"Tomorrow is a landmark of sorts for you, Emjay," Abby says. "You'll be setting recovery goals with some of the doctors."

"You mean, they'll evaluate me," Emjay says with his wry expression. "I never did like test day."

"You'll do fine. You've embraced all the goals we established." Looking down her list, she would give Emjay full points in all categories: developing positive coping actions, engaging in talk therapy, learning about his condition, practicing relaxation methods. "Good work, Emjay."

"I had a pretty good intern," he jokes. "You are going to be there tomorrow, right?"

Tomorrow . . . Abby isn't sure how much longer she can

take the strain of being in the same building with Dr. Jump. And once Jump finds out she didn't turn in all those treatment plans, he might be terminating her internship, anyway. "I'm planning on it," she tells Emjay.

"I don't know. I'd like to get out of here, but I don't know if I'm cured yet."

"There's no sudden insight or quick cure. Recovery is an ongoing, daily process, and you're chiseling away at it, bit by bit."

"One day at a time." His voice is low, melodic. "I suppose you want me to give you some more stories so's you can fill your clipboard?"

"If you want. It *is* called talk therapy."

"I suppose we can do that." He glances across the Day Room to Jake, the new soldier, who is playing solitaire. "Have you ever been on a chicken farm?"

Coming from out of the blue, the question makes Abby smile. "No, although I've driven by them on the Delaware shore." The only reason Abby remembers is because, even from fifty yards away, the stench from the long buildings can be unbearable.

"I grew up on a chicken farm. Eastern Maryland."

"How was that?"

He shakes his head. "Hated it. I signed on with the army just to get away."

"What were you trying to get away from?"

"My old man liked his whiskey. Falling-down drunk half the time. It got to the point where I couldn't leave, could never get away, 'cause I couldn't count on him to take care of the chickens. Twice a day you have to go out culling in the chicken coops. You gag at the smell, chicken shit everywhere. Gets in your boots and your pores. They say eventually the ammonia burns a hole in your sinuses and you don't smell it anymore, but that never happened to me. Nah, I smelled it every time I got downwind of the chicken coops, and stepping inside, it stings your throat . . ."

He rubs his chin, wincing at the memory. "But you have to

go inside, gotta walk through from one end to the other and pick out the dead chicks before they infect the others. Put 'em in a bucket or a bag and count the bodies. Their little chick bodies, all stiff. Legs in the air." He squeezes his eyes shut, and Abby notices his cheeks are wet with tears.

This is about more than raising chickens. She waits for him to continue, her gaze on his face, encouraging.

"You need to keep count if you want to run a business." He sucks in a breath. "Gotta keep count."

"It sounds like an unpleasant job."

"Nobody should have to do that. No one. The bodies . . ." His voice is broken by a sob.

"What bodies are you talking about, Emjay?"

"I keep seeing them, soldiers. Men and women. They keep carrying their bodies out of the ravine." He sniffs and wipes a sleeve over his face.

"This is in Iraq?"

He nods. "We were in traveling a convoy by this oil rig that somebody set on fire. It was burning like the fires of hell, damn hot, and we were doing our best to get around it fast. One of the armored vehicles took a different detour, trying to get away, but they ran into a drainage ditch. Flipped the vehicle, and the soldiers were trapped inside." He blanches, his face tight with anguish. "They drowned. Drowned in the fucking desert. What's the chance of that?"

"Bad things happen in war," Abby says. "Things that the human psyche isn't built to endure."

"They made me count them. Someone had to count the bodies." A sob slips from his throat and he drops his head into his hands. "They made me cull the bodies."

Abby reaches over and rubs his back, firm strokes between the shoulder blades.

When his breath evens out, he continues. "Now—how many months later?—I dream about it. I'm walking through the desert, picking up dead bodies as I go, tossing them onto heaps. All for the U.S. Army, so they can have a list, their statistics. Their war."

"When was the last time you had this dream?"

"Just before I took that midnight stroll down the boulevard with my rifle."

She nods. "You know, there are ways of gaining some control over your dreams. You can make your mind go to a safer place at night." The buzzing of the hospital pager at her waist disrupts Abby's train of thought. "We'll work on some strategies for programming dreams."

The page is from Admissions. After Abby finishes the session with Emjay, she takes the elevator down, expecting to be assigned a new patient. However, when she passes the waiting room on the way of that wing, she nearly runs into Sharice Stanton, who is pacing frantically.

"Sharice?"

"Abby! Oh, Abby." Tears flood Sharice's eyes as she clutches Abby's hands.. "It's Madison. Something happened. A panic attack, I think. I dropped her off here for therapy and when I came to pick her up they told me she's going to be admitted."

"I'm so sorry." Abby bites her lower lip. Would any of this have happened if Madison had been in the hands of a decent therapist? Guilt sweeps over her, a hood of regret, but Abby has to shake it off and move ahead. Right now Madison is the priority. "I'll do everything I can to help you, Sharice."

"Will she be in your ward? Maybe you can look in on her."

"We don't have minors in the psych ward. She'll probably get a room on a pediatric floor. How did she look to you?"

"I haven't been allowed to see her yet." Sharice presses a hand to her forehead. "That's one of the reasons I'm so worried."

"But you're her mother," Abby says, shaking her head. "We'll get you in. Let me see what I can find out."

At the Admissions desk she learns that Madison is "still being stabilized" in one of the Admissions bays. As a psych intern, Abby has no authority or privilege in this wing of the hospital, but she strides down the hall, checking charts and peering into the slits between curtains. At last she finds Madison, but the sight of the unconscious girl, waxen and pale against the sheets, strikes fear in her heart.

A nurse glances up from taking her vitals. "If you're the psych consult, you can come back at the end of shift. This little shorty's going to be sleeping for a long time."

"I know her." Abby reaches under the sheet and takes Madison's hand, which is cold to the touch. Her fingers are limp, her fingernails pearly with a pale blue tint. "Is she going to be okay?"

"Looks that way. Though the doctor had no business giving her that much morphine. Apparently the syringe was loaded up for some other patient and this girl went wild. Took a swing at him and he used the injection to calm her down." The nurse glances up through an artistic spray of curls to check the IV. "This girl's lucky to be alive."

When Abby brings Sharice into the curtained bay, Sharice's eyes well over at the sight of her daughter, so lifeless and sedated. She drags a plastic chair over to Madison's bedside and rocks there, holding her daughter's hand to her cheek.

"She's so still," Sharice murmurs. "Are you sure she's breathing?"

"Her breathing is shallow, but at least she's breathing on her own. There's a good chance she'll be nauseous when she wakes up. She should be okay, Sharice, but I feel responsible for this." Abby glances toward the curtain; no sign of him yet. "I should have never recommended Dr. Jump as a therapist."

Sharice holds a hand up. "Abby, it's not your fault. I know your reservations, and I have some of my own." She winces. "I found out that he lied about attending Rutgers with John. I don't know, maybe it was a ruse to put him in our good graces. But I talked to Jim about it and, little white lies aside, he thinks Dr. Jump is just great." Her hand squeezes Madison's. "Whatever happened to Maddy today, we are going to get her through this."

"Of course we are, but Sharice . . ." Abby squats beside her. "It's not Maddy. Madison is not the problem at all—it's

Dr. Jump. I've figured out what happened to John. Jump's the one who killed John, Sharice."

"What?" The older woman's eyes go wide, then she closes them. "No, Abby. That's impossible. Don't you know the creed doctors take? 'First, do no harm.'"

"But Jump is no normal doctor. He suffers from a serious personality disorder, and he has the capacity to do heinous things to people without feeling any guilt or remorse."

"Where are you getting this from?"

"From observing his behavior, catching him in a few of his lies. He's a sociopath, Sharice, and I think he's targeted me and . . ." Then it hits her. "Oh, my God. It's not just me."

"I beg your pardon?"

"I'm not the only one he's after. He's targeted all of us . . . all of John's family. That's why he injected Madison today. Oh my God, Sharice, you've got to promise me you won't leave Madison alone with him."

"Now who's having a meltdown? Listen, Abby, I appreciate all your help. But really, Jim and I thought Madison made considerable progress with Dr. Jump and it seemed to make sense to leave her under—" Her eyes grow wide as something behind Abby steals her attention. "Oh, hello, Dr. Jump."

Steeling herself, Abby rises and faces her husband's killer. Her attacker. Sofia's kidnapper.

Under the hospital's fluorescent lights, his skin looks slightly pallid, but with his broad smile and clear blue eyes he could be the poster child for MDs of America. "Sharice?" He stares right past Abby, taking Sharice's hands. "First, I don't want you to see this as a setback but as a breakthrough. Madison was trying to conquer some difficult demons today, and I'm afraid the monsters got the better of her."

Speaking of demons, Abby wants to say, *I hear you've got a direct line to hell.*

With great restraint, she stands there staring at the floor tiles while he tells Sharice his version of Madison's episode, a tale that sounds ludicrous even to Abby's unseasoned ear. First, she finds it hard to believe that a man the size of Dr. Jump could not restrain a slender girl like Madison. And even if it was a struggle, he could have called for assistance. And the drug injection . . . as if anyone would leave a loaded syringe of morphine on his desk during a therapy session? Morphine is a special class of drug kept under lock and key, even in a hospital.

"So Madison is going to have to stay with us for a few days," he says, checking the patient's pulse. "In a few minutes they'll move her to a room upstairs, which will be more comfortable for you." He turns to Sharice and claps her on the shoulder. "Give you a chance to catch up on your TV viewing. I hear *American Idol* is addictive."

Charming, charismatic—Dr. Charles Jump has honed his people skills well. It's chilling to watch him in action, frightening to think of the damage he can cause in his quest for self-gratification.

Abby wants to stay and warn Sharice further, but Jump dismisses her outright, telling her that he needs a few moments alone with the patient's guardian.

"I'll check in on you later," Abby tells Sharice, looking directly in her eyes. "You're going to stay with Maddy, right?"

Sharice nods. "Jim is bringing me some things. We'll take good care of her."

As Abby leaves the room, Jump flashes her a chilling smile that penetrates her soul. It plants a hollow feeling of fear for Madison's welfare, a feeling of dread for her own safety here at the hospital.

An hour later, as she's working on her therapy notes upstairs, she finds that she's still shivering.

Chapter 70

Seattle
Flint

The Lakeside Hospital Web site dedicates an entire page to Dr. Charles Jump, Director of Psychiatric Services. His record in the U.S. Army is lauded, as well as his educational background—a Bachelor of Science at Rutgers University and an M.D. at Harvard University School of Medicine.

"Very impressive," Flint says aloud for the benefit of anyone in the newsroom who cares to hear.

The snag here is that it's a load of bullshit.

Charles Jump didn't attend Rutgers or Harvard University.

A check with the American Medical Association revealed that Dr. Charles Jump was a Board-Certified Psychiatrist, a graduate of the University of Missouri School of Medicine.

A good guy, according to his obituary. Dr. Jump passed away in Kansas City back in 2003 at the age of seventy-four.

Something stinks here, a real rotten egger. Flint's favorite kind of story.

He's supposed to be covering the grand opening of the Potlatch Trail, a new path connecting South Lake Union to Elliott Bay. Snooze. The exposure of Charles Jump's fraudulent ways, however, is a story with mileage.

His only concern is that Abby Fitzgerald is caught in the eye of this storm.

He tries calling her for the ninetieth time, but again, the

voice mail clicks on. Damn. Where the hell is she? No answer on her home phone or her cell.

To build a story, he needs to speak with someone from the hospital's human resources department, inquire about their hiring practicing and process of checking employment history, but that will have to wait until morning, since HR people work bankers' hours.

So where does he stand now?

He's got to talk to Abby.

She needs to be warned. And if he's going to write this story, which he's itching to do, he wants her to be onboard. Although the promise was unspoken, he never intended to write about John Stanton, never wanted to use his connection to Abby for a story. But now . . . this thing is spiraling out of control, way beyond the orbit of John's celebrity, and Flint wants to be the one to lasso the moon.

He could lump this all into an e-mail, but that would be a little abrupt, considering they haven't had any contact with each other since they argued. Somehow, an attack on Jump doesn't seem to be the best way to reestablish the connection.

Hey, here's some dirt on the asshole you were shacking up with last time we tangled.

No, that's not quite right.

You know the dickhead who's been borrowing your razor? He's actually an imposter, someone who's stolen a dead man's identity.

But Suz Wollenberg said Abby and the dickhead weren't shacking up anymore. Actually, she said Abby never slept with the man, though that wasn't his take on it.

"Believe me, it never happened. Never." Suz was emphatic on the phone. "But I think Abby is embarrassed because she let him push her around and . . . well, you'll have to get the details yourself. Abby says the man is a sociopath, whatever that means, but it's clear he's targeted Abby and he's like a shark with his jaw clamped shut and just can't let go. Just this weekend, he slipped Abby drugs and scared the hell out of her by taking Sofia, but he's a careful motherfucker. We can't prove anything. The bottom line is, this guy is a psycho tyrant, and we've got to figure out what rathole he crawled out of and expose him."

"I never liked the guy but I didn't peg him as a psycho."

"Well, think again. Abby says he's a sociopath, a manipulative, charming asshole who doesn't feel guilt. Look, I've got to get to a meeting, but you get going and do some digging, okay?"

"You're pretty passionate about your cause," he told Suz.

"I'll leave the passion to you. Me, I'm just trying to watch out for my friend. She's been through a lot, and she's in an impossible situation right now. This psycho is her boss at the hospital."

"I get it. I'll do some digging under Jump's rocks," he told Suz.

Of course, when he made that promise, he had no idea that a few records checks would open a huge can of worms.

He tries Abby again, but still gets no answer. This time he leaves a message. "Dammit, Abby, call me."

"Charming," says his editor, Nina Torkelson, as she walks past him without looking. Nina possesses a luscious voice and the body of a Teletubby. When he was embedded in Iraq, speaking to her daily on the phone, he was sure she was much sexier than he remembered. Wrong. "I wouldn't wait around to hear back from that one, Flint."

Flint rakes his hair back with his fingers. "Yeah, I always stick my foot in it."

"Aren't you supposed to be at the Potlatch Path event?" Nina calls.

He checks the clock in the corner of his computer. Might as well, since there's no way he's getting through to Abby today. "I'm on it," he says, swinging his fleece-lined denim jacket over his shoulders as he heads out to the elevator.

Today he'll cover the community event. Tomorrow, Doctor Imposter.

Chapter 71

Lakeside Hospital
Sharice

In the haze of near-sleep inside Madison's room, colors dance in Sharice's mind.

Velvety evergreen branches. Emerald green fields of clover edged by wildflowers in bursts of brilliant yellow, red and violet. A dusky purple mountain ridge holding up a big cerulean sky. The rich colors come to mind when she thinks of Noah these days, having seen her youngest son standing before towering pines in a photo on the war resisters' Web site. In the picture Noah looks healthy, and his e-mails are very positive, talking about the hard work of helping some Canadians run a dairy farm and the peace he's found living in the countryside. Madison has already promised him a visit, and Sharice hopes that one day that might happen. Maybe she and Madison could travel there together, a mother-daughter trip before Madison finishes high school.

Settling into the corner chair under the blankets the nurses brought her, Sharice falls into melancholy over her failure to protect her children. Why do parents believe they can handle the navigation and growth of tiny beings when the world is riddled with hazards, dangers, evils?

How ambitious she was when her children were toddlers. How blissfully ignorant of the dangers that would appear suddenly, giant potholes in the course of a life.

Good, solid, strong John . . . all the love in the world could not keep him alive.

Sensitive, smart, diligent Noah . . . living a world apart, unable to ever rejoin them.

And Madison, her persistent baby girl who taught herself to walk at ten months, bruised shins and all. How does a mother help a child walk without worrying that she'll walk away?

Her daughter is breathing more deeply now in the nearly dark room. The light rack behind Madison's bed has been switched to night-light mode, and the only other light in the room floods in from the corridor through the glass window in the door. In the dimness, Madison's body seems so small under the sheets, as if she were still a child.

And in a way, she still is. Sixteen. A foot in each world.

Sharice rarely questions the decisions she's made regarding her kids. Somehow, a mother just knows what's right for her own kids.

But what if she and Jim were wrong about Dr. Jump? Madison, who vehemently resisted when they made her see the psychiatrist for her first session, recently softened her attitude toward Jump. Or was that the drugs making her go soft? Sharice worried about those drugs, too. Maybe they should wean Madison from them?

Or maybe Abby was right about switching to a different therapist. Sharice still had a bad feeling about Charles Jump's credentials—the lies about Rutgers and Harvard. Since that day, she has not mentioned her discoveries to a soul, but it always niggles at her.

Why did he lie about his college alma mater?

What was he trying to hide?

Really, if there was any question about the man's credentials, he shouldn't be treating her daughter. Her baby girl. It was Sharice's job to watch out for Madison, and if that meant hurting some feelings here and there, so be it.

Tomorrow morning, when Jim stops in to visit, she'll discuss changing therapists for Madison. Certainly, after the incident today, Dr. Jump would understand. In fact, he might welcome the change that would let him off the hook. She settles into the chair, relieved to have a plan.

The slightest creak of a rubber sole on the tile awakens her. She stares at the strange properties of the room, taking a moment to realize where she is.

A glance to her left reveals someone standing over her daughter.

Dr. Jump.

At first realization she is warmed by his presence. She wouldn't expect a psychiatrist to visit his hospitalized patients in the middle of the night.

Then she sees the syringe in his hand.

What?

As she watches in horror he folds down the sheet and reaches down to Madison's hips, turning her slightly in the bed. His hand snakes under her gown to her bare bottom, smoothing a path there.

He tests the syringe. In the silhouette of light from the hall she sees the tiny spirt of liquid arching through the air from the needle.

"No!" she shouts, startling him. "Don't do it. She's not going to have any more medication from you."

He swings the syringe aside, wheeling to see who's been behind him. "Mrs. Stanton! I'm sorry, did I wake you?"

She throws off the blankets and rises. "Take that away. We're done with drugs, doctor."

"This? Oh, this is just something to help her sleep peacefully."

"I said take it away."

Dr. Jump places the syringe onto its tray and steps back. "I just didn't want Madison to have a restless night."

"But I want her to wake up. Three, four in the morning. I'll be happy to have her awake, happy to have the chance to talk with her."

"That's not advisable. Madison is in such a deep depression, she'll probably be unresponsive, anyway. I hate for you to be frustrated."

"I'll deal with that when it happens. If it happens."

He folds his arms across his chest. "Oh, it'll happen, all right." Anger simmers in his words. His gaze scrutinizes her as she lowers Madison's gown and pulls the sheet up to her chin. "And I don't take kindly to people coming in here and telling me how to do my job."

Sharice smooths her daughter's hair back and turns to him. "Dr. Jump, that's the last time you will ever, ever touch my daughter." She grabs her cell phone and flips it open.

"Mrs. Stanton . . . Sharice . . ." His tone softens in appeal—back to Dr. Jekyll. "Don't do something you'll regret."

Oh, she had regrets, all right. And they started with choosing him as a therapist.

"Jim?" Her eyes never leave Dr. Jump. "Sorry to wake you, honey, but I need you, now. We're taking Madison home. No, she's not awake yet, but . . . we'll figure it out. I'll pay for an ambulance if need be."

"You're overreacting," Dr. Jump says. "And you're making a mistake. Home is a negative environment for her."

"Well, then," Sharice pushes the nurse's call button, "we'll have to work on that, won't we?"

After the nurse responds, Dr. Jump recedes to the doorway. "This is a mistake, Sharice."

"Not the first time, and it won't be the last," she says. "Goodbye, Dr. Jump."

Fury flares in his eyes, but he turns on his heel and leaves. Finally.

As Sharice packs up Madison's clothes and belongings, her duty as a mother crystallizes in her mind. She's taking her daughter home, which is where Madison needs to be right now. When Madison wakes up, Sharice is going to open the lines of communication between them and they are going to talk, every day and always. She's going to make sure Maddy attends a twelve-step program. And she's going to let her daughter march in war protests 24/7 if that's what Madison thinks is right.

I've lost one already. I am not going to lose Maddy.

Chapter 72

The last time he did this, he walked in on a half-naked man and a roomful of underwear.

"Maybe you can get it right this time," Flint tells himself as he takes the Fort Lewis exit off I-5 and cruises to a stop at the light. This time, he's got some information Abby wants. Hell, he's got stuff that should keep her away from that hospital until the real psycho is under lock and key.

He just hopes she'll listen.

The lights are on, but Abby isn't answering. He moves away from the door to the front window, looking for signs of life. "Abby? Where the hell are you?"

"I'm right here," comes a voice from the side of the house. Abby steps out from behind the shrubs, an aluminum baseball bat dangling from one hand. She's wearing a short silk leopard-print robe with sweat pants and Crocs.

"Practicing your batting stance?"

"Just taking some precautions," she says, motioning him over. "Come on. We'll go in the back door because I left it open."

"I'm impressed. You've devised your own alarm system."

"Don't be. It's more like an escape hatch so I can get the hell out. And I guess I should apologize for chasing you out last time you were here. I was kind of worn down by everything, and I lost perspective."

"I'll say. You were dating Charles Jump."

"I was *not* dating him." She tightens the belt of her robe. "I wasn't really, though he was pushing for that. But a few things have changed since the last time you were here. I've discovered that Dr. Charles Jump is a sociopath, and I've determined that I'm his next target."

"Somehow that doesn't surprise me." The cavalier attitude is a cover for the protective instincts that slammed him when he started researching Jump yesterday. He's relieved that she's being careful, that she's making an attempt to protect herself from Charles Jump, but from the research he's done on the profile of a sociopath, her baseball bat security system might not be enough.

He wants to protect her. He'd like nothing more than to keep her at arm's length until Jump is apprehended. But, being a practical person, he knows you can't have everything you want.

"Jump is one of the reasons I'm here." He pauses in front of the back door. "After you." When she passes by him in a cloud of sweet flowers, he has to restrain himself from touching her hair.

Better watch it, or she'll use that bat.

Inside, the house is not as homey as he remembered it. The kitchen walls are bare, and boxes line one wall of the dining room, stacked up to his shoulders. "What happened here?" he asks.

"I'm packing. I need to be out next month, but I haven't had time to find a new place with my internship and everything else that's going on. My stuff is going into storage and I'll be staying with Suz and Sofia in Tacoma."

A few miles closer to me. "Sounds like a plan. Honestly, I wish you were living there already. Not that the base isn't usually safe, but even the Military Police can't guard an individual twenty-four/seven." He leaves his jacket on but sits down at the kitchen table.

"And you think Suz can protect me?"

"Safety in numbers. I have to admit, after Suz called and asked me to check out Jump, it really rattled my cage."

"Suz called you . . ." She rolls her eyes. "Of course, she did."

"And it's a good thing. I don't think you realize who you're dealing with here. And I agree that he's targeted you. That's something sociopaths do, right?"

"They seem to choose victims, find the individual's weakness and prey upon it. But with Jump, I think he devised a grander scheme, starting with John."

"Back in Iraq?" He shrugs out of his jacket. "You think Jump was the killer?"

She nods. "You don't seem surprised."

"I've had some experience with reading people. I've always known that Jump was a great bullshit artist. You couldn't trust him." He puts a hand up. "Not that I knew Jump killed John when I met him back at Camp Despair. I'm not that good."

"Do you want some tea?" She turns the gas on under the kettle. "I've got decaf."

"Now you're making me feel old. Sure, but do you have straight up, conventional tea?"

"*Man* tea? Let me look."

"I'm sorry about John." She looks up from the open canister, and he continues, "I didn't mean to sound cavalier about it just now. While I suppose it must be a relief to identify the man who murdered him, it's a concern to know the killer is still out there, free."

"It's more than a concern. Jump has targeted the people who were important to John: me, John's sister, his parents. He's zeroed in to identify our weaknesses and, well, attack our vulnerable spots."

"Not if we stop him first. I've been checking up on Dr. Charles Jump, and the man is not who he claims to be."

She swings around with a mug in her hand. "What did you find?"

"First off, Jump didn't go to Harvard or Rutgers."

She points an empty mug at him. "I knew he was lying about Rutgers! You know that photo of Jump and John? It was Photoshop'd. Jump's face was plastered over Spike Montessa's. What else?"

"Dr. Charles Jump died in 2003. The guy was in his seventies, and his wife reported a burglary at his home the week after he died. Some lowlife broke in and robbed the place while the family was attending his funeral. Can you imagine that?"

Abby frowns. "I can imagine."

"So here's the thing from my angle." Flint shifts in the kitchen chair, wishing he could do more than just write Charles Jump up in a story. "Investigating Jump could be a great story for me, but I wanted to check in with you first. I don't want to write a piece that takes advantage of our relationship." Whatever that relationship might be. At the moment, he's not really sure.

"A story about Charles Jump? Write anything you want. You wouldn't need to quote me, would you?"

"Definitely not. Though I'd like to point to the possibility that Jump murdered John in the so-called friendly fire incident."

"Then go right ahead." She pours hot water into the two mugs and places one in front of him. "Here you go. One man-tea. I'm sticking with chamomile. Not that I'll ever get to sleep, but I like to think it will help." Squeezing honey into her mug, she asks: "So what's your next step to research the piece?"

"I've already sewn up interviews in Kansas City, Missouri, where the Widow Jump lives. The police there were pleased to have a lead on their old burglary complaint. I'll see what my army contacts can find out about a sociopath like Jump slipping through the screening process. And I'd like to talk with Lakeside Hospital's HR department in the morning."

"The hospital . . . are you planning to reveal the truth to them tomorrow?"

"That's not the way I usually work." A journalist's job is to find your lead, build a story, get the facts straight, and get it printed. He was not a cop or a federal prosecutor empowered to stop or punish crimes. He lifts the mug to his lips. "But I suppose I could let one or two disturbing facts slip if it helps your case."

"That would be extremely helpful." She sips the tea, then

holds the mug below her chin. "Tomorrow morning . . . that gives me opportunity to strike at the same time." Her green eyes soften with relief, and from this close proximity he can see the little flecks of gold that have always intrigued him. A man could spend days lost in those eyes.

Snapping out of it, he asks, "You have a plan in mind?"

"My first strike would be to go to the head of the psych services team and report that Dr. Jump is not really a doctor." She places her mug on the table. "After that, I'm not sure I'll have my internship anymore, but I'll deal with that when it comes. I've got a discharge review for Emjay . . . I wish I could get that done beforehand, but if Jump is relieved of duty, I'm sure the doctor who steps in will do the right thing."

"So first you get him out of the hospital." He nods.

"It's a start. Then . . . it's a matter of getting him incarcerated. I'll go to Sergeant Palumbo and my other military contacts with the theory that Dr. Jump killed John." She shrugs. "We'll see what they do with—"

The crash startles her. Her arms fly wildly, knocking her mug of tea to the kitchen floor.

Adrenaline stings right up to the top of Flint's head as he slides out of his chair and leaps over to Abby. He pauses in the doorway of the dining room, standing between Abby and the source of the noise.

"Who's there?"

He flips the light switch and the room is awash in stark white, illuminating a box that has fallen from the top of the stack. Books spill out from the top, one of them cracked open.

"A box fell," he says, leaning down to stack the books. "Looks like these are stacked too high."

"Oh my God." Abby presses a hand to her chest, her fingers flat beneath the fine bones of her clavicle. "That scared me."

"Got my blood moving, too. There's nothing like being the target of a sociopath to keep you on your toes."

She turns to the kitchen and sighs. "Look at the mess I made."

While Flint picks up the fallen box and begins to rearrange

the more tenuously stacked items, Abby cleans up the spill in the kitchen.

"So you're planning to come back here in the morning," she says. "The traffic between here and Seattle is going to be a bitch."

"Yeah, that's a given."

"You could stay here, if you want. The couch opens up to a bed."

He hesitates. "That's a great offer." It would save him a frustrating drive, and give him peace of mind knowing Abby had protection tonight. "But I don't want you to think I'm pulling a Jump on you."

"Well, first of all, I won't be doing your laundry. And second, it would be a favor to me. I'll sleep a lot better knowing I'm not alone in the house. And third, we lived together for four years in college."

She appears at the doorway of the kitchen—sweat pants, spotted silk kimono, and dish rag. *Has a woman ever been more beautiful?* "I think I can trust you for one more night."

Chapter 73

Where did Madison go?

Abby double-checks the door number—yup, room 327—and stares at a sleeping boy, around eight or nine, whose leg is suspended from a harness over the bed. This was Madison's room yesterday, and Abby didn't think to check and see if she was moved since last night.

Worry flickers in her chest as she heads to the nurses' station. What if something happened? If Jump got wind that he was about to be found out as an imposter, would he have done something rash?

The nurse on duty has a million things to do. "I came on at eight a.m. and there was no Madison Stanton on the patient list," she tells Abby, then heads off to start a procedure. Which leaves Abby at a loss as to how to find Madison.

"You looking for someone?" asks a woman lumbering down the hall.

Abby realizes that her purple scrubs and the photo ID on the lanyard around her neck carry some weight inside the hospital. "My sister-in-law was on this floor yesterday, but someone else is in her room now. I'm trying to find out what room she was moved to."

"Don't you worry, now." Dressed in pink scrubs, probably an aide, the woman settles down heavily at the desk and runs a key card through the computer. "What was her name?" She types the information in with clawlike nails dotted with pink gems in the shape of a flower. "Hmm. Okay, I see her now. She was discharged during the night."

"Really?" Abby moves in view of the screen. "Was it Dr. Jump who discharged her?"

"That information doesn't show up on this list. But that's good news, right? She got to go home?"

"Yes, thank you so much," Abby says.

As the elevator hums upward, Abby wonders what circumstances would cause Madison to be discharged in the middle of the night. She wants to call Sharice and find out what happened, but cell phone use is not permitted inside the hospital, and she doesn't have time to take a break.

The minute Abby buzzes herself into the psych ward, Cilla pounces on her with information. "You're in big trouble."

"I just got here," Abby says, "and I'm five minutes early."

"Dr. Jump has been looking for you, and he's on a rampage." Cilla's mousey little nose twitches beneath her dark glasses. "I've never seen him like this before."

He must know I'm onto him.

"Thanks for the tip," Abby tells Cilla as she heads to the locker room to stow her purse.

"That's not all. One of your patients had an episode last night and had to be subdued. He's in lockdown now."

Abby turns back. "Who?" Even as she asks, she knows the answer.

"Emjay Brown. Dr. Jump is blaming you, that you did something that set the patient off yesterday."

Shaking her head, Abby heads back to the locker room.

"Is it true? Hey, Abby, aren't you scared of being kicked out of the program?"

Abby keeps moving, pushing forward. Yesterday Madison, and now Emjay . . . two patients in two days.

What do you expect when the patients are being treated by a fraud?

Feeling precious moments slipping away, Abby quickens her step. She has to get to Dr. Steen, the director of the Psychological Services Unit.

It's up to her to stop Charles Jump.

Now.

Chapter 74

People are such morons.

Cranky, whiny babies like Madison Stanton who thinks it's so hard being a teenager with great parents and a cell phone and firm, high tits that she just has to have a little drink to dull the pain.

Uppity bitches like her mother. Sharice comes on with the manners and the reserved smile, the lipstick and skinny eyebrows. But one little bump in the path and she snaps her fingers at you as if you're a bad dog who needs to get off the table. That woman has a stick up her ass—or maybe she deserves one.

The nerve of her, pulling his patient out of treatment!

He's thought long and hard about what made Sharice Stanton turn on him, and it's got to be that whore Abby. He thought she would keep her mouth shut, knowing what he could do to her, knowing how he could get to her and the little girl.

But no . . . Abby doesn't seem to understand that he's not playing a game. This is a mission. He's going after everything that once belonged to the king, and no one's going to stop him—not an uptight shrew or a melodramatic whore who thinks she's got all the answers in psychology. Ha! He can spin circles around her with theories and jargon and bullshit terminology. The shrinks act like it's a science, but in practice it's a mushy guessing game. The blind leading the insane.

Doctors . . . what the hell do they know?

Give a man a white coat and a stethoscope and he's supposed to have all the answers. Like the nerds his mother made him see when he was a kid. Goofballs in loafers and shiny wristwatches.

Chucky does not have the capacity to love.

What we've got here is a pathological liar.

He has a grandiose sense of self.

The child displays poor behavioral control.

They had a million things to say about him, but all he had for them was contempt. A bunch of doctors, physicians, making up bad things about him when there wasn't anything wrong with him at all!

And after all these years, where are the naysayers now? All the doctors who called him a psychopath? Most of them are dead in the dust.

Look at me now, Mama. They're done, and who's the doctor now?

I am.

Dr. Charles Jump.

Chapter 75

Lakeside Hospital
Abby

Abby braces herself as she approaches the office of the director of Psychological Services. Dr. Lauren Steen is known for running her department efficiently and cheaply. Although Abby has never had occasion to speak with her personally, she knows Dr. Steen is petite, slim, and beautiful in that ice-blond sort of way. Abby can only hope she can locate the director, who is difficult to track down.

Having run from the other wing, Abby is breathless, but her pace is brisk. Halfway down the corridor, someone emerges from an office and stalks toward Abby. It's her.

"Dr. Steen!" Abby tries not to rush her words; she wants to maintain professionalism. "I'm an intern, Abby Fitzgerald, and I need to talk with you if you have a minute."

"I don't, but . . . wait. You're Ms. Fitzgerald? You are already on my agenda this morning. Dr. Jump has requested a special review of your performance. I hear you've been interfering with patient treatment?"

"My performance?"

"Don't look so surprised. He tells me you've been apprised of these breaches every step of the way."

"Dr. Steen, I don't know what he's told you, but—"

"Come, walk with me." Dr. Steen puts a hand on Abby's back and guides her down the corridor. "I was just on my way to the meeting, and frankly it's not my protocol to discuss intern evaluations in the hallways."

"But honestly, I don't know what these charges are about."

"Does the patient Emjay Brown ring a bell?" Steen asks as the doors part before them and they step out of the office wing, into a courtyard where wind is twisting dry leaves into the overhang between buildings.

"I've been working with Emjay on confidence building and stress management strategies—just as outlined in his treatment plan. He's made progress, enough so that discharge could be considered."

"Not according to Dr. Jump."

"Actually, before we see him, I need to talk with you about Dr. Jump." Abby stops walking in the courtyard, relieved that Dr. Steen pauses, too. "Charles Jump is not what he seems. I've noticed problems with dosages and his demeanor with patients. At first I thought it was me, but I've done some research and Dr. Jump is a fraud. The real Dr. Charles Jump died three years ago. This man, whoever he is, did not attend Rutgers or Harvard. His credentials are phony. He's a fraud."

Dr. Steen purses her lips, then laughs. "Twenty years in the medical profession and I thought I'd heard every excuse imaginable from interns, but this is a new one for me." She points to the door and proceeds forward. "Quickly. I don't have time for this."

"But Dr. Steen—"

"Don't say another word, Abby. You're on tenuous ground as it is."

As they step inside the wing, Abby frantically searches her mind for a fallback plan. She never anticipated that Dr. Steen would accuse her of lying. This thwarts Abby's plans to shut Jump down today, but the hospital will dismiss him soon. Flint is meeting with Human Resources, who will discover that they've been defrauded, if not today, then soon.

It's going to be okay, Abby tells herself. *It will all work out in the end.*

"I'm going to sit in on Emjay Brown's evaluation first," Lauren Steen says condescendingly, "and then the three of us will do your eval."

Although Abby is silent, she's thinking of the Native American toast before going into battle: *It's a good day to die.*

The isolation rooms are not on the psych floor, where patient doors are usually locked in the open position and patients are encouraged to spend time in the Day Room, the library, or the dining area. The isolation rooms, designated for patients who are at risk of harming themselves or someone else, are situated at the end of a med-surg floor, away from people traffic. The walls are devoid of artwork or mirrors. In Abby's view, they are not awful, simply boring and isolated.

As they pass the nurses' station in the center of the hall, an aide emerges from behind the counter. "Dr. Steen, we were just about to page you. One of the doctors from upstairs just called down. There was some kind of a scuffle in the psych ward. One patient bit another? Apparently they need you to sign off on the paperwork."

"Lovely," Steen says sarcastically as she checks her watch. "There are not enough hours in the day." She strides off, telling Abby, "I'll be right back."

Left on her own, Abby wants to check on Emjay. "Which room is Emjay Brown in?" she asks.

"End of the hall, seven thirty-eight. He won't give you any trouble. After he acted out, Dr. Jump got a tranquilizer in him."

More drugs, and probably a whopping dosage.

Through the window in the door, Abby sees soft gray light suffusing the room from a high window and Emjay prone on a mattress.

"Good morning, Emjay," she says, opening the door and propping it open.

When he doesn't respond, she enters the room tentatively. "Emjay?" He is curled on the mattress, facing her feet. His gray T-shirt is soaked with sweat, and his body trembles, almost convulsively. His breathing is shallow and quick, almost as if he is gasping for breath. Is he reacting to the medication? Overdosing? God knows what dosage Jump has prescribed for him. "Emjay, it's Abby. Can you hear me?"

"Mmm." He stirs, scratching at his face, trembling. This is different from the deep sleep he was in when she first met him; this time he's agitated, moaning.

"Emjay? How are you feeling?" She squats beside him to get her face into his line of vision, but his pupils are contracted into tiny pinpoints in his glazed eyes—one sign of a drug overdose. And that breathing is a bad sign. Emjay needs to be examined by a real doctor.

"I know it's hard for you to breathe," she tells him, "but hang in there. I'm going to get help, okay?"

"Not so fast. I cannot have you interfering with my patients." Jump's voice chills her to the bone.

She kneels beside Emjay, but does not turn to acknowledge the man watching from the open doorway.

"First Madison Stanton is withdrawn from my care, and then today I hear you've taken it upon yourself to promise one of my patients a release. And under whose authority would that be?"

"Emjay is one of my assigned patients, as you well know."

As she speaks, Emjay moans and writhes. He tries to push himself off the mat, but falls back. "I can . . ."

"Easy," Abby says, "I won't leave you now."

"Actually, it's time for you to leave, Abby." Jump steps forward. "I recommend you get out before this patient attacks you the way he attacked me."

"Are you kidding me? He's so drugged up he can barely breathe!"

"He's stronger than you think. I was lucky to have escaped unharmed. What a shame, we send these guys over to Iraq, make them kill, and then expect them to put the brakes on it once they're back home."

"Nice argument. I'm sure it will play well in your eval meeting with the other doctors," she says, straightening. "But I don't believe Emjay attacked you. In the time I've worked with him, he's shown no tendencies toward violence. We've been working on stress management and coping strategies. Ways to recover from PTSD." She snaps her head around to glare at Jump. "But wait, you wouldn't know about those things, *Dr. Jump,* since you don't have a real medical degree."

His shoulders pull back, his chest puffing out—the bully stance. "You don't know anything about me," he growls. "And as of this moment, you are removed from Mr. Brown's case. In fact, you can turn in your ID badge at the desk, because you're officially dismissed from the internship program."

"Fine. I'm out. But I'm staying here as Emjay's friend and advocate, and if you want to spare yourself a death sentence for murdering him, you'd be wise to get a nurse now. In fact . . ." she reaches for the call button. "I'll get one myself."

In a flash, Jump is on her, chopping her hand. His move takes her by surprise and she hugs her arm close before she realizes his motive—to yank the call button out of the wall and disconnect it.

"I don't think so," he says quietly, tossing the disabled cord to the floor. "We don't need any witnesses for our last procedure with Emjay Brown, do we?"

"What are you talking about? As soon as the medication wears off, and he gets over the trauma of having a doctor abuse him, he'll be ready for release."

"Wrong. You think you're so smart, but you haven't made the simplest connection." Jump reaches for the dog tags around his neck. His fingers find a gold medal hanging there, a Purple Heart replica, which he rubs between his thumb and fingers like an amulet. "Brown will never be released. He knows too much. This soldier was John's partner the night he was killed. He saw me cleaning my rifle afterward, and he may have seen things at the scene. I made sure his night-vision device was disabled, but it's hard to know what he'll piece together over time. He holds the truth, even if it's been buried in the Gordian knot of PTSD. He's a liability." He shakes his head. "He's got to go."

"Because he knows you killed John? He's not the only one,

you know." Abby moves back to Emjay, who has grown still on the floor. Oh God, has she waited too long to get a doctor?

"Don't act like you're so smart. I wanted you to know. But Emjay Brown is the only one who could testify, and I can't let that happen." Charles Jump drops the medals against his chest, reaches into the pocket of his lab coat, and holds up a syringe. "He's already loaded up with juice. This will shut him down for good."

The shiny plastic tubing of the syringe twinkles in the gray light, the taunt of death.

"There's going to be a little screw-up in meds," Jump says. "I'll figure out a way to explain it. Or maybe I'll accuse Brown of dosing himself. Junky."

"No." Abby positions herself between Emjay and Jump, her hands braced against the floor for purchase. "You're not going to do it, because you don't want to get caught. And I'll give you up in a heartbeat."

Charles shakes his head. "You have too much to lose. Your own life. Madison Stanton . . . or that cute little Sofia, so vulnerable . . ."

"You wouldn't dare," she hisses, even as she knows he would stoop to any level for self-gain.

"I *would* . . . and I *have*."

As she watches in horror, he pops the cap off the syringe.

"No!" she swipes at him, but he pushes her aside, lunging for Emjay.

"Don't fight me on this," he growls, trying to reach past her.

When she swipes at the syringe again, the needle hits her in the upper arm. She sucks air through her teeth as Jump's eyes widen in outrage . . .

And he pushes the plunger.

"There you go," he says spitefully, yanking back the syringe and tossing it down.

Stabbed, Abby sinks down with the hollow feeling of loss, failure. A tingling sensation travels along her arm, warmth jets to her head, and suddenly the floor comes up to meet her.

"You little druggy. Got yours. You can flake out here while

I go get another syringe for Brown, because there's plenty more where that came—"

Suddenly Jump is cut off by a growling mass rising from the mat as Emjay Brown rises up like an angry bear. He barrels toward Charles, grabs him by the throat, and slams him against the wall.

"No more!" Emjay bellows, grinding Charles into the wall.

Jump sucks in air. "I can't breathe."

"No more killing." The words scrape through Emjay's hoarse throat. "I saw you do it. It was you. I saw that damn gold medal, shining in your helmet. It was you. You killed John."

"Stop it, Emjay. Put me down, now!"

Abby can hear a scuffle between them, but she can't summon the strength to lift her head.

"Stop it! Nurse!" Charles shouts. "Help! Nurse!"

"Go on and call 'em." Emjay's voice is low but steady. "Get 'em all in here. I can't wait to tell them all what you're trying to do."

The rapid pounding of footsteps mixes with the sound of voices, shouts down the hall. Abby's feels herself slipping away. When she opens her eyes, the room is hot with outrage and new voices.

Her mind still processes but she cannot make her body lift itself from the floor. As she helplessly stares up, faces swim past—Dr. Steen, a uniformed hospital security guard, and Flint. *Oh, thank you, Flint.*

"What did you do to her?" Flint is shouting. "What the hell did you inject her with?"

"Ow! You're hurting my arm!"

"Tell me!"

"It's just Percocet, a painkiller. She'll sleep it off."

"What was the dosage?" Laura Steen demands.

"What the hell should I know? I had some nurse make it up for me."

"Go find out—stat!" Dr. Steen tells the nurse, and Abby hears footsteps recede down the hall.

"I don't feel so good. Better lie down." Abby feels Emjay

collapse onto the mat at her feet. "He was trying to inject me, but Abby took the hit for me. Probably would've killed me with everything he's sunk into me."

Flint's face looms before Abby. Honest brown eyes and strong lips, all framed by crazy dark curls. "Abby . . ." His long fingers cup her jaw. Fit so well there. "How you doing? How you feeling?"

"Sleep."

"It's okay, you can sleep now. You got him, kid. You snagged Jump."

"He killed Joh . . ." she mutters, wishing her mouth would wrap around the words properly. "Emjay saw 'im."

"We'll get that all wrapped up with the police," Flint promises. "We've got time, now that he'll be restrained from hurting anyone else. We've got time."

He squeezes her hand and Abby tries to squeeze back, but all she can do is bask in the warm energy of his touch as her world goes black.

Chaper 76

Well, at least his name is Charles.

Jim Stanton stands at attention, his chin and shoulders squared, his eyes on the back of Charles's head. Today is a preliminary stage of the court-martial, the Article 32 hearing in which the charges are read and the defense counsel gets a chance to learn the specific evidence and testimony the military has gathered against the defendant.

Charles Turnball stands at the front of the courtroom as the court officer reads from a long list of charges.

"Article 82, Fraudulent Enlistment, Article 118, Murder . . ."

Of my son. You killed my son, then swooped in and tried to take over the life he built. And when that didn't work, you tried to systematically disassemble it.

A soft hand clasps his, and he squeezes back. His wife. He marvels at her resilience, her undaunted spirit and strength after everything they've been through. John, Noah, Madison. Abby, nearly lost to this man who stalked her.

And me, believing in him, trusting him, letting him guide me.

Jim lifts Sharice's hand and presses it to his heart. He never would have made it without this woman. He thinks of the matching gold bands waiting for him at the engravers, a gift he's planned for their thirtieth anniversary but never got around to purchasing. When they got married back in 1976, Jim didn't get a wedding band because he never wore jewelry. Now, knowing how much it will mean to Sharice, he's willing to bite the bullet and keep the symbol of marriage around one finger. Inside each band are the words: *Now more than ever . . .*

Jim's party takes up nearly an entire row at the court-martial proceeding, and most of them will be called as witnesses during some stage. Beside Sharice, Abby sits quietly, her hair pulled back from her face, freckles bolder than ever. She's looking a little more solid these days, finally getting some meat on those bones. Suz Wollenberg sits next to Abby, nervously twitching her sandaled foot. High energy, that girl, but a big heart, and her little one is a doll.

On Jim's left are two soldiers from John and Noah's platoon who have been subpoenaed to testify. Emjay Brown will be a key witness in Turnball's court-martial, as both a witness to John's murder and a victim of abuse by Charles Turnball at Lakeside Hospital. Brown was honorably discharged last month and is now attending school on the GI Bill, actually looking to be a counselor like Abby. Emjay wants to reach out to other soldiers who suffer from PTSD. A good man, Emjay Brown.

And Luke Spinelli, the kid, has become a fixture around the Stantons' house. When he returned from Iraq, the kid sought out Jim and Sharice, wanting to share some memories about John. "I didn't know your son long," Luke told them, "but he looked out for me when I really needed it, and I'll always be grateful for that." After they got to talking, they found they had a common interest in cryptology, the study of creating and breaking down codes. Jim took the kid under his wing, tried to show him some of the ways the army could offer him a career. Since then, Spinelli has been reassigned to the U.S. Army Signal Corps, where he's got a good shot at attending cryptology school and working with the National Security Agency in Maryland. He's a good kid, and Jim likes the feeling of carrying on the goodwill his son initiated.

The army's investigating officer also issued a subpoena for Noah to testify, but he is staying in Canada, probably for the long haul. Last week, Jim actually spoke with him on the phone for the first time since he went AWOL. A little awkward, mostly because Jim has never been a phone person, but it was good to hear his son's voice. Madison and Sharice plan to head up that way this summer, when school is out. Madison e-mails Noah every day and is always reporting on what seeds are sprouting or the purchase of a new milk cow. Noah's defection is still a source of discomfort for Jim, but he's learning to separate his feelings about going AWOL from his feelings about his son. Something to work on.

"Article 120a," the court clerk reads on, "Stalking one Abby Fitzgerald. Article 123, Forgery."

Standing at the front of the room, Charles raises his cuffed hands to scratch near his face, then turns back toward the rows of seats, searching the crowd casually . . . for what? Jim would love to know. The look in Charles's eyes isn't evil or contrite. He seems bored.

How could someone so normal wreak havoc in the lives of so many?

And I'm the biggest sucker of all, Jim thinks, though he's trying to get past it. Dr. Berton, his new therapist, who's an old veteran like Jim, keeps reminding Jim not to blame himself. "For all his insanity, Jump got you on the right path in therapy," Dr. Berton keeps telling him. "Let's not discount progress you made, personally, because of circumstances beyond your control."

Some days Jim wants to beat himself up over his own stupidity, but Dr. Berton cuts the pity party short. "There are things that you cannot control, things that you cannot blame yourself for, difficult things that you need to have the grace to accept," Berton says. "And beyond that, you're allowed to make a few mistakes. We're all human."

Mostly, Jim tries to focus on moving ahead one day at a time.

"Your honor, I'd like to say something," Charles Turnball interrupts the investigative officer. "I don't understand what any of these charges are about. My guess is that they're the result of jealousy and vindictiveness from the military commu-

422 Rosalind Noonan

nity—the military that I served so bravely. Do you know that I received a Purple Heart?"

"Actually—" The judge advocate flips through a folder— "That medal is listed as stolen property in these charges, so I'd advise you to refrain from speaking during these hearings, Mr. Turnball."

"No, Judge, that's wrong," Charles insists. "That medal is mine. I could show it to you, but those leathernecks took it away from me when they brought me in."

The judge is shaking his head. "Please, Mr. Turnball, defer to your lawyer."

"The problem is that I'm dismissing my lawyer, who's done a hell of a lot of nothing so far."

Camera flashes fill the room as an excited murmur rises from behind Jim, causing the judge advocate to bang his gavel. "Order, please."

"I intend to defend myself and prove that these charges are a bunch of lies. This case is a conspiracy against me brought on by the military community I served for years."

Abby leans closer to Sharice and Jim and confides in a low voice: "And right now, he probably believes that's true. Sociopaths don't accept blame and often blame others for acts they obviously committed."

The click and whir of expensive cameras fills the back of the room. The media.

Dave Flint is back there somewhere, taking notes. His unique insight gives him an edge over all the other reporters, but Jim doesn't begrudge him that. In Jim's opinion, everything Flint has written about the case so far has been true and sympathetic toward the victims. You can't ask for more than that. And in his investigations, Flint uncovered a trail of crimes perpetrated by Charles Turnball throughout Missouri, Illinois, and Alaska, where he had apparently faked his way into the military at a small recruiting office in Nome.

Born into a middle-class family outside Kansas City, Missouri, Turnball showed signs of personality disorder as a child when he killed the family dog at the age of thirteen. His parents had tried therapy, but Charles did not respond, adamant that he did not have a problem.

"Mr. Turnball, it's always advisable to retain a defense advocate," the judge tells Charles. "Especially in a General Court-Martial where the punishment for the charges spans from life in prison to death."

Charles glances over at his lawyer, then flicks him off with one hand. "I don't need him. You're fired," he says flatly.

As the noise in the courtroom rallies once again, Jim's gut clenches with dread at the court-martial ahead. It'll be a real courtroom circus if Charles represents himself.

Will it snap his patience? Will he lash out at Charles Jump when he has a chance to testify?

Jim Stanton will simply deal with that when he gets there.

One day at a time.

Chapter 77

U.S. Army Regional Confinement Center, Fort Lewis
Charles

"You have a visitor," the officer tells him.
A visitor? Who might that be?

As Charles follows the guard down the corridor and through locked gates of the army's Regional Confinement Center, he tries to calculate who's come to see him.

When he finally hits on the answer, he grins.

Abby.

She's come to ask forgiveness, to tell him that she's always wanted him and that she'll wait for him. Maybe they can even get married while he's detained and get one of those sex visitation dates.

And once he gets Abby, he'll eventually win back Jim and Madison and Sharice. They screwed up, mistaking him for some black-hearted villain, but they would learn the truth. He'd show them. And they'd get the army to reverse the charges against him, and finally he'd be free of this place.

But when he gets to the visitation room he pauses in the doorway, pissed.

Abby isn't here. The only open booth faces some middle-aged man with acne and a cowlick.

Lifting his cuffs toward the man, Charles snaps at the guard. "What am I here for? I don't know him."

"He's your brother," the guard says. "Have a seat and visit with him, or you go back to your cell."

Goddammit. Gritting his teeth, Charles slides onto the bench.

"Hey, Chucky." Cowlick Boy has a smooth voice, like a radio host. "You botched things up again. Heard all about it. But you got pretty far this time. Really had people thinking you were a doctor. Unbelievable."

Charles lets a smile curl the corner of his lip. "I'm good at what I do."

"Yeah, until you screw it all up. But really, to think that you had them believing you were a shrink. A mental patient treating mental patients. Isn't that ironic? Cracks me up. I can't believe they didn't see you were a retard."

Fury skitters up Charles's spine. "Who the hell are you?"

"Your big brother, Chucky. Don't you remember your long-lost brother?"

"Don't call me Chucky," he snarls, wanting to lash out and whip this oaf with his cuffed hands. How could it be that his brother John is standing right here?

But I killed you, Charles thinks. *Shot you dead in the dark warehouse.* How could he have done all that work for nothing? If he killed his brother, why is he sitting on the other side of the glass booth?

"You're not real," Charles says, nodding as it begins to make sense. "You're not real, John. You're dead."

"John?" The oaf chuckles. "My name is Pete, Chucky. Your big brother Pete."

"Don't call me Chucky," he growls, looking down at the counter. He's sick of looking at this overgrown troll. He already killed him, dammit. Die, already!

"Aren't you going to thank me for coming to visit you?" Pete asks. "You better look at me, Chucky, 'cause it might be your last chance. The way I read it, you're either going to prison for life or getting executed, so you better say your good-byes now."

Charles shakes his head, turning away. He has no need for this moron. He's in the process of crafting a brilliant defense, an airtight argument that demonstrates how they've all been conspiring against him, how he has been the victim all along.

"Hey, Chucky, wait!"

But Charles is already on his feet, walking to the door. "Take me back to my room, James," he orders pompously.

Might as well make the most of things.

Until he wins his freedom, he's all squared away here. Three meals a day, his own room—a free ride. Nobody looking over his shoulder, no time card to punch.

"Lucky for me," he mutters as he is shown to his room. He's not a mouse on a wheel running nowhere like the rest of them. "Lucky me."

With a deep sigh, Charles stretches out on his cot and folds his hands behind his head. Yup. Once again, he's found the easy way out.

Epilogue

Paris, France
April, 2008

April in Paris.

Abby Fitzgerald opens the top button of her sweater to the afternoon sunshine, soaking in the light that glances off the cobblestones, the wrought iron table, the warped glass and turquoise windowpanes of the Montmartre café behind her. In this City of Light, even the breeze carries color and luminescence.

Flint peels off his leather bomber jacket—which Abby suspects he's had since college—and drapes it over the back of a chair. "Why don't you order us some coffee and croissants? I'm going to go find a newspaper in English."

"Suffering withdrawal?" she teases.

"It just seems like a Hemingway-esque thing to do, sip coffee and leaf through the paper in the sunshine."

She waves him off. "Go on, Ernest. I've got this covered."

At times like this, Abby wishes she could paint. To capture the panorama of a day in Montmartre, the colors, the balance, the textures . . . it seems like a sumptuous way to spend an afternoon. She's glad Flint pushed her to accompany him on this brief assignment in Paris, a trip that is a landmark for Abby in so many ways: the end of her internship at Seattle General, the beginning of a new facet of her relationship with Flint, and the fulfillment of a promise to John.

The breeze sweeps through again, ruffling the carnation in its small vase on the table. As it washes over her, Abby recalls the way the gentle wind carried John's ashes into the Seine early that morning.

She had planned to go it alone. "Go back to sleep." She had leaned in to kiss him, almost falling back into the white duvet and downy pillows as her lips brushed over the stubble on his cheek. "I just want to do this while there aren't too many people around." There were rules about scattering a person's ashes, some fairly strict, but Abby had turned a blind eye to them and pressed on to do what she knew in her heart was right.

"I'll go." In a second Flint was out of bed and pulling on his jeans. "I don't think it wise for a young lady to be walking around Paris alone in the dark. I promise, I'll stay out of your hair."

You could see your breath in the cool air as they walked along the Seine, mists swirling along the surface of the river. Tucked in an inner pocket of her coat, John's ashes were sealed in a Ziploc bag. The sun had not yet risen in the rosy sky.

"This is perfect." Abby chose an empty stone bench that overlooked the river. It felt like a block of ice, but Abby smoothed her trench coat to cover her bottom and sat down quietly. Flint stood behind the bench, watching the river pensively.

Minutes passed as Abby sat and watched Paris arise: people hurrying by on their way to work; cabs growling past, spinning around corners; the scent of fresh rolls baking; and the yellow ball of sun chasing away the red hues of dawn.

And just like that, it was a brand-new day.

Sensing that the time was right, Abby rose, moved to the ledge along the river, and opened the bag. A breeze coursed over the water, tugging at her hair and wooing John's ashes away from her as the words from the minister at his funeral sounded in her head: *Remember, man, that you are dust, and unto dust you shall return.*

This time there were no tears, no anxiety, no worry over

doing the right thing. Instead, Abby felt a sense of joy that today, John's life was coming full circle in the way he had intended it to end, his ashes spread in Paris.

When the bag was empty, she looked up, glad that Flint was with her, confident that John would have been glad to have him be a part of his final return to the earth.

Now, while Flint is off at a kiosk on the boulevard, Abby, at a sidewalk café, struggles with her high school French, trying to order two croissants and coffee. *"Deux croissants et deux cafés au lait, s'il vous plaît."*

There. It may have sounded hackneyed, but at least she got it out.

As the waiter heads inside to the kitchen, she hears a familiar voice asking if he can join her for a second. She looks up and—

It's John. Healthy and glowing again, eyes laughing. She wants to reach across the table and touch him, but she knows that he's a ghost and it might be a mistake to mess with things and make his image pop off.

"You look good," he says. "Happy. I always knew Flint had a crush on you."

"Really? I was too in love with someone else to notice."

When the waiter returns with two white mugs and croissants, Abby has to bite her lip to keep from laughing as John nearly topples a croissant from its plate. "Is this Flint's roll?" John says. "I'll just rub it around in the dirt a few times. Kidding. I like Flint. Always have. It's just that I liked you more, and he wasn't about to make a commitment to anyone back then, was he?"

It's true. Abby nods at him as the waiter struggles to lower the pastry to the table intact. *"Merci,"* Abby says, waiting for the waiter to leave before she continues talking with the apparition.

"So I guess I can get out of your hair now," John says. "You're gonna be okay, Abs. And good job taking down Charles Jump. He was a menace to society."

"You helped me figure that out," Abby says, thinking of the

teardrops on John's photo, the freezing temperature in her apartment when Jump was around.

He stands, moves toward her, and she feels her breath catch in her throat at the sight of John Stanton, so strong, aglow with health. Was he really this tall, his shoulders and chest so broad?

"I couldn't leave until I knew you were okay." He moves behind her and her scalp tingles as he slides a hand over her head, finally resting his thumb in the crook of her neck.

She cannot see him anymore but she can feel his touch, that steady pressure on the spot his thumb would always find. She closes her eyes and savors this last moment with him.

And then his touch fades and disappears.

A few minutes later, Flint returns, walking tentatively, with his eyes on the headlines. "Remind me never to check how the stock market is doing when I'm supposed to be on vacation," he says, folding the paper and slapping it on to the table beside his coffee. "Hey, what's up with you? You feeling okay?"

Abby takes a deep breath and removes her hand from her throat. She's ready to move on now. She's ready to live. *"Oui,"* she says, meeting his gaze and melting under the warm caramel of his eyes. Flint, in his leather jacket and Yankees cap. The second great love of her life. How lucky is that?

"I'm fine now." She pushes his warm coffee cup closer to him and their hands brush in that electrifying stir that always makes her smile. *"Très bien."*

Please turn the page
for a special conversation with
Rosalind Noonan.

What first sparked the idea for One September Morning?

There was a gut-wrenching moment in my local coffee shop in September 2004. I had moved from New York City to the Pacific Northwest a few months before that, and I was still feeling tender from the terrorist attacks of 9-11. The conversation moved to recent news events, including the war in Iraq, where the death toll of U.S. soldiers had reached one thousand that week. "One thousand . . ." A friend of mine shrugged it off. "It's not really that high."

I was aghast. How could this normally kind person minimize the deaths of others with such ease and alacrity? Whether or not he approved of American involvement in Iraq, did he really think one thousand lives were dispensable?

That got me started. I'm an advocate of non-violent solutions, but I also have the utmost respect for people who serve in the U.S. Armed Forces. I grieved the loss of those soldiers, Americans trying to do the right thing, lives ended prematurely. My heart ached for the families of those one thousand service members as I tried to imagine their grief and pain, one thousand times twelve, times twenty, times fifty . . .

That day I knew I wanted to write a story that lent support and paid tribute to people who had chosen to serve our country in the military, both the soldiers and their families. I wasn't sure precisely what the storyline of characters would entail, but my creative search started there.

Were any of these characters based on you or people you know?

A piece of me exists in every character I write. To do a character justice I need to get under her skin for a while, imagine a typical day in his life, and identify her dreams or his worst fears, even if those things never come to fruition in the story. That said, a writer has to use what she knows and feels as a springboard and launch the imagination from there. I could feel Abby's pain, though I was never married to a soldier. I have not worked as a journalist or visited Iraq, so I had to incorporate research and imagination to create Flint's experience as an embedded reporter.

Sometimes, for a minor character, I'll use a friend's name and one or two personality traits. For example, while reading over the proofs, I noticed that I used the childhood nickname for one of my husband's friends—Killer Kelly—when referring to one of John's football buddies. We never meet the character in the book, but I did crack a smile when I saw the reference.

Was John's character inspired by Pat Tillman, who left a career in professional football to serve in the U.S. Armed Forces?

When I started writing *One September Morning* there wasn't a lot of information available about Pat Tillman—which was frustrating for me. I couldn't get the facts—probably because the truth was still hidden at that point in time—but I was alarmed by witnesses' accounts of his death in Afghanistan and moved by the shining purpose that drove the man. I tried to capture Tillman's commitment to doing the right thing—that was a source of inspiration for me. Also, by making John Stanton a celebrity it helped raise the profile of the incidents within the novel, raising the stakes.

In the years since, more of the details of Pat Tillman's death have been revealed, in large part thanks to the steadfast persistence of his mother Mary and his brother Kevin, who served in Afghanistan with Pat. Some of them correspond to the plot of my novel, others diverge. From everything I've read, I admire the diligence of the Tillman family, who pursued the truth despite many obstacles. A few readers have asked me why I didn't contact the family and try to tell Pat Tillman's story, which is rich and moving and heroic in its own right. The truth is, I'm a fiction writer, not really worthy or experienced enough to do his biography justice.

The villain of the novel is absolutely chilling. How did you come up with his character?

My husband expressed interest in a nonfiction book he was reading called *The Sociopath Next Door* by Martha Stout, which I snagged as soon as he was finished. Although nonfiction is not usually my thing, I found this book riveting, well-documented, well-researched, and yet insightful and entertaining. As I tend to look for the best qualities in a person and I want to believe that humans are a benevolent race, Ms. Stout's work helped me understand that there are people in the world who have a completely different moral compass—or none at all. She defines a sociopath as a person who does not feel guilt or remorse, a person who would kill to reap some personal benefits as long as he thinks he can get away with it. This profile of a sociopath stuck with me as I was fleshing out the villain of *One September Morning*.

After I read Ms. Stout's book, I realized I had come dangerously close to a few sociopaths during my lifetime. Only a few, but even one is enough, don't you think? It's a very creepy thought.

How do you approach the process of writing a novel?

Since I was fired up with an overall idea for this book, certain scenes came to me right away—such as Abby opening her door to two soldiers who notify her that her husband has died in combat. Other scenes eluded me until I was doing rewrites.

As I was writing, I was very pleased with the way certain characters came alive, particularly the Stanton family. I enjoyed writing Madison's defiant, youthful voice. Jim Stanton's point of view and backstory grew richer with my research of the Vietnam War. And Noah Stanton's story was a gift. There was the obvious juxtaposition to the lives of his father and brother, but beyond that Noah's voice was strong in my ears. I had to work a little harder with Sharice, who's a bit of a control freak, but by the end of the writing process I was feeling her pain, too.

When I first had an idea, I sent my editor a one-page story pitch or concept, which he thought was worth pursuing. Then I developed it into an outline, a rather detailed chapter by chapter description that ran over fifty pages. Once the outline was approved, I began the actual writing, which also involves some expansion.

For example, the outline included an otherworldly element that had John actually speaking to Abby in a ghostly voice, warning her about the man who was trying to hurt her. My editor advised me to take this out—sage advice—as he thought it gave away too much of the story and might be a little weird it its actual execution. On the other hand, in the outline Jim Stanton didn't have much of a backstory or a voice, so as I was writing I explored his past and gave him some scenes of his own that tied into John's story. Of course, the novel varies from the outline. In the end, the outline is a framework—a road map for what becomes an amazing adventure, but a road map, nonetheless, so that the publisher and the writer share a sense of where the book is going.

The book immerses us in the lives of military families. Were you an army brat as a kid?

My father served in the Signal Corps, but he was a civilian by the time I was born. When I was in fourth grade an army family moved on our block, and I quickly befriended the captain's daughter Julie, who was a year older than I was. Their family of nine had just come from an assignment in Panama, and the neighborhood kids were mystified by such an exotic background. In the ensuing years Julie and I became best friends, and I fell into her family. I worried when her father was deployed to Vietnam. Her mom took us everywhere, so I was exposed to activities on the local army base.

Then, when I was in high school, my father took a position with the Department of Defense, working outside Stuttgart, Germany. Although our family lived in a small farming town, we were allowed certain military privileges at the military bases— the commissary and PX, the officer's club and subsidized APO mail. My siblings and I attended the American schools on base. During the summers I worked in the base library and for the Red Cross, which had a presence on base to serve soldiers and assist in international communications. It was a rich experience, diminished only by the fact that I was a senior in high school, and an extremely introverted individual.

How has your research for One September Morning *changed the way you view daily news stories?*

First, I cannot allow myself the luxury of not reading about the developing situation in Iraq or walking away from the *Today* show when they're doing a segment involving an American soldier or combat situations overseas. By nature, I have always been a news wimp, preferring to avoid stories that are disturbing or unpleasant, and I have had to overcome that secret desire to live in a bubble.

My research has also diminished any desire I might have had to be a journalist. I worry for any people venturing into war zones and unstable nations. I held my breath when Meredith Vieira traveled to China to cover the 2008 earthquake. Any longings I once had for international adventure are now lost to a latte and a good book by the fire!

Who are some of the authors you admire? What are some of your favorite reads?

I'm smiling because recently I was asked that question by someone I'd just met at a party and my first answer was that I love everything by Anna Quindlen. She turned to me, grabbed both my arms, jumping up and down and shouting, "Yes! Yes!" I was right with her; we spoke the same language, having lost and found ourselves in Ms. Quindlen's fiction and nonfiction work. *Rise and Shine, Blessing, Black and Blue, One True Thing*— Anna Quindlen's novels captivate me from beginning to end. My only complaint is that she doesn't write enough.

Other writers that get me in trouble because I cannot put their books down are Lolly Winston, Lisa Jackson and Nora Roberts. I admire Jodie Picoult's love of a controversial dynamic, and Alice Hoffman's ability to portray the spiritual and otherworldly as organic facets of life. Their work entertains and pulls the reader into their stories through their characters. These writers really get inside a character's skin. I'm in awe of their talents.

ONE SEPTEMBER MORNING

Rosalind Noonan

ABOUT THIS GUIDE

The suggested questions are included to
enhance your group's reading of Rosalind Noonan's
One September Morning

DISCUSSION QUESTIONS

1. If you had been in Abby's position at the beginning of the novel, would you have pursued the truth, even if it meant defying the U.S. Department of Defense? What would you have done differently?

2. How does Sharice's relationship with her daughter evolve throughout the course of this story, from the scene in which we meet Madison at the protest to the courtroom scene at the end of the novel?

3. Do you think Abby will succeed as a psychologist? Why or why not?

4. In the novel, the terrorist attacks of 9/11 had a profound effect on the lives of John, Abby and Flint. Do you remember what you were doing the morning of September 11, 2001? What effects did the events of that day have on your life?

5. How would you describe Abby and Flint's relationship? Did you root for them to be together?

6. The episode in which Emjay Brown melts down on his way home from the store was based on something that happened to a veteran of the war in Iraq. How would you suggest authorities in the military intervene so that veterans of this war do not suffer this degree of alienation and post-traumatic stress?

7. Noah's early life choices were strongly influenced by his older brother John. Do you consider the choices Noah makes later in the novel brave or cowardly? Would John have approved?

8. Despite the years he spent suffering from post-traumatic stress, Jim Stanton was reluctant to consult a mental health professional. Do you think there is still a stigma connected to being in therapy or seeing a psychologist? Do you think it's more difficult for men in law enforcement or the armed forces to ask for help?

9. Do you know anyone who is currently serving in the U.S. Armed Forces? What would you tell your son or daughter if they were about to deploy to a hazardous overseas assignment?

10. By definition, a sociopath is a person who is incapable of feeling guilt or compassion, one who has a pervasive pattern of violation of, and disregard for, the rights of others. Have you ever encountered such a person?

11. Discuss the novel's ending. What do you think the future holds for Madison Stanton? For Sharice and Jim Stanton? Do you think Noah can find happiness outside his homeland? If John Stanton had survived combat in Iraq, what would his future have entailed? Forecast the future highs and lows of Abby and Flint's relationship.

12. If you were producing *One September Morning* as a feature film, who would you cast as Abby and Flint? What actors should play the members of the Stanton family? How about Doc Jump? Emjay Brown?